TOWARDS INFINITY

Damon Knight, who has been a freelance writer since 1950, is the author and editor of over thirty books, including anthologies, translations, novels and short stories. In 1956, he won the 'Hugo' award for science fiction criticism and is at present editor of the *Orbit* series of original collections of science fiction stories. He founded and was first President (1965-6) of the Science Fiction Writers of America and is a Director of the Milford Science Fiction Writers' Conference.

Born in 1922, Damon Knight now lives with his wife, authoress Kate Wilhelm, in Florida.

D1351907

Also available in Pan Books

100 YEARS OF SCIENCE FICTION – Vol 1
Edited by Damon Knight

100 YEARS OF SCIENCE FICTION – Vol 2
Edited by Damon Knight

CONDITIONS OF SALE

This book shall not, by way of trade or otherwise, be lent, re-sold, hired out or otherwise circulated without the publisher's prior consent in any form of binding or cover other than that in which it is published and without a similar condition including this condition being imposed on the subsequent purchaser. The book is published at a net price, and is supplied subject to the Publishers Association Standard Conditions of Sale registered under the Restrictive Trade Practices Act, 1956.

TOWARDS INFINITY

Nine Science Fiction Adventures

Edited by Damon Knight

UNABRIDGED

PAN BOOKS LTD : LONDON

First published in Great Britain 1970
by Victor Gollancz Ltd.
This edition published 1973 by Pan Books Ltd,
33 Tothill Street, London, SW1.

ISBN 0 330 23431 5

Text copyright © 1968 by Damon Knight

Printed in Great Britain by
Richard Clay (The Chaucer Press), Ltd,
Bungay, Suffolk

Grateful acknowledgement is made to the following for permission to include these stories:

Theodore Sturgeon for *The Man Who Lost the Sea*, copyright © 1959 by Mercury Press, Inc.

Ford McCormack for *March Hare Mission*, copyright 1950 by Hillman Periodicals, Inc; by arrangement with Forrest J. Ackerman.

Ray Bradbury for *The Earth Men*, copyright 1948 by Standard Magazine, Inc. Reprinted by permission of Harold Matson Company, Inc.

Don A. Stuart (John W. Campbell) for *Who Goes There?* copyright 1938 by Street & Smith Publications, Inc.

Wilmar H. Shiras for *In Hiding*, copyright 1948 by Street & Smith Publications, Inc.

Isaac Asimov for *Not Final!* copyright 1941 by Street & Smith Publications, Inc. Copyright © 1968 by Isaac Asimov.

Katherine Maclean for *And Be Merry ...*, copyright 1950 by Katherine Maclean; first published in *Astounding Science Fiction*.

James H. Schmitz for *The Witches of Karres*, copyright 1949 by Street & Smith Publications, Inc.

A. E. Van Vogt for *Resurrection*, copyright 1948 by Street & Smith Publications, Inc, copyright 1952 by A. E. Van Vogt; by arrangement with Forrest J. Ackerman.

CONTENTS

TOWARDS INFINITY

INTRODUCTION

Perspective is the art of representing objects to give an illusion of depth; the Renaissance painters went temporarily mad over it – it was a craze, like Mah-Jongg; they spent days and weeks drawing complex geometric shapes according to the rules of perspective. A related problem, which they did not attempt because they didn't have the technical means, is stereoscopic vision, the curious process by which our brains are able to combine two separate images into one, so that instead of seeing just the front of an object, we see a little way around it on either side.

We are so used to seeing with two eyes that we never notice that we have this depth-vision only in the horizontal plane – we can see around an object on the left and right, but not on top and bottom. If we had three eyes, all functioning together, we could see depth in the vertical plane as well. Anatomists tell us that our amphibian ancestors did have a third eye; it was in the back of the head, however, and has since migrated inside the brain and become the pineal gland.

We sometimes speak of perspective in time rather than space – 'historical perspective', for instance, meaning the vision of the historian who can 'see' a long period as a whole because it is so distant. We don't usually talk about stereoscopic vision in this way, but it occurs to me that perhaps we ought to. Another word for this is 'parallax', the method by which astronomers measure the distance of nearby stars. If you take a photograph of the sky in January and another in July, the Earth has travelled 186,000,000 miles in the interim, so that combining the images gives the equivalent of a stereoscopic effect. When we talk about the perspective that a man has looking back over his lifetime, I think sometimes we really mean parallax. A man at forty-five, say, remembering something that happened when he was fifteen, has two images of it, taken from different angles. The contrast between the two can be startling and illuminating.

In 1937, for example, when John W. Campbell took over the editorship of *Astounding Stories* (now *Analog*) and modernized science fiction, it was a revolutionary event; it overturned something that had been established for a long time. This, at any rate, was the way I saw it then. But I was fifteen in 1937, and had been reading science fiction only since 1933. The older magazines, which I bought in second-hand bookstores – wonderful old bedsheet-sized *Amazings* and *Wonder Stories*, with gaudy covers by Frank R. Paul – were like archaeological discoveries. The oldest of them had been published in 1926, a date almost as remote to me as 1066. I never realized, until I happened to write the dates down the other day, that the pre-Campbell period in American science fiction magazines lasted only eleven years.

This isn't perspective, it's parallax. I have a double vision of that period. In one image, the Gernsback era, with its creaky writing and its naïve enthusiasm for machinery, is a vast dark gulf of prehistory; in the other, it is merely a temporary interruption. For, of course, H. G. Wells and Mark Twain knew that you must have two things in science fiction – an imaginative idea, based on real science and technology, and a strong, well-told story about believable people. And this is all that Campbell taught.

Reading through the stories in this collection, I discover that many of them seem even better now than they did when they were first published. Obviously the stories themselves haven't changed. I think it's parallax again, or maybe perspective – I see how long they have lasted, and that in itself is a quality that makes me admire them more.

If you stop to think about it, parallax is really what we are after when we read fiction. Writers are our third eyes; they give us images of the world and our own lives from unexpected angles. This is even more important in science fiction than in other fields, because the baseline is longer – the distance between the two lenses: the 186,000,000 miles across the orbit of Earth, or the two and five-eighths inches across the bridge of your nose. Science fiction, by investigating problems that are purely imaginative, can give us a broad view of what we are and what the universe is. Disciplined imagination is not a futile exercise, even when it deals with drugs that will make human beings immortal, or with monsters from another star. In John Campbell's 'Who Goes There?' (written under his pseudonym of Don A. Stuart), the problem is how to identify a monster that can change itself into an exact duplicate of a human being, right down to the structure of the individual cells. The solution, technical and specific as it is, also has something to tell us about human beings. Wilmar Shiras' 'In Hiding' is a superman story about a boy who must hide his abnormal intelligence from the world, but it has something to say about all gifted, lonely children.

Another trick you can play with parallax is to see through two writers' eyes at once. The stories in this collection were not chosen to illustrate this point, but it happens that they do. The same ideas, even the same images, turn up over and over in science fiction, transformed but recognizable, like images in a dream. These recurrent ideas are fascinating to me, and I'll have more to say about them later on in this book. Now – here are the stories.

DAMON KNIGHT

THE MAN WHO LOST THE SEA

Theodore Sturgeon

I can't tell you what this story is about, or even where it takes place: you're going to have to find that out for yourself. The vivid opening scene is like a stage setting for a surrealist play, something that might have been written by Samuel Beckett: the boy running with his toy helicopter, the man in the pressure suit half-buried in the sand ... What can they mean? Read on and see.

SAY you're a kid, and one dark night you're running along the cold sand with this helicopter in your hand, saying very fast, *witchy-witchy-witchy*. You pass the sick man and he wants you to shove off with that thing. Maybe he thinks you're too old to play with toys. So you squat next to him in the sand and tell him it isn't a toy, it's a model. You tell him, Look here, here's something most people don't know about helicopters. You take a blade of the rotor in your fingers and show him how it can move in the hub, up and down a little, back and forth a little, and twist a little, to change pitch. You start to tell him how this flexibility does away with the gyroscopic effect, but he won't listen. He doesn't want to think about flying, about helicopters, or about you, and he most especially does not want explanations about anything by anybody. Not now. Now, he wants to think about the sea. So you go away.

The sick man is buried in the cold sand with only his head and his left arm showing. He is dressed in a pressure suit and looks like a man from Mars. Built into his left sleeve is a combination timepiece and pressure gauge, the gauge with a luminous blue indicator which makes no sense, the clock hands luminous red. He can hear the pounding surf and the soft, swift pulse of his pumps. One time long ago when he was swimming he went too deep and stayed down too long and came up too fast, and when he came to it was like this: they said, 'Don't move, boy. You've got the bends. Don't even *try* to move.' He had tried anyway. It hurt. So now, this time, he lies in the sand without moving, without trying.

His head isn't working right. But he knows clearly that it isn't working right, which is a strange thing that happens to people in shock sometimes. Say you were that kid, you could say how it was, because once you woke up lying in the gym office in high school and asked what had happened. They explained how you tried something on the parallel bars and fell on your head. You understood exactly, though you couldn't remember falling. Then a minute later you asked again what had happened and they told you. You understood it. And a minute later ... forty-one times they told you, and you understood. It was just that no matter how many times they pushed it into your head, it wouldn't stick there; but all the while you *knew* that your head would start working again in time. And in time it did ... Of course, if you were that kid, always explaining things to people and to yourself, you wouldn't want to bother the sick man with it now.

Look what you've done already, making him send you away with that angry shrug of the mind (which, with the eyes, are the only things which will move just now). The motionless effort costs him a wave of nausea. He has felt seasick before but he has never *been* seasick, and the formula for that is to keep your eyes on the horizon and stay busy. Now! Then he'd better get busy – now; for there's one place especially not to be seasick in, and that's locked up in a pressure suit. Now!

So he busies himself as best he can, with the seascape, landscape, sky. He lies on high ground, his head propped on a vertical wall of black rock. There is another such outcrop before him, whip-topped with white sand and surrounded by smooth, flat sand. Beyond and down is valley, salt flat, estuary; he cannot yet be sure. He is sure of the line of footprints, which begin behind him, pass to his left, disappear in the outcrop shadows, and reappear beyond to vanish at last into the shadows of the valley.

Stretched across the sky is old mourning cloth, with starlight burning holes in it, and between the holes the black is absolute—wintertime, mountaintop sky-black.

(Far off on the horizon within himself, he sees the swell and crest of approaching nausea; he counters with an undertow of weakness, which meets and rounds and settles the wave before it can break. Get busier. *Now*.)

Burst in on him, then, with the X-15 model. That'll get him. Hey, how about this for a gimmick? Get too high for the thin air to give you any control, you have these little jets in the wing tips, see? and on the sides of the empennage: bank, roll, yaw, whatever, with squirts of compressed air.

But the sick man curls his sick lip: Oh, git, kid, git, will you? – that has nothing to do with the sea. So you git.

Out and out the sick man forces his view, etching all he sees with a meticulous intensity, as if it might be his charge, one day, to duplicate all this. To his left is only starlit sea, windless. In front of him across the valley, rounded hills with dim white epaulettes of light. To his right, the jutting corner of the black wall against which his helmet rests. He thinks the distant moundings of nausea becalmed, but he will not look yet. So he scans the sky, black and bright, calling Sirius, calling Pleiades, Polaris, Ursa Minor, calling that ... that ... Why, it *moves*. Watch it – yes, it moves! It is a fleck of light, seeming to be wrinkled, fissured rather like a chip of boiled cauliflower in the sky. (Of couse, he knows better than to trust his own eyes just now.) But that movement...

As a child he had stood on cold sand in a frosty Cape Cod evening, watching Sputnik's steady spark rise out of the haze (madly, dawning a little north of west); and after that he had sleeplessly wound special coils for his receiver, risked his life restringing high antennas, all for the brief capture of an unreadable *tweetle-eep-tweetle* in his earphones from Vanguard, Explorer, Lunik, Discoverer, Mercury. He knew them all (well, some people collect match covers, stamps) and he knew especially that unmistakable steady sliding in the sky.

This moving fleck was a satellite, and in a moment, motionless, uninstrumented but for his chronometer and his part-brain, he will know which one. (He is grateful beyond expression – without that sliding chip of light, there were only those footprints, those wandering footprints, to tell a man he was not alone in the world.)

Say you were a kid, eager and challengeable and more than a little bright, you might in a day or so work out a way to measure the period of a satellite with nothing but a timepiece and a brain; you might eventually see that the shadow in the rocks ahead had been there from the first only because of the light from the rising satellite. Now if you check the time exactly at the moment when the shadow on the sand is equal to the height of the outcrop, and time it again when the light is at the zenith and the shadow gone, you will multiply this number of minutes by eight – think why, now: horizon to zenith is one fourth of the orbit, give or take a little, and halfway up the sky is half that quarter – and you will then know this satellite's period. You know all the periods – ninety minutes, two, two and a half hours; with that and the appearance of this bird, you'll find out which one it is.

But if you were that kid, eager or resourceful or whatever, you wouldn't jabber about it to the sick man, for not only does he not want to be bothered with you, he's thought of all that long since and is even now watching the shadows for that triangular split second of measurement. *Now!* His eyes drop to the face of his chronometer: 0400, near as makes no never mind.

He has minutes to wait now – ten? ... thirty? ... twenty-three? – while this baby moon eats up its slice of shadow-pie; and that's too bad, the waiting, for though the inner sea is calm there are currents below, shadows that shift and swim. Be busy. Be busy. He must not swim near that great invisible amoeba whatever happens; its first cold pseudopod is even now reaching for the vitals.

Being a knowledgeable young fellow, not quite a kid any more, wanting to help the sick man too, you want to tell him everything you know about that cold-in-the-gut, that reaching invisible surrounding implacable amoeba. You know all about it. Listen, you want to yell at him, don't let that touch of cold bother you. Just know what it is, that's all. Know what it is that is touching your gut. You want to tell him. Listen:

Listen, this is how you met the monster and dissected it. Listen, you were skin diving in the Grenadines, a hundred tropical shoal-water islands; you had a new blue snorkel mask, the kind with face plate and breathing tube all in one, and new blue flippers on your feet, and a new blue spear gun – all this new because you'd only begun, you see; you were a beginner, aghast with pleasure at your easy intrusion into this underwater otherworld. You'd been out in a boat, you were coming back, you'd just reached the mouth of the little bay, you'd taken the notion to swim the rest of the way. You'd said as much to the boys and slipped into the warm silky water. You brought your gun.

Not far to go at all, but then beginners find wet distances deceiving. For the first five minutes or so it was only delightful, the sun hot on your back and the water so warm it seemed not to have any temperature at all and you were flying. With your face under the water, your mask was not so much attached as part of you, your wide blue flippers trod away yards, your gun rode all but weightless in your hand, the taut rubber sling making an occasional hum as your passage plucked it in the sunlit green. In your ears crooned the breathy monotone of the snorkel tube, and through the invisible disk of plate glass you saw wonders. The bay was shallow – ten, twelve feet or so – and sandy, with great growths of brain-, bone-, and fire-coral, intricate waving sea fans, and fish – such fish! Scarlet and green and aching azure, gold and rose and slate-colour studded with sparks of enamel blue, pink and peach and silver. And that *thing* got into you, that ... monster.

There were enemies in this otherworld: the sand-coloured spotted sea snake with his big ugly head and turned-down mouth, who would not retreat but lay watching the intruder pass; and the mottled moray with jaws like bolt cutters; and somewhere around, certainly, the barracuda with his undershot face and teeth turned inward so that he must take away whatever he might strike. There were urchins – the plump white sea egg with its thick fur of sharp quills and the black ones with the long slender spines that would break off in unwary flesh and fester there for weeks; and filefish and stone-fish with their poisoned barbs and lethal meat; and the stingaree who could drive his spike through a leg bone. Yet these were not *monsters*, and could not matter to you, the invader churning above them all. For you were above them in so many ways – armed, rational, comforted by the close shore (ahead the beach, the rocks on each side) and by the presence of the boat not too far behind. Yet you were . . . attacked.

At first it was uneasiness, not pressing, but pervasive, a contact quite as intimate as that of the sea; you were sheathed in it. And also there was the touch – the cold inward contact. Aware of it at last, you laughed: For Pete's sake, what's there to be scared of?

The monster, the amoeba.

You raised your head and looked back in air. The boat had edged in to the cliff at the right; someone was giving a last poke around for lobster. You waved at the boat; it was your gun you waved, and emerging from the water it gained its latent ounces so that you sank a bit, and as if you had no snorkel on, you tipped your head back to get a breath. But tipping your head back plunged the end of the tube under water; the valve closed; you drew in a hard lungful of nothing at all. You dropped your face under; up came the tube; you got your air, and along with it a bullet of seawater which struck you somewhere inside the throat. You coughed it out and floundered, sobbing as you sucked in air, inflating your chest until it hurt, and the air you got seemed no good, no good at all, a worthless, devitalized, inert gas.

You clenched your teeth and headed for the beach, kicking strongly and knowing it was the right thing to do; and then below and to the right you saw a great bulk mounding up out of the sand floor of the sea. You knew it was only the reef, rocks and coral and weed, but the sight of it made you scream; you didn't care what you knew. You turned hard left to avoid it, fought by as if it would reach for you, and you couldn't get air, couldn't get air, for all the un-obstructed hooting of your snorkel tube. You couldn't bear the mask, suddenly, not for another second, so you shoved it upwards clear of your mouth and rolled over, floating on your back and opening your mouth to the sky and breath-ing with a sort of quacking noise.

It was then and there that the monster well and truly engulfed you, mantling you round and about within itself – formless, borderless, the illimitable amoeba. The beach, mere yards away, and the rocky arms of the bay, and the not too distant boat – these you could identify but no longer distinguish, for they were all one and the same thing ... the thing called unreachable.

You fought that way for a time, on your back, dangling the gun under and behind you and straining to get enough warm, sun-stained air into your chest. And in time some particles of sanity began to swirl in the roil of your mind, and to dissolve and tint it. The air pumping in and out of your square, grinned, frightened mouth began to be mean-ingful at last, and the monster relaxed away from you.

You took stock, saw surf, beach, a leaning tree. You felt the new scent of your body as the rollers humped to be-come breakers. Only a dozen firm kicks brought you to where you could roll over and double up; your shin struck coral with a lovely agony, and you stood in foam and waded ashore. You gained the wet sand, hard sand, and ultimately with two more paces powered by bravado, you crossed high-water mark and lay in the dry sand, unable to move.

You lay in the sand, and before you were able to move or to think, you were able to feel a triumph – a triumph be-cause you were alive and knew that much without thinking at all.

When you *were* able to think, your first thought was of the gun, and the first move you were able to make was to let go at last of the thing. You had nearly died because you had not let it go before; without it you would not have been burdened and you would not have panicked. You had (you began to understand) kept it because someone else would have had to retrieve it – easily enough – and you could not have stood the laughter. You had almost died because they might laugh at you.

This was the beginning of the dissection, analysis, study of the monster. It began then; it had never finished. Some of what you had learned from it was merely important; some of the rest – vital.

You had learned, for example, never to swim farther with a snorkel than you could swim back without one. You learned never to burden yourself with the unnecessary in an emergency: even a hand or a foot might be as expendable as a gun; pride was expendable, dignity was. You learned never to dive alone, even if they laugh at you, even if you have to shoot a fish yourself and say afterwards 'we' shot it. Most of all, you learned that fear has many fingers, and one of them – a simple one, made of too great a concentration of carbon dioxide in your blood, as from too rapid breathing in and out of the same tube – is not really fear at all but feels like fear, and can turn into panic and kill you.

Listen, you want to say, listen, there isn't anything wrong with such an experience or with all the study it leads to, because a man who can learn enough from it could become fit enough, cautious enough, foresighted, unafraid, modest, teachable enough to be chosen, to be qualified for—

You lose the thought, or turn away, because the sick man feels that cold touch deep inside, feels it right now, feels it beyond ignoring, above and beyond anything that you, with all your experience and certainty, could explain to him even if he would listen, which he won't. Make him, then; tell him the cold touch is some simple explainable thing like anoxemia, like gladness even – some triumph that he will be able to appreciate when his head is working right again.

Triumph? Here he's alive after ... whatever it is, and that doesn't seem to be triumph enough, though it was in the Grenadines, and that other time, when he got the bends, saved his own life, saved two other lives. Now, somehow, it's not the same: there seems to be a reason why just being alive afterwards isn't a triumph.

Why not triumph? Because not twelve, not twenty, not even thirty minutes is it taking the satellite to complete its eighth of an orbit. Fifty minutes are gone, and still there's a slice of shadow yonder. It is this, *this* which is placing the cold finger upon his heart, and he doesn't know why, he doesn't know why, he *will* not know why; he is afraid he shall when his head is working again ...

Oh, where's the kid? Where is any way to busy the mind, apply it to something, anything else but the watch hand which outruns the moon? Here, kid: come over here – what you got there?

If you were the kid, then you'd forgive everything and hunker down with your new model, not a toy, not a helicopter or a rocket plane, but the big one, the one that looks like an overgrown cartridge. It's so big even as a model that even an angry sick man wouldn't call it a toy. A giant cartridge, but watch. The lower four-fifths is Alpha – all muscle – over a million pounds thrust. (Snap it off, throw it away.) Half the rest is Beta – all brains – it puts you on your way. (Snap it off, throw it away.) And now look at the polished fraction which is left. Touch a control somewhere and see – see? it has wings – wide triangular wings. This is Gamma, the one with wings, and on its back is a small sausage; it is a moth with a sausage on its back. The sausage (click! it comes free) is Delta. Delta is the last, the smallest: Delta is the way home.

What will they think of next? Quite a toy. Quite a toy. Beat it, kid. The satellite is almost overhead, the sliver of shadow going – going – almost gone and ... gone.

Check: 0459. Fifty-nine minutes?, give or take a few. Time: eight ... 472 ... is, uh, seven hours fifty-two minutes.

Seven hours fifty-two minutes? Why there isn't a satellite

around Earth with a period like that. In all the solar system there's only . . .

The cold finger turns fierce, implacable.

The east is paling and the sick man turns to it, wanting the light, the sun, an end to questions whose answers couldn't be looked upon. The sea stretches endlessly out to the growing light, and endlessly, somewhere out of sight, the surf roars. The paling east bleaches the sandy hilltops and throws the line of footprints into aching relief. That would be the buddy, the sick man knows, gone for help. He cannot at the moment recall who the buddy is, but in time he will, and meanwhile the footprints make him less alone.

The sun's upper rim thrusts itself above the horizon with a flash of green, instantly gone. There is no dawn, just the green flash and then a clear white blast of unequivocal sunup. The sea could not be whiter, more still, if it were frozen and snow-blanketed. In the west, stars still blaze, and overhead the crinkled satellite is scarcely abashed by the growing light. A formless jumble in the valley below begins to resolve itself into a sort of tent city, or installation of some kind, with tube-like and sail-like buildings. This would have meaning for the sick man if his head were working right. Soon, it would. Will. (Oh . . .)

The sea, out on the horizon just under the rising sun, is behaving strangely, for in that place where properly belongs a pool of unbearable brightness, there is instead a notch of brown. It is as if the white fire of the sun is drinking dry the sea – for look, look! the notch becomes a bow and the bow a crescent, racing ahead of the sunlight, white sea ahead of it and behind it a cocoa-dry stain spreading across and down toward where he watches.

Beside the finger of fear which lies on him, another finger places itself, and another, making ready for that clutch, that grip, that ultimate insane squeeze of panic. Yet beyond that again, past that squeeze when it comes, to be savoured if the squeeze is only fear and not panic, lies triumph – triumph, and a glory. It is perhaps this which constitutes his whole battle: to fit himself, prepare himself to bear the utmost that fear could do, for if he can do that, there is a triumph on the other side. But ... not yet. Please, not yet awhile.

Something flies (or flew, or will fly – he is a little confused on this point) towards him, from the far right where the stars still shine. It is not a bird and it is unlike any aircraft on earth, for the aerodynamics are wrong. Wings so wide and so fragile would be useless, would melt and tear away in any of earth's atmosphere but the outer fringes. He sees then (because he prefers to see it so) that it is the kid's model, or part of it, and for a toy, it does very well indeed.

It is the part called Gamma, and it glides in, balancing, parallels the sand, and holds away, holds away slowing, then settles, all in slow motion, throwing up graceful sheet fountains of fine sand from its skids. And it runs along the ground for an impossible distance, letting down its weight by the ounce and stingily the ounce, until *look out* until a skid *look out* fits itself into a bridged crevasse *look out, look out!* and still moving on, it settles down to the struts. Gamma then, tired, digs her wide left wing tip carefully into the racing sand, digs it in hard; and as the wing breaks off, Gamma slews, sidles, slides slowly, pointing her other triangular tentlike wing at the sky, and broadside crushes into the rocks at the valley's end.

As she rolls smashing over, there breaks from her broad back the sausage, the little Delta, which somersaults away to break its back upon the rocks, and through the broken hull spill smashed shards of graphite from the moderator of her power pile. *Look out! Look out!* and at the same instant from the finally checked mass of Gamma there explodes a doll, which slides and tumbles into the sand, into the rocks and smashed hot graphite from the wreck of Delta.

The sick man numbly watches this toy destroy itself – what will they think of next? – and with a gelid horror prays at the doll lying in the raging rubble of the atomic pile: *don't stay there, man – get away! get away! that's hot, you know?* But it seems like a night and a day and half another night before the doll staggers to its feet and, clumsy in its pressure suit, runs way up the valley-side, climbs a sand-topped outcrop, slips, falls, lies under a slow cascade of cold ancient sand until, but for an arm and the helmet, it is buried.

The sun is high now, high enough to show the sea is not a sea, but brown plain with the frost burned off it, as now it burns away from the hills, diffusing in air and blurring the edges of the sun's disc, so that in a very few minutes there is no sun at all, but only a glare in the east. Then the valley below loses its shadows, and like an arrangement in a diorama, reveals the form and nature of the wreckage below: no tent city this, no installation, but the true real ruin of Gamma and the eviscerated hulk of Delta. (Alpha was the muscle, Beta the brain; Gamma was a bird; but Delta, Delta was the way home.)

And from it stretches the line of footprints, to and by the sick man, above to the bluff, and gone with the sandslide which had buried him there. Whose footprints?

He knows whose, whether or not he knows that he knows, or wants to or not. He knows what satellite has (give or take a bit) a period like that (want it exactly? – it's 7.66 hours). He knows what world has such a night, and such a frosty glare by day. He knows these things as he knows how spilled radioactives will pour the crash and mutter of surf into a man's earphones.

Say you were that kid; say, instead, at last, that you are the sick man, for they are the same. Surely then you can understand why of all things, even while shattered, shocked, sick with radiation calculated (leaving), radiation computed (arriving), and radiation past all bearing (lying in the wreckage of Delta) you would want to think of the sea. For no farmer who fingers the soil with love and knowledge, no poet who sings of it, artist, contractor, engineer, even child bursting into tears at the inexpressible beauty of a field of daffodils – none of these is as intimate with Earth as those who live on, live with, breathe and drift in its seas. So of these things you must think; with these you must dwell until you are less sick and more ready to face the truth.

26

The truth, then, is that the satellite fading here is Phobos, that those footprints are your own, that there is no sea here, that you have crashed and are killed and will in a moment be dead. The cold hand ready to squeeze and still your heart is not anoxia or even fear, it is death. Now, if there is something more important than this, now is the time for it to show itself.

The sick man looks at the line of his own footprints, which testify that he is alone, and at the wreckage below, which states that there is no way back, and at the white east and the mottled west and the paling fleck-like satellite above. Surf sounds in his ears. He hears his pumps. He hears what is left of his breathing. The cold clamps down and folds him round past measuring, past all limits.

Then he speaks, cries out; then with joy he takes his triumph at the other side of death, as one takes a great fish, as one completes a skilled and mighty task, rebalances at the end of some great daring leap; and as he used to say, 'We shot a fish,' he uses no 'I':

'God,' he cries, dying on Mars, 'God, we made it!'

MARCH HARE MISSION

Ford McCormack

In the Introduction I mentioned the recurrent ideas and images that turn up in the work of science fiction writers. Take the landscape in the Sturgeon story, with its trail of footprints; we'll meet it again, with a difference, in Ray Bradbury's 'The Earth Men'. Or take the temporary loss of memory which Sturgeon uses as a single thread in the tapestry he is weaving.

In the story you are about to read, this idea becomes central and is transformed into an ingenious problem. As I wrote in 1950, when this story was first published in Worlds Beyond : *'How do you execute an incredibly complex and dangerous mission, without arms, without aid – and without the simple ability to recall what you're doing for more than thirty seconds at a time?'*

A distant roar sounded hollowly in the rock-walled corridor, and after a moment Lieutenant Gavin realized what it was – machine-gun fire, its familiar chatter dissipated in the maze between.

He swore fervently, drew his automatic, and stretched his wiry legs to a fast lope. The enemy must have broken through at the other stairway, since the one behind him was still being held. Only a low rumble from that direction told of the carnage beyond the huge emergency door. The elevator shafts had, of course, been irreversibly sealed off long before, by steel slabs at every level.

Bitterly, Gavin regretted having lingered for a few pot shots before the doors were closed. Now he faced the prospect of being cut off from a much more important objective. And there was only one cartridge left in his automatic.

It had been fairly certain from the first that the enemy would reject a peaceful surrender of the hospital section. The massacre of helpless patients was part of what military propaganda called 'severe retaliation' – against any and all resistance.

There had been plenty of resistance in and around Vancouver Combs. The top levels had been abandoned for a week because of radioactivity, while the mightiest battle of the war raged in the air over the disfigured terrain. Armament was about equal, but numbers were with the enemy. In the actual storming of the Combs, each successive level had cost the invader heavily. But this last, bottom level, with its handful of defenders, would come cheaper.

Gavin's stride faltered momentarily, as two grey-uniformed soldiers appeared at the far end of the corridor; then he sprinted for the nearest cross corridor twenty yards farther on. As he ducked into it, a bullet knocked chips from the wall over his head, and the sound of the shot clapped and echoed behind him.

There was no one in the cross corridor, but he had to get out of it before the men who had seen him could reach it. The noise of battle – or slaughter – was louder now, and seemed to come from all directions. Behind some of the doors he passed, there was the babble of frightened voices.

At the next main corridor he paused for a quick glance both ways. It too was empty. He turned left and raced along, his hopes rising with every step. The destination was not far now. At the third cross corridor, he turned right. Seconds later, he stood panting at the last turn, within sight of his goal – a door not fifty feet from the intersection. But in between, walking away from Gavin, was a soldier.

Perhaps a hundred yards farther down the corridor a group of five more soldiers was approaching. As yet, the group presented a minor hazard; in fact, it would fit in very well with Gavin's plan. But if he waited until the solitary soldier reached the others, they would all be too close.

He had no doubts about his ability to kill the soldier with his one remaining shot. And under the circumstances, he

29

felt not the slightest compunction about shooting him in the back. But in case he couldn't reach the door – or it just happened to be locked – he would need that last bullet for another purpose.

Gavin hefted the automatic in his hand, and his dark, rather sharp face tightened with decision. On soundless feet, he darted out into the corridor, conscious of his conspicuous lieutenant's uniform. Still, with the soldier between himself and the group, there was a chance they might not see him too soon.

They did. The soldier was ten yards beyond the door and Gavin was passing it when a shot rang along the corridor. Both Gavin and the soldier stopped instantly – but the soldier had to turn around. As he did so, Gavin's last bullet caught him high in the stomach and he dropped like an empty sack.

Gavin whirled and reached the door marked PHARMACY in one bound. It was not locked. As he snatched it open, a bullet splintered through one of the panels, and another whipped the air close behind him. Inside, he pulled the door shut and turned the lock.

He was in a small medical storeroom with shelves and bottles from floor to ceiling. It adjoined a larger room by an archway, and the other room also had a door to the hall. But that door should be locked, and there was no time to make sure.

Gavin jerked a fold of papers from his breast pocket, loosened the separate sheets, and made a wad, tossing it on the floor. He struck a match with fairly steady hands and, stooping, lighted the wad at several points. Shouts reverberated in the corridor outside, and the doorknob rattled loudly.

He stood up and turned to the shelves, running his eye along one of them to a bottle with a bright red label. Printed on it prominently was the word POISON. Gavin took the bottle quickly, pulled the stopper, and raised it to his mouth.

He was briefly aware of a sour taste, which was obliterated by a strangling sensation of liquid fire. It took intense

30

muscular effort to force several swallows past his burning throat.

Dizzily, he dropped the half-empty bottle on the floor, with a crash that seemed to shake the room.... No, the crash had been something hitting the door – the lock was bent out of shape ... The papers on the floor had burned to as many layers of black ash; Gavin lurched forward and stamped on them heavily, then dropped to his hands and knees as the floor began to rise in a mad spiral ...

His next impression, which he accepted matter-of-factly, was of having been stuffed into a coffin that was too small. But he had not yet been buried, for there was light....

Gavin opened his eyes and saw the plain ceiling and walls of a small hospital room. It was no coffin that compressed his arms and torso, but a tightly wrapped straitjacket. A lieutenant with the enemy insignia of Intelligence on his sleek grey uniform stood by the cot. Behind him was a white-smocked attendant.

The stone-faced lieutenant spoke in over-articulated but passable English: 'You are to come with us.'

Gavin nodded wearily. His head ached, his throat was raw, and the snug jacket was doing nothing to alleviate the nausea he felt. He struggled awkwardly to a sitting position.

Walking along the corridor between the two men, Gavin noticed small variations of construction which indicated that these combs had been built, rather than captured, by the enemy. But as yet there was nothing to show their probable location.

He was led through double, soundproofed doors into a large room suggesting a surgery at first glance. But there were noticeable differences: the operating table had too many clamps and adjustments; the glass case near it held an unorthodox array of instruments; there was other apparatus difficult to connect with the art of healing, some of which Gavin recognized from previous descriptions. This chamber was what the enemy euphemistically referred to as a 'question room'.

Gavin doubted that they would use torture on him – yet.

It was effective enough for certain purposes, such as breaking up an underground movement by forcing the betrayal of one's fellow conspirators. But it was not so useful in extracting scientific information, where it might take weeks of experimentation to prove the data false. And in the case of military information, a major disaster could result from any great reliance on reports so obtained.

The most innocuous piece of equipment in evidence was a lie-detector setup – a chair surrounded by half a dozen physiological recording instruments attachable to the subject. Gavin was not surprised at being escorted to it. The attendant, an owlish little man who looked withered beyond his years, began removing his straitjacket.

There was a surge of relief as the canvas loosened about Gavin's midsection. The jacket showed evidence of much use. If they put it back on him, as was probable, they would not be likely to notice that the fastenings failed to pull up so far as they had when he was unconscious. Gavin knew a certain technique for enlarging the torso imperceptibly.

The tall lieutenant stood off watchfully, holding his automatic by its barrel, while the attendant strapped Gavin securely to the chair.

They were applying the various attachments of the lie detector when the door opened and a squat, middle-aged officer entered. His tightly fitting uniform emphasized his hoglike physique, and his platinum hair and pale-blue eyes contrasted icily with the heavy, florid cheeks.

This would be the official inquisitor, no doubt, and it was perhaps significant that his rank was that of colonel. He stared with cold contempt at Gavin while the wizened attendant made the final adjustments on the lie detector and indicated that it was functioning. Then the colonel spoke in a metallic bass, his accent somewhat thicker than the lieutenant's had been:

'So this is the coward who lacked the courage to put a bullet through his brain. I must compliment you on your choice of poison, however – we located a stomach pump barely in time to save your life.'

The fools! thought Gavin. There had been a stomach

pump across the hall, in the laboratory storeroom. It shouldn't have taken them two minutes to find it. And it was known that the enemy awarded a substantial bonus for officers and key men captured alive.

'Not that we have much use for you,' the colonel went on casually. 'We have already found out a great deal about the new super-weapon.'

Gavin saw the colonel's gaze flicker past him towards the recorders, which were all strategically located in back of the chair. It had been a fairly clever remark – to be made by someone who was not even sure a super-weapon existed. A surprise reaction would be quite indicative. Gavin was reasonably sure he had not shown one: his long and rigorous schooling with every type of lie detector had more than prepared him for such simple tests.

If the colonel was annoyed by the lack of response, he did not show it. He spoke again, in the same condescending tone, but in his own language: 'How long have you been a spy?'

The designation was pure bluster, of course, based on the arrogant and familiar view that opposition agents deserved no more honourable title. But it had been a direct question, and Gavin did not wish to antagonize the man by ignoring it completely. Those petulant lips and narrowed eyes bespoke a character that might easily be prompted to an offhand but crippling act of cruelty. Gavin could not afford to have that happen. Nor did he wish to reveal his considerable fluency with the language of the enemy. He replied hesitantly, in English: 'How long – I didn't catch the question.' The words rasped painfully in his sore throat.

The colonel sneered, reverting to the same language: 'Never mind. Your lack of experience, and your ignorance, is very evident. Did you imagine, for instance, that burning those papers and stamping on them would put the information out of our reach? Even your own so-called experts could have recovered some of it; we were able to restore it completely. Every word! Every equation! What do you think of that?'

Privately, Gavin doubted it. But they had probably got

33

enough to connect him with Dr Middleton, as they were intended to. As for the rest of the data, it concerned a very interesting if unproductive line of research which had nothing to do with Dr Middleton or any known weapon. But even if they got it all, they would need considerable time to make sure it was useless.

The colonel looked up at the tall lieutenant and nodded significantly towards the door. The solemn lieutenant wheeled stiffly and marched out. Hands on hips, the colonel stood facing Gavin for a moment, then spoke quietly: 'You know, of course, that we can break down your conditioning with nepenthal in a very short time.'

Gavin waited, guessing what was coming. He knew the facts, all right. Full security conditioning took months of intensive treatment to build up. It included a violent antipathy towards all hypnotic drugs or so-called truth serums. Even a moderate dosage of any of them would cause convulsions and unconsciousness, from which the subject would not recover to any useful extent while the effects lasted. But the peculiar action of nepenthal, a non-hypnotic drug which the enemy had synthesized within the last year, would break down that conditioning in a few weeks at most.

The colonel's tone grew deadly: 'I wonder if you know how much difference it can make to you, whether you freely answer a few questions now or wait until we drag it out of you.'

He studied Gavin's face for a moment, then went on: 'If you tell us now, the truth of your answers will of course be tested later. If you have not lied, you will be well treated. You can believe this, since it is obvious that such a policy works to our advantage. Otherwise – if you refuse to answer, or lie to me – well, you will die eventually. But you will start dying long before that. What do you say?'

Gavin wondered how many times the same routine had been performed in this same room – and how many steadfast, heroic rejections had followed. As for himself, he had little choice. He could not answer those 'few questions' if he wanted to, and it would be dangerous to leave any room for argument. He spoke flatly: 'I say no.'

The colonel's beefy hand delivered a jolting slap to Gavin's face.

Fast as the motion had been, Gavin had seen it coming. He could have jerked his head sideways at the last instant and greatly reduced the force of the blow, but a split-second decision had restrained him. It would be unwise to reveal his unusual, hair-trigger coordination to this man. Gavin's only hope was to keep that weapon secret as long as possible. Besides, the sadistic satisfaction of the act might allay the other's vindictiveness.

When the bells stopped ringing in Gavin's head and his vision cleared, he became aware that the colonel was chuckling.

'So! He is not a mechanical man, after all. He is made of flesh which quivers and blood whose pressure can be made to jump!'

He turned to the attendant, who wore a cadaverous grin of appreciation. 'Give him a test dose of solanacin. He probably has the full conditioning, but we must make sure.'

The door swung wide, and the tall lieutenant appeared, pushing before him a shambling figure wearing a strait-jacket. The prisoner's head drooped low, showing only a dirty bandage and tousled grey hair. Gavin knew who it must be, even before the lieutenant shoved the head back with the butt of his hand, revealing a square, lined face and sunken eyes that stared as if with vague puzzlement.

Gavin deliberately stimulated in himself a slight momentary tension. The role he was playing called for considerable surprise at this juncture, and the colonel was watching him closely. It was just as well to jog the recorders a little.

He had studied too many photographs of the well-known physicist standing there not to recognize him despite his altered appearance. It was Dr Middleton – the man Gavin must kill, if the slightest opportunity presented itself.

Dr Middleton had been captured two weeks ago at Juneau Combs, which had fallen so unexpectedly that the usual precaution of removing key men from danger points could not be taken. The scientist had good reason to be at Juneau, which had been the nearest position to the enemy at the time. He had been supervising installations for the only really revolutionary weapon to be developed since the war began.

Gavin had only the vaguest idea of its technical nature: it seemed to be a form of focusable radiation, and in the most basic sense, it was not even destructive. Quite the contrary. It *stabilized* things. Exposure to it somehow strengthened the electrical bonds between the constituent elements of any compound. In the laboratory, Gavin had personally seen trinitrotenuin, that most sensitive of explosives, pounded harmlessly with a hammer under the inhibitory rays. But the wielder of the hammer had taken care not to expose himself for long. The stoppage of chemical change extended to life processes.

A great and useful future was foreseen for the radiation. At low power output it would preserve food indefinitely, without refrigeration. At high power, it would extinguish fires from a considerable distance by making combustion impossible.

Just now, the prime purpose was to see how efficaciously a ring of large projectors could clear the air of jet planes. Installations were being rushed to completion at Seattle, Portland, and Spokane, and should be in operation within a week. The new weapon had no effect on atomic bombs, of course – but it could do a wholesale job of crippling the planes that carried them. It was confidently expected to end the war – providing the enemy failed to duplicate it within the next few months. If they did, then the war would continue as of old on land and sea, and the advantage would inevitably revert to the side with the preponderance of manpower.

The enemy would not have been likely to arrive at the discovery soon enough by research alone. But now, the fiasco at Juneau had delivered into their hands a man who had been instrumental in the development of the new weapon from the laboratory stage. They got no critical plans or equipment – those had been destroyed. But the information in Dr Middleton's mind, once extracted, would be more than they needed. The last radio report from

Juneau Combs said that Dr Middleton had attempted suicide, but had either been restrained or had bungled the job. The head bandage and straitjacket he now wore seemed to bear out that report. Certainly, no one could have realized more keenly the disastrous implications of his capture than the doctor himself.

At home, officialdom had reacted with freshets of counter-accusations, some of which were true. Those who had ordered the installations at Juneau had certainly not allowed a sufficient margin of time – events proved that. On the other hand, if the fortunes of war had permitted only a few days more of respite, two cities and an estimated hundred thousand casualties might have been spared.

Amid the hubbub, the March Hare Project – so named for its utter foolhardiness – had been quietly born. The one-man mission had been conceived with Lieutenant Gavin's special talents in mind, and the Chief of Intelligence had personally and reluctantly outlined it to him. It was the Chief who had arranged the lab demonstration of the new weapon, so that Gavin could judge for himself what was at stake – though he was shown nothing that the enemy would not learn the first time it was used.

Gavin had not jumped at the chance – he was far from being a chauvinist – yet the very fact that no orders had been given influenced him strongly. If this war was about anything at all, it was about differences of policy at all levels. Those differences were worth preserving, even at the wildest of risks. And the war would have been lost long since if his side had been unable to muster its share of men who were willing to play for keeps. So Gavin had become the March Hare.

He was now as close to his objective as careful scheming could bring him. From now on, only luck, and the lightning synapses which had uniquely qualified him for this desperate job, could help.

'I see you know the good doctor.' The colonel smirked at Gavin, and added slyly, 'And he has probably recognized you several times already.'

37

The wizened attendant cackled, and even the tall lieu-tenant permitted himself a twisted smile.

Gavin found the joke less than amusing, for the simple reason that it might have been literally true – except for the fact that Gavin had never before met Dr Middleton. The latter was plainly under the influence of nepenthal. There were definite signs of the drug's main symptom: an odd disfunction of the memory.

While it had relatively little immediate effect on mental alertness, the drug nullified one's ability to store recollec-tions of current happenings, usually on an almost instan-taneous basis. However, the presymptomatic memory was unaffected. Thus, under its influence, the subject was un-aware of any lapse of time between the onset of the drug's full effect and the present moment. And therefore it was quite possible to recognize the same person several times within a brief period. One had only to look away to forget completely.

Protracted use of the drug would eventually cause per-manent damage to the brain. Yet the enemy used it indis-criminately on prisoners whether they had security con-ditioning or not. Since the drug made them incapable of sustained or coherent action, it reduced the problem of guarding them to a minimum.

Gavin had seen some of the mindless wrecks the enemy had exchanged for human beings. Although the drug's formula was now known to both sides, there did not seem to be any recourse against this crime of war that would not be equally inhumane. So the shameful traffic continued.

The owlish attendant approached with a hypodermic syringe, jabbed it casually into Gavin's arm just above the rubber armlet of the sphygmomanometer, and pressed the plunger. The mere injection caused a slight hypertension which must have been plainly observable on the recorders. And in a few minutes, the solanacin was kicking up a physiological disturbance out of all proportion to the minute dosage, and in contradistinction to its narcotic properties.

In spite of himself, Gavin fidgeted with acute discomfort. His breathing was becoming asthmatically difficult, and the feeling of nausea was returning with a vengeance. He was almost glad when the colonel spoke to the attendant with an air of boredom: 'There's no doubt about it. You can start the nepenthal now – and give him plenty.' He turned to the tall lieutenant. 'You might as well wait and take them both with you. Have a guard stay with the little spy until he is completely under the influence.'

He smiled sardonically at Gavin. 'Farewell, amateur! When I see you in a few weeks, you will have cause to regret your stubbornness. In the meantime – just a few days from now, in fact – Dr Middleton will have told us all you know and more. That is a pleasant little thought for you to turn over and over at your absentminded leisure.'

Obviously pleased with himself, the colonel sauntered out.

The nepenthal brought quick relief from the worst of the reactions occasioned by the narcotic, to which it was a partial antidote. But it also brought a strong sense of urgency.

From previous experience, Gavin knew that the effect would reach maximum in fifteen minutes at most. At any given moment during the next six to eight hours, his last recollections would be of the present interval. In that time he must formulate and fix in his mind the cues which would guide his subsequent behaviour.

During his ten days at Vancouver Combs, while awaiting its inevitable downfall, Gavin had experimented with nepenthal several times, and had become painfully aware of his limitations. The directives had to be simple, or even his phenomenal associative powers were unable to reconstruct the pattern and retain it long enough to accomplish the most elementary purpose. If the purpose involved several steps, it was advisable to anticipate some characteristic of each one and select cues accordingly.

For this occasion, he had long since decided what the first and predominant directive must be, on which the separate cues would depend, in those isolated moments which lay ahead . . .

*　　*　　*

39

Look around! Gavin's gaze swung quickly about the rough and pitted rock walls of his cell, whose single furnishing was the cot on which he was sitting. He was alone: the guard had left.

Simultaneously, the slight motion of his body made him aware of the confining straitjacket. That awareness was the cue which launched a cyclical writhing of his entire torso. He felt his outer arm slip slightly in its canvas sheath. This was a critical point, at which untrained individuals usually made the mistake of trying to loosen the inner arm as well: instead, Gavin preserved the small amount of slack between them with care, and set about the strenuous process of making more . . .

Look around! But he could not. His head and shoulders were engulfed in suffocating folds of rough cloth. He was not immediately aware of the position of his arms: they were upraised and numb, and as a result, his efforts to disentangle them were rather feeble. . . .

Look around! As Gavin did so, he was conscious of an aching weariness in the muscles of his arms and shoulders. The straitjacket lay on the floor at his feet. He was free to attempt the plan whose initial steps he had visualized while sitting here before the drug had taken full effect – seemingly, seconds ago.

He had been well aware of the plan's inflexibility. Its failure could easily have the result of immobilizing him. But that was a risk he had already accepted, and he wasted no irreplaceable moments considering it now.

Instead, orientation congealed into stimulus; he twisted from his sitting position, clutched the cot pad by the near edge and slung it with some precision to the floor and against one wall. That wall contained the cell's only opening other than its metal-sheathed door – a heavy-grilled ventilator near the ceiling.

With a continuous motion, Gavin spun back to the bare cot and grasped it by the sides of its rusted steel frame. It was not anchored in any way – that had been the first thing he had checked on entering the room. The cell itself was too large – or too small – to have been intended as such. This part of the Combs had probably been converted from a hospital or residential section, and the usual precautions were no longer considered necessary since the enemy had adopted the practice of using the new drug to render its prisoners helpless.

But he made no attempt to lift the cot just then. There had been a warning protest from his tired muscles – he would be too slow. First he must rest ...

Look around! In the act of turning his head, Gavin stopped, then returned his attention to the cot over which he was bending, as the plan took priority in his mind. With a heave, he swung the cot over his head, inverting it, stepped forward and placed its end against the wall under the ventilator grill.

Straining on tiptoe, he raised the cot so that one of its tubular steel legs passed between the closely meshed bars of the slightly protruding grill. A final thrust with his fingertips caused the crossbar of the cot's end section to catch on the rough surface of the wall. It held – the cot hung straight out from the wall, its full length providing leverage in probable excess of its strength. But the legs were well braced, and there were four of them ...

The cot pad on the floor was not altogether successful in mitigating the noise of the crash. Gavin was unable to prevent the cot from scraping the wall on the way down, and the grill, joined to a foot-long section of heavy-gauge duct that had pulled out with it, bounced on the cot springs with a disconcerting clamour. The incident would have been excellent cause for worry, if Gavin had not promptly forgotten it ...

Look around! The upended cot under him swayed dangerously, and Gavin oriented himself barely in time to hook his hand in the ventilator hole for stability. But the glance had informed him that there was no one else in the cell.

The weak spot of the ventilator had been where it had joined the main duct, and the torn bolt-holes made a hazard in squeezing his body through the narrow opening. There was also a baffle partly blocking the way, which he was able to bend sufficiently.

There was no doubt about which way to turn. Dr Middleton's cell lay somewhere to the left. The lieutenant had taken him on down the corridor after leaving Gavin and the guard. The doctor's cell was most likely on the same side – there were only two doors on the other – but whether it was one or a dozen cells away, there had been no way of telling. Not that it mattered much. There was no practicable way of counting them, either...

Gavin quite literally found himself in the near-blackness of a tube so flat in its cross-section that he could not raise his belly from the dust-caked surface far enough to crawl normally. There was only room to squirm, which he promptly did. The cold air blowing around his body from behind carried the disturbed dust to his face in choking eddies as he inched forward.

It had been easy to deduce where he was, in a general way. But that in itself told him virtually nothing regarding the all-important question: Had he accomplished his mission? Fortunately, there was an indirect answer to that. There was no pain in his right earlobe.

A week ago, a small capsule had been inserted under the skin on the inner side of that lobe. The capsule could be ruptured by the firm pressure of a thumbnail, releasing an irritant into the tissues which would keep them inflamed for days. Only when and if he felt this soreness would Gavin be free to indulge in the frail hope of his own escape...

He was looking down through a ventilator at a familiar bandaged head and mass of grey hair. The head was drooping so that the face was not visible. How many other cells Gavin had peered into – how long he had waited at this one for more certain identification to become possible – he would never know. But as he watched now, the man beneath heaved a sigh and the blunt, seamed features of Dr Middleton came briefly but unmistakably into view.

Instantly, Gavin pressed his shoulder against the baffle which partly blocked the opening, and bent it clear. Simultaneously, he plucked a button off the fly of his pants. They and his shirt were the only parts of his uniform that had been left on him. The buttons were of tough steel and had various potentialities in an emergency. He inserted the thin edge of this one into the slot of the nearest bolt securing the ventilator grill, and twisted with all the strength of fingers that could bend a twenty-penny nail held in one hand . . .

The button itself provided an adequate clue as to what he was doing, and by convention he took the bolts in clockwise order around the grill. In each case, he applied the maximum force at the first approach. If the bolt would not turn, due to corrosion, or its slot disintegrated under the strain for the same reason, he went quickly to the next one . . .

Two empty holes in succession – one would not have been conclusive – told him at a glance that he had done all he could to weaken the attachment. With one writhing twist of his torso he reversed position and jabbed both feet at the grill. It came free gratingly and disappeared from view. Its unrelieved clatter was still sounding from the floor below, as Gavin followed through with his legs and hips. At that point, his shirt caught on a ragged edge of metal, tore wide open, and caught again . . .

In spite of the fact that his own body shut off most of the light, Gavin's mind leaped to the simplest explanation of his position. He was halfway into the air duct through the only opening his memory had registered: the ventilator in his own cell. Then, as he started to work himself farther in, he became aware of the metal button he was holding in his fingers. After a slight hesitation, he projected himself outwards with a strong thrust of his arms. . . .

*   *   *

Look around! As he picked himself up off the floor, Gavin's swinging gaze paused with a slight shock of recognition on the sitting figure of Dr Middleton, then went on with sudden purpose. He could kill the doctor with his bare hands, quite easily – but not quickly enough, under the circumstances, to be sure of carrying through.

His eyes fell on the grill assembly, lying in the middle of the floor. At the same instant, there was the metallic rasp of a key being inserted in the lock of the cell door.

As he automatically lunged towards the grill, Gavin's racing mind weighed the situation.

There was a chance that he could kill Dr Middleton before being apprehended – and complete his mission. His normal, deep-seated reluctance to kill a helpless person – one who was nominally a friend – would be no deterrent whatever. Dr Middleton's continued existence was a threat to the lives of millions and, in all probability, to the freedom of mankind for generations. In this vital sense, the good doctor was an archenemy.

But the grill was bulky, and there was no assurance that he might not be defeated by the mental fog which was due to descend at any instant. Also, the guards all wore side arms and were trained, he knew, to use them fast. Whether he finished off the doctor or not, the outcome for himself would be certain death, within seconds at most. Yet he would not be here if fear of death had been a guiding factor.

The key was still turning noisily in the lock as Gavin paused, bending over the grill with his fingers clutching its crossbars. His thoughts had been scarcely more than unresolved flashes of insight. In the same overall manner, he considered the alternative.

It was simple enough in its conception – as it had to be. Kill the guard and escape, taking the doctor along. In its execution, the plan's basic difficulties would be rendered fantastic by Gavin's condition. Yet there was the prospect of a certain amount of latitude beyond that first big step. With the guard out of the way, Dr Middleton could possibly be disposed of any time the going got too rough.

Acting on the gravest decision of his career, Gavin re-

44

leased his hold on the grill and flung himself towards the corner of the room where the door was. The latch clicked and the door swung wide as he flattened himself against the wall behind it.

And forgot why he was there ...

A moment later he had partially reconstructed the situation. The door behind which he stood was located differently than in his own cell: this could be Dr Middleton's. The heavy footsteps were undoubtedly those of a guard, who was muttering something in his own language about noise and twenty devils.

Without hesitation Gavin moved out from behind the door. There was simply no time to stalk the guard, and he could only hope for the advantage of surprise.

Luck was momentarily with him. The guard, a heavyset six-footer, was turned partly away, looking up at the uncovered ventilator hole. But he must have caught a glimpse of Gavin's motion, for he whirled around, raising an automatic pistol. As he did so, Gavin lashed out with a well-gauged kick, connecting solidly with the guard's wrist, and the gun continued on up, spinning slowly. Before it hit the floor, Gavin had launched his body straight at the larger man, lowering his head at the last instant and butting it rather painfully but with brutal effect into the other's face. At the same time, his crossed hands gripped the collar of the guard's uniform just above the lapels, and his knee came up sharply to the groin.

The disabled guard went down heavily, the beginnings of a scream cut off by the pressure of Gavin's forearms on his throat. From the feel of the initial kick, Gavin judged the guard's wrist was badly damaged, if not broken. Since the problem was not only to kill the man but to do it quickly and silently, that was so much the better. This particular stranglehold was very hard to break with one hand ...

A loud groan from the barely conscious man beneath him brought Gavin's senses into focus, and he instantly tightened his grip ...

*　　*　　*

Look around! He was standing in a cell with a dead guard at his feet and with Dr Middleton staring blankly at him from the cot. The door was open.

Gavin sprang quickly to close it, first removing the cluster of keys that hung from its lock, then returned to the body. Dropping to his knees, he began working at the buttons of the oversized uniform . . .

It was not such a bad fit as might be expected, judging by the beefy, underwear-clad corpse on the floor. Gavin's shoulders were deceptively broad; the gunbelt gathered in the fullness at the waist acceptably; the roomy pants, worn over his own, pulled up high under the coat and turned under at the cuffs, merely made him look stouter. And the cap was actually a bit snug. Swiftly, he caught up the gun from the floor, slipped it into the holster at his side, and continued across the room towards Dr Middleton . . .

He was escorting Dr Middleton by the arm along a corridor otherwise empty. Walking, he had long since discovered, was a sufficiently automatic process that its own momentum made it fairly continuous. This was not altogether advantageous. Gavin stopped them just in time to prevent their barging across the intersection of a larger corridor.

But a discreet glance showed that it, too, was empty. And it showed something else. A hundred feet to the right was the open door of a brightly lighted room, from which could be heard the mumble of men's voices. An equal distance farther on, a ten-foot iron fence and gate spanned the corridor, marking an entrance to the prison. Beyond that, in the next cross corridor, the recessed edge of an elevator door could be seen. Immediately, he was able to orient their position to the mental map of this part of the Combs that he had carefully formulated on his way here – seemingly minutes ago. The trouble with a map was that it could not tell you how to proceed unless you knew where you were. Here, the landmarks showed they were still on the wrong side of the fence.

It was unguarded – a degree of laxity compatible only with the enemy's methods of imprisonment. The gate itself, he recalled, had an old-style lock which conveniently narrowed down his choice to the two largest of the keys dangling from his belt. And Gavin was sure he could open it much less noisily than the guard who had originally admitted them – providing they could reach it undetected.

There was no choice but to walk past that open door and hope intensely to be unnoticed. To search for other egress from the section would even more decidedly invite disaster. Gripping Dr Middleton's arm more firmly, he urged him to a fairly rapid walk...

Approaching the doorway, Gavin became aware of a number of things simultaneously: the doorway itself, Dr Middleton, the gate ahead, the jingling keys at his waist and the weight of an automatic at his side. The last called his attention to his ill-fitting clothes, which he identified wonderingly as the uniform of an enemy guard.

He quickly grasped the keys with his free hand to silence them, but the doctor's shuffling feet were making more noise on the stone floor than the murmur of voices in the room could be expected to drown out. Gavin held his breath as they came abreast of the doorway. If they were seen at all, they were lost. It would do no good to avert his head – no matter whom they mistook him for, the circumstances would undoubtedly seem peculiar enough to investigate. He glanced in.

A group of men sat at a table not fifteen feet from the doorway playing cards. One of them was almost directly facing the doorway, with nothing in his line of sight. He was in the act of slapping a card triumphantly down on the table, after which he turned to grin at the man at his left. Then Gavin and the doctor were past the seemingly wide doorway, safe for the moment. Gavin felt briefly grateful for the comparatively dim lighting of the corridor, and for the winning guard's luck...

Look around! He and Dr Middleton were standing before a row of elevators, and there was no one else in sight. As Gavin assessed the important factors of the situation, including his weapon and disguise, he felt a rising excitement, combined with a touch of awe at the incredible luck which must have brought him this far.

Yet there was still a tremendous – even hopeless – distance to go. The improbable achievement of reaching topside would leave the matter of at least a few thousand miles between them and safety. If – but the concern of the moment was that they were still on the same level as the prison where they had been confined. Painted in the recess at each end of the row of five doors was the same symbol he had noticed in coming down, a letter corresponding to the English R. The enemy, he knew, followed the worldwide convention of alphabetical sequence for their underground levels, starting from the top so that levels could be added without confusion when the Combs expanded downwards.

The indicator above one of the doors showed that an elevator was rising from the bottom of the shaft, only three levels below. Gavin was standing within reach of the signal buttons, which probably meant that he had already pushed one. Nevertheless, he pressed the upper one firmly, mentally approving the earlier choice implied by their presence here. Stairwells were usually widely separated from elevator shafts, for military reasons, and even if he had known where the nearest one was, the climb would be too time-consuming and strenuous, especially for the debilitated doctor. And it would greatly increase the chances of disastrous encounter. This way, with luck, there might be only the elevator operator to deal with. Gavin rested his free hand on his hip, in contact with the butt of the automatic, and hoped it would stay there as an instantaneous reminder...

As the elevator door before him began to slide open, he identified the cold metal touching his hand, and oriented himself sufficiently to restrain an impulse to draw the weapon. There were two men in the elevator: the operator, who was a soldier of the rank corresponding to corporal, and an officer. As the latter stepped from the car, Gavin saw that he was a captain of ordnance. The officer glanced at them with no more than mild curiosity and turned down the corridor. As quickly as possible, Gavin led the stumbling doctor into the elevator, and was aware of the doors gliding shut behind them...

He was in an elevator with Dr Middleton and the operator, a soldier, who was looking at him curiously. The car's motion was changing, yet because it was completely enclosed, there were no visual clues. Gavin's first impression was of coming to a stop in a downward direction. Then as the pressure of his shoe-soles eased off and the sighing sound of movement in the shaft continued, he realized the car had been accelerating upwards. On the assumption that it had started from the prison level, there was a long way to go to the top one, and there would be time enough to—

Gavin drew his pistol and waved the astonished operator away from the controls. As the soldier released the lever and stepped aside with hands upraised, the car slowed sharply in its ascent. Quickly, Gavin grasped the lever, swung it hard over and half-sat on it, with his back against the panel. Gesturing towards Dr Middleton, he curbed a growing sense of urgency well enough to speak distinctly to the soldier in his own language: 'The jacket – take it off him!'

Fortunately, the man turned submissively, almost without hesitation, and began to unfasten the doctor's straps. At that moment, a buzzer sounded within the car, in short, angry bursts. Someone had evidently been passed up, and didn't like it...

There was an almost continual buzzing in the moving elevator, accompanied by a dull roaring from without which was increasing in volume. An enemy soldier stood with his back turned toward Gavin, who tensed, then relaxed as the situation explained itself in part. The soldier was in the act of unwrapping the straitjacket from Dr Middleton.

The next instant, he whirled and lashed out with the jacket. It caught Gavin in the head and whipped his face, blinding him momentarily; then he was grappling with the soldier, grimly aware of the hampering effect of the studded panel against which his back was pressed.

The pistol was slowly being twisted from his grasp – not expertly, but irresistibly, because of superior leverage. Gavin took a chance and let go of the gun, which the soldier was holding by its barrel. It was then that the latter revealed his amateur status. He attempted to jump back and shift the gun to his other hand to reverse it.

Gavin jumped with him, knocked the man's gun arm upward and followed through with a swift hammerlock. Seconds later, he relieved the soldier of the excruciating pain of a broken arm by clubbing him unconscious with the gun butt.

Gavin had identified the roaring sound. The elevator was stopped near one of the factory levels. He reached for the control lever . . .

The insistent buzzing made it difficult to tell, but the car seemed to be moving very slowly, though the lever was all the way over, in the 'up' position. It could mean they were approaching the top of the shaft. And this car would not be the only one doing that. Others would be coming to investigate – if they were not there already. Yet the cars which had been near the top level would have had to go down quite a way to place the source of trouble. And if those cars were also operated by common soldiers, no investigation would be undertaken without orders. There was a chance that the top level would still be clear.

The elevator stopped. As Gavin released the lever, the car settled slowly, evidently seeking alignment with the top level. When it stopped, both doors would open automatically.

Hastily, Gavin grasped the unconscious soldier by his collar and pulled him closer, then ripped open the man's coat and tugged it off him. It would be useful to Dr Middleton, when and if there were time to put it on him.

With a heave, he propped the soldier in a sitting position under the control lever. Catching up the straitjacket from the floor, he passed it around the man's chest under his arms and tied the ends to the handle of the control lever, just as the elevator stopped again and the doors slid open.

Gavin grabbed Dr Middleton's arm with one hand, the soldier's coat with the other, and hauled them both from the car. There was no time for caution – but a quick glance showed no one close by. Reaching into the elevator he clutched the soldier by his shirt sleeve and toppled him over. At once, the doors started to shut, and a moment later the indicator showed the car on its way – to the bottom....

Look around! The letter painted in the recess corresponded to the top level of the Combs, and stirred in Gavin a brief feeling of astonishment. It also posed a problem, being the only means yet apparent for distinguishing this level from any other.

Whether or not they had come up on one of these elevators, as was probable, it was obviously not safe to remain here. A quick glance at the indicators above the doors showed that two of the cars were only a few levels below and rising steadily.

And there were several people visible along the corridor, both civilians and soldiers. The former, from what Gavin knew of the enemy's martial caste system, would offer little hazard. In fact, the uniform he wore might very well get them past all save officers – until the alarm was sounded.

Making an automatic connexion in his mind between the coat in his hand and Dr Middleton's lack of one, he quickly stepped behind the doctor and caught his dangling hands in the sleeve holes. The coat went on easily, being somewhat large, and Gavin noted with approval that the loss of its metal buttons made it look less military.

At that moment, Gavin heard the noise, faint with distance, and realized that it had existed for several seconds, at least. They were only a few steps from the intersection of another corridor. He led the doctor hastily around the corner – and kept on walking, past two men whose heavy clothing and ruddy faces suggested outdoor workers, and who glanced at them with weary indifference.

The sound was louder now, and unmistakable. It was the guttural roar of jet engines, somewhere ahead . . .

Look around! Several matters pressed for Gavin's attention all at once. He and Dr Middleton were at an intersection of two corridors, one of which ended twenty feet away at a big door. Over it was a sign which translated, amazingly enough, into HANGAR 3. Built into the large door was a smaller one, which an armed guard was holding open to admit a worker into the corridor. The noise of jet engines rolled loudly from the opening, yet did not quite drown out the insistent clangour of a bell – or bells, since it seemed to come from all directions. A general alarm, it must be, and there was little question as to its object.

Not too abruptly, for the guard had not yet noticed them, Gavin drew the automatic from its holster and released the safety. Whatever miracle had got them this far, no sort of pretence would get them any farther.

Suddenly, a new sound obtruded itself: the sharp reverberations of several shots along the corridor. If they had been aimed this way, the bullets had not come close enough to be audible above the general noise. Without taking his eyes off the guard, Gavin clutched the doctor's arm more tightly and moved quickly forward. At that moment the civilian stopped just inside the door, looking at them doubtfully, and the guard noticed them for the first time.

As Gavin had half expected, the soldier reached for his gun, ignoring the one which was pointed at him – and which promptly shot him down. The guard had had no real choice. He was responsible for this gateway, and under the enemy system, the alternatives confronting him had been virtual suicide or – worse.

On the other hand, no such handicap to survival attached to the civilian, who had scuttled back through the doorway and disappeared before the soldier had hit the floor. Gavin might have winged him, but it was doubtful that the man would spread the alarm within the hangar – or, in fact, do anything but make himself scarce. Iron discipline the enemy had in abundance, but *esprit de corps*, even among its military, was known to be rare ...

The broad hangar room, dim-lit and cluttered with a variety of small and medium-sized war planes, was like most chambers of its kind: thick columns supported the arched steel and concrete ceiling, which in turn supported a sizeable part of the mountain, or of one of the hills, under which these Combs had undoubtedly been built. Across the room, fifty yards away, some of the heavy steel doors stood open, admitting grey daylight, along with a chill wind and an ear-splitting noise. Yet within the hangar itself, the steady ringing of a bell was faintly audible. Here and there in the general gloom, bright portable lights showed mechanics at work on some of the planes. Gavin led Dr Middleton toward the far doors in as fast a walk as possible, and with little regard for concealment ...

The deafening roar was coming from the twin jets of a black night fighter on the runway just outside the hangar. Beyond it was the high, camouflaged wall of a revetment, and looming vaguely in the dusky background was a rugged, snow-covered landscape. Since the month was only October, these Combs must be situated quite far north. The deep twilight indicated that the day was either coming or going; Gavin hoped it was the latter.

The night fighter was not being warmed up for a take-off as Gavin had supposed. He could now see that two mechanics were apparently testing its engines; that could mean there was something serious wrong with one, or even both. It could also mean the plane was not fully fuelled – and in any case, the type did not begin to have the necessary range.

He paused in the partial shadow of one of the great steel doors, tensely clutching the arm of Dr Middleton, who was shivering with cold. Directly beyond the night fighter, but several hundred yards farther down the runway was a larger plane of a type familiar to Gavin as the Osprey fighter-bomber, although the enemy had got this version into production only recently. Differences of detail were not noticeable in the half-light, and the stubby fuselage and offset wings were characteristic. It was powered by an engine of radical design, without moving parts, which utilized fuel so efficiently as to provide truly global range. Its top speed approached that of rocket planes, whose scope was much more restricted. Just now, it seemed hopelessly far away....

Look around! Halfway across the hangar, two soldiers with drawn pistols were running towards them, and Gavin could see the legs of several others beneath intervening planes. The first soldier raised his gun and fired; the bullet screeched against the door beside them leaving a bright furrow in the metal, but the sound of the shot was lost in the noise from outside. The next instant, Gavin had hustled Dr Middleton out, and with the temporary protection of the door behind them, he started for the black fighter.

The two mechanics, who were lifting a section of housing from the near engine, looked up in surprise, then dropped the housing on the ground and moved aside as Gavin motioned with his gun. Since they were unarmed, he gave them no further thought. Half dragging the stumbling doctor, Gavin ducked under the plane and heaved the other man sprawling on the wing.

Jumping on it himself, he stretched half his length down into the cockpit, pulled the throttle over to maximum and released the brakes. Immediately, the plane began to move forward...

As he straightened up, puzzled, a hole appeared in the plastic canopy before his eyes, then another not far from it. A glance showed soldiers running out of the hangar nearby, the foremost of them trying to circle out far enough to get a direct shot at this side of the plane, which was beginning to outdistance them.

A sudden thrust against his feet nearly toppled him from the wing. Instinctively, he stepped clear – then bent and grabbed with one hand at the sliding, squirming form of Dr Middleton, just in time. Shifting his grip to the man's coat

54

collar, Gavin lifted him high. With one knee under the other's buttocks, he was about to boost the doctor headlong into the cockpit, when he caught sight of another plane standing on the runway a few hundred yards ahead. It was the enemy equivalent of an Osprey, and there seemed to be no one near it. If he could take that...

Gavin hesitated the merest instant, then, with grim logic, he swung the doctor pickaback, between himself and the pursuing soldiers. Reaching precariously into the cockpit, he slacked off on the throttle – and waited...

Look around! Through the viewports of the Osprey's small control cabin, throbbing bands of eerie light were visible, sweeping erratically across a starry sky. The plane was flying smoothly, high above a black and silver wasteland.

By the dim glow from the instrument panel, Gavin noticed with a start the limp form of a man in the seat beside him. The lined face was that of Dr Middleton, and there was dried blood on his shirt, though he seemed to be sleeping normally. Gavin pulled the man's coat farther back and tore open his shirt, exposing the blood-caked flesh beneath. Somewhere along the line, the doctor had taken a bullet through the latissimal muscles under his right arm, but the wound had stopped bleeding and with caution would probably keep all right for a few hours—

Gavin's gaze flew to the instrument panel. The fuel gauge showed almost one half of capacity, which should be more than enough to take them home – though it would not be safe to take an enemy plane farther than the first friendly outpost that the radio could contact.

Altitude, seventeen thousand; speed, just over eight hundred; course—

Gavin grinned, suddenly aware that a considerable time had passed with no lapse of memory. He was now fairly sure one would not occur, for in order to be where they seemed to be, several hours must have passed. Also, while his vitals ached with a hunger that was making him a little light-headed, he did not feel overly tired, which could only mean that he had slept. In all probability, the effect of the

drug had fallen below the neural-dissociative level. He relaxed systematically – and, as the tautness left his nerves, he
realized that he was wearier than he had thought.

According to the somewhat demented magnetic compass,
their course was approximately north. The plane had not
been guided thus far by that venerable instrument, however, but by a gyroscopic grandson known as the ortho-
compass, especially developed for trans-polar navigation.
For once, Gavin was glad the enemy had contrived to steal
it. Just now, the indicator under its calibrated bell-crystal
was pointing straight up. More significant was the reading
of its geared-in longitude recorder, which was in the slow
process of changing from 98° E to 82° W.

Actually, their course was due south. Since they were
moving, it had to be. For there was little doubt that they
were sitting on top of the world.

THE EARTH MEN

Ray Bradbury

I don't know how many stories have been written in which the first men from Earth reach another planet, find it inhabited by people much like themselves, then proceed to battle the bad guys, get lost in jungles, marry local princesses, and so on: there must be hundreds. Who but Bradbury would have thought of writing a story in which the first men reach Mars, meet the inhabitants ... and find that nobody cares?

WHOEVER was knocking at the door didn't want to stop.

Mrs Ttt threw the door open. 'Well?'

'You speak *English*!' The man standing there was astounded.

'I speak what I speak,' she said.

'It's wonderful *English*!' The man was in uniform. There were three men with him, in a great hurry, all smiling, all dirty.

'What do you want?' demanded Mrs Ttt.

'You are a *Martian*!' The man smiled. 'The word is not familiar to you, certainly. It's an Earth expression.' He nodded at his men. 'We are from Earth. I'm Captain Williams. We've landed on Mars within the hour. Here we are, the *Second* Expedition! There was a First Expedition, but we don't know what happened to it. But here we are, anyway. And you are the first Martian we've met!'

'Martian?' Her eyebrows went up.

'What I mean to say is, you live on the fourth planet from the sun. Correct?'

'Elementary,' she snapped, eyeing them.

'And we' – he pressed his chubby pink hand to his chest – 'we are from Earth. Right, men?'

'Right, sir!' A chorus.

'This is the planet Tyrr,' she said, 'if you want to use the proper name.'

'Tyrr, Tyrr.' The captain laughed exhaustedly. 'What a *fine* name! But, my good woman, how is it you speak such perfect English?'

'I'm not speaking, I'm thinking,' she said. 'Telepathy! Good day!' And she slammed the door.

A moment later there was that dreadful man knocking again.

She whipped the door open. 'What now?' she wondered.

The man was still there, trying to smile, looking bewildered. He put out his hands. 'I don't think you *understand*—'

'What?' she snapped.

The man gazed at her in surprise. 'We're from *Earth*!'

'I haven't time,' she said. 'I've a lot of cooking today and there's cleaning and sewing and all. You evidently wish to see Mr Ttt; he's upstairs in his study.'

'Yes,' said the Earth man confusedly, blinking. 'By all means, let us see Mr Ttt.

'He's busy.' She slammed the door again.

This time the knock on the door was most impertinently loud.

'See here!' cried the man when the door was thrust open again. He jumped in as if to surprise her. 'This is no way to treat visitors!'

'All over my clean floor!' she cried. 'Mud! Get out! If you come in my house, wash your boots first.'

The man looked in dismay at his muddy boots. 'This,' he said, 'is no time for trivialities. I think,' he said, 'we should be celebrating.' He looked at her for a long time, as if looking might make her understand.

'If you've made my crystal buns fall in the oven,' she exclaimed, 'I'll hit you with a piece of wood!' She peered into a little hot oven. She came back, red, steamy-faced. Her eyes were sharp yellow, her skin was soft brown, she was thin and quick as an insect. Her voice was metallic and

58

sharp. 'Wait here. I'll see if I can let you have a moment with Mr Ttt. What was your business?'

The man swore luridly, as if she'd hit his hand with a hammer. 'Tell him we're from Earth and it's never been done before!'

'What hasn't?' She put her brown hand up. 'Never mind. I'll be back.'

The sound of her feet fluttered through the stone house.

Outside, the immense blue Martian sky was hot and still as a warm deep sea water. The Martian desert lay broiling like a prehistoric mud pot, waves of heat rising and shimmering. There was a small rocket ship reclining upon a hilltop nearby. Large footprints came from the rocket to the door of this stone house.

Now there was a sound of quarrelling voices upstairs. The men within the door stared at one another, shifting on their boots, twiddling their fingers, and holding on to their hip belts. A man's voice shouted upstairs. The woman's voice replied. After fifteen minutes the Earth men began walking in and out the kitchen door, with nothing to do.

'Cigarette?' said one of the men.

Somebody got out a pack and they lit up. They puffed slow streams of pale white smoke. They adjusted their uniforms, fixed their collars. The voices upstairs continued to mutter and chant. The leader of the men looked at his watch.

'Twenty-five minutes,' he said. 'I wonder what they're up to up there.' He went to a window and looked out.

'Hot day,' said one of the men.

'Yeah,' said someone else in the slow warm time of early afternoon. The voices had faded to a murmur and were now silent. There was not a sound in the house. All the men could hear was their own breathing.

An hour of silence passed. 'I hope we didn't cause any trouble,' said the captain. He peered into the living-room.

Mrs Ttt was there, watering some flowers that grew in the centre of the room.

'I knew I had forgotten something,' she said when she saw the captain. She walked out to the kitchen. 'I'm sorry.' She handed him a slip of paper. 'Mr Ttt is much too busy.'

59

She turned to her cooking. 'Anyway, it's not Mr Ttt you want to see; it's Mr Aaa. Take that paper over to the next farm, by the blue canal, and Mr Aaa'll advise you about whatever it is you want to know.'

'We don't want to know anything,' objected the captain, pouting out his thick lips. 'We already *know* it.'

'You have the paper. What more do you want?' she asked him straight off. And she would say no more.

'Well,' said the captain, reluctant to go. He stood as if waiting for something. He looked like a child staring at an empty Christmas tree. 'Well,' he said again. 'Come on, men.'

The four men stepped out into the hot silent day.

Half an hour later, Mr Aaa, seated in his library sipping a bit of electric fire from a metal cup, heard the voices outside in the stone causeway. He leaned over the windowsill and gazed at the four uniformed men who squinted up at him.

'Are you Mr Aaa?' they called.

'I am.'

'Mr Ttt sent us to see you!' shouted the captain.

'Why did he do that?' asked Mr Aaa.

'He was busy!'

'Well, that's a shame,' said Mr Aaa sarcastically. 'Does he think I have nothing else to do but entertain people he's too busy to bother with?'

'That's not the important thing, sir,' shouted the captain.

'Well, it is to me. I have much reading to do. Mr Ttt is inconsiderate. This is not the first time he has been this thoughtless of me. Stop waving your hands, sir, until I finish. And pay attention. People usually listen to me when I talk. And you'll listen courteously or I won't talk at all.'

Uneasily the four men in the court shifted and opened their mouths, and once the captain, the veins on his face bulging, showed a few little tears in his eyes.

'Now,' lectured Mr Aaa, 'do you think it fair of Mr Ttt to be so ill-mannered?'

The four men gazed up through the heat. The captain said, 'We're from Earth!'

'I think it very ungentlemanly of him,' brooded Mr Aaa.

'A *rocket* ship. We came in it. Over there!'

'Not the first time Ttt's been unreasonable, you know.'

'All the way from Earth.'

'Why, for half a mind, I'd call him up and tell him off.'

'Just the four of us; myself and these three men, my crew.'

'I'll call him up, yes, that's what I'll do!'

'Earth. Rocket. Men. Trip. Space.'

'Call him and give him a good lashing!' cried Mr Aaa. He vanished like a puppet from a stage. For a minute there were angry voices back and forth over some weird mechanism or other. Below, the captain and his crew glanced longingly back at their pretty rocket ship lying on the hillside, so sweet and lovely and fine.

Mr Aaa jerked up in the window, wildly triumphant. 'Challenged him to a duel, by the gods! A duel!'

'Mr Aaa—' the captain started all over again, quietly.

'I'll shoot him dead, do you hear!'

'Mr Aaa, I'd like to *tell* you. We came sixty million miles.'

Mr Aaa regarded the captain for the first time. 'Where'd you say you were from?'

The captain flashed a white smile. Aside to his men he whispered, '*Now* we're getting someplace!' To Mr Aaa he called, 'We travelled sixty million miles. From Earth!'

Mr Aaa yawned. 'That's only *fifty* million miles this time of year.' He picked up a frightful-looking weapon. 'Well, I have to go now. Just take that silly note, though I don't know what good it'll do you, and go over that hill into the little town of Iopr and tell Mr Iii all about it. *He's* the man you want to see. Not Mr Ttt, he's an idiot; I'm going to kill him. Not me, because you're not in my line of work.'

'Line of work, line of work!' bleated the captain. 'Do you have to be in a certain line of work to welcome Earth men!'

'Don't be silly, everyone knows *that*!' Mr Aaa rushed downstairs. 'Goodbye!' And down the causeway he raced, like a pair of wild calipers.

The four travellers stood shocked. Finally the captain said, 'We'll find someone yet who'll listen to us.'

'Maybe we could go out and come in again,' said one of the men in a dreary voice. 'Maybe we should take off and land again. Give them time to organize a party.'

'That might be a good idea,' murmured the tired captain.

The little town was full of people drifting in and out of doors, saying hello to one another, wearing golden masks and blue masks and crimson masks for pleasant variety, masks with silver lips and bronze eyebrows, masks that smiled or masks that frowned, according to the owners' dispositions.

The four men, wet from their long walk, paused and asked a little girl where Mr Iii's house was.

'There.' The child nodded her head.

The captain got eagerly, carefully, down on one knee, looking into her sweet young face. 'Little girl, I want to talk to you.'

He seated her on his knee and folded her small brown hands neatly in his own big ones, as if ready for a bedtime story which he was shaping in his mind slowly and with a great patient happiness in details.

'Well, here's how it is, little girl. Six months ago another rocket came to Mars. There was a man named York in it, and his assistant. Whatever happened to them, we don't know. Maybe they crashed. They came in a rocket. So did we. You should see it! A *big* rocket! So we're the *Second* Expedition, following up the First. And we came all the way from Earth . . .'

The little girl disengaged one hand without thinking about it and clapped an expressionless golden mask over her face. Then she pulled forth a golden spider toy and dropped it to the ground while the captain talked on. The toy spider climbed back up to her knee obediently, while she speculated upon it coolly through the slits of her emotionless mask and the captain shook her gently and urged his story upon her.

'We're Earth men,' he said. 'Do you believe me?'

'Yes.' The little girl peeped at the way she was wiggling her toes in the dust.

'Fine.' The captain pinched her arm, a little bit with

joviality, a little bit with meanness, to get her to look at him. 'We built our own rocket ship. Do you believe *that*?'

The little girl dug in her nose with a finger. 'Yes.'

'And – take your finger out of your nose, little girl – *I* am the captain, and—'

'Never before in history has anybody come across space in a big rocket ship,' recited the little creature, eyes shut.

'Wonderful! How do you know?'

'Oh, telepathy.' She wiped a casual finger on her knee.

'Well, aren't you just *ever* so excited?' cried the captain. 'Aren't you glad?'

'You just better go see Mr Iii right away.' She dropped her toy to the ground. 'Mr Iii will like talking to you.' She ran off, with the toy spider scuttling obediently after her.

The captain squatted there, looking after her with his hand out. His eyes were watery in his head. He looked at his empty hands. His mouth hung open. The other three men stood with their shadows under them. They spat on the stone street...

Mr Iii answered his door. He was on his way to a lecture, but he had a minute, if they would hurry inside and tell him what they desired...

'A little attention,' said the captain, red-eyed and tired. 'We're from Earth, we have a rocket, there are four of us, crew and captain, we're exhausted, we're hungry, we'd like a place to sleep. We'd like someone to give us the key to the city or something like that, and we'd like somebody to shake our hands and say, "Hooray" and say, "Congratulations, old man!" That about sums it up.'

Mr Iii was a tall, vaporous, thin man with thick, blind, blue crystals over his yellowish eyes. He bent over his desk and brooded upon some papers, glancing now and again with extreme penetration at his guests.

'Well, I haven't the forms with me here, I don't *think*.' He rummaged through the desk drawers. 'Now, where *did* I put the forms?' He mused. 'Somewhere. Somewhere. Oh, *here* we are! Now!' He handed the papers over crisply. 'You'll have to sign these papers, of course.'

'Do we have to go through all this rigmarole?'

Mr Iii gave him a thick glassy look. 'You say you're from Earth, don't you? Well, then there's nothing for it but you sign.'

The captain wrote his name. 'Do you want my crew to sign also?'

Mr Iii looked at the captain, looked at the three others, and burst into a shout of derision. '*Them* sign! Ho! How marvellous! Them, oh, *them* sign!' Tears sprang from his eyes. He slapped his knee and bent to let his laughter jerk out of his gaping mouth. He held himself up with the desk. '*Them* sign!'

The four men scowled. 'What's funny?'

'Them sign!' sighed Mr Iii, weak with hilarity. 'So very funny. I'll have to tell Mr Xxx about this!' He examined the filled-out form, still laughing. 'Everything seems to be in order.' He nodded. 'Even the agreement for euthanasia if final decision on such a step is necessary.' He chuckled.

'Agreement for *what*?'

'Don't talk. I have something for you. Here. Take this key.'

The captain flushed. 'It's a great honour.'

'Not the key to the city, you fool!' snapped Mr Iii. 'Just a key to the House. Go down that corridor, unlock the big door, and go inside and shut the door tight. You can spend the night there. In the morning I'll send Mr Xxx to see you.'

Dubiously the captain took the key in hand. He stood looking at the floor. His men did not move. They seemed to be emptied of all their blood and their rocket fever. They were drained dry.

'What is it? What's wrong?' inquired Mr Iii. 'What are you waiting for? What do you want?' He came and peered up into the captain's face, stooping. 'Out with it, you!'

'I don't suppose you could even—' suggested the captain. 'I mean, that is, try to, or think about...' He hesitated. 'We've worked hard, we've come a long way, and maybe you could just shake our hands and say "Well done!" Do you – think?' His voice faded.

Mr Iii stuck out his hand stiffly. 'Congratulations!' He smiled a cold smile. 'Congratulations.' He turned away. 'I must go now. Use that key.'

Without noticing them again, as if they had melted down through the floor, Mr Iii moved about the room, packing a little manuscript case with papers. He was in the room another five minutes but never again addressed the solemn quartet that stood with heads down, their heavy legs sagging, the light dwindling from their eyes. When Mr Iii went out the door, he was busy looking at his fingernails...'

They straggled along the corridor in the dull, silent afternoon light. They came to a large, burnished silver door, and the silver key opened it. They entered, shut the door, and turned.

They were in a vast sunlit hall. Men and women sat at tables and stood in conversing groups. At the sound of the door they regarded the four uniformed men.

One Martian stepped forward, bowing. 'I am Mr Uuu,' he said.

'And I am Captain Jonathan Williams, of New York City, on Earth,' said the captain without emphasis.

Immediately the hall exploded!

The rafters trembled with shouts and cries. The people, rushing forward, waved and shrieked happily, knocking down tables, swarming, rollicking, seizing the four Earth men, lifting them swiftly to their shoulders. They charged about the hall six times, six times making a full and wonderful circuit of the room, jumping, bounding, singing.

The Earth men were so stunned that they rode the toppling shoulders for a full minute before they began to laugh and shout at each other: 'Hey! This is more *like* it!' 'This is the life! Boy! Yay! Yow! Whoopee!'

They winked tremendously at each other. They flung up their hands to clap the air. 'Hey!'

'Hooray!' said the crowd.

They set the Earth men on a table. The shouting died.

The captain almost broke into tears. 'Thank you. It's good, it's good.'

'Tell us about yourselves,' suggested Mr Uuu.

The captain cleared his throat.

The audience ohed and ahed as the captain talked. He introduced his crew; each made a small speech and was embarrassed by the thunderous applause.

Mr Uuu clapped the captain's shoulder. 'It's good to see another man from Earth. I am from Earth also.'

'How was that again?'

'There are many of us here from Earth.'

'You? From Earth?' The captain stared. 'But is that possible? Did you come by rocket? Has space travel been going on for centuries?' His voice was disappointed. 'What – what country are you from?'

'Tuiereol. I came by the spirit of my body, years ago.'

'Tuiereol.' The captain mouthed the word. 'I don't know that country. What's this about spirit of body?'

'And Miss Rrr over here, she's from Earth, too, *aren't* you, Miss Rrr?'

Miss Rrr nodded and laughed strangely.

'And so is Mr Www and Mr Qqq and Mr Vvv!'

'I'm from Jupiter,' declared one man, preening himself.

'I'm from Saturn,' said another, eyes glinting slyly.

'Jupiter, Saturn,' murmured the captain, blinking.

It was very quiet now; the people stood around and sat at the tables which were strangely empty for banquet tables. Their yellow eyes were glowing, and there were dark shadows under their cheekbones. The captain noticed for the first time that there were no windows; the light seemed to permeate the walls. There was only one door. The captain winced. 'This is confusing. Where on Earth is this Tuiereol? Is it near America?'

'What is America?'

'You never heard of America! You say you're from Earth and yet you don't know!'

Mr Uuu drew himself up angrily. 'Earth is a place of seas and nothing but seas. There is no land. I am from Earth, and know.'

'Wait a minute.' The captain sat back. 'You look like a regular Martian. Yellow eyes. Brown skin.'

'Earth is a place of all *jungle*,' said Miss Rrr proudly. 'I am from Orri, on Earth, a civilization built of silver!'

Now the captain turned his head from and then to Mr Uuu and then to Mr Www and Mr Zzz and Mr Nnn and Mr Hhh and Mr Bbb. He saw their yellow eyes waxing and waning in the light, focusing and unfocusing. He began to shiver. Finally he turned to his men and regarded them sombrely.

'Do you realize what this is?'

'What, sir?'

'This is no celebration,' replied the captain tiredly. 'This is no banquet. These aren't government representatives. This is no surprise party. Look at their eyes. Listen to them!'

Nobody breathed. There was only a soft white move of eyes in the closed room.

'Now I understand' – the captain's voice was far away – 'why everyone gave us notes and passed us on, one from the other, until we met Mr Iii, who sent us down a corridor with a key to open a door and shut a door. And here we are . . .'

'Where are we, sir?'

The captain exhaled. 'In an insane asylum.'

It was night. The large hall lay quiet and dimly illumined by hidden light sources in the transparent walls. The four Earth men sat around a wooden table, their bleak heads bent over their whispers. On the floor, men and women lay huddled. There were little stirs in the dark corners, solitary men or women gesturing their hands. Every half-hour one of the captain's men would try the silver door and return to the table. 'Nothing doing, sir. We're locked in proper.'

'They think we're really insane, sir?'

'Quite. That's why there was no hullabaloo to welcome us. They merely tolerated what, to them, must be a constantly recurring psychotic condition.' He gestured at the dark sleeping shapes all about them. 'Paranoids, every single one! What a welcome they gave us! For a moment there' – a little fire rose and died in his eyes – 'I thought we were getting our true reception. All the yelling and singing and speeches. Pretty nice, wasn't it – while it lasted?'

'How long will they keep us here, sir?'

'Until we prove we're not psychotics.'

'That should be easy.'

'I *hope* so.'

'You don't sound very certain, sir.'

'I'm not. Look in that corner.'

A man squatted alone in darkness. Out of his mouth issued a blue flame which turned into the round shape of a small naked woman. It flourished on the air softly in vapours of cobalt light, whispering and sighing.

The captain nodded at another corner. A woman stood there, changing. First she was embedded in a crystal pillar, then she melted into a golden statue, finally a staff of polished cedar, and back to a woman.

All through the midnight hall people were juggling thin violet flames, shifting, changing, for night-time was the time of change and affliction.

'Magicians, sorcerers,' whispered one of the Earth men.

'No, hallucination. They pass their insanity over into us so that we see their hallucinations too. Telepathy. Auto-suggestion and telepathy.'

'Is that what worries you, sir?'

'Yes. If hallucinations can appear this "real" to us, to anyone, if hallucinations are catching and almost believable, it's no wonder they mistook us for psychotics. If that man can produce little blue fire women and that woman there melt into a pillar, how natural if normal Martians think we produce our rocket ship with *our* minds.'

'Oh,' said his men in the shadows.

Around them, in the vast hall, flames leaped blue, flared, evaporated. Little demons of red sand ran between the teeth of sleeping men. Women became oily snakes. There was a smell of reptiles and animals.

In the morning everyone stood around looking fresh, happy, and normal. There were no flames or demons in the room. The captain and his men waited by the silver door, hoping it would open.

Mr Xxx arrived after about four hours. They had a suspicion that he had waited outside the door, peering in at them for at least three hours before he stepped in, beckoned, and led them to his small office.

He was a jovial, smiling man, if one could believe the mask he wore, for upon it was painted not one smile, but three. Behind it, his voice was the voice of a not so smiling psychologist. 'What seems to be the trouble?'

'You think we're insane, and we're not,' said the captain.

'Contrarily, I do not think *all* of you are insane.' The psychologist pointed a little wand at the captain. 'No. Just *you* sir. The others are secondary hallucinations.'

The captail slapped his knee. 'So *that's* it! That's why Mr Iii laughed when I suggested my men sign the papers too!'

'Yes, Mr Iii told me.' The psychologist laughed out of the carved, smiling mouth. 'A good joke. Where was I? Secondary hallucinations, yes. Women come to me with snakes crawling from their ears. When I cure them the snakes vanish.'

'We'll be glad to be cured. Go right ahead.'

Mr Xxx seemed surprised. 'Unusual. Not many people want to be cured. The cure is drastic, you know.'

'Cure ahead! I'm confident you'll find we're all sane.'

'Let me check your papers to be sure they're in order for a "cure".' He checked a file. 'Yes. You know, such cases as yours need special "curing". The people in that hall are simpler forms. But once you've gone this far, I must point out, with primary, secondary, auditory, olfactory, and labial hallucinations, as well as tactile and optical fantasies, it is pretty bad business. We have to resort to euthanasia.'

The captain leaped up with a roar. 'Look here, we've stood quite enough! Test us, tap our knees, check our hearts, exercise us, ask questions!'

'You are free to speak.'

The captain raved for an hour. The psychologist listened.

'Incredible,' he mused. 'Most detailed dream fantasy I've ever heard.'

'God damn it, we'll show you the rocket ship!' screamed the captain.

'I'd like to see it. Can you manifest it in this room?'

'Oh, certainly. It's in that file of yours, under *R*.'

Mr Xxx peered seriously into his file. He went 'Tsk' and shut the file solemnly. 'Why did you tell me to look? The rocket isn't there.'

'Of course not, you idiot! I was joking. Does an insane man joke?'

'You find some odd senses of humour. Now, take me out to your rocket. I wish to see it.'

It was noon. The day was very hot when they reached the rocket.

'So.' The psychologist walked up to the ship and tapped it. It gonged softly. 'May I go inside?' he asked slyly.

'You may.'

Mr Xxx stepped in and was gone for a long time.

'Of all the silly, exasperating things.' The captain chewed a cigar as he waited. 'For two cents I'd go back home and tell people not to bother with Mars. What a suspicious bunch of louts.'

'I gather that a good number of their population are insane, sir. That seems to be their main reason for doubting.'

'Nevertheless, this is all so damned irritating.'

The psychologist emerged from the ship after half an hour of prowling, tapping, listening, smelling, tasting.

'*Now* do you believe!' shouted the captain, as if he were deaf.

The psychologist shut his eyes and scratched his nose. 'This is the most incredible example of sensual hallucination and hypnotic suggestion I've ever encountered. I went through your "rocket", as you call it.' He tapped the hull. 'I hear it. Auditory fantasy.' He drew a breath. 'I smell it. Olfactory hallucination, induced by sensual telepathy.' He kissed the ship. 'I taste it. Labial fantasy!'

He shook the captain's hand. 'May I congratulate you? You are a psychotic genius! You have done a most complete job! The task of projecting your psychotic image life into the mind of another via telepathy and keeping the hallucinations from becoming sensually weaker is almost impossible. Those people in the House usually concentrate on visuals or, at the most, visuals and auditory fantasies combined. You have balanced the whole conglomeration! Your insanity is beautifully complete!'

'My insanity.' The captain was pale.

'Yes, yes, what a lovely insanity. Metal, rubber, gravitizers, foods, clothing, fuel, weapons, ladders, nuts, bolts, spoons. Ten thousand separate items I checked on your vessel. Never have I seen such a complexity. There were even *shadows* under the bunks and under *everything*! Such concentration of will! And everything, no matter how or when tested, had a smell, a solidity, a taste, a sound! Let me embrace you!'

He stood back at last. 'I'll write this into my greatest monograph! I'll speak of it at the Martian Academy next month! *Look* at you! Why, you've even changed your eye colour from yellow to blue, your skin to pink from brown. And those clothes, and your hands having five fingers instead of six! Biological metamorphosis through psychological imbalance! And your three friends—'

He took out a little gun. 'Incurable, of course. You poor, wonderful man. You will be happier dead. Have you any last words?'

'Stop, for God's sake! Don't shoot!'

'You sad creature. I shall put you out of your misery which has driven you to imagine this rocket and these three men. It will be most engrossing to watch your friends and your rocket vanish once I have killed you. I will write a neat paper on the dissolvement of neurotic images from what I perceive here today.'

'I'm from Earth! My name is Jonathan Williams, and these—'

'Yes, I know,' soothed Mr Xxx, and fired his gun.

The captain fell with a bullet in his heart. The other three men screamed.

Mr Xxx stared at them. 'You continue to exist? This is superb! Hallucinations with time and spatial persistence!'

He pointed the gun at them. 'Well, I'll scare you into dissolving.'

'No!' cried the three men.

'An auditory appeal, even with the patient dead,' observed Mr Xxx as he shot the three men down.

They lay on the sand, intact, not moving.

He kicked them. Then he rapped on the ship.

'*It* persists! *They* persist!' He fired his gun again and again at the bodies. Then he stood back. The smiling mask dropped from his face.

Slowly the little psychologist's face changed. His jaw sagged. The gun dropped from his fingers. His eyes were dull and vacant. He put his hands up and turned in a blind circle. He fumbled at the bodies, saliva filling his mouth.

'Hallucinations,' he mumbled frantically. 'Taste. Sight. Smell. Sound. Feeling.' He waved his hands. His eyes bulged. His mouth began to give off a faint froth.

'Go away!' he shouted at the bodies. 'Go away!' he screamed at the ship. He examined his trembling hands. 'Contaminated,' he whispered wildly. 'Carried over into me. Telepathy. Hypnosis. Now *I'm* insane. Now *I'm* contaminated. Hallucinations in all their sensual forms.' He stopped and searched around with his numb hands for the gun. 'Only one cure. Only one way to make them go away, vanish.'

A shot rang out. Mr Xxx fell.

The four bodies lay in the sun. Mr Xxx lay where he fell.

The rocket reclined on the little sunny hill and didn't vanish.

When the town people found the rocket at sunset, they wondered what it was. Nobody knew, so it was sold to a junkman and hauled off to be broken up for scrap metal.

That night it rained all night. The next day was fair and warm.

WHO GOES THERE?

Don A. Stuart
(John W. Campbell)

Stories about mammoths perfectly preserved in the Siberian ice have fascinated us for generations. What if something else were dug up out of the polar ice, thawed and brought back to life – some prehistoric man, perhaps, or some monster? This story is a strictly disciplined work of science fiction, with a tricky problem and a brilliant solution. It is also a classic of horror. Don't read it late at night unless your nerves are good.

THE place stank. A queer, mingled stench that only the ice-buried cabins of an Antarctic camp know, compounded of reeking human sweat, and the heavy, fish-oil stench of melted seal blubber. An overtone of liniment combated the musty smell of sweat-and-snow-drenched furs. The acrid odour of burnt cooking fat, and the animal, not-unpleasant smell of dogs, diluted by time, hung in the air.

Lingering odours of machine oil contrasted sharply with the taint of harness dressing and leather. Yet, somehow, through all that reek of human beings and their associates – dogs, machines, and cooking – came another taint. It was a queer, neck-ruffling thing, a faintest suggestion of an odour alien among the smells of industry and life. And it was a life smell. But it came from the thing that lay bound with cord and tarpaulin on the table, dripping slowly, methodically onto the heavy planks, dank and gaunt under the unshielded glare of the electric light.

Blair, the little bald-pated biologist of the expedition, twitched nervously at the wrappings, exposing clear dark ice beneath and then pulling the tarpaulin back into place restlessly. His little birdlike motions of suppressed eagerness danced his shadow across the fringe of dingy grey underwear hanging from the low ceiling, the equatorial fringe of stiff, greying hair around his naked skull a comical halo about the shadow's head.

Commander Garry brushed aside the lax legs of a suit of underwear, and stepped towards the table. Slowly his eyes traced around the rings of men sardined into the Administration Building. His tall, stiff body straightened finally, and he nodded. 'Thirty-seven. All here.' His voice was low, yet carried the clear authority of the commander by nature, as well as by title.

'You know the outline of the story back of that find of the Secondary Magnetic Expedition. I have been conferring with Second-in-Command McReady and Norris as well as Blair and Dr Copper. There is a difference of opinion, and because it involves the entire group, it is only just that the entire expedition personnel act on it.

'I am going to ask McReady to give you the details of the story, because each of you has been too busy with his own work to follow closely the endeavours of the others. McReady?'

Moving from the smoke-blued background, McReady was a figure from some forgotten myth, a looming, bronze statue that held life, and walked. Six feet four inches he stood as he halted beside the table, and, with a characteristic glance upwards to assure himself of room under the low ceiling beams, straightened. His rough, clashingly orange windproof jacket he still had on, yet on his huge frame it did not seem misplaced. Even here, four feet beneath the driftwind that droned across the Antarctic waste above the ceiling, the cold of the frozen continent leaked in, and gave meaning to the harshness of the man. And he was bronze – his great red-bronze beard, the heavy hair that matched it. The gnarled, corded hands gripping, relaxing, gripping and relaxing on the table planks were bronze. Even the deep-sunken eyes beneath heavy brows were bronzed.

Age-resisting endurance of the metal spoke in the cragged heavy outlines of his face, and the mellow tones of the heavy voice. 'Norris and Blair agree on one thing: that animal we found was not – terrestrial in origin. Norris fears there may be danger in that; Blair says there is none.

'But I'll go back to how, and why, we found it. To all that was known before we came here, it appeared that this point was exactly over the South Magnetic Pole of Earth. The compass does point straight down here, as you all know. The more delicate instruments of the physicists, instruments especially designed for this expedition and its study of the magnetic pole, detected a secondary effect, a secondary, less powerful magnetic influence about eighty miles south-west of here.

'The Secondary Magnetic Expedition went out to investigate it. There is no need for details. We found it, but it was not the huge meteorite or magnetic mountain Norris had expected to find. Iron ore is magnetic of course, iron more so – and certain special steels even more magnetic. From the surface indications, the secondary pole we found was small, so small that the magnetic effect it had was preposterous. No magnetic material conceivable could have that effect. Soundings through the ice indicated it was within one hundred feet of the glacier surface.

'I think you should know the structure of the place. There is a broad plateau, a level sweep that runs more than one hundred and fifty miles due south from the Secondary station, Van Wall says. He didn't have time or fuel to fly farther, but it was running smoothly due south then. Right there, where that buried thing was, there is an ice-drowned mountain ridge, a granite wall of unshakable strength that has dammed back the ice creeping from the south.

'And four hundred miles due south is the South Polar Plateau. You have asked me at various times why it gets warmer here when the wind rises, and most of you know. As a meteorologist I'd have staked my word that no wind could blow at minus seventy degrees – that no more than a five-mile wind could blow at minus fifty – without causing warming due to friction with ground, snow and ice, and the air itself.

'We camped there on the lip of that ice-drowned mountain range for twelve days. We dug our camp into the blue ice that formed the surface, and escaped most of it. But for twelve consecutive days the wind blew at forty-five miles an hour. It went as high as forty-eight and fell to forty-one at times. The temperature was minus sixty-three degrees. It rose to minus sixty and fell to minus sixty-eight. It was meteorologically impossible, and it went on uninterruptedly for twelve days and twelve nights.

'Somewhere to the south, the frozen air of the South Polar Plateau slides down from that eighteen-thousand-foot bowl, down a mountain pass, over a glacier, and starts north. There must be a funnelling mountain chain that directs it, and sweeps it away for four hundred miles to hit that bald plateau where we found the secondary pole, and three hundred and fifty miles farther north reaches the Antarctic Ocean.

'It's been frozen there since the Antarctica froze twenty million years ago. There never has been a thaw there.

'Twenty million years ago Antarctica was beginning to freeze. We've investigated, thought, and built speculations. What we believe happened was about like this.

'Something came down out of space, a ship. We saw it there in the blue ice, a thing like a submarine without a conning tower or directive vanes, two hundred and eighty feet long and forty-five feet in diameter at its thickest.

'Eh, Van Wall? Space? Yes, but I'll explain that better later.' McReady's steady voice went on.

'It came down from space, driven and lifted by forces men haven't discovered yet, and somehow – perhaps something went wrong then – it tangled with Earth's magnetic field. It came south here, out of control probably, circling the magnetic pole. That's a savage country there, but when Antarctica was still freezing it must have been a thousand times more savage. There must have been blizzard snow, as well as drift, new snow falling as the continent glaciated. The swirl there must have been particularly bad, the wind hurling a solid blanket of white over the lip of that now-buried mountain.

'The ship struck solid granite head-on, and cracked up.

Not every one of the passengers in it was killed, but the ship must have been ruined, her driving mechanism locked. It tangled with Earth's field, Norris believes. No thing made by intelligent beings can tangle with the dead immensity of a planet's natural forces and survive.

'One of its passengers stepped out. The wind we saw there never fell below forty-one, and the temperature never rose above minus sixty. Then, the wind must have been stronger. And there was drift falling in a solid sheet. The *thing* was lost completely in ten paces.' He paused for a moment, the deep, steady voice giving way to the drone of wind overhead and the uneasy, malicious gurgling in the pipe of the galley stove.

Drift – a driftwind was sweeping by overhead. Right now the snow picked up by the mumbling wind fled in level, blinding lines across the face of the buried camp. If a man stepped out of the tunnels that connected each of the camp buildings beneath the surface, he'd be lost in ten paces. Out there the slim, black finger of the radio mast lifted three hundred feet into the air, and at its peak was the clear night sky. A sky of thin, whining wind rushing steadily from beyond to another beyond under the licking, curling mantle of the aurora. And off north, the horizon flamed with queer, angry colours of the midnight twilight. That was spring three hundred feet above Antarctica.

At the surface – it was white death. Death of a needle-fingered cold driven before the wind, sucking heat from any warm thing. Cold – and white mist of endless, everlasting drift, the fine, fine particles of licking snow that obscured all things.

Kinner, the little, scar-faced cook, winced. Five days ago he had stepped out to the surface to reach a cache of frozen beef. He had reached it, started back – and the driftwind leapt out of the south. Cold, white death that streamed across the ground blinded him in twenty seconds. He stumbled on wildly in circles. It was half an hour before rope-guided men from below found him in the impenetrable murk.

It was easy for man – or *thing* – to get lost in ten paces.

77

'And the driftwind then was probably more impenetrable than we know.' McReady's voice snapped Kinner's mind back. Back to welcome, dank warmth of the Ad Building. 'The passenger of the ship wasn't prepared either, it appears. It froze within ten feet of the ship.

'We dug down to find the ship, and our tunnel happened to find the frozen – animal. Barclay's ice axe struck its skull.

'When we saw what it was, Barclay went back to the tractor, started the fire up, and when the steam pressure built, sent a call for Blair and Dr Copper. Barclay himself was sick then. Stayed sick for three days, as a matter of fact.

'When Blair and Copper came, we cut out the animal in a block of ice, as you see, wrapped it, and loaded it on the tractor for return here. We wanted to get into that ship.

'We reached the side and found the metal was something we didn't know. Our beryllium-bronze, non-magnetic tools wouldn't touch it. Barclay had some tool steel on the tractor, and that wouldn't scratch it either. We made reasonable tests – even tried some acid from the batteries with no results.

'They must have had a passivating process to make magnesium metal resist acid that way, and the alloy must have been at least ninety-five per cent magnesium. But we had no way of guessing that, so when we spotted the barely opened lock door, we cut around it. There was clear, hard ice inside the lock, where we couldn't reach it. Through the little crack we could look in and see that only metal and tools were in there, so we decided to loosen the ice with a bomb.

'We had decanite bombs and thermite. Thermite is the ice softener; decanite might have shattered valuable things, where the thermite's heat would just loosen the ice. Dr Copper, Norris, and I placed a twenty-five-pound thermite bomb, wired it, and took the connector up the tunnel to the surface, where Blair had the steam tractor waiting. A hundred yards the other side of that granite wall we set off the thermite bomb.

'The magnesium metal of the ship caught, of course. The

glow of the bomb flared and died, then it began to flare again. We ran back to the tractor, and gradually the glare built up. From where we were we could see the whole ice field illuminated from beneath with an unbearable light; the ship's shadow was a great, dark cone reaching off toward the north, where the twilight was just about gone. For a moment it lasted, and we counted three other shadow-things that might have been other – passengers – frozen there. Then the ice was crashing down and against the ship.

'That's why I told you about that place. The wind sweeping down from the Pole was at our backs. Steam and hydrogen flame were torn away in white ice-fog; the flaming heat under the ice there was yanked away towards the Antarctic Ocean before it touched us. Otherwise we wouldn't have come back, even with the shelter of that granite ridge that stopped the light.

'Somehow in the blinding inferno we could see great hunched things, black bulks glowing, even so. They shed even the furious incandescence of the magnesium for a time. Those must have been the engines, we knew. Secrets going in blazing glory – secrets that might have given man the planets. Mysterious things that could lift and hurl that ship, and had soaked in the force of the Earth's magnetic field. I saw Norris' mouth move, and ducked. I couldn't hear him.

'Insulation – something – gave way. All Earth's field they'd soaked up twenty million years before broke loose. The aurora in the sky above licked down, and the whole plateau there was bathed in cold fire that blanketed vision. The ice axe in my hand got red hot, and hissed on the ice. Metal buttons on my clothes burned into me. And a flash of electric blue seared upward from beyond the granite wall.

'Then the walls of ice crashed down on it. For an instant it squealed the way dry ice does when it's pressed between metal.

'We were blind and groping in the dark for hours while our eyes recovered. We found every coil within a mile was fused rubbish, the dynamo and every radio set, the earphones and speakers. If we hadn't had the steam tractor, we wouldn't have got over to the Secondary Camp.

'Van Well flew in from Big Magnet at sunup, as you know. We came home as soon as possible. That is the history of – that.' McReady's great bronze beard gestured towards the thing on the table.

II

Blair stirred uneasily, his little bony fingers wriggling under the harsh light. Little brown freckles on his knuckles slid back and forth as the tendons under the skin twitched. He pulled aside a bit of the tarpaulin and looked impatiently at the dark icebound thing inside.

McReady's big body straightened somewhat. He'd ridden the rocking, jarring steam tractor forty miles that day, pushing on to Big Magnet here. Even his calm will had been pressed by the anxiety to mix again with humans. It was lone and quiet out there in Secondary Camp, where a wolf-wind howled down from the Pole. Wolf-wind howling in his sleep – winds droning and the evil, unspeakable face of that monster leering up as he'd first seen it through clear, blue ice, with a bronze ice axe buried in its skull.

The giant meteorologist spoke again. 'The problem is this. Blair wants to examine the thing. Thaw it out and make microslides of its tissues and so forth. Norris doesn't believe that is safe, and Blair does. Dr Copper agrees pretty much with Blair. Norris is a physicist, of course, not a biologist. But he makes a point I think we should all hear. Blair has described the microscopic life-forms biologists find living, even in this cold and inhospitable place. They freeze every winter, and thaw every summer, for three months, and live.

'The point Norris makes is – they thaw, and live again. There must have been microscopic life associated with this creature. There is with every living thing we know. And Norris is afraid that we may release a plague, some germ disease unknown to Earth, if we thaw those microscopic things that have been frozen there for twenty million years.

'Blair admits that such micro life might retain the power of living. Such unorganized things as individual cells can retain life for unknown periods, when solidly frozen. The beast itself is as dead as those frozen mammoths they find in Siberia. Organized, highly developed life-forms can't stand that treatment.

'But micro life could. Norris suggests that we may release some disease form that man, never having met it before, will be utterly defenceless against.

'Blair's answer is that there may be such still-living germs, but that Norris has the case reversed. They are utterly non-immune to man. Our life chemistry probably—'

'Probably!' The little biologist's head lifted in a quick, birdlike motion. The halo of grey hair about his bald head ruffled as though angry. 'Heh. One look—'

'I know,' McReady acknowledged. 'The thing is not Earthly. It does not seem likely that it can have a life chemistry sufficiently like ours to make cross infection remotely possible. I would say that there is no danger.'

McReady looked towards Dr Copper. The physician shook his head slowly. 'None whatever,' he asserted confidently. 'Man cannot infect or be infected by germs that live in such comparatively close relatives as the snakes. And they are, I assure you' – his clean-shaven face grimaced uneasily – '*much* nearer to us than – *that.*'

Vance Norris moved angrily. He was comparatively short in this gathering of big men, some five feet eight, and his stocky, powerful build tended to make him seem shorter. His black hair was crisp and hard, like short steel wires, and his eyes were the grey of fractured steel. If McReady was a man of bronze, Norris was all steel. His movements, his thoughts, his whole bearing had the quick, hard impulse of a steel spring. His nerves were steel – hard, quick-acting – swift-corroding.

He was decided on his point now, and he lashed out in its defence with a characteristic quick, clipped flow of words. 'Different chemistry be damned. That thing may be dead – or, by God, it may not – but I don't like it. Damn it, Blair, let them see the monstrosity you are petting over there. Let them see the foul thing and decide for themselves whether they want that thing thawed out in this camp.

'Thawed out, by the way. That's got to be thawed out in one of the shacks tonight, if it is thawed out. Somebody – who's watchman tonight? Magnetic – oh, Connant. Cosmic rays tonight. Well, you get to sit up with that twenty-million-year-old mummy of his.

'Unwrap it, Blair. How the hell can they tell what they are buying, if they can't see it? It may have a different chemistry. I don't care what else it has, but I know it has something I don't want. If you can judge by the look on its face – it isn't human so maybe you can't – it was annoyed when it froze. Annoyed, in fact, is just about as close an approximation of the way it felt as crazy, mad, insane hatred. Neither one touches the subject.

'How the hell can these birds tell what they are voting on? They haven't seen those three red eyes, and that blue hair like crawling worms. Crawling – damn, it's crawling there in the ice right now!

'Nothing Earth ever spawned had the unutterable sublimation of devastating wrath that thing let loose in its face when it looked around his frozen desolation twenty million years ago. Mad? It was mad clear through – searing, blistering mad!

'Hell, I've had bad dreams ever since I looked at those three red eyes. Nightmares. Dreaming the thing thawed out and came to life – that it wasn't dead, or even wholly unconscious all those twenty million years, but just slowed, waiting – waiting. You'll dream, too, while that damned thing that Earth wouldn't own is dripping, dripping in the Cosmos House tonight.

'And Connant' – Norris whipped toward the cosmic ray specialist – 'won't you have fun sitting up all night in the quiet. Wind whining above, and that thing dripping—' He stopped for a moment and looked around.

'I know. That's not science. But this is, it's psychology. You'll have nightmares for a year to come. Every night since I looked at that thing I've had 'em. That's why I hate it – sure I do – and don't want it around. Put it back where

82

it came from and let it freeze for another twenty million years. I had some swell nightmares – that it wasn't made like we are, which is obvious, but of a different kind of flesh that it can really control. That it can change its shape, and look like a man – and wait to kill and eat—

'That's not a logical argument. I know it isn't. The thing isn't Earth logic anyway.

'Maybe it has an alien body chemistry, and maybe its bugs do have a different body chemistry. A germ might not stand that, but, Blair and Copper, how about a virus? That's just an enzyme molecule, you've said. That wouldn't need anything but a protein molecule of any body to work on.

'And how are you so sure that, of the million varieties of microscopic life it may have, *none* of them are dangerous? How about diseases like hydrophobia – rabies – that attacks any warm-blooded creature, whatever its body chemistry may be? And parrot fever? Have you a body like a parrot, Blair? And plain rot – gangrene – necrosis if you want? *That* isn't choosy about body chemistry!'

Blair looked up from his puttering long enough to meet Norris' angry, grey eyes for an insant. 'So far the only thing you have said this thing gave off that was catching was dreams. I'll go so far as to admit that.' An impish, slightly malignant grin crossed the little man's seamed face. 'I had some, too. So. It's dream-infectious. No doubt an exceedingly dangerous malady.

'So far as your other things go, you have a badly mistaken idea about viruses. In the first place, nobody has shown that the enzyme-molecule theory, and that alone, explains them. And in the second place, when you catch tobacco mosaic or wheat rust, let me know. A wheat plant is a lot nearer your body chemistry than this otherworld creature is.

'And your rabies is limited, strictly limited. You can't get it from, or give it to, a wheat plant or a fish – which is a collateral descendant of a common ancestor of yours. Which this, Norris, is not.' Blair nodded pleasantly towards the tarpaulined bulk on the table.

'Well, thaw the damned thing in a tub of formalin if you must thaw it. I've suggested that—'

'And I've said there would be no sense in it. You can't compromise. Why did you and Commander Garry come down here to study magnetism? Why weren't you content to stay at home? There's magnetic force enough in New York. I could no more study the life this thing once had from a formalin-pickled sample than you could get the information you wanted back in New York. And – if this one is so treated, *never in all time to come can there be a duplicate*! The race it came from must have passed away in the twenty million years it lay frozen, so that even if it came from Mars then, we'd never find its like. And – the ship is gone.

'There's only one way to do this, and that is the best possible way. It must be thawed slowly, carefully, and not in formalin.'

Commander Garry stood forward again, and Norris stepped back, muttering angrily. 'I think Blair is right, gentlemen. What do you say?'

Connant grunted. 'It sounds right to us, I think – only perhaps he ought to stand watch over it while it's thawing.' He grinned ruefully, brushing a stray lock of ripe-cherry hair back from his forehead. 'Swell idea, in fact – if he sits up with his jolly little corpse.'

Garry smiled slightly. A general chuckle of agreement rippled over the group. 'I should think any ghost it may have had would have starved to death if it hung around here that long, Connant,' Garry suggested. 'And you look capable of taking care of it. "Ironman" Connant ought to be able to take out any opposing players, still.'

Connant shook himself uneasily. 'I'm not worrying about ghosts. Let's see that thing. I—'

Eagerly Blair was stripping back the ropes. A single throw of the tarpaulin revealed the thing. The ice had melted somewhat in the heat of the room, and it was clear and blue as thick, good glass. It shone wet and sleek under the harsh light of the unshielded globe above.

The room stiffened abruptly. It was face up there on the plain, greasy planks of the table. The broken half of the bronze ice axe was still buried in the queer skull. Three mad, hate-filled eyes blazed up with a living fire, bright as fresh-spilled blood, from a face ringed with a writhing, loathsome nest of worms, blue, mobile worms that crawled where hair should grow—

Van Wall, six feet and two hundred pounds of ice-nerved pilot, gave a queer, strangled gasp and butted, stumbled his way out to the corridor. Half the company broke for the doors. The others stumbled away from the table.

McReady stood at one end of the table watching them, his great body planted solid on his powerful legs. Norris from the opposite end glowered at the thing with smouldering hate. Outside the door, Garry was talking with half a dozen of the men at once.

Blair had a tack hammer. The ice that cased the thing *schluffed* crisply under its steel claw as it peeled from the thing it had cased for twenty million years—

III

'I know you don't like the thing, Connant, but it just has to be thawed out right. You say leave it as it is till we get back to civilization. All right, I'll admit your argument that we could do a better and more complete job there is sound. But – how are we going to get this across the Line? We have to take this through one temperate zone, the equatorial zone, and halfway through the other temperate zone before we get it to New York. You don't want to sit with it one night, but you suggest, then, that I hang its corpse in the freezer with the beef?' Blair looked up from his cautious chipping, his bald, freckled skull nodding triumphantly.

Kinner, the stocky, scar-faced cook, saved Connant the trouble of answering. 'Hey, you listen, mister. You put that thing in the box with the meat, and by all the gods there ever were, I'll put you in to keep it company. You birds have brought everything movable in this camp in onto my mess tables here already, and I had to stand for that. But you go putting things like that in my meat box or even my meat cache here, and you cook your damn grub.'

'But, Kinner, this is the only table in Big Magnet that's big enough to work on,' Blair objected. 'Everybody's explained that.'

'Yeah, and everybody's brought everything in here. Clark brings his dogs every time there's a fight and sews them up on that table. Ralsen brings in his sledges. Hell, the only thing you haven't had on that table is the Boeing. And you'd 'a' had that in if you coulda figured a way to get it through the tunnels.'

Commander Garry chuckled and grinned at Van Wall, the huge chief pilot. Van Wall's great blond beard twitched suspiciously as he nodded gravely to Kinner. 'You're right, Kinner. The aviation department is the only one that treats you right.'

'It does get crowded, Kinner,' Garry acknowledged. 'But I'm afraid we all find it that way at times. Not much privacy in an Antarctic camp.'

'Privacy? What the hell's that? You know, the thing that really made me weep was when I saw Barclay marchin' through here chantin' "The last lumber in the camp! The last lumber in the camp!" and carryin' it out to build that house on his tractor. Damn it, I missed that moon cut in the door he carried out more'n I missed the sun when it set. That wasn't just the last lumber Barclay was walkin' off with. He was carryin' off the last bit of privacy in this blasted place.'

A grin rode even on Connant's heavy face as Kinner's perennial good-natured grouch came up again. But it died away quickly as his dark, deep-set eyes turned again to the red-eyed thing Blair was chipping from its cocoon of ice. A big hand ruffed Connant's shoulder-length hair and tugged at a twisted lock that fell behind his ear in a familiar gesture. 'I know that cosmic ray shack's going to be too crowded if I have to sit up with that thing,' he growled. 'Why can't you go on chipping the ice away from around it – you can do that without anybody butting in, I assure you –

86

and then hang the thing up over the power-plant boiler? That's warm enough. It'll thaw out a chicken, even a whole side of beef, in a few hours.'

'I know,' Blair protested, dropping the tack hammer to gesture more effectively with his bony, freckled fingers, his small body tense with eagerness, 'but this is too important to take any chances. There never was a find like this; there never can be again. It's the only chance men will ever have, and it has to be done exactly right.

'Look, you know how the fish we caught down near the Ross Sea would freeze almost as soon as we got them on deck, and come to life again if we thawed them gently? Low forms of life aren't killed by quick freezing and slow thawing. We have—'

'Hey, for the love of Heaven – you mean that damned thing will come to life!' Connant yelled. 'You get the damned thing— Let me at it! That's going to be in so many pieces—'

'NO! *No*, you fool—' Blair jumped in front of Connant to protect his precious find. 'No. Just *low* forms of life. For Pete's sake let me finish. You can't thaw higher forms of life and have them come to. Wait a moment now – hold it! A fish can come to after freezing because it's so low a form of life that the individual cells of its body can revive, and that alone is enough to re-establish life. Any higher forms thawed out that way are dead. Though the individual cells revive, they die because there must be organization and cooperative effort to live. That cooperation cannot be re-established. There is a sort of potential life in any un-injured, quick-frozen animal. But it can't – can't under any circumstances – become active life in higher animals. The higher animals are too complex, too delicate. This is an intelligent creature as high in its evolution as we are in ours. Perhaps higher. It is as dead as a frozen man would be.'

'How do you know?' demanded Connant, hefting the ice axe he had seized a moment before.

Commander Garry laid a restraining hand on his heavy shoulder. 'Wait a minute, Connant. I want to get this straight. I agree that there is going to be no thawing of this thing if there is the remotest chance of its revival. I quite agree it is much too unpleasant to have alive, but I had no idea there was the remotest possibility.'

Dr Copper pulled his pipe from between his teeth and heaved his stocky, dark body from the bunk he had been sitting in. 'Blair's being technical. That's dead. As dead as the mammoths they find frozen in Siberia. Potential life is like atomic energy – there, but nobody can get it out, and it certainly won't release itself except in rare cases, as rare as radium in the chemical analogy. We have all sorts of proof that things don't live after being frozen – not even fish, generally speaking – and no proof that higher animal life can under any circumstances. What's the point, Blair?'

The little biologist shook himself. The little ruff of hair standing out around his bald pate waved in righteous anger. 'The point is,' he said in an injured tone, 'that the individual cells might show the characteristics they had in life, if it is properly thawed. A man's muscle cells live many hours after he has died. Just because they live, and a few things like hair and fingernail cells still live, you wouldn't accuse a corpse of being a zombie, or something.

'Now if I thaw this right, I may have a chance to determine what sort of world it's native to. We don't, and can't know by any other means, whether it came from Earth or Mars or Venus or from beyond the stars.

'And just because it looks unlike men, you don't have to accuse it of being evil, or vicious or something. Maybe that expression on its face is its equivalent to a resignation to fate. White is the colour of mourning to the Chinese. If men can have different customs, why can't a so-different race have different understandings of facial expressions?'

Connant laughed softly, mirthlessly. 'Peaceful resignation! If that is the best it could do in the way of resignation, I should exceedingly dislike seeing it when it was looking mad. That face was never designed to express peace. It just didn't have any philosophical thoughts like peace in its makeup.

'I know it's your pet, but be sane about it. That thing

grew up on evil, adolesced slowly roasting alive the local equivalent of kittens, and amused itself through maturity on new and ingenious torture.'

'You haven't the slightest right to say that,' snapped Blair. 'How do you know the first thing about the meaning of a facial expression inherently inhuman? It may well have no human equivalent whatever. That is just a different development of nature, another example of nature's wonderful adaptability. Growing on another, perhaps harsher world, it has different form and features. But it is just as much a legitimate child of nature as you are. You are displaying that childish human weakness of hating the different. On its own world it would probably class you as a fish-belly, white monstrosity with an insufficient number of eyes and a fungoid body pale and bloated with gas.

'Just because its nature is different, you haven't any right to say it's necessarily evil.'

Norris burst out a single, explosive, 'Haw!' He looked down at the thing. 'May be that things from other worlds don't *have* to be evil just because they're different. But that thing *was*! Child of nature, eh? Well, it was a hell of an evil nature.'

'Aw, will you mugs cut crabbing at each other and get the damned thing off my table?' Kinner growled. 'And put a canvas over it. It looks indecent.'

'Kinner's gone modest,' jeered Connant.

Kinner slanted his eyes up to the big physicist. The scarred cheek twisted to join the line of his tight lips in a twisted grin. 'All right, big boy, and what were you grousing about a minute ago? We can set the thing in a chair next to you tonight, if you want.'

'I'm not afraid of its face,' Connant snapped. 'I don't like keeping a wake over its corpse particularly, but I'm going to do it.'

Kinner's grin spread. 'Uh-huh.' He went off to the galley stove and shook down ashes vigorously, drowning the brittle chipping of the ice as Blair fell to work again.

IV

'*Cluck*,' reported the cosmic ray counter, '*cluck-brrrp-cluck*.' Connant started and dropped his pencil.

'Damnation.' The physicist looked towards the far corner, back at the Geiger counter on the table near that corner, and crawled under the desk at which he had been working to retrieve the pencil. He sat down at his work again, trying to make his writing more even. It tended to have jerks and quavers in it, in time with the abrupt proud-hen noises of the Geiger counter. The muted *whoosh* of the pressure lamp he was using for illumination, the mingled gargles and bugle calls of a dozen men sleeping down the corridor in Paradise House formed the background sounds for the irregular, clucking noises of the counter, the occasional rustle of falling coal in the copper-bellied stove. And a soft, steady drip-drip-drip from the thing in the corner.

Connant jerked a pack of cigarettes from his pocket, snapped it so that a cigarette protruded, and jabbed the cylinder into his mouth. The lighter failed to function, and he pawed angrily through the pile of papers in search of a match. He scratched the wheel of the lighter several times, dropped it with a curse, and got up to pluck a hot coal from the stove with the coal tongs.

The lighter functioned instantly when he tried it on returning to the desk. The counter ripped out a series of chuckling guffaws as a burst of cosmic rays struck through to it. Connant turned to glower at it, and tried to concentrate on the interpretation of data collected during the past week. The weekly summary—

He gave up and yielded to curiosity, or nervousness. He lifted the pressure lamp from the desk and carried it over to the table in the corner. Then he returned to the stove and picked up the coal tongs. The beast had been thawing for nearly eighteen hours now. He poked at it with an unconscious caution; the flesh was no longer hard as armour plate, but had assumed a rubbery texture. It looked like wet blue rubber glistening under droplets of water like little round jewels in the glare of the gasoline pressure lantern.

Connant felt an unreasoning desire to pour the contents of the lamp's reservoir over the thing in its box and drop the cigarette into it. The three red eyes glared up at him sightlessly, the ruby eyeballs reflecting murky, smoky rays of light.

He realized vaguely that he had been looking at them for a very long time, even vaguely understood that they were no longer sightless. But it did not seem of importance, of no more importance than the laboured, slow motion of the tentacular things that sprouted from the base of the scrawny, slowly pulsing neck.

Connant picked up the pressure lamp and returned to his chair. He sat down, staring at the pages of mathematics before him. The clucking of the counter was strangely less disturbing, the rustle of the coals in the stove no longer distracting.

The creak of the floorboards behind him didn't interrupt his thoughts as he went about his weekly report in an automatic manner, filling in columns of data and making brief, summarizing notes.

The creak of the floorboards sounded nearer.

V

Blair came up from the nightmare-haunted depths of sleep abruptly. Connant's face floated vaguely above him; for a moment it seemed a continuance of the wild horror of the dream. But Connant's face was angry, and a little frightened. 'Blair – Blair, you damned log, wake up.'

'Uh-eh?' the little biologist rubbed his eyes, his bony, freckled fingers crooked to a mutilated child-fist. From surrounding bunks other faces lifted to stare down at them.

Connant straightened up. 'Get up – and get a lift on. Your damned animal's escaped.'

'Escaped – what!' Chief Pilot Van Wall's bull voice roared out with a volume that shook the walls. Down the communication tunnels other voices yelled suddenly. The dozen inhabitants of Paradise House tumbled in abruptly,

Barclay, stocky and bulbous in long woollen underwear, carrying a fire extinguisher.

'What the hell's the matter?' Barclay demanded.

'Your damned beast got loose. I fell asleep about twenty minutes ago, and when I woke up, the thing was gone. Hey, Doc, the hell you say those things can't come to life. Blair's blasted potential life developed a hell of a lot of potential and walked out on us.'

Copper stared blankly. 'It wasn't – Earthly,' he sighed suddenly. 'I – I guess Earthly laws don't apply.'

'Well, it applied for leave of absence and took it. We've got to find it and capture it somehow.' Connant swore bitterly, his deep-set black eyes sullen and angry. 'It's a wonder the hellish creature didn't eat me in my sleep.'

Blair started back, his pale eyes suddenly fear-struck. 'Maybe it di – er – uh – we'll have to find it.'

'You find it. It's your pet. I've had all I want to do with it, sitting there for seven hours with the counter clicking every few seconds, and you birds in here singing night music. It's a wonder I got to sleep. I'm going through to the Ad Building.'

Commander Garry ducked through the doorway, pulling his belt tight. 'You won't have to. Van's roar sounded like the Boeing taking off downwind. So it wasn't dead?'

'I didn't carry it off in my arms, I assure you,' Connant snapped. 'The last I saw, that split skull was oozing green goo, like a squashed caterpillar. Doc just said our laws don't work – it's unearthly. Well, it's an unearthly monster, with an unearthly disposition, judging by the face, wandering around with a split skull and brains oozing out.'

Norris and McReady appeared in the doorway, a doorway filling with other shivering men. 'Has anybody seen it coming over here?' Norris asked innocently. 'About four feet tall – three red eyes – brains oozing out— Hey, has anybody checked to make sure this isn't a cracked idea of humour? If it is, I think we'll unite in tying Blair's pet around Connant's neck like the Ancient Mariner's albatross.'

'It's no humour.' Connant shivered. 'Lord, I wish it were. I'd rather wear—' He stopped. A wild, weird howl shrieked through the corridors. The men stiffened abruptly, and half turned.

'I think it's been located,' Connant finished. His dark eyes shifted with a queer unease. He darted back to his bunk in Paradise House, to return almost immediately with a heavy .45 revolver and an ice axe. He hefted both gently as he started for the corridor towards Dogtown. 'It blundered down the wrong corridor, and landed among the huskies. Listen – the dogs have broken their chains—'

The half-terrorized howl of the dog pack had changed to a wild hunting mêlée. The voices of the dogs thundered in the narrow corridors, and through them came a low rippling snarl of distilled hate. A shrill of pain, a dozen snarling yelps.

Connant broke for the door. Close behind him, McReady, then Barclay and Commander Garry came. Other men broke for the Ad Building and weapons – the Sledge House. Pomroy, in charge of Big Magnet's five cows, started down the corridor in the opposite direction. He had a six-foot-handled, long-pronged pitchfork in mind.

Barclay slid to a halt, as McReady's giant bulk turned abruptly away from the tunnel leading to Dogtown and vanished off at an angle. Uncertainly, the mechanism wavered a moment, the fire extinguisher in his hands, hesitating from one side to the other. Then he was racing after Connant's broad back. Whatever McReady had in mind, he could be trusted to make it work.

Connant stopped at the bend in the corridor. His breath hissed suddenly through his throat. 'Great God—' The revolver exploded thunderously; three numbing, palpable waves of sound crashed through the confined corridors. Two more. The revolver dropped to the hard-packed snow of the trail, and Barclay saw the ice axe shift into defensive position. Connant's powerful body blocked his vision, but beyond he heard something mewing and, insanely, chuckling. The dogs were quieter; there was a deadly seriousness in their low snarls. Taloned feet scratched at hard-packed snow; broken chains were clinking and tangling.

Connant shifted abruptly, and Barclay could see what lay

93

beyond. For a second he stood frozen; then his breath went out in a gusty curse. The thing launched itself at Connant; the powerful arms of the man swung the ice axe flatside first at what might have been a head. It scrunched horribly, and the tattered flesh, ripped by a half-dozen savage huskies, leapt to its feet again. The red eyes blazed with an unearthly hatred, an unearthly, unkillable vitality.

Barclay turned the fire extinguisher on it; the blinding, blistering stream of chemical spray confused it, baffled it, together with the savage attacks of the huskies, who, not for long afraid of anything that did or could live, held it at bay.

McReady wedged men out of his way and drove down the narrow corridor packed with men unable to reach the scene. There was a sure foreplanned drive to McReady's attack. One of the giant blowtorches used in warming the plane's engines was in his bronzed hands. It roared gustily as he turned the corner and opened the valve. The mad mewing hissed louder. The dogs scrambled back from the three-foot lance of blue-hot flame.

'Bar, get a power cable, run it in somehow. And a handle. We can electrocute this – monster, if I don't incinerate it.' McReady spoke with an authority of planned action. Barclay turned down the long corridor to the power plant, but already before him Norris and Van Wall were racing down.

Barclay found the cable in the electrical cache in the tunnel wall. In a half minute he was hacking at it, walking back. Van Wall's voice rang out in a warning shout of 'Power!' as the emergency gasoline-powered dynamo thudded into action. Half a dozen other men were down in the tunnel now; the coal and kindling were going into the firebox of the steam power plant. Norris, cursing in a low, deadly monotone, was working with quick, sure fingers on the other end of Barclay's cable, splicing in a contactor in one of the power leads.

The dogs had fallen back when Barclay reached the corridor bend, fallen back before a furious monstrosity that glared from baleful red eyes, mewing in trapped hatred. The dogs were a semicircle of red-dipped muzzles with a fringe of glistening white teeth, whining with a vicious eagerness that near matched the fury of the red eyes. McReady stood confidently alert at the corridor bend, the gustily muttering torch held loose and ready for action in his hands. He stepped aside without moving his eyes from the beast as Barclay came up. There was a slight, tight smile on his lean, bronzed face.

Norris' voice called down the corridor, and Barclay stepped forward. The cable was taped to the long handle of a snow-shovel, the two conductors split and held eighteen inches apart by a scrap of lumber lashed at right angles across the far end of the handle. Bare copper conductors, charged with 220 volts, glinted in the light of pressure lamps. The thing mewed and halted and dodged. McReady advanced to Barclay's side. The dogs beyond sensed the plan with the almost telepathic intelligence of trained huskies. Their whining grew shriller, softer, their mincing steps carried them nearer. Abruptly a huge, night-black Alaskan leapt onto the trapped thing. It turned squalling, sabre-clawed feet slashing.

Barclay leapt forward and jabbed. A weird, shrill scream rose and choked out. The smell of burnt flesh in the corridor intensified; greasy smoke curled up. The echoing pound of the gas-electric dynamo down the corridor became a slogging thud.

The red eyes clouded over in a stiffening, jerking travesty of a face. Armlike, leglike members quivered and jerked. The dogs leapt forward, and Barclay yanked back his shovel-handled weapon. The thing on the snow did not move as gleaming teeth ripped it open.

VI

Garry looked about the crowded room. Thirty-two men, some tensed nervously standing against the wall, some uneasily relaxed, some sitting, most perforce standing, as intimate as sardines. Thirty-two, plus the five engaged in sewing up wounded dogs, made thirty-seven, the total personnel.

Garry started speaking. 'All right, I guess we're here.

Some of you – three or four at most – saw what happened. All of you have seen that thing on the table, and can get a general idea. Anyone hasn't, I'll lift—' His hand strayed to the tarpaulin bulking over the thing on the table. There was an acrid odour of singed flesh seeping out of it. The men stirred restlessly – hasty denials.

'It looks rather as though Charnauk isn't going to lead any more teams,' Garry went on. 'Blair wants to get at this thing and make some more detailed examination. We want to know what happened and make sure right now that this is permanently, totally dead. Right?'

Connant grinned. 'Anybody that doesn't agree can sit up with it tonight.'

'All right then, Blair, what can you say about it? What was it?' Garry turned to the little biologist.

'I wonder if we ever saw its natural form.' Blair looked at the covered mass. 'It may have been imitating the beings that built that ship, but I don't think it was. I think that was its true form. Those of us who were up near the bend saw the thing in action; the thing on the table is the result. When it got loose, apparently, it started looking around. Antarctica still frozen as it was ages ago when the creature first saw it – and froze. From my observations while it was thawing out, and the bits of tissue I cut and hardened then, I think it was native to a hotter planet than Earth. It couldn't, in its natural form, stand the temperature. There is no life-form on Earth that can live in Antarctica during the winter, but the best compromise is the dog. It found the dogs, and somehow got near enough to Chernauk to get him. The others smelled it – heard it – I don't know – anyway they went wild and broke chains and attacked it before it was finished. The thing we found was part Charnauk, queerly only half-dead, part Charnauk half-digested by the jellylike protoplasm of that creature, and part the remains of the thing we originally found, sort of melted down to the basic protoplasm.

'When the dogs attacked it, it turned into the best fighting thing it could think of. Some otherworld beast apparently.'

'Turned,' snapped Garry. 'How?'

'Every living thing is made up of jelly – protoplasm and minute, submicroscopic things called nuclei, which control the bulk, the protoplasm. This thing was just a modification of that same worldwide plan of nature; cells made up of protoplasm, controlled by infinitely tinier nuclei. You physicists might compare it – an individual cell of any living thing – with an atom; the bulk of the atom, the space-filling part, is made up of the electron orbits, but the character of the thing is determined by the atomic nucleus.

'This isn't wildly beyond what we already know. It's just a modification we haven't seen before. It's as natural, as logical, as any other manifestation of life. It obeys exactly the same laws. The cells are made of protoplasm, their character determined by the nucleus.

'Only in this creature, the cell nuclei can control those cells at *will*. It digested Charnauk, and as it digested, studied every cell of his tissue, and shaped its own cells to imitate them exactly. Parts of it – parts that had time to finish changing – are dog cells. But they don't have dog-cell nuclei.' Blair lifted a fraction of the tarpaulin. A torn dog's leg with stiff grey fur protruded. 'That, for instance, isn't dog at all; it's imitation. Some parts I'm uncertain about; the nucleus was hiding itself, covering up with dog-cell imitation nucleus. In time, not even a microscope would have shown the difference.'

'Suppose,' asked Norris bitterly, 'it had had lots of time?'

'Then it would have been a dog. The other dogs would have accepted it. We would have accepted it. I don't think anything would have distinguished it, not microscope, nor X ray, nor any other means. This is a member of a supremely intelligent race, a race that has learned the deepest secrets of biology, and turned them to its use.'

'What was it planning to do?' Barclay looked at the humped tarpaulin.

Blair grinned unpleasantly. The wavering halo of thin hair round his bald pate wavered in a stir of air. 'Take over the world, I imagine.'

'Take over the world! Just it, all by itself?' Connant gasped. 'Set itself up as a lone dictator?'

'No,' Blair shook his head. The scalpel he had been fumbling in his bony fingers dropped; he bent to pick it up, so that his face was hidden as he spoke. 'It would become the population of the world.'

'Become – populate the world? Does it reproduce asexually?'

Blair shook his hand and gulped. "It's – it doesn't have to. It weighed eighty-five pounds. Charnauk weighed about ninety. It would have become Charnauk, and had eighty-five pounds left, to become – oh, Jack for instance, or Chinook. It can imitate anything – that is, become anything. If it had reached the Antarctic Ocean, it would have become a seal, maybe two seals. They might have attacked a killer whale, and become either killers, or a herd of seals. Or maybe it would have caught an albatross, or a skua gull, and flown to South America.'

Norris cursed softly. 'And every time it digested something, and imitated it—'

'It would have had its original bulk left, to start again,' Blair finished. 'Nothing would kill it. It has no natural enemies, because it becomes whatever it wants to. If a killer whale attacked it, it would become a killer whale. If it was an albatross and an eagle attacked it, it would become an eagle. Lord, it might become a female eagle. Go back – build a nest and lay eggs!'

'Are you sure that thing from hell is dead?' Dr Copper asked softly.

'Yes, thank Heaven,' the little biologist gasped. 'After they drove the dogs off, I stood there poking Bar's electrocution thing into it for five minutes. It's dead and – cooked.'

'Then we can only give thanks that this is Antarctica, where there is not one, single, solitary, living thing for it to imitate, except these animals in camp.'

'Us,' Blair giggled. 'It can imitate us. Dogs can't make four hundred miles to the sea; there's no food. There aren't any skua gulls to imitate at this season. There aren't any penguins this far inland. There's nothing that can reach the sea from this point – except us. We've got brains. We can do it. Don't you see – *it's got to imitate us – it's got to be one of us – that's the only way it can fly an aeroplane – fly a plane for two hours, and rule – be – all Earth's inhabitants. A world for the taking – if it imitates us!*

'It didn't know yet. It hadn't had a chance to learn. It was rushed – hurried – took the thing nearest its own size. Look – I'm Pandora! I opened the box! And the only hope that can come out is – that nothing can come out. You didn't see me. I did it. I fixed it. I smashed every magneto. Not a plane can fly. Nothing can fly.' Blair giggled and lay down on the floor crying.

Chief Pilot Van Wall made a dive for the door. His feet were fading echoes in the corridors as Dr Copper bent un-hurriedly over the little man on the floor. From his office at the end of the room he brought something, and injected a solution into Blair's arm. 'He might come out of it when he wakes up,' he sighed, rising. McReady helped him lift the biologist onto a nearby bunk. 'It all depends on whether we can convince him that thing is dead.'

Van Wall ducked into the shack, brushing his heavy blond beard absently. 'I didn't think a biologist would do a thing like that up thoroughly. He missed the spares in the second cache. It's all right. I smashed them.'

Commander Garry nodded. 'I was wondering about the radio.'

Dr Copper snorted. 'You don't think it can leak out on a radio wave, do you? You'd have five rescue attempts in the next three months if you stop the broadcasts. The thing to do is talk loud and not make a sound. Now I wonder—'

McReady looked speculatively at the doctor. 'It might be like an infectious disease. Everything that drank any of its blood—'

Copper shook his head. 'Blair missed something. Imitate it may, but it has, to a certain extent, its own body chem-istry, its own metabolism. If it didn't, it would become a dog – and be a dog and nothing more. It has to be an imitation dog. Therefore you can detect it by serum tests. And its chemistry, since it comes from another world, must be so wholly, radically different that a few cells, such as gained by drops of blood, would be treated as disease germs by the dog, or human body.'

'Blood – would one of those imitations bleed?' Norris demanded.

'Surely. Nothing mystic about blood. Muscle is about ninety per cent water; blood differs only in having a couple per cent more water, and less connective tissue. They'd bleed all right,' Copper assured him.

Blair sat up in his bunk suddenly. 'Connant – where's Connant?'

The physicist moved over towards the little biologist. 'Here I am. What do you want?'

'Are you?' giggled Blair. He lapsed back into the bunk contorted with silent laughter.

Connant looked at him blankly. 'Huh? Am I what?'

'*Are* you there?' Blair burst into gales of laughter. 'Are you Connant? The beast wanted to be a *man* – not a dog—'

VII

Dr Copper rose wearily from the bunk, and washed the hypodermic carefully. The little tinkles it made seemed loud in the packed room, now that Blair's gurgling laughter had finally quieted. Copper looked toward Garry and shook his head slowly. 'Hopeless, I'm afraid. I don't think we can ever convince him the thing is dead now.'

Norris laughed uncertainly. 'I'm not sure you can convince me. Oh, damn you, McReady.'

'McReady?' Commander Garry turned to look from Norris to McReady curiously.

'The nightmares,' Norris explained. 'He had a theory about the nightmares we had at the Secondary Station after finding that thing.'

'And that was?' Garry looked at McReady levelly.

Norris answered for him, jerkily, uneasily. 'That the creature wasn't dead, had a sort of enormously slowed existence, an existence that permitted it, nonetheless, to be vaguely aware of the passing of time, of our coming, after endless years. I had a dream it could imitate things.'

'Well,' Copper grunted, 'it can.'

'Don't be an ass,' Norris snapped. 'That's not what's bothering me. In the dream it could read minds, read thoughts and ideas and mannerisms.'

'What's so bad about that? It seems to be worrying you more than the thought of the joy we're going to have with a mad man in an Antarctic camp.' Copper nodded towards Blair's sleeping form.

McReady shook his great head slowly. 'You know that Connant is Connant, because he not merely looks like Connant – which we're beginning to believe that beast might be able to do – but he thinks like Connant, talks like Connant, moves himself around as Connant does. That takes more than merely a body that looks like him; that takes Connant's own mind, and thoughts and mannerisms. Therefore, though you know that the thing might make itself *look* like Connant, you aren't much bothered, because you know it has a mind from another world, a totally un-human mind, that couldn't possibly react and think and talk like a man we know, and do it so well as to fool us for a moment. The idea of the creature imitating one of us is fascinating, but unreal because it is too completely un-human to deceive us. It doesn't have a human mind.'

'As I said before,' Norris repeated, looking steadily at McReady, 'you can say the damnedest things at the damnedest times. Will you be so good as to finish that thought – one way or the other?'

Kinner, the scar-faced expedition cook, had been standing near Connant. Suddenly he moved down the length of the crowded room towards his familiar galley. He shook the ashes from the galley stove noisily.

'It would do it no good,' said Dr Copper, softly as though thinking out loud, 'to merely look like something it was trying to imitate; it would have to understand its feelings, its reactions. It *is* unhuman; it has powers of imitation beyond any conception of man. A good actor, by training himself, can imitate another man, another man's mannerisms, well enough to fool most people. Of course no actor could imitate so perfectly as to deceive men who had been living with the imitated one in the complete lack of privacy of an Antarctic camp. That would take a superhuman skill.'

'Oh, you've got the bug too?' Norris cursed softly.

Connant, standing alone at one end of the room, looked about him wildly, his face white. A gentle eddying of the men had crowded them slowly down towards the other end of the room, so that he stood quite alone. 'My God, will you two Jeremiahs shut up?' Connant's voice shook. 'What am I? Some kind of a microscopic specimen you're dissecting? Some unpleasant worm you're discussing in the third person?'

McReady looked up at him; his slowly twisting hands stopped for a moment. 'Having a lovely time. Wish you were here. Signed: Everybody.

'Connant, if you think you're having a hell of a time, just move over on the other end for a while. You've got one thing we haven't; you know what the answer is. I'll tell you this, right now you're the most feared and respected man in Big Magnet.'

'Lord, I wish you could see your eyes,' Connant gasped. 'Stop staring, will you! What the hell are you going to do?'

'Have you any suggestions, Dr Copper?' Commander Garry asked steadily. 'The present situation is impossible.'

'Oh, is it?' Connant snapped. 'Come over here and look at that crowd. By Heaven, they look exactly like that gang of huskies around the corridor bend. Benning, will you stop hefting that damned ice axe?'

The coppery blade rang on the floor as the aviation mechanic nervously dropped it. He bent over and picked it up instantly, hefting it slowly, turning it in his hands, his brown eyes moving jerkily about the room.

Copper sat down on the bunk beside Blair. The wood creaked noisily in the room. Far down a corridor, a dog yelped in pain, and the dog drivers' tense voices floated softly back. 'Microscopic examination,' said the doctor thoughtfully, 'would be useless, as Blair pointed out. Considerable time has passed. However, serum tests would be definitive.'

'Serum tests? What do you mean exactly?' Commander Garry asked.

'If I had a rabbit that had been injected with human blood – a poison to rabbits, of course, as is the blood of any animal save that of another rabbit – and the injections continued in increasing doses for some time, the rabbit would be human-immune. If a small quantity of its blood were drawn off, allowed to separate in a test tube, and to the clear serum, a bit of human blood were added, there would be a visible reaction, proving the blood was human. If cow, or dog blood were added – or any protein material other than that one thing, human blood – no reaction would take place. That would prove definitely.'

'Can you suggest where I might catch a rabbit for you, Doc?' Norris asked. 'That is, nearer than Australia; we don't want to waste time going that far.'

'I know there aren't any rabbits in Antarctica,' Copper nodded, 'but that is simply the usual animal. Any animal except man will do. A dog for instance. But it will take several days, and due to the greater size of the animal, considerable blood. Two of us will have to contribute.'

'Would I do?' Garry asked.

'That will make two.' Copper nodded. 'I'll get to work on it right away.'

'What about Connant in the meantime?' Kinner demanded. 'I'm going out that door and head off for the Ross Sea before I cook for him.'

'He may be human—' Copper started.

Connant burst out in a flood of curses. 'Human! *May* be human, you damned sawbones! What in hell do you think I am?'

'A monster,' Copper snapped sharply. 'Now shut up and listen.' Connant's face drained of colour and he sat down heavily as the indictment was put in words. 'Until we know – you know as well as we do that we have reason to question the fact, and only you know how that question is to be answered – we may reasonably be expected to lock you up. If you are – unhuman, you're a lot more dangerous than poor Blair there, and I'm going to see that he's locked up thoroughly. I expect that his next stage will be a violent desire to kill you, all the dogs, and probably all of us. When he wakes, he will be convinced we're all unhuman, and nothing on the planet will ever change his conviction. It would be kinder to let him die, but we can't do that, of course. He's going in one shack, and you can stay in Cosmos House with your cosmic ray apparatus. Which is about what you'd do anyway. I've got to fix up a couple of dogs.'

Connant nodded bitterly. 'I'm human. Hurry that test. Your eyes – Lord, I wish you could see your eyes staring—'

Commander Garry watched anxiously as Clark, the dog handler, held the big brown Alaskan husky, while Copper began the injection treatment. The dog was not anxious to cooperate; the needle was painful, and already he'd experienced considerable needle work that morning. Five stitches held closed a slash that ran from his shoulder across the ribs halfway down his body. One long fang was broken off short; the missing part was to be found half buried in the shoulder bone of the monstrous thing on the table in the Ad Building.

'How long will that take?' Garry asked, pressing his arm gently. It was sore from the prick of the needle Dr Copper had used to withdraw blood.

Copper shrugged. 'I don't know, to be frank. I know the general method, I've used it on rabbits. But I haven't experimented with dogs. They're big clumsy animals to work with; naturally rabbits are preferable, and serve ordinarily. In civilized places you can buy a stock of human-immune rabbits from suppliers, and not many investigators take the trouble to prepare their own.'

'What do they want with them back there?' Clark asked.

'Criminology is one large field. A says he didn't murder B, but that the blood on his shirt came from killing a chicken. The State makes a test, then it's up to A to explain how it is the blood reacts on human-immune rabbits, but not on chicken-immunes.'

'What are we going to do with Blair in the meantime?' Garry asked wearily. 'It's all right to let him sleep where he is for a while, but when he wakes up—'

'Barclay and Benning are fitting some bolts on the door of Cosmos House,' Copper replied grimly. 'Connant's acting like a gentleman. I think perhaps the way the other men look at him makes him rather want privacy. Lord knows, heretofore we've all of us individually prayed for a little privacy.'

Clark laughed brittlely. 'Not any more, thank you. The more the merrier.'

'Blair,' Copper went on, 'will also have to have privacy – and locks. He's going to have a pretty definite plan in mind when he wakes up. Ever hear the old story of how to stop hoof-and-mouth disease in cattle?'

Clark and Garry shook their heads silently.

'If there isn't any hoof-and-mouth disease, there won't be any hoof-and-mouth disease,' Copper explained. 'You get rid of it by killing every animal that exhibits it, and every animal that's been near the diseased animal. Blair's a biologist, and knows that story. He's afraid of this thing we loosed. The answer is probably pretty clear in his mind now. Kill everybody and everything in this camp before a skua gull or a wandering albatross coming in with the spring chances out this way and – catches the disease.'

Clark's lips curled in a twisted grin. 'Sounds logical to me. If things get too bad, maybe we'd better let Blair get loose. It would save us committing suicide. We might also make something of a vow that if things get bad, we see that that does happen.'

Copper laughed softly. 'The last man alive in Big Magnet – wouldn't be a man,' he pointed out. 'Somebody's got to kill those – creatures that don't desire to kill themselves, you know. We don't have enough thermite to do it all at once, and the decanite explosive wouldn't help much. I have an idea that even small pieces of one of those beings would be self-sufficient.'

'If,' said Garry thoughtfully, 'they can modify their protoplasm at will, won't they simply modify themselves to birds and fly away? They can read all about birds and imitate their structure without even meeting them. Or imitate, perhaps, birds of their home planet.'

Copper shook his head, and helped Clark to free the dog. 'Man studied birds for centuries, trying to learn how to make a machine to fly like them. He never did do the trick; his final success came when he broke away entirely and tried new methods. Knowing the general idea, and knowing the detailed structure of wing and bone and nerve-tissue is something far, far different. And as for otherworld birds, perhaps, in fact very probably, the atmospheric conditions here are so vastly different that their birds couldn't fly. Perhaps, even, the being came from a planet like Mars with such a thin atmosphere that there were no birds.'

Barclay came into the building, trailing a length of aeroplane control cable. "It's finished, Doc. Cosmos House can't be opened from the inside. Now where do we put Blair?'

Copper looked toward Garry. 'There wasn't any biology building. I don't know where we can isolate him.'

'How about East Cache?' Garry said after a moment's thought. 'Will Blair be able to look after himself – or need attention?'

'He'll be capable enough. We'll be the ones to watch out,' Copper assured him grimly. 'Take a stove, a couple of bags of coal, necessary supplies, and a few tools to fix it up. Nobody's been out there since last fall, have they?'

Garry shook his head. 'If he gets noisy – I thought that might be a good idea.'

Barclay hefted the tools he was carrying and looked up at Garry. 'If the muttering he's doing now is any sign, he's going to sing away the night hours. And we won't like his song.'

'What's he saying?' Copper asked.

Barclay shook his head. 'I didn't care to listen much. You can if you want to. But I gathered that the blasted idiot had all the dreams McReady had, and a few more. He slept beside the thing when we stopped on the trail coming in from Secondary Magnetic, remember. He dreamt the thing was alive, and dreamt more details. And – damn his soul – knew it wasn't all dream, or had reason to. He knew it had telepathic powers that were stirring vaguely, and that it could not only read minds, but project thoughts. They weren't dreams, you see. They were stray thoughts that thing was broadcasting, the way Blair's broadcasting his thoughts now – a sort of telepathic muttering in its sleep. That's why he knew so much about its powers. I guess you and I, Doc, weren't so sensitive – if you want to believe in telepathy.'

'I have to,' Copper sighed. 'Dr Rhine of Duke University has shown that it exists, shown that some are much more sensitive than others.'

'Well, if you want to learn a lot of details, go listen in on Blair's broadcast. He's driven most of the boys out of the Ad Building; Kinner's rattling pans like coal going down a chute. When he can't rattle a pan, he shakes ashes.'

'By the way, Commander, what are we going to do this spring, now the planes are out of it?'

Garry sighed. 'I'm afraid our expedition is going to be a loss. We cannot divide our strength now.'

'It won't be a loss, if we continue to live, and come out of this,' Copper promised him. 'The find we've made, if we can get it under control, is important enough. The cosmic ray data, magnetic work, and atmospheric work won't be greatly hindered.'

Garry laughed mirthlessly. 'I was just thinking of the radio broadcasts. Telling half the world about the wonderful results of our exploration flights, trying to fool men like Byrd and Ellsworth back home there that we're doing something.'

Copper nodded gravely. 'They'll know something's wrong. But men like that have judgement enough to know we wouldn't do tricks without some sort of reason, and will wait for our return to judge us. I think it comes to this: men who know enough to recognize our deception will wait for our return. Men who haven't discretion and faith enough to wait will not have the experience to detect any fraud. We know enough of the conditions here to put through a good bluff.'

'Just so they don't send "rescue" expeditions,' Garry prayed. 'When – if – we're ever ready to come out, we'll have to send word to Captain Forsythe to bring a stock of magnetos with him when he comes down. But – never mind that.'

'You mean if we don't come out?' asked Barclay. 'I was wondering if a nice running account of an eruption or an earthquake via radio, with a swell windup by using a stick of decanite under the microphone, would help. Nothing, of course, will entirely keep people out. One of those swell, melodramatic "last-man-alive" scenes might make 'em go easy though.'

Garry smiled with genuine humour. 'Is everybody in camp trying to figure that out too?'

Copper laughed. 'What do you think, Garry? We're confident we can win out. But not too easy about it, I guess.'

Clark grinned up from the dog he was petting into calmness. 'Confident, did you say, Doc?'

VIII

Blair moved restlessly around the small shack. His eyes jerked and quivered in vague, fleeting glances at the four men with him; Barclay, six feet tall and weighing over 190 pounds; McReady, a bronze giant of a man; Dr Copper, short, squatly powerful; and Benning, five feet ten of wiry strength.

Blair was huddled up against the far wall of the East Cache cabin, his gear piled in the middle of the floor beside the heating stove, forming an island between him and the four men. His bony hands clenched and fluttered, terrified. His pale eyes wavered uneasily as his bald, freckled head darted about in birdlike motion.

'I don't want anybody coming here. I'll cook my own food,' he snapped nervously. 'Kinner may be human now, but I don't believe it. I'm going to get out of here, but I'm not going to eat any food you send me. I want cans. Sealed cans.'

'Okay, Blair, we'll bring 'em tonight,' Barclay promised. 'You've got coal, and the fire's started. I'll make a last—' Barclay started forward.

Blair instantly scurried to the farthest corner. 'Get out! Keep away from me, you monster!' the little biologist shrieked, and tried to claw his way through the wall of the shack. 'Keep away from me – keep away – I won't be absorbed – I won't be—'

Barclay relaxed and moved back. Dr Copper shook his head. 'Leave him alone, Bar. It's easier for him to fix the thing himself. We'll have to fix the door, I think—'

The four men let themselves out. Efficiently, Benning and Barclay fell to work. There were no locks in Antarctica; there wasn't enough privacy to make them needed. But powerful screws had been driven in each side of the door frame, and the spare aviation control cable, immensely strong, woven steel wire, was rapidly caught between them and drawn taut. Barclay went to work with a drill and a keyhole saw. Presently he had a trap cut in the door through which goods could be passed without unlashing the entrance. Three powerful hinges from a stock crate, two hasps, and a pair of three-inch cotter pins made it proof against opening from the other side.

Blair moved about restlessly inside. He was dragging something over to the door with panting gasps and muttering, frantic curses. Barclay opened the hatch and glanced in, Dr Copper peering over his shoulder. Blair had moved the heavy bunk against the door. It could not be opened without his cooperation now.

'Don't know but what the poor man's right at that,' McReady sighed. 'If he gets loose, it is his avowed intention to kill each and all of us as quickly as possible, which is something we don't agree with. But we've something on our side of that door that is worse than a homicidal maniac. If one or the other has to get loose, I think I'll come up and undo those lashings here.'

Barclay grinned. 'You let me know, and I'll show you how to get these off fast. Let's go back.'

The sun was painting the northern horizon in multicoloured rainbows still, though it was two hours below the horizon. The field of drift swept off to the north, sparkling under its flaming colours in a million reflected glories. Low mounds of rounded white on the northern horizon showed the Magnet Range was barely awash above the sweeping drift. Little eddies of wind-lifted snow swirled away from their skies as they set out toward the main encampment two miles away. The spidery finger of the broadcast radiator lifted a gaunt black needle against the white of the Antarctic continent. The snow under their skis was like fine sand, hard and gritty.

'Spring,' said Benning bitterly, 'is come. Ain't we got fun! I've been looking forward to getting away from this blasted hole in the ice.'

'I wouldn't try it now, if I were you.' Barclay grunted. 'Guys that set out from here in the next few days are going to be marvellously unpopular.'

'How is your dog getting along, Dr Copper?' McReady asked. 'Any results yet?'

'In thirty hours? I wish there were. I gave him an injection of my blood today. But I imagine another five days will be needed. I don't know certainly enough to stop sooner.'

'I've been wondering – if Connant were – changed, would he have warned us so soon after the animal escaped? Wouldn't he have waited long enough for it to have a real chance to fix itself? Until we woke up naturally?' McReady asked slowly.

'The thing is selfish. You didn't think it looked as though it were possessed of a store of the higher justices, did you?' Dr Copper pointed out. 'Every part of it is all of it, every part of it is all for itself, I imagine. If Connant were changed, to save his skin, he'd have to. But Connant's feelings aren't changed; they're imitated perfectly, or they're his own. Naturally, the imitation, imitating perfectly Connant's feelings, would do exactly what Connant would do.'

'Say, couldn't Norris or Vane give Connant some kind of a test? If the thing is brighter than men, it might know more physics than Connant should, and they'd catch it out,' Barclay suggested.

Copper shook his head wearily. 'Not if it reads minds. You can't plan a trap for it. Vane suggested that last night. He hoped it would answer some of the questions of physics he'd like to know answers to.'

'This expedition-of-four idea is going to make life happy.' Benning looked at his companions. 'Each of us with an eye on the others to make sure he doesn't do something – peculiar. Man, aren't we going to be a trusting bunch! Each man eyeing his neighbours with the grandest exhibition of faith and trust – I'm beginning to know what Connant meant by "I wish you could see your eyes." Every now and then we all have it, I guess. One of you looks around with a sort of "I-wonder-if-the-other-*three*-are look." Incidentally, I'm not excepting myself.'

'So far as we know, the animal is dead, with a slight question as to Connant. No other is suspected,' McReady stated slowly. 'The "always-four" order is merely a precautionary measure.'

'I'm waiting for Garry to make it four-in-a-bunk,' Barclay sighed. 'I thought I didn't have any privacy before, but since that order—'

None watched more tensely than Connant. A little sterile glass test tube, half filled with straw-coloured fluid. One – two – three – four – five drops of the clear solution Dr Copper had prepared from the drops of blood from Connant's arm. The tube was shaken carefully, then set in a beaker of clear, warm water. The thermometer read blood heat, a little thermostat clicked noisily, and the electric hot plate began to glow as the lights flickered slightly.

Then – little white flecks of precipitation were forming, snowing down in the clear straw-coloured fluid. 'Lord,' said Connant. He dropped heavily into a bunk, crying like a baby. 'Six days—' Connant sobbed, 'six days in there, wondering if that damned test would lie—'

Garry moved over silently and slipped his arm across the physicist's back.

'It couldn't lie,' Dr Copper said. 'The dog was human-immune, and the serum reacted.'

'He's – all right?' Norris gasped. 'Then – the animal is dead – dead forever?'

'He is human,' Copper spoke definitely, 'and the animal is dead.'

Kinner burst out laughing, laughing hysterically. Mc-Ready turned toward him and slapped his face with a methodical one-two, one-two action. The cook laughed, gulped, cried a moment, and sat up rubbing his cheeks, mumbling his thanks vaguely. 'I was scared. Lord, I was scared—'

Norris laughed brittlely. 'You think we weren't, you ape? You think maybe Connant wasn't?'

The Ad Building stirred with a sudden rejuvenation. Voices laughed; the men clustering around Connant spoke with unnecessarily loud voices, jittery, nervous voices relievedly friendly again. Somebody called out a suggestion, and a dozen started for their skis. Blair. Blair might recover – Dr Copper fussed with his test tubes in nervous relief, trying solutions. The party of relief for Blair's shack started out the door, skis clapping noisily. Down the corridor, the dogs set up a quick yelping howl as the air of excited relief reached them.

Dr Copper fussed with his tubes. McReady noticed him first, sitting on the edge of the bunk, with two precipitin-whitened test tubes of straw-coloured fluid, his face whiter than the stuff in the tubes, silent tears slipping down from horror-widened eyes.

McReady felt a cold knife of fear pierce through his heart and freeze in his breast. Dr Copper looked up.

'Garry,' he called hoarsely. 'Garry, for God's sake, come here.'

Commander Garry walked toward him sharply. Silence clamped down on the Ad Building. Connant looked up, rose stiffly from his seat.

'Garry – tissue from the monster – precipitates too. It proves nothing. Nothing but – but the dog was monster-immune too. That *one of the two contributing blood – one of us two*, you and I, Garry – *one of us is a monster.*'

IX

'Bar, call back those men before they tell Blair,' McReady said quietly. Barclay went to the door; faintly his shouts came back to the tensely silent men in the room. Then he was back.

'They're coming,' he said. 'I didn't tell them why. Just that Dr Copper said not to go.'

'McReady,' Garry sighed, 'you're in command now. May God help you. I cannot.'

The bronzed giant nodded slowly, his deep eyes on Commander Garry.

'I may be the one,' Garry added. 'I know I'm not, but I cannot prove it to you in any way. Dr Copper's test has broken down. The fact that he showed it was useless, when it was to the advantage of the monster to have that uselessness not known, would seem to prove he was human.'

Copper rocked back and forth slowly on the bunk. 'I know I'm human. I can't prove it either. One of us two is a liar, for that test cannot lie, and it says one of us is. I gave proof that the test was wrong, which seems to prove I'm human, and now Garry has given that argument which proves me human – which he, as the monster, should not do. Round and round and round and round and—'

Dr Copper's head, then his neck and shoulders began circling slowly in time to the words. Suddenly he was lying back on the bunk, roaring with laughter. It doesn't have to prove one of us is a monster! It doesn't have to prove that at all! Ho-ho. If we're *all* monsters it works the same! We're all monsters – all of us – Connant and Garry and I – and all of you.'

'McReady,' Van Wall, the blond-bearded Chief Pilot, called softly, 'you were on the way to an MD when you took up meteorology, weren't you? Can you make some kind of test?'

McReady went over to Copper slowly, took the hypodermic from his hand, and washed it carefully in ninety-five per cent alcohol. Garry sat on the bunk edge with wooden face, watching Copper and McReady expressionlessly.

'What Copper said is possible,' McReady sighed. 'Van, will you help here? Thanks.' The filled needle jabbed into Copper's thigh. The man's laughter did not stop, but slowly faded into sobs, then sound sleep as the morphia took hold.

McReady turned again. The men who had started for Blair stood at the far end of the room, skis dripping snow, their faces as white as their skis. Connant had a lighted cigarette in each hand, one he was puffing absently while staring at the floor. The heat of the one in his left hand attracted him and he stared at it and the one in the other hand stupidly for a moment. He dropped one and crushed it under his heel slowly.

'Dr Copper,' McReady repeated, 'could be right. I know I'm human – but of course can't prove it. I'll repeat the test for my own information. Any of you others who wish to may do the same.'

Two minutes later, McReady held a test tube with white precipitin settling slowly from straw-coloured serum. It reacts to human blood too, so they aren't both monsters.'

'I didn't think they were,' Van Wall sighed. 'That wouldn't suit the monster either; we could have destroyed them if we knew. Why hasn't the monster destroyed us, do you suppose? It seems to be loose.'

McReady snorted, then laughed softly. 'Elementary, my dear Watson. The monster wants to have life forms available. It cannot animate a dead body, apparently. It is just waiting – waiting until the best opportunities come. We who remain human, it is holding in reserve.'

Kinner shuddered violently. 'Hey. Hey, Mac. Mac, would I know if I was a monster? Would I know if the monster had already got me? Oh Lord, I may be a monster already.'

'You'd know,' McReady answered.

'But we wouldn't,' Norris laughed shortly, half-hysterically.

McReady looked at the vial of serum remaining. 'There's one thing this damned stuff is good for, at that,' he said thoughtfully. 'Clark, will you and Van help me? The rest of the gang better stick together here. Keep an eye on each other,' he said bitterly. 'See that you don't get into mischief, shall we say?'

McReady started down the tunnel towards Dogtown, with Clark and Van Wall behind him. 'You need more serum?' Clark asked.

McReady shook his head. 'Tests. There's four cows and a bull, and nearly seventy dogs down there. This stuff reacts only to human blood and – monsters.'

McReady came back to the Ad Building and went silently to the washstand. Clark and Van Wall joined him a moment later. Clark's lips had developed a tic, jerking into sudden, unexpected sneers.

'What did you do?' Connant exploded suddenly. 'More immunizing?'

Clark snickered, and stopped with a hiccough. 'Immunizing. Haw! Immune all right.'

'That monster,' said Van Wall steadily, 'is quite logical. Our immune dog was quite all right, and we drew a little more serum for the tests. But we won't make any more.'

'Can't – can't you use one man's blood on another dog—' Norris began.

'There aren't,' said McReady softly, 'any more dogs. Nor cattle, I might add.'

'No more dogs?' Benning sat down slowly.

'They're very nasty when they start changing,' Van Wall said precisely, 'but slow. That electrocution iron you made up, Barclay, is very fast. There is only one dog left – our immune. The monster left that for us, so we could play with our little test. The rest—' He shrugged and dried his hands.

'The cattle—' gulped Kinner.

'Also. Reacted very nicely. They look funny as hell when they start melting. The beast hasn't any quick escape, when it's tied in dog chains, or halters, and it had to be to imitate.'

Kinner stood up slowly. His eyes darted around the room, and came to rest horribly quivering on a tin bucket in the galley. Slowly, step by step, he retreated towards the door, his mouth opening and closing silently, like a fish out of water.

'The milk—' he gasped. 'I milked 'em an hour ago—' His voice broke into a scream as he dived through the door. He was out on the ice cap without windproof or heavy clothing.

Van Wall looked after him for a moment thoughtfully. 'He's probably hopelessly mad,' he said at length, 'but he might be a monster escaping. He hasn't skis. Take a blow-torch – in case.'

The physical motion of the chase helped them; something that needed doing. Three of the other men were quietly being sick. Norris was lying flat on his back, his face greenish, looking steadily at the bottom of the bunk above him.

'Mac, how long have the – cows been not-cows—?'

McReady shrugged his shoulders hopelessly. He went over to the milk bucket, and with his little tube of serum went to work on it. The milk clouded it, making certainty difficult. Finally he dropped the test tube in the stand and shook his head. 'It tests negatively. Which means either they were cows then, or that, being perfect imitations, they gave perfectly good milk.'

Copper stirred restlessly in his sleep and gave a gurgling cross between a snore and a laugh. Silent eyes fastened on him. 'Would morphia – a monster—' somebody started to ask.

'Lord knows,' McReady shrugged. 'It affects every Earthly animal I know of.'

Connant suddenly raised his head. 'Mac! The dogs must have swallowed pieces of the monster, and the pieces destroyed them! The dogs were where the monster resided. I was locked up. Doesn't that prove—'

Van Wall shook his head. 'Sorry. Proves nothing about what you are, only proves what you didn't do.'

'It doesn't do that,' McReady sighed. 'We are helpless because we don't know enough, and so jittery we don't think straight. Locked up! Ever watch a white corpuscle of the blood go through the wall of a blood vessel? No? It sticks out a pseudopod. And there it is – on the far side of the wall.'

'Oh,' said Van Wall unhappily. 'The cattle tried to melt

down, didn't they? They could have melted down – become just a thread of stuff and leaked under a door to re-collect on the other side. Ropes – no – no, that wouldn't do it. They couldn't live in a sealed tank or—'

'If,' said McReady, 'you shoot it through the heart, and it doesn't die, it's a monster. That's the best test I can think of, offhand.'

'No dogs,' said Garry quietly, 'and no cattle. It has to imitate men now. And locking up doesn't do any good. Your test might work, Mac, but I'm afraid it would be hard on the men.'

X

Clark looked up from the galley stove as Van Wall, Barclay, McReady, and Benning came in, brushing the drift from their clothes. The other men jammed into the Ad Building continued studiously to do as they were doing, playing chess, poker, reading. Ralsen was fixing a sledge on the table; Van and Norris had their heads together over magnetic data, while Harvey read tables in a low voice.

Dr Copper snored softly on the bunk. Garry was working with Dutton over a sheaf of radio messages on the corner of Dutton's bunk and a small fraction of the radio table. Connant was using most of the table for cosmic ray sheets.

Quite plainly through the corridor, despite two closed doors, they could hear Kinner's voice. Clark banged a kettle onto the galley stove and beckoned McReady silently. The meteorologist went over to him.

'I don't mind the cooking so damn much,' Clark said nervously, 'but isn't there some way to stop that bird? We all agreed that it would be safe to move him into Cosmos House.'

'Kinner?' McReady nodded towards the door. 'I'm afraid not. I can dope him, I suppose, but we don't have an un-limited supply of morphia, and he's not in danger of losing his mind. Just hysterical.'

'Well, we're in danger of losing ours. You've been out for

an hour and a half. That's been going on steadily ever since and it was going for two hours before. There's a limit, you know.'

Garry wandered over slowly, apologetically. For an instant, McReady caught the feral spark of fear – horror – in Clark's eyes, and knew at the same instant it was in his own. Garry – Garry or Copper – was certainly a monster.

'If you could stop that, I think it would be a sound policy, Mac.' Garry spoke quietly. 'There are – tensions enough in this room. We agreed that it would be safe for Kinner in there, because everyone else in camp is under constant eyeing.' Garry shivered slightly. 'And try, try in God's name, to find some test that will work.'

McReady sighed. 'Watched or unwatched, everyone's tense. Blair's jammed the trap so it won't open now. Says he's got food enough, and keeps screaming, "Go away, go away – you're monsters. I won't be absorbed. I won't. I'll tell men when they come. Go away." So – we went away.'

'There's no other test?' Garry pleaded.

McReady shrugged his shoulders. 'Copper was perfectly right. The serum test could be absolutely definitive if it hadn't been – contaminated. But that's the only dog left, and he's fixed now.'

'Chemicals? Chemical tests?'

McReady shook his head. 'Our chemistry isn't that good. I tried the microscope, you know.'

Garry nodded. 'Monster-dog and real dog were identical. But – you've got to go on. What are we going to do after dinner?'

Van Wall had joined them quietly. 'Rotation sleeping. Half the crowd sleep; half awake. I wonder how many of us are monsters? All the dogs were. We thought we were safe, but somehow it got Copper – or you.' Van Wall's eyes flashed uneasily. 'It may have got every one of you. All of you but myself may be wondering, looking. No, that's not possible. You'd just spring then. I'd be helpless. We humans must somehow have the greater numbers now. But—' He stopped.

McReady laughed shortly. 'You're doing what Norris

complained of in me. Leaving it hanging. "But if one more is changed – that may shift the balance of power." It doesn't fight. I don't think it ever fights. It must be a peaceable thing, in its own – inimitable – way. It never had to, because it always gained its end – otherwise.'

Van Wall's mouth twisted in a sickly grin. 'You're suggesting, then, that perhaps it already *has* the greater numbers, but is just waiting – waiting, all of them – all of you, for all I know – waiting till I, the last human, drop my wariness in sleep. Mac, did you notice their eyes, all looking at us?'

Garry sighed. 'You haven't been sitting here for four straight hours, while all their eyes silently weighed the information that one of us two, Copper or I, is a monster certainly – perhaps both of us.'

Clark repeated his request. 'Will you stop that bird's noise? He's driving me nuts. Make him tone down, anyway.'

'Still praying?' McReady asked.

'Still praying,' Clark groaned. 'He hasn't stopped for a second. I don't mind his praying if it relieves him, but he yells, he sings psalms and hymns and shouts prayers. He thinks God can't hear well way down here.'

'Maybe he can't,' Barclay grunted. 'Or he'd have done something about this thing loosed from hell.'

'Somebody's going to try that test you mentioned, if you don't stop him,' Clark stated grimly. 'I think a cleaver in the head would be as positive a test as a bullet in the heart.'

'Go ahead with the food. I'll see what I can do. There may be something in the cabinets.' McReady moved wearily towards the corner Copper had used as his dispensary. Three tall cabinets of rough boards, two locked, were the repositories of the camp's medical supplies. Twelve years ago McReady had graduated, had started for an internship, and been diverted to meteorology. Copper was a picked man, a man who knew his profession thoroughly and modernly. More than half the drugs available were totally unfamiliar to McReady; many of the others he had forgotten. There was no huge medical library here, no series of journals available to learn the things he had forgotten, the elementary, simple things to Copper, things that did not merit inclusion in the small library he had been forced to content himself with. Books are heavy, and every ounce of supplies had been freighted in by air.

McReady picked a barbiturate hopefully. Barclay and Van Wall went with him. One man never went anywhere alone in Big Magnet.

Ralsen had his sledge put away, and the physicists had moved off the table, the poker game broken up when they got back. Clark was putting out the food. The click of spoons and the muffled sounds of eating were the only signs of life in the room. There were no words spoken as the three returned; simply all eyes focused on them questioningly, while the jaws moved methodically.

McReady stiffened suddenly. Kinner was screeching out a hymn in a hoarse, cracked voice. He looked wearily at Van Wall with a twisted grin and shook his head. 'Uh-uh.'

Van Wall cursed bitterly, and sat down at the table. 'We'll just plumb have to take that till his voice wears out. He can't yell like that forever.'

'He's got a brass throat and a cast-iron larynx,' Norris declared savagely. 'Then we could be hopeful, and suggest he's one of our friends. In that case he could go on renewing his throat till doomsday.'

Silence clamped down. For twenty minutes they ate without a word. Then Connant jumped up with an angry violence. 'You sit as still as a bunch of graven images. You don't say a word, but oh, Lord, what expressive eyes you've got. They roll around like a bunch of glass marbles spilling down a table. They wink and blink and stare – and whisper things. Can you guys look somewhere else for a change, please?

'Listen, Mac, you're in charge here. Let's run movies for the rest of the night. We've been saving those reels to make 'em last. Last for what? Who is it's going to see those last reels, eh? Let's see 'em while we can, and look at something other than each other.'

'Sound idea, Connant. I, for one, am quite willing to change this in any way I can.'

'Turn the sound up loud, Dutton. Maybe you can drown out the hymns,' Clark suggested.

'But don't,' Norris said softly, 'don't turn off the lights altogether.'

'The lights will be out.' McReady shook his head. 'We'll show all the cartoon movies we have. You won't mind seeing the old cartoons, will you?'

'Goody, goody – a moom pitcher show. I'm just in the mood.' McReady turned to look at the speaker, a lean, lanky New Englander, by the name of Caldwell. Caldwell was stuffing his pipe slowly, a sour eye cocked up to McReady.

The bronze giant was forced to laugh. 'Okay, Bart, you win. Maybe we aren't quite in the mood for Popeye and trick ducks, but it's something.'

'Let's play Classifications,' Caldwell suggested slowly. 'Or maybe you call it Guggenheim. You draw lines on a piece of paper and put down classes of things – like animals, you know. One for H and one for U and so on. Like Human and Unknown for instance. I think that would be a hell of a lot better game. Classification, I sort of figure, is what we need right now a lot more than movies. Maybe somebody's got a pencil that he can draw lines with, draw lines between the U animals and the H animals for instance.'

'McReady's trying to find that kind of a pencil,' Van Wall answered quietly, 'but we've got three kinds of animals here, you know. One that begins with M. We don't want any more.'

'Mad ones, you mean. Uh-uh. Clark, I'll help you with those pots so we can get our little peep show going.' Caldwell got up slowly.

Dutton and Barclay and Benning, in charge of the projector and sound mechanism arrangements, went about their job silently, while the Ad Building was cleared and the dishes and pans disposed of. McReady drifted over towards Van Wall slowly, and leaned back in the bunk beside him. 'I've been wondering, Van,' he said with a wry grin, 'whether or not to report my ideas in advance. I forgot the "U animals", as Caldwell named it, could read minds. I've a vague idea of something that might work. It's too vague to bother with though. Go ahead with your show, while I try to figure out the logic of the thing. I'll take this bunk.'

Van Wall glanced up and nodded. The movie screen would be practically on a line with his bunk, hence making the pictures least distracting here, because least intelligible. 'Perhaps you should tell us what you have in mind. As it is, only the unknowns know what you plan. You might be – unknown before you got it into operation.'

'Won't take long, if I get it figured out right. But I don't want any more all-but-the-test-dog-monsters things. We better move Copper into this bunk directly above me. He won't be watching the screen either.' McReady nodded towards Copper's gently snoring bulk. Garry helped them lift and move the doctor.

McReady leaned back against the bunk and sank into a trance, almost, of concentration, trying to calculate chances, operations, methods. He was scarcely aware as the others distributed themselves silently, and the screen lit up. Vaguely Kinner's hectic, shouted prayers and his rasping hymn singing annoyed him till the sound accompaniment started. The lights were turned out, but the large, light-coloured areas of the screen reflected enough light for ready visibility. It made men's eyes sparkle as they moved restlessly. Kinner was still praying, shouting, his voice a raucous accompaniment to the mechanical sound. Dutton stepped up the amplification.

So long had the voice been going on, that only vaguely at first was McReady aware that something seemed missing. Lying as he was, just across the narrow room from the corridor leading to Cosmos House, Kinner's voice had reached him fairly clearly, despite the sound accompaniment of the pictures. It struck him abruptly that it had stopped.

'Dutton, cut that sound,' McReady called as he sat up abruptly. The pictures flickered a moment, soundless and strangely futile in the sudden, deep silence. The rising wind on the surface above bubbled melancholy tears of sound down the stovepipes. 'Kinner's stopped,' McReady said softly.

'For God's sake start that sound then; he may have stopped to listen,' Norris snapped.

McReady rose and went down the corridor. Barclay and Van Wall left their places at the far end of the room to follow him. The flickers bulged and twisted on the back of Barclay's grey underwear as he crossed the still-functioning beam of the projector. Dutton snapped on the lights, and the pictures vanished.

Norris stood at the door as McReady had asked. Garry sat down quietly in the bunk nearest the door, forcing Clark to make room for him. Most of the others had stayed exactly where they were. Only Connant walked slowly up and down the room, in steady, unvarying rhythm.

'If you're going to do that, Connant,' Clark spat, 'we can get along without you altogether, whether you're human or not. Will you stop that damned rhythm?'

'Sorry.' The physicist sat down in a bunk and watched his toes thoughtfully. It was almost five minutes, five ages, while the wind made the only sound, before McReady appeared at the door.

'We,' he announced, 'haven't got enough grief here already. Somebody's tried to help us out. Kinner has a knife in his throat, which was why he stopped singing probably. We've got monsters, madmen, and murderers. Any more M's you can think of, Caldwell? If there are, we'll probably have 'em before long.'

XI

'Is Blair loose?' someone asked.

'Blair is not loose. Or he flew in. If there's any doubt about where our gentle helper came from – this may clear it up.' Van Wall held a foot-long, thin-bladed knife in a cloth. The wooden handle was half burnt, charred with the peculiar pattern of the top of the galley stove.

Clark stared at it. 'I did that this afternoon. I forgot the damn thing and left it on the stove.'

Van Wall nodded, 'I smelled it, if you remember. I knew the knife came from the galley.'

'I wonder,' said Benning, looking around at the party warily, 'how many more monsters have we? If somebody could slip out of his place, go back of the screen to the galley and then down to the Cosmos House and back – he did come back, didn't he? Yes – everybody's here. Well, if one of the gang could do all that—'

'Maybe a monster did it,' Garry suggested quietly. 'There's that possibility.'

'The monster, as you pointed out today, has only men left to imitate. Would he decrease his – supply, shall we say?' Van Wall pointed out. 'No, we just have a plain, ordinary louse, a murderer, to deal with. Ordinarily we'd call him an inhuman murderer I suppose, but we have to distinguish now. We have inhuman murderers, and now we have human murderers. Or one at least.'

'There's one less human,' Norris said softly. 'Maybe the monsters have the balance of power now.'

'Never mind that,' McReady sighed, and turned to Barclay. "Bar, will you get your electric gadget? I'm going to make certain—'

Barclay turned down the corridor to get the pronged electrocuter, while McReady and Van Wall went back towards Cosmos House. Barclay followed them in some thirty seconds.

The corridor to Cosmos House twisted, as did nearly all corridors in Big Magnet, and Norris stood at the entrance again. But they heard, rather muffled, McReady's sudden shout. There was a savage flurry of blows, dull *ch-thunk*, *shluff* sounds. 'Bar – Bar—' And a curious, savage mewing scream, silenced before even quick-moving Norris had reached the bend.

Kinner – or what had been Kinner – lay on the floor, cut half in two by the great knife McReady had had. The meteorologist stood against the wall, the knife dripping red in his hand. Van Wall was stirring vaguely on the floor, moaning, his hand half-consciously rubbing at his jaw. Barclay, an unutterably savage gleam in his eyes, was methodically leaning on the pronged weapon in his hand, jabbing – jabbing, jabbing.

Kinner's arms had developed a queer, scaly fur, and the flesh had twisted. The fingers had shortened, the hands rounded, the fingernails become three-inch-long things of dull red horn, keened to steel-hard, razor-sharp talons.

McReady raised his head, looked at the knife in his hand, and dropped it. 'Well, whoever did it can speak up now. He was an inhuman murderer at that – in that he murdered an inhuman. I swear by all that's holy, Kinner was a lifeless corpse on the floor here when we arrived. But when it found we were going to jab it with the power – it changed.'

Norris stared unsteadily. 'Oh, Lord, those things can act. Ye gods – sitting in here for hours, mouthing prayers to a God it hated! Shouting hymns in a cracked voice – hymns about a church it never knew. Driving us mad with its ceaseless howling—

'Well. Speak up, whoever did it. You didn't know it, but you did the camp a favour. And I want to know how in blazes you got out of that room without anyone seeing you. It might help in guarding ourselves.'

'His screaming – his singing. Even the sound projector couldn't drown it.' Clark shivered. "It was a monster.'

'Oh,' said Van Wall in sudden comprehension. 'You *were* sitting right next to the door, weren't you! And almost behind the projection screen already.'

Clark nodded dumbly. 'He – it's quiet now. It's dead – Mac, your test's no damn good. It was dead anyway, monster or man, it was dead.'

McReady chuckled softly. 'Boys, meet Clark, the only one we know is human! Meet Clark, the one man who proves he's human by trying to commit murder – and failing. Will the rest of you please refrain from trying to prove you're human for a while? I think we may have another test.'

'A test!' Connant snapped joyfully, then his face sagged in disappointment. 'I suppose it's another either-way-you-want it.'

'No,' said McReady steadily. 'Look sharp and be careful. Come into the Ad Building. Barclay, bring your electrocuter. And somebody – Dutton – stand with Barclay to make sure he does it. Watch every neighbour, for by the hell these monsters came from, I've got something, and they know it. They're going to get dangerous!'

The group tensed abruptly. An air of crushing menace entered into every man's body, sharply they looked at each other. More keenly than ever before – *is that man next to me an inhuman monster?*

'What is it?' Garry asked, as they stood again in the main room. 'How long will it take?'

'I don't know, exactly,' said McReady, his voice brittle with angry determination. 'But I *know* it will work, and no two ways about it. It depends on a basic quality of the *monsters*, not on us. "*Kinner*" just convinced me.' He stood heavy and solid in bronzed immobility, completely sure of himself again at last.

'This,' said Barclay, hefting the wooden-handled weapon, tipped with its two sharp-pointed, charged conductors, 'is going to be rather necessary, I take it. Is the power plant assured?'

Dutton nodded sharply. 'The automatic stoker bin is full. The gas power plant is on standby. Van Wall and I set it for the movie operation and we've checked it over rather carefully several times, you know. Anything those wires touch, dies,' he assured them grimly. '*I* know that.'

Dr Copper stirred vaguely in his bunk, rubbed his eyes with fumbling hand. He sat up slowly, blinked his eyes blurred with sleep and drugs, widened with an unutterable horror of drug-ridden nightmares. 'Garry,' he mumbled, 'Garry – listen. Selfish – from hell they came, and hellish shellfish – I mean self— Do I? What do I mean?' he sank back in his bunk, and snored softly.

McReady looked at him thoughtfully. 'We'll know presently,' he nodded slowly. 'But selfish is what you mean all right. You may have thought of that, half-sleeping, dreaming there. I didn't stop to think what dreams you might be having. But that's all right. Selfish is the word. They must be, you see.' He turned to the men in the cabin, tense, silent men staring with wolfish eyes each at his neighbour. 'Selfish, and as Dr Copper said – *every part is a whole*. Every piece is self-sufficient, an animal in itself.

'That, and one other thing, tell the story. There's nothing mysterious about blood; it's just as normal a body tissue as a piece of muscle, or a piece of liver. But it hasn't so much connective tissue, though it has millions, billions of life cells.'

McReady's great bronze beard ruffled in a grim smile. 'This is satisfying, in a way. I'm pretty sure we humans still outnumber you – others. Others standing here. And we have what you, your otherworld race, evidently doesn't. Not an imitated, but a bred-in-the-bone instinct, a driving un-quenchable fire that's genuine. We'll fight, fight with a ferocity you may attempt to imitate, but you'll never equal! We're human. We're real. You're imitations, false to the core of your every cell.

'All right. It's a showdown now. *You* know. You, with your mind reading. You've lifted the idea from my brain. You can't do a thing about it.'

'Standing here—

'Let it pass. Blood is tissue. They have to bleed. If they don't bleed when cut, then, by heaven they're phoney! Phoney from hell! If they bleed, then that blood, separated from them, is an individual – *a newly formed individual in its own right, just as they, split, all of them, from one origi-nal, are individuals!*

'Get it, Van? See the answer Bar?'

Van Wall laughed very softly. 'The blood – the blood will not obey. It's a new individual, with all the desire to protect its own life that the original – the main mass from which it was split – has. The blood will live, and try to crawl away from a hot needle, say!'

McReady picked up the scalpel from the table. From the cabinet, he took a rack of test tubes, a tiny alcohol lamp, and a length of platinum wire set in a little glass rod. A smile of grim satisfaction rode his lips. For a moment he glanced up at those around him. Barclay and Dutton moved toward him slowly, the wooden-handled electric instrument alert.

'Dutton,' said McReady, 'suppose you stand over by the splice there where you've connected that in. Just make sure no – thing pulls it loose.'

Dutton moved away. 'Now, Van, suppose you be the first on this.'

White-faced, Van Wall stepped forward. With a delicate precision, McReady cut a vein in the base of his thumb. Van Wall winced slightly, then held steady as a half-inch of bright blood collected in the tube. McReady put the tube in the rack, gave Van Wall a bit of alum, and indicated the iodine bottle.

Van Wall stood motionlessly watching. McReady heated the platinum wire in the alcohol lamp flame, then dipped it into the tube. It hissed softly. Five times he repeated the test. 'Human, I'd say.' McReady sighed, and straightened. 'As yet, my theory hasn't been actually proven – but I have hopes. I have hopes.

'Don't, by the way, get too interested in this. We have with us some unwelcome ones, no doubt. Van, will you relieve Barclay at the switch? Thanks. Okay, Barclay, and may I say I hope you stay with us? You're a damned good guy.'

Barclay grinned uncertainly; winced under the keen edge of the scalpel. Presently, smiling widely, he retrieved his long-handled weapon.

'Mr Samuel Dutt – *Bar!*'

The tensity was released in that second. Whatever of hell the monsters may have had within them, the men in that instant matched it. Barclay had no chance to move his weapon as a score of men poured down on that thing that had seemed Dutton. It mewed, and spat, and tried to grow fangs – and was a hundred broken, torn pieces. Without knives, or any weapon save the brute-given strength of a staff of picked men, the thing was crushed, rent.

Slowly they picked themselves up, their eyes smouldering, very quiet in their emotions. A curious wrinkling of their lips betrayed a species of nervousness.

Barclay went over with the electric weapon. Things smouldered and stank. The caustic acid Van Wall dropped on each spilled drop of blood gave off tickling cough-provoking fumes.

McReady grinned, his deep-set eyes alight and dancing. 'Maybe,' he said softly, 'I underrated man's abilities when I said nothing human could have the ferocity in the eyes of that thing we found. I wish we could have the opportunity to treat in a more befitting manner these things. Something with boiling oil, or melted lead in it, or maybe slow roasting in the power boiler. When I think what a man Dutton was—

'Never mind. My theory is confirmed by – by one who knew? Well, Van Wall and Barclay are proven. I think then, that I'll try to show you what I already know. That I too am human.' McReady swished the scalpel in absolute alcohol, burned it off the metal blade, and cut the base of his thumb expertly.

Twenty seconds later he looked up from the desk at the waiting men. There were more grins out there now, friendly grins, yet withal, something else in the eyes.

'Connant,' McReady laughed softly, 'was right. The huskies watching that thing in the corridor bend had nothing on you. Wonder why we think only the wolf blood has the right to ferocity? Maybe on spontaneous viciousness a wolf takes tops, but after these seven days – abandon all hope, ye wolves who enter here!

'Maybe we can save time. Connant, would you step for—'

Again Barclay was too slow. There were more grins, less tensity still, when Barclay and Van Wall finished their work.

Garry spoke in a low, bitter voice. 'Connant was one of the finest men we had here – and five minutes ago I'd have sworn he was a man. Those damnable things are more than imitation.' Garry shuddered and sat back in his bunk.

And thirty seconds later, Garry's blood shrank from the hot platinum wire, and struggled to escape the tube, struggled as frantically as a suddenly feral, red-eyed, dissolving imitation of Garry struggled to dodge the snake-tongue weapon Barclay advanced at him, white-faced and sweating. The thing in the test tube screamed with a tiny, tinny voice as McReady dropped it into the glowing coal of the galley stove.

XII

'The last of it?' Dr Copper looked down from his bunk with bloodshot, saddened eyes. 'Fourteen of them—'

McReady nodded shortly. 'In some ways – if only we could have permanently prevented their spreading – I'd like to have even the imitations back. Commander Garry – Connant – Dutton – Clark—'

'Where are they taking those things?' Copper nodded to the stretcher Barclay and Norris were carrying out.

'Outside. Outside on the ice, where they've got fifteen smashed crates, half a ton of coal, and presently will add ten gallons of kerosene. We've dumped acid on every spilled drop, every torn fragment. We're going to incinerate those.'

'Sounds like a good plan.' Copper nodded wearily. 'I wonder, you haven't said whether Blair—'

McReady started. 'We forgot him! We had so much else! I wonder – do you suppose we can cure him now?'

'If—' began Dr Copper, and stopped meaningly.

McReady started a second time. 'Even a madman. It imitated Kinner and his praying hysteria—' McReady turned toward Van Wall at the long table. 'Van, we've got to make an expedition to Blair's shack.'

Van looked up sharply, the frown of worry faded for an instant in surprised remembrance. Then he rose, nodded. 'Barclay better go along. He applied the lashings, and may figure how to get in without frightening Blair too much.'

Three-quarters of an hour, through minus thirty-seven-degree cold, while the aurora curtain bellied overhead. The twilight was nearly twelve hours long, flaming in the north on snow like white, crystalline sand under their skis. A five-mile wind piled it in drift lines pointing off to the north-west. Three quarters of an hour to reach the snow-buried shack. No smoke came from the little shack, and the men hastened.

'Blair!' Barclay roared into the wind when he was still a hundred yards away. 'Blair!'

'Shut up,' said McReady softly. 'And hurry. He may be trying a lone hike. If we have to go after him – no planes, the tractors disabled—'

'Would a monster have the stamina a man has?'

'A broken leg wouldn't stop it for more than a minute,' McReady pointed out.

Barclay gasped suddenly and pointed aloft. Dim in the twilit sky, a winged thing circled in curves of indescribable grace and ease. Great white wings tipped gently, and the bird swept over them in silent curiosity. 'Albatross,' Barclay said softly. 'First of the season, and wandering way inland for some reason. If a monster's loose—'

Norris bent down on the ice, and tore hurriedly at his heavy, windproof clothing. He straightened, his coat flapping open, a grim blue-metalled weapon in his hand. It roared a challenge to the white silence of Antarctica.

The thing in the air screamed hoarsely. Its great wings worked frantically as a dozen feathers floated down from its tail. Norris fired again. The bird was moving swiftly now, but in an almost straight line of retreat. It screamed again, more feathers dropped, and with beating wings it soared behind a ridge of pressure ice, to vanish.

Norris hurried after the others. 'It won't come back,' he panted.

Barclay cautioned him to silence, pointing. A curiously, fiercely blue light beat out from the cracks of the shack's door. A very low, soft humming sounded inside, a low, soft humming and a clink and click of tools, the very sounds somehow bearing a message of frantic haste.

McReady's face paled. 'Lord help us if that thing has—' He grabbed Barclay's shoulder, and made snipping motions with his fingers, pointing towards the lacing of control cables that held the door.

Barclay drew the wire cutters from his pocket, and kneeled soundlessly at the door. The snap and twang of cut wires made an unbearable racket in the utter quiet of the Antarctic hush. There was only that strange, sweetly soft hum from within the shack, and the queerly, hectically clipped clicking and rattling of tools to drown their noises.

McReady peered through a crack in the door. His breath sucked in huskily and his great fingers clamped cruelly on Barclay's shoulder. The meteorologist backed down. 'It isn't,' he explained very softly, 'Blair. It's kneeling on something on the bunk – something that keeps lifting. Whatever it's working on is a thing like a knapsack – and it lifts.'

'All at once,' Barclay said grimly. 'No. Norris, hang back, and get that iron of yours out. It may have – weapons.'

Together, Barclay's powerful body and McReady's giant strength struck the door. Inside, the bunk jammed against the door screeched madly and crackled into kindling. The door flung down from broken hinges, the patched lumber of the doorpost dropping inward.

Like a blue rubber ball, a thing bounced up. One of its four tentaclelike arms looped out like a striking snake. In a seven-tentacled hand a six-inch pencil of winking, shining metal glinted and swung upward to face them. It's line-thin lips twitched back from snake-fangs in a grin of hate, red eyes blazing.

Norris' revolver thundered in the confined space. The hate-washed face twitched in agony, the looping tentacle snatched back. The silvery thing in its hand a smashed ruin of metal, the seven-tentacled hand became a mass of mangled flesh oozing greenish-yellow ichor. The revolver thundered three times more. Dark holes drilled each of the three eyes before Norris hurled the empty weapon against its face.

The thing screamed in feral hate, a lashing tentacle wiping at blinded eyes. For a moment it crawled on the floor, savage tentacles lashing out, the body twitching. Then it staggered up again, blinded eyes working, boiling hideously, the crushed flesh sloughing away in sodden gobbets.

Barclay lurched to his feet and dove forward with an ice axe. The flat of the weighty thing crushed against the side of the head. Again the unkillable monster went down. The tentacles lashed out, and suddenly Barclay fell to his feet in the grip of a living, livid rope. The thing dissolved as he held it, a white-hot band that ate into the flesh of his hands like living fire. Frantically he tore the stuff from him, held his hands where they could not be reached. The blind thing felt and ripped at the tough, heavy, wind-proof cloth, seeking flesh – flesh it could convert—

The huge blowtorch McReady had brought coughed solemnly. Abruptly it rumbled disapproval throatily. Then it laughed gurglingly, and thrust out a blue-white, three-foot tongue. The thing on the floor shrieked, flailed out blindly with tentacles that writhed and withered in the bubbling wrath of the blowtorch. It crawled and turned on the floor, it shrieked and hobbled madly, but always McReady held the blowtorch on the face, the dead eyes burning and bubbling uselessly. Frantically the thing crawled and howled.

A tentacle sprouted a savage talon – and crisped in the flame. Steadily McReady moved with a planned, grim campaign. Helpless, maddened, the thing retreated from the grunting torch, the caressing, licking tongue. For a moment it rebelled, squalling in inhuman hatred at the touch of the icy snow. Then it fell back before the charring breath of the torch, the stench of its flesh bathing it. Hopelessly it retreated – on and on across the Antarctic snow. The bitter wind swept over it twisting the torch-tongue; vainly it flopped, a trail of oily, stinking smoke bubbling away from it—

McReady walked back towards the shack silently. Barclay met him at the door. 'No more?' the giant meteorologist asked grimly.

Barclay shook his head. 'No more. It didn't split?'

'It had other things to think about,' McReady assured him. 'When I left it, it was a glowing coal. What was it doing?'

Norris laughed shortly. 'Wise boys, we are. Smash magnetos so planes won't work. Rip the boiler tubing out of the tractors. And leave that thing alone for a week in this shack. Alone and undisturbed.'

McReady looked in at the shack more carefully. The air,

despite the ripped door, was hot and humid. On a table at the far end of the room rested a thing of coiled wires and small magnets, glass tubing and radio tubes. At the centre a block of rough stone rested. From the centre of the block came the light that flooded the place, the fiercely blue light bluer than the glare of an electric arc, and from it came the sweetly soft hum. Off to one side was another mechanism of crystal glass, blown with an incredible neatness and delicacy, metal plates and a queer, shimmery sphere of insubstantiality.

'What is that?' McReady moved nearer.

Norris grunted. 'Leave it for investigation. But I can guess pretty well. That's atomic power. That stuff to the left – that's a neat little thing for doing what men have been trying to do with one-hundred-ton cyclotrons and so forth. It separates neutrons from heavy water, which he was getting from the surrounding ice.'

'Where did he get all – oh. Of course. A monster couldn't be locked in – or out. He's been through the apparatus caches.' McReady stared at the apparatus. 'Lord, what minds that race must have—'

'The shimmery sphere – I think it's a sphere of pure force. Neutrons can pass through any matter, and he wanted a supply reservoir of neutrons. Just project neutrons against silica – calcium – beryllium – almost anything, and the atomic energy is released. That thing is the atomic generator.'

McReady plucked a thermometer from his coat. 'It's a hundred and twenty degrees in here, despite the open door. Our clothes have kept the heat out to an extent, but I'm sweating now.'

Norris nodded. 'The light's cold. I found that. But it gives off heat to warm the place through the coil. He had all the power in the world. He could keep it warm and pleasant, as his race thought of warmth and pleasantness. Did you notice the light, the colour of it?'

McReady nodded. 'Beyond the stars is the answer. From beyond the stars. From a hotter planet that circled a brighter, bluer sun they came.'

McReady glanced out the door towards the blasted, smoke-stained trail that flopped and wandered blindly off across the drift. 'There won't be any more coming, I guess. Sheer accident it landed here, and that was twenty million years ago. What did it do all that for?' He nodded towards the apparatus.

Barclay laughed softly. 'Did you notice what it was working on when we came? Look.' He pointed towards the ceiling of the shack.

Like a knapsack made of flattened coffee tins, with dangling cloth straps and leather belts, the mechanism clung to the ceiling. A tiny, glaring heart of supernal flame burned in it, yet burned through the ceiling's wood without scorching it. Barclay walked over to it, grasped two of the dangling straps in his hands and pulled it down with an effort. He strapped it about his body. A slight jump carried him in a weirdly slow arc across the room.

'Antigravity,' said McReady softly.

'Antigravity.' Norris nodded. 'Yes, we had 'em stopped, with no planes and no birds. The birds hadn't come. But they had coffee tins and radio parts, and glass and the machine shop at night. And a week – a whole week – all to itself. America in a single jump – with antigravity powered by the atomic energy of matter.

'We had 'em stopped. Another half-hour – it was just tightening these straps on the device so it could wear it – and we'd have stayed in Antarctica, and shot down any moving thing that came from the rest of the world.'

'The albatross—' McReady said softly. 'Do you suppose—'

'With this thing almost finished? With that death weapon it held in its hand?

'No, by the grace of God, who evidently does hear very well, even down here, and the margin of half an hour, we keep our world, and the planets of the system too. Antigravity, you know, and atomic power. Because *they* came from another sun, a star beyond the stars. *They* came from a world with a bluer sun.'

IN HIDING

Wilmar H. Shiras

Stories about supermen are among the most difficult to write in science fiction; there are not many good ones. Some readers will remember Olaf Stapledon's Odd John *and A. E. van Vogt's* Slan. *Here is a third, a little more human than the other two – no tendrils, no superpowers, double hearts or telepathy ... just the loneliness of a boy who is too intelligent to be considered 'normal'.*

Peter Welles, psychiatrist, eyed the boy thoughtfully. Why had Timothy Paul's teacher sent him for examination?

'I don't know, myself, that there's really anything wrong with Tim,' Miss Page had told Dr Welles. 'He seems perfectly normal. He's rather quiet as a rule, doesn't volunteer answers in class or anything of that sort. He gets along well enough with other boys and seems reasonably popular, although he has no special friends. His grades are satisfactory – he gets B faithfully in all his work. But when you've been teaching as long as I have, Peter, you get a feeling about certain ones. There is a tension about him – a look in his eyes sometimes – and he is very absentminded.'

'What would your guess be?' Welles had asked. Sometimes these hunches were very valuable. Miss Page had taught school for thirty-odd years; she had been Peter's teacher in the past, and he thought highly of her opinion.

'I ought not to say,' she answered. 'There's nothing to go on – yet. But he might be starting something, and if it could be headed off—'

'Physicians are often called before the symptoms are

sufficiently marked for the doctor to be able to see them,' said Welles. 'A patient, or the mother of a child, or any practised observer can often see that something is going to be wrong. But it's hard for the doctor in such cases. Tell me what you think I should look for.'

'You won't pay too much attention to me? It's just what occurred to me, Peter; I know I'm not a trained psychiatrist. But it could be delusions of grandeur. Or it could be a withdrawing from the society of others. I always have to speak to him twice to get his attention in class, and he has no real chums.'

Welles had agreed to see what he could find, and promised not to be too much influenced by what Miss Page herself called 'an old woman's notions'.

Timothy, when he presented himself for examination, seemed like an ordinary boy. He was perhaps a little small for his age, he had big dark eyes and close-cropped dark curls, thin sensitive fingers and – yes, a decided air of tension. But many boys were nervous on their first visit to the – psychiatrist. Peter often wished that he was able to concentrate on one or two schools, and spend a day a week or so getting acquainted with all the youngsters.

In response to Welles' preliminary questioning, Tim replied in a clear, low voice, politely and without wasting words. He was thirteen years old, and lived with his grandparents. His mother and father had died when he was a baby, and he did not remember them. He said that he was happy at home, and that he liked school 'pretty well', that he liked to play with other boys. He named several boys when asked who his friends were.

'What lessons do you like at school?'

Tim hesitated, then said: 'English, and arithmetic ... and history ... and geography,' he finished thoughtfully. Then he looked up, and there was something odd in the glance.

'What do you like to do for fun?'

'Read, and play games.'

'What games?'

'Ball games ... and marbles ... and things like that. I like to play with other boys,' he added, after a barely perceptible pause, 'anything they play.'

'Do they play at your house?'

'No; we play on the school grounds. My grandmother doesn't like noise.'

Was that the reason? When a quiet boy offers explanations, they may not be the right ones.

'What do you like to read?'

But about his reading Timothy was vague. He liked, he said, to read 'boys' books', but could not name any.

Welles gave the boy the usual intelligence tests. Tim seemed willing, but his replies were slow in coming. *Perhaps*, Welles thought, I'm imagining this, but he is too careful – too *cautious*. Without taking time to figure exactly, Welles knew what Tim's IQ would be – about 120.

'What do you do outside of school?' asked the psychiatrist.

'I play with the other boys. After supper, I study my lessons.'

'What did you do yesterday?'

'We played ball on the school playground.'

Welles waited a while to see whether Tim would say anything of his own accord. The seconds stretched into minutes.

'Is that all?' said the boy finally. 'May I go now?'

'No; there's one more test I'd like to give you today. A game, really. How's your imagination?'

'I don't know.'

'Cracks on the ceiling – like those over there – do they look like anything to you? Faces, animals, or anything?'

Tim looked.

'Sometimes. And clouds, too. Bob saw a cloud last week that was like a hippo.' Again the last sentence sounded like something tacked on at the last moment, a careful addition made for a reason.

Welles got out the Rorschach cards. But at the sight of them, his patient's tension increased, his wariness became unmistakably evident. The first time they went through the cards, the boy could scarcely be persuaded to say any-thing but 'I don't know.'

'You can do better than this,' said Welles. 'We're going through them again. If you don't see anything in these pictures, I'll have to mark you a failure,' he explained. 'That won't do. You did all right on the other things. And maybe next time we'll do a game you'll like better.'

'I don't feel like playing this game now. Can't we do it again next time?'

'May as well get it done now. It's not only a game, you know, Tim; it's a test. Try harder, and be a good sport.'

So Tim, this time, told what he saw in the inkblots. They went through the cards slowly, and the test showed Tim's fear, and that there was something he was hiding; it showed his caution, a lack of trust, and an unnaturally high emotional self-control.

Miss Page had been right; the boy needed help.

'Now,' said Welles cheerfully, 'that's all over. We'll just run through them again quickly and I'll tell you what other people have seen in them.'

A flash of genuine interest appeared on the boy's face for a moment.

Welles went through the cards slowly, seeing that Tim was attentive to every word. When he first said, 'And some see what you saw here,' the boy's relief was evident. Tim began to relax, and even to volunteer some remarks. When they had finished he ventured to ask a question.

'Dr Welles, could you tell me the name of this test?'

'It's sometimes called the Rorschach test, after the man who worked it out.'

'Would you mind spelling that?'

Welles spelled it, and added, 'Sometimes it's called the inkblot test.'

Tim gave a start of surprise, and then relaxed again with a visible effort.

'What's the matter? You jumped.'

'Nothing.'

'Oh, come on! Let's have it.' And Welles waited.

'Only that I thought about the ink pool in the Kipling

stories,' said Tim, after a minute's reflection. 'This is different.'

'Yes, very different,' laughed Welles. 'I've never tried that. Would you like to?'

'Oh, no, sir,' cried Tim earnestly.

'You're a little jumpy today,' said Welles. 'We've time for some more talk, if you are not too tired.'

'No, I'm not very tired,' said the boy warily.

Welles went to a drawer and chose a hypodermic needle. It wasn't usual, but perhaps – 'I'll just give you a little shot to relax your nerves, shall I? Then we'd get on better.'

When he turned around, the stark terror on the child's face stopped Welles in his tracks.

'Oh, no! Don't! Please, please, don't!'

Welles replaced the needle and shut the drawer before he said a word.

'I won't,' he said quietly. 'I didn't know you didn't like shots. I won't give you any, Tim.'

The boy, fighting for self-control, gulped and said nothing.

'It's all right,' said Welles, lighting a cigarette and pretending to watch the smoke rise. Anything rather than appear to be watching the badly shaken small boy shivering in the chair opposite him. 'Sorry. You didn't tell me about the things you don't like, the things you're afraid of.'

The words hung in the silence.

'Yes,' said Timothy slowly. 'I'm afraid of shots. I hate needles. It's just one of those things.' He tried to smile.

'We'll do without them, then. You've passed all the tests, Tim, and I'd like to walk home with you and tell your grandmother about it. Is that all right with you?'

'Yes, sir.'

'We'll stop for something to eat,' Welles went on, opening the door for his patient. 'Ice cream, or a hot dog.'

They went out together.

Timothy Paul's grandparents, Mr and Mrs Herbert Davis, lived in a large old-fashioned house that spelled money and position. The grounds were large, fenced, and bordered with shrubbery. Inside the house there was little that was new, everything was well kept. Timothy led the psychiatrist to Mr Davis' library, and then went in search of his grandmother.

When Welles saw Mrs Davis, he thought he had some of the explanation. Some grandmothers are easygoing, jolly, comparatively young. This grandmother was, as it soon became apparent, quite different.

'Yes, Timothy is a pretty good boy,' she said, smiling on her grandson. 'We have always been strict with him, Dr Welles, but I believe it pays. Even when he was a mere baby, we tried to teach him right ways. For example, when he was barely three I read him some little stories. And a few days later he was trying to tell us, if you will believe it, that he could read! Perhaps he was too young to know the nature of a lie, but I felt it my duty to make him understand. When he insisted, I spanked him. The child had a remarkable memory, and perhaps he thought that was all there was to reading. Well! I don't mean to brag of my brutality,' said Mrs Davis, with a charming smile. 'I assure you, Dr Welles, it was a painful experience for me. We've had very little occasion for punishments. Timothy is a good boy.'

Welles murmured that he was sure of it.

'Timothy, you may deliver your papers now,' said Mrs Davis. 'I am sure Dr Welles will excuse you.' And she settled herself for a good long talk about her grandson.

Timothy, it seemed, was the apple of her eye. He was a quiet boy, an obedient boy, and a bright boy.

'We have our rules, of course. I have never allowed Timothy to forget that children should be seen and not heard, as the good old-fashioned saying is. When he first learned to turn somersaults, when he was three or four years old, he kept coming to me and saying, "Grandmother, see me!" I simply had to be firm with him. "Timothy," I said, "let us have no more of this! It is simply showing off. If it amuses you to turn somersaults, well and good. But it doesn't amuse me to watch you endlessly doing it. Play if you like, but do not demand admiration."'

'Did you never play with him?'

'Certainly I played with him. And it was a pleasure to me also. We – Mr Davis and I – taught him a great many games, and many kinds of handicraft. We read stories to him and taught him rhymes and songs. I took a special course in kindergarten craft, to amuse the child – and I must admit that it amused me also!' added Tim's grandmother, smiling reminiscently. 'We made houses of toothpicks, with balls of clay at the corners. His grandfather took him for walks and drives. We no longer have a car, since my husband's sight has begun to fail him slightly, so now the garage is Timothy's workshop. We had windows cut in it, and a door, and nailed the large doors shut.'

It soon became clear that Tim's life was not all strictures by any means. He had a workshop of his own, and upstairs beside his bedroom was his own library and study.

'He keeps his books and treasures there,' said his grandmother, 'his own little radio, and his schoolbooks, and his typewriter. When he was only seven years old, he asked us for a typewriter. But he is a careful child, Dr Welles, not at all destructive, and I had read that in many schools they make use of typewriters in teaching young children to read and write and to spell. The words look the same as in printed books, you see; and less muscular effort is involved. So his grandfather got him a very nice noiseless typewriter, and he loved it dearly. I often hear it purring away as I pass through the hall. Timothy keeps his own rooms in good order, and his shop also. It is his own wish. You know how boys are – they do not wish others to meddle with their belongings. "Very well, Timothy," I told him, "if a glance shows me that you can do it yourself properly, nobody will go into your rooms; but they must be kept neat." And he has done so for several years. A very neat boy, Timothy.'

'Timothy didn't mention his paper route,' remarked Welles. 'He said only that he plays with other boys after school.'

'Oh, but he does,' said Mrs Davis. 'He plays until five o'clock, and then he delivers his papers. If he is late, his grandfather walks down and calls him. The school is not very far from here, and Mr Davis frequently walks down and watches the boys at their play. The paper route is Timothy's way of earning money to feed his cats. Do you care for cats, Dr Welles?'

'Yes, I like cats very much,' said the psychiatrist. 'Many boys like dogs better.'

'Timothy had a dog when he was a baby – a collie.' Her eyes grew moist. 'We all loved Ruff dearly. But I am no longer young, and the care and training of a dog is difficult. Timothy is at school or at the Boy Scout camp or something of the sort a great part of the time, and I thought it best that he should not have another dog. But you wanted to know about our cats, Dr Welles. I raise Siamese cats.'

'Interesting pets,' said Welles cordially. 'My aunt raised them at one time.'

'Timothy is very fond of them. But three years ago he asked me if he could have a pair of black Persians. At first I thought not; but we like to please the child, and he promised to build their cages himself. He had taken a course in carpentry at vacation school. So he was allowed to have a pair of beautiful black Persians. But the very first litter turned out to be short-haired, and Timothy confessed that he had mated his queen to my Siamese tom, to see what would happen. Worse yet, he had mated his tom to one of my Siamese queens. I really was tempted to punish him. But, after all, I could see that he was curious as to the outcome of such cross-breeding. Of course I said the kittens must be destroyed. The second litter was exactly like the first – all black, with short hair. But you know what children are. Timothy begged me to let them live, and they were his first kittens. Three in one litter, two in the other. He might keep them, I said, if he would take full care of them and be responsible for all the expense. He mowed lawns and ran errands and made little footstools and bookcases to sell, and did all sorts of things, and probably used his allowance, too. But he kept the kittens and has a whole row of cages in the yard beside his workshop.'

'And their offspring?' inquired Welles, who could not see what all this had to do with the main question, but was willing to listen to anything that might lead to information.

143

'Some of the kittens appear to be pure Persian, and others pure Siamese. These he insisted on keeping, although, as I have explained to him, it would be dishonest to sell them, since they are not pure-bred. A good many of the kittens are black short-haired and these we destroy. But enough of cats, Dr Welles. And I am afraid I am talking too much about my grandson.'

'I can understand that you are very proud of him,' said Welles.

'I must confess that we are. And he is a bright boy. When he and his grandfather talk together, and with me also, he asks very intelligent questions. We do not encourage him to voice his opinions – I detest the smart-aleck type of small boy – and yet I believe they would be quite good opinions for a child of his age.'

'Has his health always been good?' asked Welles.

'On the whole, very good. I have taught him the value of exercise, play, wholesome food, and suitable rest. He has had a few of the usual childish ailments, not seriously. And he never has colds. But, of course, he takes his cold shots twice a year when we do.'

'Does he mind the shots?' asked Welles, as casually as he could.

'Not at all. I always say that he, though so young, sets an example I find hard to follow. I still flinch, and really rather dread the ordeal.'

Welles looked toward the door at a sudden, slight sound.

Timothy stood there, and he had heard. Again, fear was stamped on his face and terror looked out of his eyes.

'Timothy,' said his grandmother, 'don't stare.'

'Sorry, sir,' the boy managed to say.

'Are your papers all delivered? I did not realize we had been talking for an hour, Dr Welles. Would you like to see Timothy's cats?' Mrs Davis inquired graciously. 'Timothy, take Dr Welles to see your pets. We have had quite a talk about them.'

Welles got Tim out of the room as fast as he could. The boy led the way around the house and into the side yard where the former garage stood.

There the man stopped.

'Tim,' he said, 'you don't have to show me the cats if you don't want to.'

'Oh, that's all right.'

'Is that part of what you are hiding? If it is, I don't want to see it until you are ready to show me.'

Tim looked up at him then.

'Thanks,' he said. 'I don't mind about the cats. Not if you like cats really.'

'I really do. But Tim, this I would like to know: you're not afraid of the needle; could you tell me why you were afraid . . . why you said you were afraid . . . of my shot? The one I promised not to give you after all?'

Their eyes met.

'You won't tell?' asked Tim.

'I won't tell.'

'Because it was pentothal. Wasn't it?'

Welles gave himself a slight pinch. Yes, he was awake. Yes, this was a little boy asking him about pentothal. A boy who – yes, certainly, a boy who knew about it.

'Yes, it was,' said Welles. 'A very small dose. You know what it is?'

'Yes, sir. I . . . I read about it somewhere. In the papers.'

'Never mind that. You have a secret – something you want to hide. That's what you are afraid about, isn't it?'

The boy nodded dumbly.

'If it's anything wrong, or that might be wrong, perhaps I could help you. You'll want to know me better, first. You'll want to be sure you can trust me. But I'll be glad to help, any time you say the word, Tim. Or I might stumble on to things the way I did just now. One thing though – I never tell secrets.'

'Never?'

'Never. Doctors and priests don't betray secrets. Doctors seldom, priests never. I guess I am more like a priest, because of the kind of doctoring I do.'

He looked down at the boy's bowed head.

'Helping fellows who are scared sick,' said the psychiatrist very gently. 'Helping fellows in trouble, getting things straight again, fixing things up, unsnarling tangles. When I can, that's what I do. And I don't tell anything to anybody. It's just between that one fellow and me.'

But, he added to himself, I'll have to find out. I'll have to find out what ails this child. Miss Page is right – he needs me.

They went to see the cats.

There were the Siamese in their cages, and the Persians in their cages, and there, in several small cages, the short-haired black cats and their hybrid offspring. 'We take them into the house or let them into this big cage, for exercise,' explained Tim. 'I take mine into my shop sometimes. These are all mine. Grandmother keeps hers on the sun porch.'

'You'd never know these were not all pure-bred,' observed Welles. 'Which did you say were the full Persians? Any of their kittens here?'

'No; I sold them.'

'I'd like to buy one. But these look just the same. It wouldn't make any difference to me. I want a pet, and wouldn't use it for breeding stock. Would you sell me one of these?'

Timothy shook his head.

'I'm sorry. I never sell any but the purebreds.'

It was then that Welles began to see what problem he faced. Very dimly he saw it, with joy, relief, hope, and wild enthusiasm.

'Why not?' urged Welles. 'I can wait for a purebred, if you'd rather, but why not one of these? They look just the same. Perhaps they'd be more interesting.'

Tim looked at Welles for a long, long minute.

'I'll show you,' he said. 'Promise to wait here? No, I'll let you come into the workroom. Wait a minute, please.'

The boy drew a key from under his blouse, where it had hung suspended from a chain, and unlocked the door of his shop. He went inside, closed the door, and Welles could hear him moving about for a few moments. Then he came to the door and beckoned.

'Don't tell Grandmother,' said Tim. 'I haven't told her yet. If it lives, I'll tell her next week.'

In the corner of the shop under a table there was a box, and in the box there was a Siamese cat. When she saw a stranger she tried to hide her kittens; but Tim lifted her gently, and then Welles saw. Two of the kittens looked like little white rats with stringy tails and smudgy paws, ears and noses. But the third – yes, it was going to be a different sight. It was going to be a beautiful cat if it lived. It had long, silky white hair like the finest Persian, and the Siamese markings were showing up plainly.

Welles caught his breath.

'Congratulations, old man! Haven't you told anyone yet?'

'She's not ready to show. She's not a week old.'

'But you're going to show her?'

'Oh, yes, Grandmother will be thrilled. She'll love her. Maybe there'll be more.'

'You knew this would happen. You made it happen. You planned it all from the start,' accused Welles.

'Yes,' admitted the boy.

'How did you know?'

The boy turned away.

'I read it somewhere,' said Tim.

The cat jumped back into the box and began to nurse her babies. Welles felt as if he could endure no more. Without a glance at anything else in the room – and everything else was hidden under tarpaulins and newspapers – he went to the door.

'Thanks for showing me, Tim,' he said. 'And when you have any to sell, remember me. I'll wait. I want one like that.'

The boy followed him out and locked the door carefully.

'But Tim,' said the psychiatrist, 'that's not what you were afraid I'd find out. I wouldn't need a drug to get you to tell me this, would I?'

Tim replied carefully, 'I didn't want to tell this until I was ready. Grandmother really ought to know first. But you made me tell you.'

'Tim,' said Peter Welles earnestly, 'I'll see you again. Whatever you are afraid of, don't be afraid of me. I often guess secrets. I'm on the way to guessing yours already. But nobody else need ever know.'

He walked rapidly home, whistling to himself from time to time. Perhaps he, Peter Welles, was the luckiest man in the world.

He had scarcely begun to talk to Timothy on the boy's next appearance at the office, when the phone in the hall rang. On his return, when he opened the door he saw a book in Tim's hands. The boy made a move as if to hide it, and thought better of it.

Welles took the book and looked at it.

'Want to know more about Rorschach, eh?' he asked.

'I saw it on the shelf. I—'

'Oh, that's all right,' said Welles, who had purposely left the book near the chair Tim would occupy. 'But what's the matter with the library?'

'They've got some books about it, but they're on the closed shelves. I couldn't get them.' Tim spoke without thinking first, and then caught his breath.

But Welles replied calmly: 'I'll get it out for you. I'll have it next time you come. Take this one along today when you go. Tim, I mean it – you can trust me.'

'I can't tell you anything,' said the boy. 'You've found out some things. I wish . . . oh, I don't know what I wish! But I'd rather be let alone. I don't need help. Maybe I never will. If I do, can't I come to you then?'

Welles pulled out his chair and sat down slowly.

'Perhaps that would be the best way, Tim. But why wait for the axe to fall? I might be able to help you ward it off – what you're afraid of. You can kid people along about the cats; tell them you were fooling around to see what would happen. But you can't fool all of the people all of the time, they tell me. Maybe with me to help, you could. Or with me to back you up, the blowup would be easier. Easier on your grandparents, too.'

'I haven't done anything wrong!'

'I'm beginning to be sure of that. But things you try to keep hidden may come to light. The kitten – you could hide it, but you don't want to. You've got to risk something to show it.'

'I'll tell them I read it somewhere.'

'That wasn't true, then. I thought not. You figured it out.'
There was silence.

Then Timothy Paul said, 'Yes, I figured it out. But that's my secret.'

'It's safe with me.'

But the boy did not trust him yet. Welles soon learned that he had been tested. Tim took the book home, and returned it, took the library books which Welles got for him, and in due course returned them also. But he talked little and was still wary. Welles could talk all he liked, but he got little or nothing out of Tim. Tim had told all he was going to tell. He would talk about nothing except what any boy would talk about.

After two months of this, during which Welles saw Tim officially once a week and unofficially several times – showing up at the school playground to watch games, or meeting Tim on the paper route and treating him to a soda after it was finished – Welles had learned very little more. He tried again. He had probed no more during the two months, respected the boy's silence, trying to give him time to get to know and trust him.

But one day he asked, 'What are you going to do when you grow up, Tim? Breed cats?'

Tim laughed a denial.

'I don't know what, yet. Sometimes I think one thing, sometimes another.'

This was a typical boy answer. Welles disregarded it.

'What would you like to do best of all?' he asked.

Tim leaned forward eagerly. 'What you do!' he cried.

'You've been reading up on it, I suppose,' said Welles, as casually as he could. 'Then you know, perhaps, that before anyone can do what I do, he must go through it himself, like a patient. He must also study medicine and be a full-fledged doctor, of course. You can't do that yet. But you can have the works now, like a patient.'

'Why? For the experience?'

'Yes. And for the cure. You'll have to face that fear and lick it. You'll have to straighten out a lot of other things, or at least face them.'

'My fear will be gone when I'm grown up,' said Timothy. 'I think it will. I hope it will.'

'Can you be sure?'

'No,' admitted the boy. 'I don't know exactly why I'm afraid. I just know I *must* hide things. Is that bad, too?'

'Dangerous, perhaps.'

Timothy thought a while in silence. Welles smoked three cigarettes and yearned to pace the floor, but dared not move.

'What would it be like?' asked Tim finally.

'You'd tell me about yourself. What you remember. Your childhood. The way your grandmother runs on when she talks about you.'

'She sent me out of the room. I'm not supposed to think I'm bright,' said Tim, with one of his rare grins.

'And you're not supposed to know how well she reared you?'

'She did fine,' said Tim. 'She taught me all the wisest things I ever knew.'

'Such as what?'

'Such as shutting up. Not telling all you know. Not showing off.'

'I see what you mean,' said Welles. 'Have you heard the story of St Thomas Aquinas?'

'No.'

'When he was a student in Paris, he never spoke out in class, and the others thought him stupid. One of them kindly offered to help him, and went over all the work very patiently to make him understand it. And then one day they came to a place where the other student got all mixed up and had to admit he didn't understand. Then Thomas suggested a solution and it was the right one. He knew more than any of the others all the time; but they called him the Dumb Ox.'

Tim nodded gravely.

'And when he grew up?' asked the boy.

'He was the greatest thinker of all time,' said Welles. 'A fourteenth-century super-brain. He did more original work than any other ten great men; and he died young.'

After that, it was easier.

'How do I begin?' asked Timothy.

'You'd better begin at the beginning. Tell me all you can remember about your early childhood, before you went to school.'

Tim gave this his consideration.

'I'll have to go forward and backward a lot,' he said. 'I couldn't put it all in order.'

'That's all right. Just tell me today all you can remember about that time of your life. By next week you'll have remembered more. As we go on to later periods of your life, you may remember things that belonged to an earlier time; tell them then. We'll make some sort of order out of it.'

Welles listened to the boy's revelations with growing excitement. He found it difficult to keep outwardly calm.

'When did you begin to read?' Welles asked.

'I don't know when it was. My grandmother read me some stories, and somehow I got the idea about the words. But when I tried to tell her I could read, she spanked me. She kept saying I couldn't, and I kept saying I could, until she spanked me. For a while I had a dreadful time, because I didn't know any word she hadn't read to me. I guess I sat beside her and watched, or else I remembered and then went over it by myself right after. I must have learned as soon as I got the idea that each group of letters on the page was a word.'

'The word-unit method,' Welles commented. 'Most self-taught readers learned like that.'

'Yes. I have read about it since. And Macaulay could read when he was three, but only upside down, because of standing opposite when his father read the Bible to the family.'

'There are many cases of children who learned to read as you did, and surprised their parents. Well? How did you get on?'

'One day I noticed that two words looked almost alike and sounded almost alike. They were "can" and "man". I remember staring at them, and then it was like something beautiful boiling up in me. I began to look carefully at the words, but in a crazy excitement. I was a long while at it, because when I put down the book and tried to stand up I was stiff all over. But I had the idea, and after that it wasn't hard to figure out almost any words. The really hard words are the common ones that you get all the time in easy books. Other words are pronounced the way they are spelled.'

'And nobody knew you could read?'

'No. Grandmother told me not to say I could, so I didn't. She read to me often, and that helped. We had a great many books, of course. I liked those with pictures. Once or twice they caught me with a book that had no pictures, and then they'd take it away and say, "I'll find a book for a little boy."'

'Do you remember what books you liked then?'

'Books about animals, I remember. And geographies. It was funny about animals—'

Once you got Timothy started, thought Welles, it wasn't hard to get him to go on talking.

'One day I was at the zoo,' said Tim, 'and by the cages alone. Grandmother was resting on a bench and she let me walk along by myself. People were talking about the animals and I began to tell them all I knew. It must have been funny in a way, because I had read a lot of words I couldn't pronounce correctly, words I had never heard spoken. They listened and asked me questions and I thought I was just like Grandfather, teaching them the way he sometimes taught me. And then they called another man to come, and said, "Listen to this kid; he's a scream!" and I saw they were all laughing at me.'

Timothy's face was redder than usual, but he tried to smile as he added, 'I can see now how it must have sounded funny. And unexpected, too; that's a big point in humour. But my little feelings were so dreadfully hurt that I ran back to my grandmother crying, and she couldn't find out why. But it served me right for disobeying her. She always told me not to tell people things; she said a child had nothing to teach its elders.'

'Not in that way, perhaps – at that age.'

'But honestly, some grown people don't know very much,' said Tim. 'When we went on the train last year, a woman came up and sat beside me and started to tell me things a little boy should know about California. I told her I'd lived here all my life, but I guess she didn't even know we are taught things in school, and she tried to tell me things, and almost everything was wrong.'

'Such as what?' asked Welles, who had also suffered from tourists.

'We . . . she said so many things . . . but I thought this was the funniest: She said all the missions were so old and interesting, and I said yes, and she said, "You know, they were all built long before Columbus discovered America," and I thought she meant it for a joke, so I laughed. She looked very serious and said, "Yes, those people all come up here from Mexico." I suppose she thought they were Aztec temples.'

Welles, shaking with laughter, could not but agree that many adults were sadly lacking in the rudiments of knowledge.

'After that zoo experience, and a few others like it, I began to get wise to myself,' continued Tim. 'People who knew things didn't want to hear me repeating them, and people who didn't know, wouldn't be taught by a four-year-old baby. I guess I was four when I began to write.'

'How?'

'Oh, I just thought if I couldn't say anything to anybody at any time, I'd burst. So I began to put it down – in printing, like in books. Then I found out about writing, and we had some old-fashioned schoolbooks that taught how to write. I'm left-handed. When I went to school, I had to use my right hand. But by then I had learned how to pretend that I didn't know things. I watched the others and did as they did. My grandmother told me to do that.'

'I wonder why she said that,' marvelled Welles.

'She knew I wasn't used to other children, she said, and it was the first time she had left me to anyone else's care. So, she told me to do what the others did and what my teacher said,' explained Tim simply, 'and I followed her advice literally. I pretended I didn't know anything, until the others began to know it, too. Lucky I was so shy. But there were things to learn, all right. Do you know, when I was first sent to school, I was disappointed because the teacher dressed like other women. The only picture of teachers I had noticed were those in an old Mother Goose book, and I thought that all teachers wore hoop skirts. But as soon as I saw her, after the little shock of surprise, I knew it was silly, and I never told.'

The psychiatrist and the boy laughed together.

'We played games. I had to learn to play with children and not be surprised when they slapped or pushed me. I just couldn't figure out why they'd do that, or what good it did them. But if it was to surprise me, I'd say, "Boo" and surprise them some time later; and if they were mad because I had taken a ball or something they wanted, I'd play with them.'

'Anybody ever try to beat you up?'

'Oh, yes. But I had a book about boxing, with pictures. You can't learn much from pictures, but I got some practice too, and that helped. I didn't want to win anyway. That's what I like about games of strength or skill – I'm fairly matched, and I don't have to be always watching in case I might show off or try to boss somebody around.'

'You must have tried bossing sometimes.'

'In books, they all cluster around the boy who can teach new games and think up new things to play. But I found out that doesn't work. They just want to do the same thing all the time – like hide and seek. It's no fun if the first one to be caught is IT next time. The rest just walk in any old way and don't try to hide or even to run, because it doesn't matter whether they are caught. But you can't get the boys to see that, and play right, so the last one caught is IT.'

Timothy looked at his watch.

'Time to go,' he said. 'I've enjoyed talking to you, Dr Welles. I hope I haven't bored you too much.'

Welles recognized the echo and smiled appreciatively at the small boy.

'You didn't tell me about the writing. Did you start to keep a diary?'

'No. It was a newspaper. One page a day, no more and no less. I still keep it,' confided Tim. 'But I get more on the page now. I type it.'

'And you write with either hand now?'

'My left hand is my own secret writing. For school and things like that I use my right hand.'

When Timothy had left, Welles congratulated himself. But for the next month he got no more. Tim would not reveal a single significant fact. He talked about ball-playing, he described his grandmother's astonished delight over the beautiful kitten, he told of its growth and the tricks it played. He gravely related such enthralling facts as that he liked to ride on trains, that his favourite wild animal was the lion, and that he greatly desired to see snow falling. But not a word of what Welles wanted to hear. The psychiatrist, knowing that he was again being tested, waited patiently.

Then one afternoon when Welles, fortunately unoccupied with a patient, was smoking a pipe on his front porch, Timothy Paul strode into the yard.

'Yesterday Miss Page asked me if I was seeing you, and I said yes. She said she hoped my grandparents didn't find it too expensive, because you had told her I was all right and didn't need to have her worrying about me. And then I said to Grandma, was it expensive for you to talk to me, and she said, "Oh no, dear; the school pays for that. It was your teacher's idea that you have a few talks with Dr Welles." '

'I'm glad you came to me, Tim, and I'm sure you didn't give me away to either of them. Nobody's paying me. The school pays for my services if a child is in a bad way and his parents are poor. It's a new service, since 1956. Many maladjusted children can be helped – much more cheaply to the state than the cost of having them go crazy or become criminals or something. You understand all that. But – sit down, Tim! I can't charge the state for you, and I can't charge your grandparents. You're adjusted marvellously well in every way, as far as I can see; and when I see the rest, I'll be even more sure of it.'

'Well – gosh! I wouldn't have come—' Tim was stammering in confusion. 'You ought to be paid. I take up so much of your time. Maybe I'd better not come any more.'

'I think you'd better. Don't you?'

'Why are you doing it for nothing, Dr Welles?'

'I think you know why.'

The boy sat down in the glider and pushed himself meditatively back and forth. The glider squeaked.

'You're interested. You're curious,' he said.

'That's not all, Tim.'

Squeak-squeak. Squeak-squeak.

'I know,' said Timothy. 'I believe it. Look, is it all right if I call you Peter? Since we're friends.'

At their next meeting, Timothy went into details about his newspaper. He had kept all the copies, from the first smudged, awkwardly printed pencil issues to the very latest neatly typed ones. But he would not show Welles any of them.

'I just put down every day the things I most wanted to say, the news or information or opinion I had to swallow unsaid. So it's a wild medley. The earlier copies are awfully funny. Sometimes I guess what they were all about, what made me write them. Sometimes I remember. I put down the books I read too, and mark them like school grades, on two points – how I liked the book, and whether it was good. And whether I had read it before, too.'

'How many books do you read? What's your reading speed?'

It proved that Timothy's reading speed on new books of adult level varied from eight hunded to nine hundred fifty words a minute. The average murder mystery – he loved them – took him a little less than an hour. A year's homework in history Tim performed easily by reading his textbook through three or four times during the year. He apologized for that, but explained that he had to know what was in the book so as not to reveal in examinations too much that he had learned from other sources. Evenings, when his grandparents believed him to be doing homework, he spent his time reading other books, or writing his newspaper, 'or something'. As Welles had already guessed, Tim had read everything in his grandfather's library, everything of interest in the public library that was not on the closed shelves, and everything he could order from the state library.

'What do the librarians say?'

'They think the books are for my grandfather. I tell them that, if they ask what a little boy wants with such a big book. Peter, telling so many lies is what gets me down. I have to do it, don't I?'

'As far as I can see, you do,' agreed Welles. 'But here's material for a while in my library. There'll have to be a closed shelf here, too, though, Tim.'

'Could you tell me why? I know about the library books. Some of them might scare people, and some are—'

'Some of my books might scare you too, Tim. I'll tell you a little about abnormal psychology if you like, one of these days, and then I think you'll see that until you're actually trained to deal with such cases, you'd be better off not knowing too much about them.'

'I don't want to be morbid,' agreed Tim. 'All right. I'll read only what you give me. And from now on I'll tell you things. There was more than the newspaper, you know.'

'I thought as much. Do you want to go on with your tale?'

'It started when I first wrote a letter to a newspaper – of course, under a pen name. They printed it. For a while I had a high old time of it – a letter almost every day, using all sorts of pen names. Then I branched out to magazines, letters to the editor again. And stories – I tried stories.'

He looked a little doubtfully at Welles, who said only, 'How old were you when you sold the first story?'

'Eight,' said Timothy. 'And when the cheque came, with

my name on it, T. Paul, I didn't know what in the world to do.'

'That's a thought. What did you do?'

'There was a sign in the window of the bank. I always read signs, and that one came back to my mind: "Banking by Mail". You can see I was pretty desperate. So I got the name of a bank across the Bay and I wrote them, on my typewriter, and said I wanted to start an account, and here was a cheque to start it with. Oh, I was scared stiff, and had to keep saying to myself that after all, nobody could do much to me. It was my own money. But you don't know what it's like to be only a small boy! They sent the cheque back to me and I died ten deaths when I saw it. But the letter explained. I hadn't endorsed it. They sent me a blank to fill out about myself. I didn't know how many lies I dared to tell. But it was my money and I had to get it. If I could get it into the bank then some day I could get it out. I gave my business as author and I gave my age as twenty-four. I thought that was awfully old.'

'I'd like to see the story. Do you have a copy of the magazine around?'

'Yes,' said Tim. 'But nobody noticed it – I mean, T. Paul could be anybody. And when I saw magazines for writers on the newsstands and bought them, I got onto the way to use a pen name on the story and my own name and address up in the corner. Before that I used a pen name and sometimes never got the things back or heard about them. Sometimes I did, though.'

'What then?'

'Oh, then I'd endorse the cheque payable to me and sign the pen name, and then sign my own name under it. Was I scared to do that! But it was my money.'

'Only stories?'

'Articles, too. And things. That's enough of that for today. Only – I just wanted to say – a while ago, T. Paul told the bank he wanted to switch some of the money over to a banking account. To buy books by mail and such. So, I could pay you, Dr Welles—' with sudden formality.

'No, Tim,' said Peter Welles firmly. 'The pleasure is all

mine. What I want is to see the story that was published when you were eight. And some of the other things that made T. Paul rich enough to keep a consulting psychiatrist on the pay-roll. And, for the love of Pete, will you tell me how all this goes on without your grandparents' knowing a thing about it?'

'Grandmother thinks I send in box tops and fill out coupons,' said Tim. 'She doesn't bring in the mail. She says her little boy gets such a big bang out of that little chore. Anyway that's what she said when I was eight. I played mailman. And there were box tops – I showed them to her, until she said, about the third time, that really she wasn't greatly interested in such matters. By now she has the habit of waiting for me to bring in the mail.'

Peter Welles thought that was quite a day of revelation. He spent a quiet evening at home, holding his head and groaning, trying to take it all in.

And that IQ – 120, nonsense! The boy had been holding out on him. Tim's reading had obviously included enough about IQ tests, enough puzzles and oddments in magazines and such, to enable him to stall successfully. What could he do if he would cooperate?

Welles made up his mind to find out.

He didn't find out. Timothy Paul went swiftly through the whole range of superior adult tests without a failure of any sort. There were no tests yet devised that could measure his intelligence. While he was still writing his age with one figure, Timothy Paul had faced alone, and solved alone, problems that would have baffled the average adult. He had adjusted to the hardest task of all – that of appearing to be a fairly normal, B-average, small boy.

And it must be that there was more to find out about him. What did he write? And what did he do besides read and write, learn carpentry, and breed cats and magnificently fool his whole world?

When Peter Welles had read some of Tim's writings, he was surprised to find that the stories the boy had written were vividly human, the product of close observation of human nature. The articles, on the other hand, were closely reasoned and showed thorough study and research. Apparently Tim read every word of several newspapers and a score or more of periodicals.

'Oh, sure,' said Tim, when questioned. 'I read everything. I go back once in a while and review old ones, too.'

'If you can write like this,' demanded Welles, indicating a magazine in which a staid and scholarly article had appeared, 'and this' – this was a man-to-man political article giving the arguments for and against a change in the whole congressional system – 'then why do you always talk to me in the language of an ordinary stupid schoolboy?'

'Because I'm only a boy,' replied Timothy. 'What would happen if I went around talking like that?'

'You might risk it with me. You've showed me these things.'

'I'd never dare to risk talking like that. I might forget and do it again before others. Besides, I can't pronounce half the words.'

'What!'

'I never look up a pronunciation,' explained Timothy. 'In case I do slip and use a word beyond the average, I can anyway hope I didn't say it right.'

Welles shouted with laughter, but was sober again as he realized the implications back of that thoughtfulness.

'You're just like an explorer living among savages,' said the psychiatrist. 'You have studied the savages carefully and tried to imitate them so they won't know there are differences.'

'Something like that,' acknowledged Tim.

'That's why your stories are so human,' said Welles. 'That one about the awful little girl—'

They both chuckled.

'Yes, that was my first story,' said Tim. 'I was almost eight, and there was a boy in my class who had a brother, and the boy next door was the other one, the one who was picked on.'

'How much of the story was true?'

'The first part. I used to see, when I went over there, how

that girl picked on Bill's brother's friend, Steve. She wanted to play with Steve all the time herself and whenever he had boys over, she'd do something awful. And Steve's folks were like I said. They wouldn't let Steve do anything to a girl. When she threw all the watermelon rinds over the fence into his yard, he just had to pick them all up and say nothing back; and she'd laugh at him over the fence. She got him blamed for things he never did, and when he had work to do in the yard she'd hang out of her window and scream at him and make fun. I thought first what made her act like that, and then I made up a way for him to get even with her, and wrote it out the way it might have happened.'

'Didn't you pass the idea on to Steve and let him try it?'

'Gosh, no! I was only a little boy. Kids seven don't give ideas to kids ten. That's the first thing I had to learn – to be always the one that kept quiet, especially if there was any older boy or girl around, even only a year or two older. I had to learn to look blank and let my mouth hang open and say, "I don't get it," to almost everything.'

'And Miss Page thought it was odd that you had no close friends of your own age,' said Welles. 'You must be the loneliest boy that ever walked this earth, Tim. You've lived in hiding like a criminal. But tell me, what are you afraid of?'

'I'm afraid of being found out, of course. The only way I can live in this world is in disguise – until I'm grown up, at any rate. At first it was just my grandparents' scolding me and telling me not to show off, and the way people laughed if I tried to talk to them. Then I saw how people hate anyone who is better or brigher or luckier. Some people sort of trade off; if you're bad at one thing you're good at another, but they'll forgive you for being good at some things, if you're not good at others so they can balance it off. They can beat you at something. You have to strike a balance. A child has no chance at all. No grown-up can stand it to have a child know anything he doesn't. Oh, a little thing if it amuses them. But not much of anything. There's an old story about a man who found himself in a country where everyone else was blind. I'm like that – but they shan't put out my eyes. I'll never let them know I can see anything.'

'Do you see things that no grown person can see?'

Tim waved his hand towards the magazines.

'Only like that, I meant. I hear people talking in street cars and stores and while they work, and around. I read about the way they act – in the news. I'm like them, just like them, only I seem about a hundred years older – more matured.'

'Do you mean that none of them have much sense?'

'I don't mean that exactly. I mean that so few of them have any, or show it if they do have. They don't even seem to want to. They're good people in their way, but what could they make of me? Even when I was seven, I could understand their motives, but they couldn't understand their own motives. And they're so lazy – they don't seem to want to know or to understand. When I first went to the library for books, the books I learned from were seldom touched by any of the grown people. But they were meant for ordinary grown people. But the grown people didn't want to know things – they only wanted to fool around. I feel about most people the way my grandmother feels about babies and puppies. Only she doesn't have to pretend to be a puppy all the time,' Tim added, with a little bitterness.

'You have a friend now, in me.'

'Yes, Peter,' said Tim, brightening up. 'And I have pen friends, too. People like what I write, because they can't see I'm only a little boy. When I grow up—'

Tim did not finish that sentence. Welles understood, now, some of the fears that Tim had not dared to put into words at all. When he grew up, would he be as far beyond all other grown-ups as he had, all his life, been above his contemporaries? The adult friends whom he now met on fairly equal terms – would they then, too, seem like babies or puppies?

Peter did not dare to voice the thought, either. Still less did he venture to hint at another thought. Tim, so far, had no great interest in girls; they existed for him as part of the human race, but there would come a time when Tim would be a grown man and would wish to marry. And where among the puppies could he find a mate?

'When you're grown up, we'll still be friends,' said Peter. 'And who are the others?'

It turned out that Tim had pen friends all over the world. He played chess by correspondence – a game he never dared to play in person, except when he forced himself to move the pieces about idly and let his opponent win at least half the time. He had, also, many friends who had read something he had written, and had written to him about it, thus starting a correspondence-friendship. After the first two or three of these, he had started some on his own account, always with people who lived at a great distance. To most of these he gave a name which, although not false, looked it. That was Paul T. Lawrence. Lawrence was his middle name; and with a comma after the Paul, it was actually his own name. He had a post office box under that name, for which T. Paul of the large bank account was his reference.

'Pen friends abroad? Do you know languages?'

Yes, Tim did. He had studied by correspondence, also; many universities gave extension courses in that manner, and lent the student records to play so that he could learn the correct pronunciation. Tim had taken several such courses, and learned other languages from books. He kept all these languages in practice by means of the letters to other lands and the replies which came to him.

'I'd buy a dictionary, and then I'd write to the mayor of some town, or to a foreign newspaper, and ask them to advertise for some pen friends to help me learn the language. We'd exchange souvenirs and things.'

Nor was Welles in the least surprised to find that Timothy had also taken other courses by correspondence. He had completed within three years, more than half the subjects offered by four separate universities, and several other courses, the most recent being architecture. The boy, not yet fourteen, had completed a full course in that subject, and had he been able to disguise himself as a full-grown man, could have gone out at once and built almost anything you'd like to name, for he also knew much of the trades involved.

'It always said how long an average student took, and I'd take that long,' said Tim, 'so, of course, I had to be working several schools at the same time.'

'And carpentry at the playground summer school?'

'Oh, yes. But there I couldn't do too much, because people could see me. But I learned how, and it made a good cover-up, so I could make cages for the cats, and all that sort of thing. And many boys are good with their hands. I like to work with my hands. I built my own radio, too – it gets all the foreign stations, and that helps me with my languages.'

'How did you figure it out about the cats?' said Welles.

'Oh, there had to be recessives, that's all. The Siamese colouring was a recessive, and it had to be mated with another recessive. Black was one possibility, and white was another, but I started with black because I liked it better. I might try white too, but I have so much else on my mind—'

He broke off suddenly and would say no more.

Their next meeting was by prearrangement at Tim's workshop. Welles met the boy after school and they walked to Tim's home together; there the boy unlocked his door and snapped on the lights.

Welles looked around with interest. There was a bench, a tool chest. Cabinets, padlocked. A radio, clearly not store-purchased. A file cabinet, locked. Something on a table, covered with a cloth. A box in the corner – no, two boxes in two corners. In each of them was a mother cat with kittens. Both mothers were black Persians.

'This one must be all black Persian,' Tim explained. 'Her third litter and never a Siamese marking. But this one carries both recessives in her. Last time she had a Siamese short-haired kitten. This morning – I had to go to school. Let's see.'

They bent over the box where the newborn kittens lay. One kitten was like the mother. The other two were Siamese-Persian; a male and a female.

'You've done it again, Tim!' shouted Welles. 'Congratulations!'

They shook hands in jubilation.

'I'll write it in the record,' said the boy blissfully.

In a nickel book marked 'Compositions' Tim's left hand added the entries. He had used the correct symbols – F_1, F_2, F_3; Ss, Bl.

'The dominants in capitals,' he explained, 'B for black, and S for short hair; the recessives in small letters – s for Siamese, l for long hair. Wonderful to write ll or ss again, Peter! Twice more. And the other kitten is carrying the Siamese marking as a recessive.'

He closed the book in triumph.

'Now' – and he marched to the covered thing on the table – 'my latest big secret.'

Tim lifted the cloth carefully and displayed a beautifully built dollhouse. No, a model house – Welles corrected himself swiftly. A beautiful model, and – yes, built to scale.

'The roof comes off. See, it has a big storage room and a room for a playroom or a maid or something. Then I lift off the attic—'

'Good heavens!' cried Peter Welles. 'Any little girl would give her soul for this!'

'I used fancy wrapping papers for the wallpapers. I wove the rugs on a little hand loom,' gloated Timothy. 'The furniture's just like real, isn't it? Some I bought; that's plastic. Some I made of construction paper and things. The curtains were the hardest; but I couldn't ask Grandmother to sew them—'

'Why not?' the amazed doctor managed to ask.

'She might recognize this afterwards,' said Tim, and he lifted off the upstairs floor.

'Recognize it? You haven't showed it to her? Then when would she see it?'

'She might not,' admitted Tim. 'But I don't like to take some risks.'

'That's a very liveable floor plan you've used,' said Welles, bending closer to examine the house in detail.

'Yes, I thought so. It's awful how many house plans leave

no clear wall space for books or pictures. Some of them have doors placed so you have to detour around the dining-room table every time you go from the living-room to the kitchen, or so that a whole corner of a room is good for nothing, with doors at all angles. Now, I designed this house to—'

'You designed it, Tim!'

'Why, sure. Oh, I see – you thought I built it from blue-prints I'd bought. My first model home I did, but the architecture courses gave me so many ideas that I wanted to see how they would look. Now, the cellar and game room—'

Welles came to himself an hour later, and gasped when he looked at his watch.

'It's too late. My patient has gone home again by this time. I may as well stay – how about the paper route?'

'I gave that up. Grandmother offered to feed the cats as soon as I gave her the kitten. And I wanted the time for this. Here are the pictures of the house.'

The colour prints were very good.

'I'm sending them and an article to the magazines,' said Tim. 'This time I'm T. L. Paul. Sometimes I used to pretend all the different people I am were talking together – but now I talk to you instead, Peter.'

'Will it bother the cats if I smoke? Thanks. Nothing I'm likely to set on fire, I hope? Put the house together and let me sit here and look at it. I want to look in through the windows. Put its lights on. There.'

The young architect beamed, and snapped on the little lights.

'Nobody can see in here. I got Venetian blinds; and when I work in here, I even shut them sometimes.'

'If I'm to know all about you, I'll have to go through the alphabet from A to Z,' said Peter Welles. 'This is Archi-tecture. What else in the A's?'

'Astronomy. I showed you those articles. My calculations proved correct. Astrophysics – I got A in the course, but haven't done anything original so far. Art, no. I can't paint or draw very well, except mechanical drawing. I've done all the merit badge work in Scouting, all through the alphabet.'

'Darned if I can see you as a Boy Scout,' protested Welles.

'I'm a very good Scout. I have almost as many badges as any other boy my age in the troop. And at camp I do as well as most city boys.'

'Do you do a good turn every day?'

'Yes,' said Timothy. 'Started that when I first read about Scouting – I was a Scout at heart before I was old enough to be a Cub. You know, Peter, when you're very young, you take all that seriously about the good deed every day, and the good habits and ideals and all that. And then you get older and it begins to seem funny and childish and posed and artificial, and you smile in a superior way and make jokes. But there is a third step, too, when you take it all seriously again. People who make fun of the Scout Law are doing the boys a lot of harm; but those who believe in things like that don't know how to say so, without sounding priggish and platitudinous. I'm going to do an article on it before long.'

'Is the Scout Law your religion – if I may put it that way?'

'No,' said Timothy. 'But "A Scout is reverent". Once I tried to study the churches and find out what was the truth. I wrote letters to pastors of all denominations, all those in the phone book and the newspapers. When I was on a vacation in the East, I got the names and then wrote after I got back. I couldn't write to people here in the city. I said I wanted to know which church was true, and expected them to write to me and tell me about theirs, and argue with me, you know. I could read library books, and all they had to do was recommend some, I told them, and then correspond with me a little about them.'

'Did they?'

'Some of them answered,' said Tim, 'but nearly all of them told me to go to somebody near me. Several said they were very busy men. Some gave me the name of a few books, but none of them told me to write again, and ... and I was only a little boy. Nine years old, so I couldn't talk to anybody. When I thought it over, I knew that I couldn't very well join any church so young, unless it was my grandparents' church. I keep on going there. It is a good church and it teaches a great deal of truth, I am sure. I'm reading all I can find, so when I am old enough I'll know what I must do. How old would you say I should be, Peter?'

'College age,' replied Welles. 'You are going to college? By then, any of the pastors would talk to you – except those that are too busy!'

'It's a moral problem, really. Have I the right to wait? But I have to wait. It's like telling lies – I have to tell some lies, but I hate to. If I have a moral obligation to join the true church as soon as I find it, well, what then? I can't until I'm eighteen or twenty?'

'If you can't you can't. I should think that settles it. You are legally a minor, under the control of your grandparents, and while you might claim the right to go where your conscience leads you, it would be impossible to justify and explain your choice without giving yourself away entirely – just as you are obliged to go to school until you are at least eighteen, even though you know more than most PhDs. It's all part of the game, and He who made you must understand that.'

'I'll never tell you any lies,' said Tim. 'I was getting so desperately lonely. My pen pals don't know anything about me really. I told them only what was right for them to know. Little kids are satisfied to be with other people, but when you get a little older you have to make friends, really.'

'Yes, that's a part of growing up. You have to reach out to others and share thoughts with them. You've kept to yourself too long as it is.'

'It wasn't that I wanted to. But without a real friend, it was only pretence, and I never could let my playmates know anything about me. I studied them and wrote stories about them and it was all of them, but it was only a tiny part of me.'

'I'm proud to be your friend, Tim. Every man needs a friend. I'm proud that you trust me.'

Tim patted the cat a moment in silence and then looked up with a grin.

'How would you like to hear my favourite joke?' he asked.

'Very much,' said the psychiatrist, bracing himself for almost any major shock.

'It's records. I recorded this from a radio programme.'

Welles listened. He knew little of music, but the symphony which he heard pleased him. The announcer praised it highly in little speeches before and after each movement. Timothy giggled.

'Like it?'

'Very much. I don't see the joke.'

'I wrote it.'

'Tim, you're beyond me! But I still don't get the joke.'

'The joke is that I did it by mathematics. I calculated what ought to sound like joy, grief, hope, triumph, and all the rest, and – it was just after I had studied harmony; you know how mathematical that is.'

Speechless, Welles nodded.

'I worked out the rhythms from different metabolisms – the way you function when under the influences of these emotions; the way your metabolic rate varies, your heart-beats and respiration and things. I sent it to the director of that orchestra, and he didn't get the idea that it was a joke – of course I didn't explain. He produced the music. I get nice royalties from it, too.'

'You'll be the death of me yet,' said Welles in deep sincerity. 'Don't tell me anything more today; I couldn't take it. I'm going home. Maybe by tomorrow I'll see the joke and come back to laugh. Tim, did you ever fail at anything?'

'There are two cabinets full of articles and stories that didn't sell. Some of them I feel bad about. There was the chess story. You know, in *Through the Looking Glass* it wasn't a very good game, and you couldn't see the relation of the moves to the story very well.'

'I never could see it at all.'

'I thought it would be fun to take a championship game and write a fantasy about it, as if it were a war between two little old countries, with knights and foot soldiers, and fortified walls in charge of captains, and the bishops couldn't fight like warriors, and, of course, the queens were women – people don't kill them, not in hand-to-hand fighting and . . . well, you see? I wanted to make up the attacks and captures, and keep the people alive, a fairy-tale war you see, and make the strategy of the game and the strategy of the war coincide, and have everything fit. It took me ever so long to work it out and write it. To understand the game as a chess game and then to translate it into human actions and motives, and put speeches to it to fit different kinds of people. I'll show it to you. I loved it. But nobody would print it. Chess players don't like fantasy, and nobody else likes chess. You have to have a very special kind of mind to like both. But it was a disappointment. I hoped it would be published, because the few people who like that sort of thing would like it *very* much.'

'I'm sure I'll like it.'

'Well, if you do like that sort of thing, it's what you've been waiting all your life in vain for. Nobody else has done it.' Tim stopped, and blushed as red as a beet. 'I see what Grandmother means. Once you get started bragging, there's no end to it. I'm sorry, Peter.'

'Give me the story. I don't mind, Tim – brag all you like to me; I understand. You might blow up if you never expressed any of your legitimate pride and pleasure in such achievements. What I don't understand is how you have kept it all under for so long.'

'I had to,' said Tim.

The story was all its young author had claimed. Welles chuckled as he read it that evening. He read it again, and checked all the moves and the strategy of them. It was really a fine piece of work. Then he thought of the symphony, and this time he was able to laugh. He sat up until after midnight, thinking about the boy. Then he took a sleeping pill and went to bed.

The next day he went to see Tim's grandmother. Mrs Davis received him graciously.

'Your grandson is a very interesting boy,' said Peter

Welles carefully. 'I'm asking a favour of you. I'm making a study of various boys and girls in this district, their abilities and backgrounds and environment and character traits and things like that. No names will ever be mentioned, of course, but a statistical report will be kept, for ten years or longer, and some case histories might later be published. Could Timothy be included?'

'Timothy is such a good, normal little boy, I fail to see what would be the purpose of including him in such a survey.'

'That is just the point. We are not interested in maladjusted persons in this study. We eliminate all psychotic boys and girls. We are interested in boys and girls who succeed in facing their youthful problems and making satisfactory adjustments to life. If we could study a selected group of such children, and follow their progress for the next ten years at least, and then publish a summary of the findings with no names used—'

'In that case, I see no objection,' said Mrs Davis.

'If you'd tell me, then, something about Timothy's parents – their history?'

Mrs Davis settled herself for a good long talk.

'Timothy's mother, my only daughter, Emily,' she began, 'was a lovely girl. So talented. She played the violin charmingly. Timothy is like her, in the face, but has his father's dark hair and eyes. Edwin had very fine eyes.'

'Edwin was Timothy's father?'

'Yes. The young people met while Emily was at college in the East. Edwin was studying atomics there.'

'Your daughter was studying music?'

'No; Emily was taking the regular liberal arts course. I can tell you little about Edwin's work, but after their marriage he returned to it and ... you understand, it is painful for me to recall this, but their deaths were such a blow to me. They were so young.'

Welles held his pencil ready to write.

'Timothy has never been told. After all, he must grow up in this world, and how dreadfully the world has changed in the past thirty years, Dr Welles! But you would not remember the day before 1945. You have heard, no doubt, of the terrible explosion in the atomic plant, when they were trying to make a new type of bomb? At the time, none of the workers seemed to be injured. They believed the protection was adequate. But two years later they were all dead or dying.'

Mrs Davis shook her head, sadly. Welles held his breath, bent his head, scribbled.

'Tim was born just fourteen months after the explosion, fourteen months to the day. Everyone still thought that no harm had been done. But the radiation had some effect which was very slow – I do not understand such things. Edwin died, and then Emily came home to us with the boy. In a few months she, too, was gone.

'Oh, but we do not sorrow as those who have no hope. It is hard to have lost her, Dr Welles, but Mr Davis and I have reached the time of life when we can look forward to seeing her again. Our hope is to live until Timothy is old enough to fend for himself. We are so anxious about him; but you see he is perfectly normal in every way.'

'Yes.'

'The specialists made all sorts of tests. But nothing is wrong with Timothy.'

The psychiatrist stayed a little longer, took a few more notes, and made his escape as soon as he could. Going straight to the school, he had a few words with Miss Page and then took Tim to his office, where he told him what he had learned.

'You mean – I'm a mutation?'

'A mutant. Yes, very likely you are. I don't know. But I had to tell you at once.'

'Must be a dominant, too,' said Tim, 'coming out this way in the first generation. You mean – there may be more? I'm not the only one?' he added in great excitement. 'Oh, Peter, even if I grow up past you I won't have to be lonely?'

There. He had said it.

'It could be, Tim. There's nothing else in your family that could account for you.'

'But I have never found anyone at all like me. I would have known. Another boy or girl my age – like me – I would have known.'

'You came west with your mother. Where did the others go, if they existed? The parents must have scattered everywhere, back to their homes all over the country, all over the world. We can trace them, though. And, Tim, haven't you thought it's just a little bit strange that with all your pen names and various contacts, people don't insist more on meeting you? Everything gets done by mail? It's almost as if the editors are used to people who hide. It's almost as if people are used to architects and astronomers and composers whom nobody ever sees, who are only names in care of other names at post office boxes. There's a chance – just a chance, mind you – that there are others. If there are, we'll find them.'

'I'll work out a code they will understand,' said Tim, his face screwed up in concentration. 'In articles – I'll do it – several magazines and in letters I can enclose copies – some of my pen friends may be the ones—'

'I'll hunt up the records – they must be on file somewhere – psychologists and psychiatrists know all kinds of tricks – we can make some excuse to trace them all – the birth records—'

Both of them were talking at once, but all the while Peter Welles was thinking sadly, perhaps he had lost Tim now. If they did find those others, those to whom Tim rightfully belonged, where would poor Peter be? Outside, among the puppies—

Timothy Paul looked up and saw Peter Welles' eyes on him. He smiled.

'You were my first friend, Peter, and you shall be forever,' said Tim. 'No matter what, no matter who.'

'But we must look for the others,' said Peter.

'I'll never forget who helped me,' said Tim.

An ordinary boy of thirteen may say such a thing sincerely, and a week later have forgotten all about it. But Peter Welles was content. Tim would never forget. Tim would be his friend always. Even when Timothy Paul and those like him should unite in a maturity undreamed of, to control the world if they chose, Peter Welles would be Tim's friend – not a puppy, but a beloved friend – as a loyal dog loved by a good master is never cast out.

NOT FINAL!

Isaac Asimov

To people who dream of journeys to other planets, Jupiter has been an object of mystery and fascination because the depth of its gravity field and the tremendous pressure of its atmosphere make a landing on its surface (if any) seem almost impossible. Such difficulties make good science fiction stories. John Jacob Astor, in his Journey in Other Worlds *(1894), simply ignored this problem – he had his space travellers land on Jupiter, get out dressed in ordinary clothing, and shoot duck and quail – but more recent writers have faced the problem and suggested answers. (See 'Bridge', by James Blish, 'Desertion', by Clifford D. Simak, and 'Call Me Joe', by Poul Anderson.) Here Isaac Asimov proposes a solution which is unwanted – because this time it's the Jovians who want to leave their planet ... and exterminate us.*

NICHOLAS ORLOFF inserted a monocle in his left eye with all the incorruptible Briticism of a Russian educated at Oxford, and said reproachfully, 'But, my dear Mr Secretary! Half a billion dollars!'

Leo Birnam shrugged his shoulders wearily and allowed his lank body to cramp up still farther in the chair. 'The appropriation must go through, Commissioner. The Dominion government here at Ganymede is becoming desperate. So far I've been holding them off, but as secretary of scientific affairs, my powers are small.'

'I know, but—' and Orloff spread his hands helplessly.

'I suppose so,' agreed Birnam. 'The Empire government finds it easier to look the other way. They've done it consistently up to now. I've tried for a year now to have them understand the nature of the danger that hangs over the entire System, but it seems that it can't be done. But I'm appealing to you, Mr Commissioner. You're new in your post and can approach this Jovian affair with an unjaundiced eye.'

Orloff coughed and eyed the tips of his boots. In the three months since he had succeeded Gridley as colonial commissioner, he had tabled unread everything relating to 'those damned Jovian DTs'. That had been according to the established cabinet policy which had labelled the Jovian affair as 'deadwood' long before he had entered office.

But now that Ganymede was becoming nasty, he found himself sent out to Jovopolis with instructions to hold the 'blasted provincials' down. It was a nasty spot.

Birnam was speaking. 'The Dominion government has reached the point where it needs the money so badly, in fact, that if they don't get it, they're going to publicize everything.'

Orloff's phlegm broke completely, and he snatched at the monocle as it dropped. 'My dear fellow!'

'I know what it would mean. I've advised against it, but they're justified. Once the inside of the Jovian affair is out, once the people know about it, the Empire government won't stay in power a week. And when the Technocrats come in, they'll give us whatever we ask. Public opinion will see to that.'

'But you'll also create a panic and hysteria—'

'Surely! That is why we hesitate. But you might call this an ultimatum. We want secrecy, we *need* secrecy; but we need money more.'

'I see.' Orloff was thinking rapidly, and the conclusions he came to were not pleasant. 'In that case, it would be advisable to investigate the case further. If you have the papers concerning the communications with the planet Jupiter—'

'I have them,' replied Birnam dryly, 'and so has the Empire government at Washington. That won't do, Commissioner. It's the same cud that's been chewed by Earth officials for the last year, and it's got us nowhere. I want you to come to Ether Station with me.'

The Ganymedan had risen from his chair, and he glowered down upon Orloff from his six and a half feet of height.

Orloff flushed. 'Are you ordering me?'

'In a way, yes. I tell you there is no time. If you intend acting, you must act quickly or not at all.' Birnam paused, then added, 'You don't mind walking, I hope. Power vehicles aren't allowed to approach Ether Station ordinarily, and I can use the walk to explain a few of the facts. It's only two miles off.'

'I'll walk,' was the brusque reply.

The trip upward to subground level was made in silence, which was broken by Orloff when they stepped into the dimly lit anteroom.

'It's chilly here.'

'I know. It's difficult to keep the temperature up to norm this near the surface. But it will be colder outside. Here!'

Birnam had kicked open a closet door and was indicating the garments suspended from the ceiling. 'Put them on. You'll need them.'

Orloff fingered them doubtfully. 'Are they heavy enough?'

Birnam was pouring into his own costume as he spoke. 'They're electrically heated. You'll find them plenty warm. That's it! Tuck the trouser legs inside the boots and lace them tight.'

He turned then and, with a grunt, brought out a double compressed-gas cylinder from its rack in one corner of the closet. He glanced at the dial reading and then turned the stopcock. There was a thin wheeze of escaping gas, at which Birnam sniffed with satisfaction.

'Do you know how to work one of these?' he asked, as he screwed onto the jet a flexible tube of metal mesh, at the other end of which was a curiously curved object of thick, clear glass.

'What is it?'

'Oxygen nosepiece! What there is of Ganymede's atmosphere is argon and nitrogen, just about half and half. It

177

isn't particularly breathable.' He heaved the double cylinder into position and tightened it in its harness on Orloff's back.

Orloff staggered. 'It's heavy. I can't walk two miles with this.'

'It won't be heavy out there.' Birnam nodded carelessly upward and lowered the glass nosepiece over Orloff's head. 'Just remember to breathe in through the nose and out through the mouth, and you won't have any trouble. By the way, did you eat recently?'

'I lunched before I came to your place.'

Birnam sniffed dubiously. 'Well, that's a little awkward.' He drew a small metal container from one of his pockets and tossed it to the commissioner. 'Put one of those pills in your mouth and keep sucking on it.'

Orloff worked clumsily with gloved fingers and finally managed to get a brown spheroid out of the tin and into his mouth. He followed Birnam up a gently sloped ramp. The blind-alley ending of the corridor slid aside smoothly when they reached it, and there was a faint soughing as air slipped out into the thinner atmosphere of Ganymede.

Birnam caught the other's elbow and fairly dragged him out.

'I've turned your air tank on full,' he shouted. 'Breathe deeply and keep sucking at that pill.'

Gravity had flicked to Ganymedan normality as they crossed the threshold, and Orloff, after one horrible moment of apparent levitation, felt his stomach turn a somersault and explode.

He gagged, and fumbled the pill with his tongue in a desperate attempt at self-control. The oxygen-rich mixture from the air cylinders burned his throat, and gradually Ganymede steadied. His stomach shuddered back into place. He tried walking.

'Take it easy, now,' came Birnam's soothing voice. 'It gets you that way the first few times you change gravity fields quickly. Walk slowly and get the rhythm, or you'll take a tumble. That's right, you're getting it.'

The ground seemed resilient. Orloff could feel the pressure of the other's arm holding him down at each step to keep him from springing too high. Steps were longer now, and flatter, as he got the rhythm. Birnam continued speaking, a voice a little muffled from behind the leather flap drawn loosely across mouth and chin.

'Each to his own world,' he grinned. 'I visited Earth a few years back, with my wife, and had a hell of a time. I couldn't get myself to learn to walk on a planet's surface without a nosepiece. I kept choking – I really did. The sunlight was too bright and the sky was too blue and the grass was too green. And the buildings were right out on the surface. I'll never forget the time they tried to get me to sleep in a room twenty storeys up in the air, with the window wide open and the moon shining in.

'I went back on the first spaceship going my way and don't ever intend returning. How are you feeling now?'

'Fine! Splendid!' Now that the first discomfort had gone, Orloff found the low gravity exhilarating. He looked about him. The broken, hilly ground, bathed in a drenching yellow light, was covered with ground-hugging, broad-leaved shrubs that showed the orderly arrangement of careful cultivation.

Birnam answered the unspoken question. 'There's enough carbon dioxide in the air to keep the plants alive, and they all have the power to fix atmospheric nitrogen. That's what makes agriculture Ganymede's greatest industry. Those plants are worth their weight in gold as fertilizers back on Earth and worth double or triple that as sources for half a hundred alkaloids that can't be got anywhere else in the System. And, of course, everyone knows that Ganymedan green-leaf has Terrestrial tobacco beat hollow.'

There was the drone of a strato-rocket overhead, shrill in the thin atmosphere, and Orloff looked up.

He stopped – stopped dead – and forgot to breathe!

It was his first glimpse of Jupiter in the sky.

It is one thing to see Jupiter, coldly harsh, against the ebon backdrop of space. At six hundred thousand miles, it is majestic enough. But on Ganymede, barely topping the hills, its outlines softened and ever so faintly hazed by the thin atmosphere, shining mellowly from a purple sky in which only a few fugitive stars dare compete with the Jovian giant – it can be described by no conceivable combination of words.

At first, Orloff absorbed the gibbous disc in silence. It was gigantic, thirty-two times the apparent diameter of the sun as seen from Earth. Its stripes stood out in faint washes of colour against the yellowness beneath, and the Great Red Spot was an oval splotch of orange near the western rim.

And finally Orloff murmured weakly, 'It's beautiful!'

Leo Birnam stared, too, but there was no awe in his eyes. There was the mechanical weariness of viewing a sight often seen, and besides that, an expression of sick revulsion. The chin flap hid his twitching smile, but his grasp upon Orloff's arm left bruises through the tough fabric of the surface suit.

He said slowly, 'It's the most horrible sight in the System.'

Orloff turned reluctant attention to his companion. 'Eh?' Then, disagreeably, 'Oh, yes, those mysterious Jovians.'

At that, the Ganymedan turned away angrily and broke into swinging, fifteen-foot strides. Orloff followed clumsily after, keeping his balance with difficulty.

'Here, now,' he gasped.

But Birnam wasn't listening. He was speaking coldly, bitterly. 'You on Earth can afford to ignore Jupiter. You know nothing of it. It's a little pinprick in your sky, a little flyspeck. You don't live here on Ganymede, watching that damned colossus gloating over you. Up and over fifteen hours – hiding God knows what on its surface. Hiding something that's waiting and waiting and *trying to get out*. Like a giant bomb just waiting to explode!'

'Nonsense!' Orloff managed to jerk out. '*Will* you slow down. I can't keep up.'

Birnam cut his strides in half and said tensely, 'Everyone knows that Jupiter is inhabited, but practically no one ever stops to realize what that means. I tell you that those Jovians, whatever they are, are born to the purple. *They are the natural rulers of the Solar System.*'

'Pure hysteria,' muttered Orloff. 'The Empire government has been hearing nothing else from your Dominion for a year.'

'And you've shrugged it off. Well, listen! Jupiter, discounting the thickness of its colossal atmosphere, is eighty thousand miles in diameter. That means it possesses a surface one hundred times that of Earth and more than fifty times that of the entire Terrestrial Empire. Its population, its resources, its war potential are in proportion.'

'Mere numbers—'

'I know what you mean,' Birnam drove on passionately. 'Wars are not fought with numbers but with science and with organization. The Jovians have both. In the quarter of a century during which we have communicated with them, we've learned a bit. They have atomic power and they have radio. And in a world of ammonia under great pressure – a world, in other words, in which almost none of the metals can exist *as* metals for any length of time because of the tendency to form soluble ammonia complexes – they have managed to build up a complicated civilization. That means they have had to work through plastics, glasses, silicates, and synethetic building materials of one sort or another. *That* means a chemistry developed just as far as ours is, and I'd put odds on its having developed further.'

Orloff waited long before answering. And then, 'But how certain are you people about the Jovians' last message? We on Earth are inclined to doubt that the Jovians can possibly be as unreasonably belligerent as they have been described.'

The Ganymedan laughed shortly. 'They broke off all communication after that last message, didn't they? That doesn't sound friendly on their part, does it? I assure you that we've all but stood on our ears trying to contact them.

'Here, now, don't talk. Let me explain something to you. For twenty-five years here on Ganymede a little group of men have worked their hearts out trying to make sense out of a static-ridden, gravity-distorted set of variable clicks in our radio apparatus, for those clicks were our only connexion with living intelligence upon Jupiter. It was a job for a world of scientists, but we never had more than two dozen at the station at any one time. I was one of them from the very beginning and, as a philologist, did my part in helping construct and interpret the code that developed between ourselves and the Jovians, so that you can see I am speaking from the real inside.

'It was a devil of a heartbreaking job. It was five years before we got past the elementary clicks of arithmetic: three and four are seven; the square root of twenty-five is five; factorial six is seven hundred and twenty. After that, months sometimes passed before we could work out and check by further communication a single new fragment of thought.

'*But* – and this is the point – by the time the Jovians broke off relations, we understood them *thoroughly*. There was no more chance of a mistake in comprehension than there was of Ganymede's suddenly cutting loose from Jupiter. And their last message was a threat and a promise of destruction. Oh, there's no doubt – there's no doubt!'

They were walking through a shallow pass in which the yellow Jupiter light gave way to a clammy darkness.

Orloff was disturbed. He had never had the case presented to him in this fashion before. He said, 'But the reason, man. What reason did we give them—'

'No reason! It was simply this: the Jovians had finally discovered from our messages – just where and how I don't know – that *we* were *not* Jovians.'

'Well, of course.'

'It wasn't "of course" to them. In their experiences they had never come across intelligences that were not Jovian. Why should they make an exception in favour of those from outer space?'

'You say they were scientists.' Orloff's voice had assumed a wary frigidity. 'Wouldn't they realize that alien environments would breed alien life? *We* knew it. We never thought the Jovians were Earth men, though we had never met intelligences other than those of Earth.'

They were back in the drenching wash of Jupiter light

again, and a spreading region of ice glimmered amberly in a depression to the right.

Birnam answered, 'I said they were chemists and physicists – but I never said they were astronomers. Jupiter, my dear Commissioner, has an atmosphere three thousand miles or more thick, and those miles of gas block off everything but the sun and the four largest of Jupiter's moons. The Jovians know nothing of alien environments.'

Orloff considered. 'And so they decided we were aliens. What next?'

'If we weren't Jovians, then, in their eyes, we weren't people. It turned out that a non-Jovian was "vermin" by definition.'

Orloff's automatic protest was cut off sharply by Birnam. 'In their eyes, I said, vermin we were; and vermin we are. Moreover, we were vermin with the peculiar audacity of having dared to attempt to treat with Jovians – with *human beings*. Their last message was this, word for word: "Jovians are the masters. There is no room for vermin. We will destroy you immediately." I doubt if there was any animosity in that message – simply a cold statement of fact. But they meant it.'

'But why?'

'Why did man exterminate the housefly?'

'Come sir. You're not seriously presenting an analogy of that nature.'

'Why not, since it is certain that the Jovian considers us a sort of housefly, an insufferable type of housefly that dares aspire to intelligence.'

Orloff made a last attempt. 'But truly, Mr Secretary, it seems impossible for intelligent life to adopt such an attitude.'

'Do you possess much of an acquaintance with any other type of intelligent life than our own?' came with immediate sarcasm. 'Do you feel competent to pass on Jovian psychology? Do you know just *how* alien Jovians must be physically? Just think of their world, with its gravity at two and one half Earth normal; with its ammonia oceans, oceans that you might throw all Earth into without raising

183

a respectable splash; with its three-thousand-mile atmosphere, dragged down by the colossal gravity into densities and pressures in its surface layers that make the sea bottoms of Earth resemble a medium-thick vacuum. I tell you, we've tried to figure out what sort of life could exist under those conditions and we've given up. It's thoroughly incomprehensible. Do you expect their mentality, then, to be any more understandable? Never! Accept it as it is. They intend destroying us. That's all we know and all we need to know.'

He lifted a gloved hand as he finished, and one finger pointed. 'There's Ether Station just ahead.'

Orloff's head swivelled. 'Underground?'

'Certainly! All except the observatory. That's that steel and quartz dome to the right – the small one.'

They had stopped before two large boulders that flanked an earthy embankment, and from behind either one a nose-pieced, suited soldier in Ganymedan orange, with blasters ready, advanced upon the two.

Birnam lifted his face into Jupiter's light, and the soldiers saluted and stepped aside. A short word was barked into the wrist mike of one of them, and the camouflaged opening between the boulders fell into two and Orloff followed the secretary into the yawning air lock.

The Earth man caught one last glimpse of sprawling Jupiter before the closing door cut off the surface altogether.

It was no longer quite so beautiful.

Orloff did not feel quite normal again until he had seated himself in the overstuffed chair in Dr Edward Prosser's private office. With a sigh of utter relaxation he propped his monocle under his eyebrow.

'Would Dr Prosser mind if I smoked in here while we're waiting?' he asked.

'Go ahead,' replied Birnam carelessly. 'My own idea would be to drag Prosser away from whatever he's fooling with just now, but he's a queer chap. We'll get more out of him if we wait until he's ready for us.' He withdrew a gnarled stick of greenish tobacco from its case and bit off the edge viciously.

Orloff smiled through the smoke of his own cigarette. 'I don't mind waiting. I still have something to say. You see, for the moment, Mr Secretary, you gave me the jitters, but, after all, granted that the Jovians intend mischief once they get at us, it remains a fact,' and here he spaced his words emphatically, 'that they can't get at us.'

'A bomb without a fuse, hey?'

'Exactly! It's simplicity itself, and not really worth discussing. You will admit, I suppose, that under no circumstances can the Jovians get away from Jupiter.'

'Under *no* circumstances?' There was a quizzical tinge to Birnam's slow reply. 'Shall we analyse that?'

He stared hard at the purple flame of his cigar. 'It's an old trite saying that the Jovians can't leave Jupiter. The fact has been highly publicized by the sensation mongers of Earth and Ganymede, and a great deal of sentiment has been drivelled about the unfortunate intelligences who are irrevocably surface-bound and must forever stare into the universe without, watching, watching, wondering, and never attaining.

'But, after all, what holds the Jovians to their planet? Two factors! That's all! The first is the immense gravity field of the planet. Two and a half Earth normal.'

Orloff nodded. 'Pretty bad!' he agreed.

'And Jupiter's gravitational potential is even worse, for, because of its greater diameter, the intensity of its gravitational field decreases with distance only one-tenth as rapidly as Earth's field does. It's a terrible problem – *but it's been solved.*'

'Hey?' Orloff straightened.

'They've got atomic power. Gravity – even Jupiter's – means nothing once you've put unstable atomic nuclei to work for you.'

Orloff crushed his cigarette to extinction with a nervous gesture. 'But their atmosphere—'

'Yes, that's what's stopping them. They're living at the bottom of a three-thousand-mile-deep ocean of it, where the hydrogen of which it is composed is collapsed by sheer pressure to something approaching the density of *solid* hydrogen. It stays a gas because the temperature of Jupiter is above the critical point of hydrogen, but you just try to figure out the pressure that can make hydrogen *gas* half as heavy as water. You'll be surprised at the number of zeros you'll have to put down.

'No spaceship of metal or of any kind of matter can stand that pressure. No Terrestrial spaceship can land on Jupiter without smashing like an eggshell, and no Jovian spaceship can leave Jupiter without exploding like a soap bubble. That problem has not yet been solved, but it will be some day. Maybe tomorrow, maybe not for a hundred years, or a thousand. We don't know, but when it is solved, the Jovians will be on top of us. And it can be solved in a specific way.'

'I don't see how—'

'Force fields! We've got them now, you know.'

'Force fields!' Orloff seemed genuinely astonished, and he chewed the word over and over to himself for a few moments. 'They're used as meteor shields for ships in the asteroid zone – but I don't see the application to the Jovian problem.'

'The ordinary force field,' explained Birnam, 'is a feeble, rarefied zone of energy extending over a hundred miles or more outside the ship. It'll stop meteors, but it's just so much empty ether to an object like a gas molecule. *But* what if you took that same zone of energy and compressed it to a thickness of a tenth of an inch. Molecules would bounce off it like this – *ping-g-g-g!* And if you used stronger generators, and compressed the field to a hundredth of an inch, molecules would bounce off even when driven by the unthinkable pressure of Jupiter's atmosphere. And then if you build a ship inside—' He left the sentence dangling.

Orloff was pale. 'You're not saying it can be done?'

'I'll bet you anything you like that the Jovians are *trying* to do it. And *we're* trying to do it right here at Ether Station.'

The colonial commissioner jerked his chair closer to

Birnam and grabbed the Ganymedan's wrist. 'Why can't we bombard Jupiter with atomic bombs? Give it a thorough going over, I mean! With her gravity and her surface area, we can't miss.'

Birnam smiled faintly. 'We've thought of that. But atomic bombs would merely tear holes in the atmosphere. And even if you could penetrate, just divide the surface of Jupiter by the area of damage of a single bomb and find how many years we must bombard Jupiter at the rate of a bomb a minute before we begin to do significant damage. Jupiter's *big*! Don't ever forget that!'

His cigar had gone out, but he did not pause to relight. He continued in a low, tense voice. 'No, we can't attack the Jovians as long as they're on Jupiter. We must wait for them to come out. And once they do, they're going to have the edge on us in numbers. A terrific, heartbreaking edge. So we'll just have to have the edge on them in science.'

'But,' Orloff broke in, and there was a note of fascinated horror in his voice, 'how can we tell in advance what they'll have?'

'We can't. We've got to scrape up everything we can lay our hands on and hope for the best. But there's one thing we *do* know they'll have, and that's force fields. They can't get out without them. And if they have them, we must, too, and that's the problem we're trying to solve here. They will not insure us victory, but without them we will suffer certain defeat. And now you know why we need money – and more than that. We want Earth itself to get to work. It's got to start a drive for scientific armaments and subordinate everything to that. You see?'

Orloff was on his feet. 'Birnam, I'm with you – a hundred per cent with you. You can count on me back in Washington.'

There was no mistaking his sincerity. Birnam gripped the hand outstretched towards him and wrung it – and at that moment the door flew open and a little pixie of a man hurtled in.

The newcomer spoke in rapid jerks, and exclusively to Birnam. 'Where'd you come from? Been trying to get in touch with you. Secretary said you weren't in. Then five minutes later you show up on your own. Can't understand it.' He busied himself furiously at his desk.

Birnam grinned. 'If you'll take time out, Doc, you might say hello to Colonial Commissioner Orloff.'

Dr Edward Prosser turned on his toe like a ballet dancer and looked the Earth man up and down twice. 'The new un, hey? We getting any money? We ought to. Been working on a shoestring ever since. At that we might not be needing any. It depends.' He was back at the desk.

Orloff seemed a trifle disconcerted, but Birnam winked impressively, and he contented himself with a glassy stare through the monocle.

Prosser pounced upon a black leather booklet in the recesses of a pigeonhole, threw himself into his swivel chair, and wheeled about.

'Glad you came, Birnam,' he said, leafing through the booklet. 'Got something to show you. Commissioner Orloff, too.'

'What were you keeping us waiting for?' demanded Birnam. 'Where were you?'

'Busy! Busy as a pig! No sleep for three nights.' He looked up and his small puckered face fairly flushed with delight. 'Everything fell into place of a sudden. Like a jigsaw puzzle. Never saw anything like it. Kept us hopping, I tell you.'

'You've got the dense force fields you're after?' asked Orloff in sudden excitement.

Prosser seemed annoyed. 'No, not that. Something else. Come on.' He glared at his watch and jumped out of his seat. 'We've got half an hour. Let's go.'

An electric-motored flivver waited outside, and Prosser spoke excitedly as he sped the purring vehicle down the ramps into the depths of the Station.

'Theory!' he said. 'Theory! Damned important, that. You set a technician on a problem. He'll fool around. Waste lifetimes. Get nowhere. Just putter about at random. A true scientist works with theory. Lets maths solve his problems.' He overflowed with self-satisfaction.

The flivver stopped on a dime before a huge double door, and Prosser tumbled out, followed by the other two at a more leisurely pace.

'Through here! Through here!' he said. He shoved the door open and led them down the corridor and up a narrow flight of stairs onto a wall-hugging passageway that circled a huge three-level room. Orloff recognized the gleaming quartz-and-steel, pipe-sprouting ellipsoid two levels below as an atomic generator.

He adjusted his monocle and watched the scurrying activity below. An earphoned man on a high stool before a control board studded with dials looked up and waved. Prosser waved back and grinned.

Orloff said, 'You create your force fields here?'

'That's right! Ever see one?'

'No.' The commissioner smiled ruefully. 'I don't even know what one *is*, except that it can be used as a meteor shield.'

Prosser said, 'It's very simple. Elementary matter. All matter is composed of atoms. Atoms are held together by interatomic forces. Take away atoms. Leave interatomic forces behind. *That's* a force field.'

Orloff looked blank, and Birnam chuckled deep in his throat and scratched the back of his ear.

'That explanation reminds me of our Ganymedan method of suspending an egg a mile high in the air. It goes like this. You find a mountain just a mile high and put the egg on top. Then, keeping the egg where it is, you take the mountain away. That's all.'

The colonial commissioner threw his head back to laugh, and the irascible Dr Prosser puckered his lips into a pursed symbol of disapproval.

'Come, come. No joke, you know. Force fields most important. Got to be ready for the Jovians when they come.'

A sudden rasping burr from below sent Prosser back from the railing.

'Get behind screen here,' he babbled. 'The twenty-milli-metre field is going up. Bad radiation.'

The burr muted almost into silence, and the three walked

189

out onto the passageway again. There was no apparent change, but Prosser shoved his hand out over the railing and said, 'Feel!'

Orloff extended a cautious finger, gasped, and slapped out with the palm of his hand. It was like pushing against very soft sponge rubber or super-resilient steel springs.

Birnam tried, too. 'That's better than anything we've done yet, isn't it?' He explained to Orloff, 'A twenty-millimetre screen is one that can hold an atmosphere of a pressure of twenty millimetres of mercury against a vacuum without appreciable leakage.'

The commissioner nodded. 'I see! You'd need a seven-hundred-sixty-millimetre screen to hold Earth's atmosphere, then.'

'Yes! That would be a unit atmosphere screen. Well, Prosser, is this what got you excited?'

'This twenty-millimetre screen. Of course not. I can go up to two hundred fifty millimetres, using the activated vanadium pentasulphide in the praseodymium breakdown. But it's not necessary. Technician would do it and blow up the place. Scientist checks on theory and goes slow.' He winked. 'We're hardening the field now. Watch!'

'Shall we get behind the screen?'

'Not necessary now. Radiation bad only at beginning.'

The burring waxed again, but not as loudly as before. Prosser shouted to the man at the control board, and a spreading wave of the hand was the only reply.

Then the control man waved a clenched fist and Prosser cried, 'We've passed fifty millimetres! Feel the field!'

Orloff extended his hand and poked it curiously. The sponge rubber had hardened! He tried to pinch it between finger and thumb, so perfect was the illusion, but here the 'rubber' faded to unresisting air.

Prosser *tch-tched* impatiently. 'No resistance at right angles to force. Elementary mechanics that is.'

The control man was gesturing again. 'Past seventy,' explained Prosser. 'We're slowing down now. Critical point is eighty-three point forty-two.'

He hung over the railing and kicked out with his feet at the other two. 'Stay away! Dangerous!'

And then he yelled, 'Careful! The generator's bucking!'

The burr had risen to a hoarse maximum and the control man worked frantically at his switches. From within the quartz heart of the central atomic generator the sullen red glow of the bursting atoms had brightened dangerously.

There was a break in the burr, a reverberant roar, and a blast of air that threw Orloff hard against the wall.

Prosser dashed up. There was a cut over his eye. 'Hurt? No? Good, good! I was expecting something of the sort. Should have warned you. Let's go down. Where's Birnam?'

The tall Ganymedan picked himself up off the floor and brushed at his clothes. 'Here I am. What blew up?'

'Nothing blew up. Something buckled. Come on, down we go.' He dabbed at his forehead with a handkerchief and led the way downward.

The control man removed his earphones as Prosser approached, and got off his stool. He looked tired, and his dirt-smeared face was greasy with perspiration.

'The damn thing started going at eighty-two point eight, boss. It almost caught me.'

'It did, did it?' growled Prosser. 'Within limits of error, isn't it? How's the generator? Hey, Stoddard!'

The technician addressed replied from his station at the generator, 'Tube Five died. It'll take two days to replace.'

Prosser turned in satisfaction and said, 'It worked. Went exactly as presumed. Problem solved, gentlemen. Trouble over. Let's get back to my office. I want to eat. And then I want to sleep.'

He did not refer to the subject again until once more behind the desk in his office, and then he spoke between huge bites of a liver and onion sandwich.

He addressed Birnam. 'Remember the work on space strain last June? It flopped, but we kept at it. Finch got a lead last week and I developed it. Everything fell into place. Slick as goose grease. Never saw anything like it.'

'Go ahead,' said Birnam calmly. He knew Prosser sufficiently well to avoid showing impatience.

'You saw what happened. When a field tops eighty-three point forty-two millimetres, it becomes unstable. Space won't stand the strain. It buckles and the field blows. *Boom!*'

Birnam's mouth dropped open, and the arms of Orloff's chair creaked under sudden pressure. Silence for a while, and then Birnam said unsteadily, 'You mean force fields stronger than that are impossible.'

'They're possible. You can create them. But the denser they are, the more unstable they are. If I had turned on the two-hundred-and-fifty millimetre field, it would have lasted one tenth of a second. Then, blooie! Would have blown up the Station! *And* myself! Technician would have done it. Scientist is warned by theory. Works carefully, the way I did. No harm done.'

Orloff tucked his monocle into his vest pocket and said tremulously, 'But if a force field is the same thing as interatomic forces, why is it that steel has such a strong interatomic binding force without buckling space? There's a flaw there.'

Prosser eyed him in annoyance. 'No flaw. Critical strength depends on numbers of generators. In steel, each atom is a force-field generator. That means about three hundred billion trillion generators for every ounce of matter. If we could use that many— As it is, one hundred generators would be the practical limit. That only raises the critical point to ninety-seven or thereabouts.'

He got to his feet and continued with sudden fervour, 'No. Problem's over, I tell you. Absolutely impossible to create a force field capable of holding Earth's atmosphere for more than a hundredth of a second. Jovian atmosphere entirely out of question. Cold figures say that; backed by experiment. *Space won't stand it!*

'Let the Jovians do their damnedest. They can't get out! That's final! That's final! *That's final!*'

Orloff said, 'Mr Secretary, can I send a spacegram anywhere in the Station? I want to tell Earth that I'm return-

ing by the next ship and that the Jovian problem is liqui-
dated – entirely and for good.'

Birnam said nothing, but the relief on his face as he
shook hands with the colonial commissioner transfigured its
gaunt homeliness unbelievably.

And Dr Prosser repeated, with a birdlike jerk of his head,
'That's *final!*'

Hal Tuttle looked up as Captain Everett, of the spaceship
Transparent, newest ship of the Comet Space Lines, entered
his private observation room in the nose of the ship.

The captain said, 'A spacegram has just reached me from
the home offices at Tucson. We're to pick up Colonial
Commissioner Orloff at Jovopolis, Ganymede, and take him
back to Earth.'

'Good. We haven't sighted any ships?'

'No, no! We're way off the regular space lanes. The first
the System will know of us will be the landing of the *Transparent* on Ganymede. It will be the greatest thing in space
travel since the first trip to the Moon.' His voice softened
suddenly. 'What's wrong, Hal? This is *your* triumph, after
all.'

Hal Tuttle looked up and out into the blackness of space.
'I suppose it is. Ten years of work, Sam. I lost an arm and
an eye in that first explosion, but I don't regret them. It's
the reaction that's got me. The problem is solved; my lifework is finished.'

'So is every steel-hulled ship in the System.'

Tuttle smiled. 'Yes. It's hard to realize, isn't it?' He
gestured outward. 'You see the stars? Part of the time
there's nothing between them and us. It gives us a queasy
feeling.' His voice brooded, 'Nine years I worked for nothing. I wasn't a theoretician, and never really knew where I
was headed – just tried everything. I tried a little too hard,
and space wouldn't stand it. I paid an arm and an eye and
started fresh.'

Captain Everett balled his fist and pounded the hull – the
hull through which the stars shone unobstructed. There
was the muffled thud of flesh striking an unyielding sur-

face, but no response whatever from the invisible wall.

Tuttle nodded. 'It's solid enough, now, though it flicks on and off eight hundred thousand times a second. I got the idea from the stroboscopic lamp. You know them – they flash on and off so rapidly that it gives the impression of steady illumination.

'And so it is with the hull. It's not on long enough to buckle space. It's not off long enough to allow appreciable leakage of the atmosphere. And the net effect is a strength better than steel.'

He paused and added slowly, 'And there's no telling how far we can go. Speed up the intermission effect. Have the field flick off and on millions of times per second – billions of times. You can get fields strong enough to hold an atomic explosion. My lifework!'

Captain Everett pounded the other's shoulder. 'Snap out of it, man. Think of the landing on Ganymede. The devil! It will be great publicity. Think of Orloff's face, for instance, when he finds he is to be the first passenger in history ever to travel in a spaceship with a force-field hull. How do you suppose he'll feel?'

Hal Tuttle shrugged. 'I imagine he'll be rather pleased.'

AND BE MERRY...

Katherine Maclean

Like Wilmar Shiras' 'In Hiding', this is a story about an improvement in human beings, and about fear. First published in 1950, it marks a new concern in science fiction for the human values of new discoveries: It asks not only 'How can we solve this problem?' but 'Will we wish we hadn't?'

It was afternoon. The walls of the room glared back the white sunlight, their smooth plaster coating concealing the rickety bones of the building. Through the barred window drifted miasmic vapours, laden with microscopic living things that could turn food to poison while one ate, bacteria that could find root in lungs or skin and multiply, swarming through the blood.

And yet it seemed to be a nice day. A smoky hint of burning leaves blurred the other odours into a pleasant autumn tang, and sunlight streaming in the windows reflected brightly from the white walls. The surface of things was harmless enough. The knack of staying calm was to think only of the surface, never of the meaning, to try to ignore what could not be helped. After all, one cannot refuse to eat, one cannot refuse to breathe. There was nothing to be done.

One of her feet had gone to sleep. She shifted her elbow to the other knee and leaned her chin in her hand again, feeling the blood prickling back into her toes. It was not good to sit on the edge of the bed too long without moving. It was not good to think too long. Thinking opened the gates to fear. She looked at her fingernails. They were pale, cyanotic. She had been breathing reluctantly, almost holding her breath. Fear is impractical. One cannot refuse to breathe.

And yet, to solve the problems of safety it was necessary to think, it was necessary to look at the danger clearly, to weigh it, to sum it up and consider it as a whole. But each time she tried to face it her imagination would flinch away. Always her thinking trailed off in a blind impulse to turn to Alec for rescue.

When someone tapped her shoulder she made sure that her face was calm and blank before raising it from her hands. A man in a white coat stood before her, proffering a pill and a cup of water. He spoke tonelessly.

'Swallow.'

There was no use fighting back. There was no use provoking them to force. Putting aside the frantic futile images of escape, she took the pill, her hands almost steady.

She scarcely felt the prick of the needle.

It was afternoon.

Alexander Berent stood in the middle of the laboratory kitchen, looking around vaguely. He had no hope of seeing her.

His wife was missing.

She was not singing in the living-room or cooking at the stove or washing dishes at the sink. Helen was not in the apartment.

She was not visiting any of her friends' houses. The hospitals had no one of her description in their accident wards. The police had not found her body on any slab of the city morgue.

Helen Berent was missing.

In the corner cages the guinea pigs whistled and chirred for food, and the rabbits snuffled and tried to shove their pink noses through the grille. They looked gaunt. He fed them and refilled their water bottles automatically.

There was something different about the laboratory. It was not the way he had left it. Naturally after five months of the stupendous deserts and mountains of Tibet any room

196

seemed small and cramped and artificial, but there were other changes. The cot had been dragged away from the wall, toward the icebox. Beside the cot was a wastebasket and a small table that used to be in the living room. On top of the table were the telephone and the dictation recorder surrounded by hypodermics, small bottles cryptically labelled with a red pencil scrawl, and an alcohol jar with its swab of cotton still in it. Alec touched the cotton. It was dusty to his fingers, and completely dry.

The dictation recorder and the telephone had been oddly linked into one circuit with a timer clock, but the connexions were open, and when he picked up the receiver the telephone buzzed as it should.

Alec replaced the receiver and sombrely considered the number of things that could be reached by a woman lying down. She could easily spend days there. Even the lower drawers of the filing cabinet were within reach.

He found what he was looking for in the lowest drawer of the filing cabinet, filed under A – a special folder marked 'ALEC'. In it were a letter and two voice records dated and filed in order.

The letter was dated the day he had left, four months ago. He held it in his hand a minute before beginning to read.

Dear Alec,

You never guessed how silly I felt with my foot in that idiotic bandage. You were so considerate I didn't know whether to laugh or to cry. After you got on board I heard the plane officials paging a tardy passenger. I knew his place was empty, and it took all my willpower to keep from running up the walk into the plane. If I had yielded to the temptation, I would be on the plane with you now, sitting in that vacant seat, looking down at the cool blue Atlantic, and in a month hiking across those windy horizons to the diggings.

But I can't give up all my lovely plans, so I sublimated the impulse to confess by promising myself to write this letter, and then made myself watch the plane take off with the proper attitude of sad resignation, like a dutiful wife with a hurt foot.

This is the confession. The bandage was a fake. My foot is all right. I just pretended to be too lame to hike to have an excuse to stay home this summer. Nothing else would have made you leave without me.

New York seems twice as hot and sticky now that the plane has taken you away. Honestly, I love you and my vacations too much to abandon the expedition to the unsanitary horrors of native cooking for just laziness. Remember, Alec, once when I was swearing at the gnats along the Whangpoo, you quoth, 'I could not love you so, my dear, loved I not science more.' I put salt in your coffee for that, but you were right. I am the wife of an archaeologist. Whither thou goest I must go, your worries are my worries, your job, my job.

What you forget is that besides being your wife, I am an endocrinologist, and an expert. If you can cheerfully expose me to cliffs, swamps, man-eating tigers and malarial mosquitoes, all in the name of Archaeology, I have an even better right to stick hypodermics in myself in the name of Endocrinology.

You know my experiments in cell metabolism. Well naturally the next step in the investigation is to try something on myself to see how it works. But for ten years, ever since you caught me with that hypodermic and threw such a fit, I have given up the personal guinea pig habit so as to save you worry. Mosquitoes can beat hypos any day, but there is no use trying to argue with a husband.

So I pretended to have broken one of the small phalanges of my foot instead. Much simpler.

I am writing this letter in the upstairs lobby of the Paramount, whither I escaped from the heat. I will write other letters every so often to help you keep up with the experiment, but right now I am going in to see this movie and have a fine time weeping over Joan Crawford's phoney troubles, then home and to work.

G'by darling. Remember your airsick tablets, and don't fall out.

Yours always,

Helen

PS Don't eat anything the cook doesn't eat first. And have a good time.

After the letter there were just two voice records in envelopes. The oldest was dated July 24th. Alec put it on the turntable and switched on the playback arm. For a moment the machine made no sound but the faint scratching of the needle, and then Helen spoke, sounding close to the microphone, her voice warm and lazy.

'Hello, Alec. The day after writing that first letter, while I was looking for a stamp, I suddenly decided not to mail it. There is no use worrying you with my experiment until it is finished. I resolved to write daily letters and save them for you to read all together when you get home.

'Of course, after making that good resolution I didn't write anything for a month but the bare clinical record of symptoms, injections, and reactions.

'I concede you that any report has to include the human detail to be readable, but honestly, the minute I stray off the straight and narrow track of formulas, my reports get so chatty they read like a gossip column. It's hopeless.

'When you get back you can write in the explanatory material yourself, from what I tell you on this disk. You write better anyhow. Here goes:

'It's hard to organize my words. I'm not used to talking at a faceless dictaphone. A typewriter is more my style, but I can't type lying down, and every time I try writing with a pen, I guess I get excited and clutch too hard, and my finger bones start bending, and I have to stop and straighten them out. Bending one's finger bones is no fun. The rubbery feel of them bothers me, and if I get scared enough, the adrenaline will upset my whole endocrine balance and set me back a week's work.

'Let's see: Introduction. Official purpose of experiment –

to investigate the condition of old age. Ageing is a progressive failure of anabolism. Old age is a disease. No one has ever liked growing old, so when you write this into beautiful prose you can call it The Age-Old Old-Age Problem.

'Nowadays there is no evolutionary reason why we should be built to get old. Since we are learning animals, longevity is a survival factor. It should be an easy conquest, considering that each cell is equipped to duplicate itself and leave a couple of young successor cells to carry on the good work. The trouble is, some of them just *don't*. Some tissues brace themselves to hang on fifty years, and you have to get along with the same deteriorating cells until death do you part.

'From nature's point of view that is reasonable. The human race evolved in an environment consisting mainly of plagues, famines, blizzards, and sabre-toothed tigers. Any man's chances of staying unkilled for fifty years were pretty thin. Longevity was not worth much those days. What good is longevity to a corpse?

'We have eliminated plagues, famines, and sabre-toothed tigers, but old age is still with us. One was meant to go with the other, but evolution hasn't had time to adjust to the change.

'That Russian scientist started me on this idea. He gave oldsters a little of their lost elasticity by injections of an antibody that attacked and dissolved some of their old connective tissue and forced a partial replacement.

'I just want to go him one better, and see if I can coax a replacement for every creaking cell in the body.

'You can see how it would be a drastic process – halfway between being born again and being run through a washing machine. There is nobody I dare try it on except myself, for I'll have to feel my way, working out each step from the reactions to the last step, like making up a new recipe by adding and tasting.

'Item: The best way to test your theories is to try them on yourself. Emergency is the mother of exertion.

'Thirty-eight is just old enough to make a good guinea pig. I am not so old and fragile that I would break down under the first strain, but I am not so young that a little added youth won't show.

'One question is – just how many tissues of any kind dare I destroy at once. The more I clear away at once, the more complete the replacement, but it is rather like replacing parts in a running motor. You wonder just how many bolts you can take out before the flywheel comes off its shaft and flies away. Speed should help. A quick regrowth can replace dissolved tissue before the gap is felt. The human machine is tough and elastic. It can run along on its own momentum when it should be stopped.

'This winter I bred a special strain of mould from some hints I had found in the wartime research reports on the penicillia. The mould makes an art of carrying on most of the processes of life outside of itself. Digestion and even most of the resynthesis of assimilation is finished before the food touches the plant. It's roots secrete enzymes that attack protein, dismantle it neatly down to small soluble molecules, and leave them linked to catalytic hooks, ready to be reassembled like the parts of a prefabricated house.

'The food below the mould becomes a pool. The mould plants draw the liquid up through their roots, give it the last touch that converts it to protoplasm, provide it with nucleus, and throw it up in a high waving fur of sporangia.

'But that liquid is magic. It could become the protoplasm of any creature with the same ease and speed. It could be put into the bloodstream and be as harmless as the normal rough aminos, and yet provide for an almost instantaneous regrowth of missing flesh, a regrowth complete enough, I hope, to allow the drastic destruction and replacement I need.

'That may provide the necessary regeneration, but to have the old cells missing at the proper time and place, in the proper controlled amounts, is another problem entirely. The Russians used the antibody technique on horses to get a selectively destructive serum. That is all right for them, but it sounds too slow and troublesome for me. The idea of inoculating a horse with some of my connective tissue doesn't appeal to me somehow. How am I supposed to get this connective tissue? Besides I don't have a horse. The serum farms charge high.

'After watching a particularly healthy colony of mould melting down a tough piece of raw beef I decided that there are other destructives than antibodies.

'I forced alternate generations of the mould to live on the toughest fresh meat I could find, and then on the dead mould mats of its own species. To feed without suicide it had to learn a fine selectivity, attacking only flesh that had passed the thin line between death and life. Twice, variants went past the line and dissolved themselves back to puddles, but the other strains learned to produce what was needed.

'Then I took some of the enzyme juice from under a mat, and shot the deadly stuff into a rabbit – the brown bunny with the white spot. Nothing happened to Bunny, she just grew very hungry and gained an ounce. I cut myself, and swabbed the juice on the cut. It skinned the callus from my fingertips, but nothing happened to the cut. So then I sent a sample over to the hospital for a test, with a note to Williams that this was a trial sample of a fine selective between dead and live tissue, to be used cautiously in cleaning out ragged infected wounds and small local gangrene.

'Williams is the same irresponsible old goat he always was. There was an ancient patient dying of everything in the book, including a gangrenous leg. Williams shot the whole tube of juice into the leg at once, just to see what would happen. Of course it made a sloppy mess that he had to clean up himself. It served him right. He said that the surprise simply turned his stomach, but the stuff fixed the gangrene all right, just as I said it would. It was as close and clean as a surgical amputation. Nevertheless he came back with what was left of the sample and was glad to be rid of it. He guessed it to be a super catalyst, somehow trained to be selective, and he wanted to get rid of it before it forgot its training.

'When I asked about the old patient later, they said that he woke up very hungry, and demanded a steak, so they satisfied him with intravenous amino acids, and he lived five days longer than expected.

'That was not a conclusive check, but it was enough. I labelled the juice H for the acid ion. H seemed a good name somehow.

'The first treatment on schedule was bone replacement. Middle age brings a sort of acromegaly. People ossify, their bones thicken, their gristle turns to bone and their arteries cake and stiffen. My framework needs a polishing down.

'For weeks I had cut my calcium intake down to almost nothing. Now I brought the calcium level in my blood down below the safe limit. The blood tried to stay normal by dissolving the treated bone. For safety, I had to play with parathyroid shots, depressants, and even a little calcium lactate on an hour-to-hour observation basis, to keep from crossing the spasm level of muscle irritability.

'But the hullabaloo must have upset my own endocrines, for they started behaving erratically, and yesterday suddenly they threw me into a fit before I could reach the depressant. I didn't break any bones, but I came out of the fit with one of my ulna uncomfortably bent. The sight of it almost gave me another fit.

'When one's bones start bending it is time to stop. I must have overdone the treatment a bit. There seems to be almost no mineral left in the smaller bones, just stiff healthy gristle. I am now lying flat on the cot drinking milk, eggnogs, and cod liver oil. I dreamed of chop suey last night, but until I ossify properly, I refuse to get up and go out for a meal. The icebox is within easy reach. Maybe my large bones are still hard, and maybe not, but I'll take no chances on bow legs and flat feet just for an oriental dinner.

'Darling, I'm having a wonderful time, and I wish you were here to look over my shoulder and make sarcastic remarks. Every step is a guess based on the wildest deductions, and almost every guess checks and has to be written down as right. At this rate, when I get through I'll be way ahead of the field. I'll be one of the best cockeyed endocrinologists practising.

'I hope you are having a good time too, and finding hundreds of broken vases and old teeth.

'I've got to switch back to the notes and hours record now and take down my pulse rate, irritability level, PH, and so on. The time is now seven ten, I'll give you another record soon.

'G'by, hon—'

Her voice stopped and the needle ran onto the label and scratched with a heavy tearing noise. Alec turned the record over. The label on the other side was dated one week later.

Helen spoke cheerfully:

'Hello, Alec. This is a week later. I took a chance today and walked. Flat on my back again now, just a bit winded, but unbowed.

'Remember the time the obelisk fell on me? They set my arm badly, and it healed crooked with a big bump in the bones where the broken ends knitted. That bump made a good test to check the amount of chromosome control in this replacement business. If it approaches true regeneration, the bump should be noticeably reduced and the knitting truer, to conform better to the gene blueprint of how an arm should be.

'The minute I thought of that test I had to try it. Risking flattened arches I got up and took the elevator down to the second floor office of Dr Stanton, and walked right through an anteroom of waiting patients to the consulting room, where I promptly lay down on his examination table.

'He was inspecting a little boy's tonsils and said irritably, "I really *must* ask you to wait your turn— Oh, it's Dr Berent. Really, Dr Berent, you shouldn't take advantage of your professional position to— Do you feel faint?'

' "Oh, I feel fine," I told him charmingly. "I just want to borrow your fluoroscope a minute to look at an old break in the right humerus."

' "Oh, yes, I understand," he says, blinking. "But why are you lying down?"

'Well, Alec, you remember how that young man is – rather innocent, and trying to be dignified and stuffy to make up for it. The last time we spoke to him, and you made those wonderful cracks, I could see him thinking that we were somewhat odd, if not completely off our rockers. If I tried to tell him now that I was afraid my legs would bend, he would have called for a padded wagon to come and take me away.

'I said, "I am afraid that I have upset my parathyroids. They are on a rampage. Just a momentary condition, but I have to stay relaxed for a while. You should see my irritability index! A little higher and ... ah ... I feel rather twitchy. Do you happen to have any curare around?"

'He looked at me as if I had just stabbed him with a hatpin, and then pulled out the fluoroscope so fast it almost ran over him, screened my arm bones, and hustled me out of there before I could even say "Aha". Apparently the idea of my throwing a fit right there didn't arouse his professional ardour one bit.

'Alec, when I saw those bone shadows it was as much as I could do to keep from frightening the poor boy with war whoops. I put both arms under together, and I couldn't see any bumps at all. *They were exactly the same.*

'This means that cells retain wider gene blueprints than they need. And they just need a little encouragement to rebuild injuries according to specifications. Regeneration must be an unused potential of the body. I don't see why. We can't evolve *unused* abilities. Natural selection only works in life-and-death trials – probably evolution had no part in this. It is just a lucky break from being foetal apes, a hangover bit of arrested development.

'I wonder how wide a blueprint each cell retains. Can a hand sprout new fingers, a wrist a new hand, a shoulder a new arm? Where does the control stop?

'The problem is a natural for the data I am getting now. Next winter when I am through with this silly rejuvenation business I'll get down to some solid work on regeneration, and try sprouting new arms on amputees. Maybe we can pry a grant from the government, through that military bureau for the design of artificial limbs. After all, new legs would be the artificial limbs to end all artificial limbs.

'But that is all for next year. Right now all I can use it for is to speed up replacement. If I can kid my cells into moving up onto embryo level activity, they would regrow fast enough to keep the inside works ticking after a really stiff jolt of that bottled dissolution. I'd have to follow it fast with the liquid protein— No, if they regrew that fast they would be using the material from the dissolved old cells. It could telescope treatment down to a few hours. And the nucleus control so active that it rebuilds according to its ideal.

'Demolition and reconstruction going on simultaneously. Business as usual.

'Next step is the replacement of various soft tissues. If I were not in such a hurry, I would do it in two long slow simple Gandhi-like fasts, with practically no scientific mumbo jumbo. The way a sea squirt does it, I mean – though I'd like to see someone starve himself down to a foot high.

'I have to start working now. The record is running out anyhow, so goodbye until the next record, whenever that is.

'Having a wonderful time.

'Wish you were here.'

He took the record off hurriedly and put on the next one. It was recorded on only one face, and dated September 17th, about fifty days later, seven weeks.

Helen started speaking without any introduction, her voice clearer and more distant as if she were speaking a few feet from the microphone.

'I'm rather upset, Alec. Something rather astonishing has happened. Have to get you up to date first.

'The fasting treatment went fine. Of course I had to stay indoors and keep out of sight until I was fit to be seen. I'm almost back to normal now, gaining about a pound a day. The embryo status treatment stimulated my cells to really get to work. They seem to be rebuilding from an adult blueprint and not a foetal one, so I am getting flesh again in proper proportion and not like an overgrown baby.

'If I am talking disjointedly it is because I am trying hard not to get to the point. The point is too big to be said easily.

'Of course you know that I started this experimenting just to check my theoretical understanding of cell metabolism. Even the best available theory is sketchy, and my own guesses are doubtful and tentative. I never could be sure whether a patient recovered because of my treatment, in spite of my treatment – or just reacted psychosomatically to the size of my consultant fee.

'The best way to correct faulty theory is to carry it to its logical absurdity, and then to use the silliness as a clue to the initial fault.

'Recipe: To test theories of some process take one neutral subject – that's me – and try to induce a specific stage of that process by artificial means dictated by the theories. The point of failure will be the clue to the revision of the theories.

'I expected to spend the second half of my vacation in the hospital, checking over records of the experiment, and happily writing an article on the meaning of its failure.

'To be ready for the emergency, I had hitched one of the electric timer clocks to the dictaphone and the telephone. If I didn't punch it at five-hour intervals, the alarm would knock off the telephone receiver, and the dictaphone would yell for an ambulance.

'Pinned to a big sign just inside the door was an explanation and full instructions for the proper emergency treatment. At every step in the experiment I would rewrite the instructions to match. "Be prepared" was the motto. "Plan for every contingency". No matter when the experiment decided to blow up in my face, I would be ready for it.

'There was only one contingency I did not plan for.

'Alec, I was just looking in the mirror. The only mirror that is any good is the big one in the front bedroom, but I had put off looking into it. For a week I lounged around reading and sleeping on the lab cot and the chair beside the window. I suppose I was still waiting for something to go wrong, but nothing did, and the skin of my hands was obviously different – no scars, no calluses, no tan, just smooth pink translucent skin – so I finally went and looked.

'Then I checked it with a medical exam. You'll find that data in with the other medical notes. Alec, I'm eighteen years old. That is as young as an adult can *get*.

'I wonder how Aladdin felt after rubbing a rusty lamp just to polish it up a bit.

'Surprised I suppose. The most noticeable feature of this new face so far is its surprised expression. It looks surprised from every angle, and sometimes it looks pale, and alarmed.

'Alarmed. Einstein was not alarmed when he discovered relativity, but they made a bomb out of it anyhow. I don't see how they could make a bomb out of this, but people are a wild, unpredictable lot. How will they react to being ageless? I can't guess, but I'm not reckless enough to hand out another Pandora's box to the world. The only safe way is to keep the secret until you get back, and then call a quiet council of experts for advice.

'But meanwhile, what if one of our friends happens to see me on the street looking like eighteen years old? What am I supposed to say?

'It is hard to be practical, darling. My imagination keeps galloping off in all directions. Did you know your hair is getting thin in back? Another two years with that crewcut and you would have begun to look like a monk.

'I know, I know, you'll tell me it is not fair for you to be a juvenile when everyone else is grey, but what is fair? To be fair at all everyone will have to have the treatment available free, for *nothing*. And I mean *everyone*. We can leave it to an economist to worry out how. Meanwhile we will have to change our names and move to California. You don't want people to recognize you, and wonder who I am, do you? You don't want to go around looking twice as old as your wife and have people calling you a cradle snatcher, now do you?

'Wheedling aside, it is fair enough. The process is still dangerous. You can call yourself Guinea Pig Number Two. That's fair. We can sign hotel registers G. Igpay and wife. Pardon me, Alec, I digress. It *is* hard to be practical, darling.

'If the treatment gets safely out of the lab and into circu-

lation – rejuvenation worked down to a sort of official vacci-
nation against old age – it would be good for the race I
think. It may even help evolution. Regeneration would re-
move environmental handicaps, old scars of bad raising,
and give every man a body as good as his genes. A world
full of the age-proof would be a sort of sound-mind, sound-
body health marathon, with the longest breeding period
won by the people with the best chromosomes and the
healthiest family tradition.

'Thank heavens I can strike a blow for evolution at last.
Usually I find myself on the opposite side, fighting to preserve the life of some case whose descendants will give
doctors a headache.

'And look at cultural evolution! For the first time we
humans will be able to use our one talent, learning, the way
it should be used, the way it was meant to be used from the
beginning, an unstoppable growth of skill and humour and
understanding, experience adding layer on layer like the
bark of a California redwood.

'And we need thinkers with time to boil the huge accu-
mulation of science down to some reasonable size. It is an
emergency job – and not just for geniuses; the rest of us
will have to help look for common denominators, too. Even
ordinary specialists will have time to learn more, do some
integrating of their own, join hands with specialists of related fields.

'Take us, a good sample of disjointed specialities. You
could learn neurology, and I could learn anthropology and
psychology, and then we could talk the same language and
still be like Jack Spratt and his wife, covering the field of
human behaviour between us. We would be close enough to
collaborate – without *many* gaps of absolute ignorance – to
write the most wonderful books. We could even ... ah— We
can even—'

(There was a silence, and then a shaky laugh.)

'I forgot. I said, "Take us for example," as if we weren't
examples already. Research is supposed to be for other
people. This is for us. It *is* a shock. Funny – funny how it
keeps taking me by surprise.

209

'It shouldn't make that much difference. After all one lifetime is like another. We'll be the same people on the same job – with more time. Time enough to see the sequoias grow, and watch the ripening of the race. A long time.

'But the outside of the condemned cell is not very different from the inside. It is the same world full of the same hare-brained human beings. And yet here I am, as shaky as if I've just missed being run over by a truck.'

(There was another uncertain laugh.)

'I can't talk just now, Alec. I have to think.'

For some minutes after the record stopped Alec stared out of the window, his hands locked behind his back, the knuckles working and whitening with tension. It was the last record, the only clue he had. The quaver in her voice, her choice of words, had emphatically filled his mind with the nameless emotion that had held her. It was almost a thought, a concept half felt, half seen, lying on the borderline of logic.

Before his eyes persistently there grew a vision of the great pyramid of Cheops, half completed, with slaves toiling and dying on its slopes. He stared blindly out over the rooftops of the city, waiting, not daring to force the explanation. Presently the vision began to slip away, and his mind wandered to other thoughts. Somewhere down in that maze of buildings was Helen. Where?

It was no use. Unclenching his stiffening fingers Alec jotted down a small triangle on the envelope of the record, to remind himself that a pyramid held some sort of clue. As he did it, suddenly he remembered that Helen, when she was puzzled, liked to jot the problem down on paper as she thought.

On the bedroom vanity table there was a tablet of white paper, and beside it an ashtray holding a few cigarette stubs. The tablet was blank, but he found two crumpled sheets of paper in the wastebasket and smoothed them carefully out on the table.

It began 'Dear Alec,' and then there were words crossed and blotted out. 'Dear Alec' was written again halfway down the sheet, and the letters absently embroidered into elaborate script. Under it were a few doodles, and then a clear surrealistic sketch of a wisdom tooth marked with neat dental work, lying on its side in the foreground of a desert. Subscribed was the title 'TIME', and beside it was written critically, 'Derivative: The lone and level sands stretch far away.' Doodles and vague figures and faces covered the bottom of the page and extended over the next page. In the midst of them was written the single stark thought, 'There is something wrong.'

That was all. Numbly Alec folded the two sheets and put them into the envelope of the record. A tooth and a triangle. It should have been funny, but he could not laugh. He took the record out and considered it. There was another concentric ribbon of sound on the face of the disk. Helen had used it again, but the needle had balked at a narrow blank line where she had restarted the recorder and placed the stylus a little too far in.

He put the record back on the turntable and placed the needle by hand.

'Alec darling, I wish you were here. You aren't as good a parlour psychologist as any woman, but you do know human nature in a broad way, and can always explain its odder tricks. I thought I was clever at interpreting other people's behaviour, but tonight I can't even interpret my own. Nothing startling has happened. It is just that I have been acting unlike myself all day and I feel that it is a symptom of something unpleasant.

'I walked downtown to stretch my legs and see the crowds and bright lights again. I was looking at the movie stills in a theatre front when I saw Lucy Hughes hurrying by with a package under one arm. I didn't turn around, but she recognized me and hurried over.

' "Why Helen Berent! I thought you were in Tibet."

'I turned around and looked at her. Lucy, with her baby ways and feminine intuition. It would be easy to confide in her but she was not the kind to keep a secret. I didn't say anything. I suppose I just looked at her with that blank expression you say I wear when I am thinking.

'She looked back, and her eyes widened slowly.

' "Why you're too young. You're not— Heavens! I'm awfully sorry. I thought you were someone else. Silly of me, but you look just like a friend of mine – when she was younger I mean. It's almost uncanny!"

'I put on a slight western drawl, and answered politely, as a stranger should, and she went away shaking her head. Poor Lucy!

'I went in to see the movie. Alec, what happened next worries me. I stayed in that movie eight hours. It was an obnoxious movie, a hard-boiled detective story full of blood and violence and slaughter. I saw it three and a half times. You used to make critical remarks on the mental state of a public that battens on that sort of thud and blunder – something about Roman circuses. I wish I could remember how you explained it, because I need that explanation. When the movie house closed for the night I went home in a taxi. It drove too fast but I got home all right. There was some meat stew contaminated with botulinus in the icebox, but I tasted the difference and threw it out. I have to be very careful. People are too careless. I never realized it before, but they are.

'I had better go to bed now and see if I can get some sleep.'

Automatically Alec took the record off and slid it back into its envelope. The pencilled triangle caught his eye, and his hands slowed and stopped. For a long time he looked at it without moving – the pyramids, the tombs of kings. An ancient religion that taught that one of a man's souls lived on in his mummy, a ghostly spark that vanished if the human form was lost. A whisper of immortality on earth. Cheops, spending the piled treasures of his kingdom and the helpless lives of slaves merely for a tomb to shield his corpse, building a pitiful mountain of rock to mock his name down the centuries. Hope – and fear.

There are wells of madness in us never tapped.

Alec put away the record and stepped to the window. The brown towers of Columbia Medical Center showed in the distance, Cornell Medical was downtown. Bellevue— 'Hope,' said Alec. 'When there is life there is hope,' said Alec, and laughed harshly at the pun. He knew now what he had to do. He turned away from the window, and picking up a classified telephone directory, turned to 'Hospitals'.

It was evening. The psychiatric resident doctor escorted him down the hall, talking companionably.

'She wouldn't give her name. Part of the complex. A symptom for us, but pretty hard on you. It would have helped you to find her if she had some identifying marks, I suppose, like scars I mean. It is unusual to find anyone without any—'

'What's her trouble?' asked Alec. 'Anxiety? Afraid of things, germs, falls—?'

'She's afraid all right. Even afraid of me! Says I have germs. Says I'm incompetent. It's all a symptom of some other fear, of course. These things are not what she is really afraid of. Once we find the single repressed fear and explain it to her—' He checked Alec's objection. 'It's not rational to be afraid of little things. Those little dangers are not what she is really afraid of anyhow. Now suppression—'

Alec interrupted with a slight edge to his voice.

'Are you afraid of death?'

'Not much. There is nothing you can do about it, after all, so normal people must manage to get used to the idea. Now she—'

'You have a religion?'

'Vedanta. What of it? Now her attitude in this case is—'

'Even a mouse can have a nervous breakdown!' Alec snapped. 'Where is the repression there? Vedanta you said? Trouble is, Helen is just too rational!' They had stopped. 'Is this the room?'

'Yeah,' said the doctor sullenly, making no move to open the door. 'She is probably still asleep.' He looked at his watch. 'No, she would be coming out of it now.'

'Drugs,' said Alec coldly. 'I suppose you have been psycho-analysing her, trying to trace her trouble back to some time when her mother slapped her with a lollypop, eh? Or shock

213

treatment perhaps, burning out the powers of imagination, eh?'

The young psychiatrist let his annoyance show. 'We know our jobs, sir. Sedatives and analysis – without them she would be screaming the roof off. She's too suspicious to consciously confide her warp to us, but under scopolamine she seems to think she is a middle-aged woman. How rational is *that*?' With an effort he regained his professional blandness. 'She has not said much so far, but we expect to learn more after the next treatment. Of course being told her family history will help us immeasurably. We would like to meet her father and mother.'

'I'll do everything in my power to help,' Alec replied. 'Where there is life there is hope.' He laughed harshly, on a note that drew a keen professional glance from the doctor. The young man put his hand to the knob, his face bland.

'You may go in and identify her now. Remember, be very careful not to frighten her.' He opened the door and stood aside, then followed Alec in.

Helen lay on the bed asleep, her dark hair lying across one cheek. She looked like a tired kid of nineteen, but to Alec there seemed to be no change. She had always looked this way. It was Helen.

The doctor called gently. 'Miss ... ah ... Berent. Miss Berent.'

Helen's body stiffened, but she did not open her eyes. 'Go away,' she said in a small flat voice. 'Please!'

'It is just Dr Marro,' the young man said soothingly.

'How do I know you are a doctor?' she said without stirring. 'You'd say that anyway. Maybe you escaped and disguised yourself as a doctor. Maybe you are a paranoiac.'

'I'm just myself,' said the resident, shrugging. 'Just Dr Marro. How can I prove it to you if you don't look at me?'

The small voice sounded like a child reciting. It said, 'If you are a doctor, you will see that having you here upsets me. You won't want to upset me, so you will go away.' She smiled secretly at the wall. 'Go away please.'

Then, abruptly terrified, she was sitting up, staring. 'You

214

called me Miss Berent. Oh, Alec!' Her eyes dilated like dark pools in a chalk face, and then Helen crumpled up and rolled to face the wall, gasping in dry sobs, 'Please, please—'

'You are exciting her, Mr Berent,' said the resident. 'I'm sorry, but I'm afraid you'll have to leave.'

It had to be done. Alec swallowed with a dry mouth, and then said in a loud clear voice, enunciating every syllable, 'Helen, honey, you are dying.'

For a moment there was a strange silence. The doctor was looking at him with a shocked white face; then he moved, fumbling for an arm lock, fumbling with his voice for the proper cheerful tone. 'Come, Mr Berent, you . . . we must be going now.'

Alec swung his clenched fist into the babbling white face. The jolt on his knuckles felt right. He did not bother to watch the doctor fall. It only meant that he would have a short time without interruption. Helen was cowering in the far corner of the bed, muttering, 'No-no-no-no—' in a meaningless voice. The limp weight of the psychiatrist leaned against his leg and then slipped down and pressed across the toes of his shoes.

'Helen,' Alec called clearly, 'Helen, you are dying. You have cancer.'

She answered only with a wordless animal whimper. Alec looked away. The gleaming white walls began to lean at crazy angles. He shut his eyes and thought of darkness and silence. Presently the whimpering stopped. A voice faltered: 'No, I am never going to d— No, I am not.'

'Yes,' he said firmly, 'you are.' The darkness ebbed. Alec opened his eyes. Helen had turned around and was watching him, a line of puzzlement on her forehead. 'Really?' she asked childishly.

His face was damp, but he did not move to wipe it. 'Yes,' he stated, 'absolutely certain. Cancer, incurable cancer.'

'Cancer,' she murmured wonderingly. 'Where?'

He had that answer ready. He had picked it from an atlas of anatomy as an inaccessible spot, hard to confirm or deny, impossible to operate for. He told her.

She considered for a second, a vague puzzlement wrinkling her face. 'Then ... I can't do anything about it. It would happen just the same. It's there now.' She looked up absently, rubbing a hand across her forehead. 'The deadline?'

'It's very small and encysted.' Casually he waved a hand. 'Maybe even ten, twenty years.'

Thinking, she got out of bed and stood looking out the window, her lips pursed as if she were whistling.

Alec turned to watch her, a polite smile fixed on his lips. He could feel the doctor's weight shifting as his head cleared.

'Cells.' Helen murmured, once, then exclaimed suddenly to herself. 'Of course not!' She chuckled, and chuckling spoke in her own warm voice, the thin note of fear gone. 'Alec, you'll never guess what I have been doing. Wait until you hear the records!' She laughed delightedly. 'A wild goose chase! I'm ashamed to face you. And I didn't see it until this minute!'

'Didn't see what, honey?'

The doctor got to his knees and softly crawled away.

Helen swung around gaily. 'Didn't see that all cells are mutable, not just germ cells, but all cells. If they keep on multiplying – each cell with the same probability of mutation – and some viable mutations would be cancerous, then everybody— Work it out on a slide rule for me, hon, with so many million cells in the body, with—'

She had been looking past him at the new idea, but now her gaze focused and softened. 'Alec, you look so tired. You shouldn't be pale after all your tramping around in—' The mists of thought cleared. She saw him. 'Alec, you're back.'

And now there was no space or time separating them and she was warm and alive in his arms, nuzzling his cheek, whispering a chuckle in his ear. 'And I was standing there lecturing you about cells! I must have been crazy.'

He could hear the doctor padding up the hall with a squad of husky attendants, but he didn't care. Helen was back.

From too much love of living
From hope and fear set free
We thank with brief thanksgiving
Whatever gods may be
That no life lives for ever;
That dead men rise up never;
That even the weariest river
Winds somewhere safe to sea.

Swinburne

THE WITCHES OF KARRES

James H. Schmitz

*Here is a tale about a young interstellar trader from a
world with the ridiculous name of Nikkeldepain. It was
Captain Pausert's first voyage, he had a cargo of unwanted
odds and ends, and his intentions were better than his navigation. Still, everything might have gone smoothly enough,
if only he had never met those three juvenile witches,
Maleen, the Leewit and Goth.*

IT was around the hub of the evening on the planet of
Porlumma that Captain Pausert, commercial traveller from
the Republic of Nikkeldepain, met the first of the Witches
of Karres.

It was just plain fate, so far as he could see.

He was feeling pretty good as he left a high-priced bar on
a cobbly street near the spaceport, with the intention of
returning straight to his ship. There hadn't been an argument, exactly. But someone grinned broadly, as usual, when
the captain pronounced the name of his native system;
and the captain had pointed out then, with considerable wit, how much more ridiculous it was to call a
planet Porlumma, for instance, than to call it Nikkeldepain.

He proceeded to collect a gradually increasing number of
pained stares by a detailed comparison of the varied, interesting, and occasionally brilliant role Nikkeldepain had
played in history with Porlumma's obviously dull and
dumpy status as a sixth-rate Empire outpost.

In conclusion, he admitted frankly that he wouldn't be
found dead on Porlumma.

Somebody muttered loudly in Imperial Universum that

in that case it might be better if he didn't hang around Porlumma too long. But the captain only smiled politely, paid for his two drinks, and left.

There was no point in getting into a rhubarb on one of these border planets. Their citizens still had an innocent notion that they ought to act like frontiersmen – but then the law always showed up at once.

He felt pretty good. Up to the last four months of his young life, he had never looked on himself as being particularly patriotic. But compared to most of the Empire's worlds, Nikkeldepain was downright attractive in its stuffy way. Besides, he was returning there solvent – would they ever be surprised!

And awaiting him, fondly and eagerly, was Illyla, the Miss Onswud, fair daughter of the mighty Councillor Onswud, and the captain's secretly affianced for almost a year. She alone had believed in him!

The captain smiled and checked at a dark cross street to get his bearings on the spaceport beacon. Less than half a mile away— He set off again. In about six hours, he'd be beyond the Empire's space borders and headed straight for Illyla.

Yes, she alone had believed! After the prompt collapse of the captain's first commercial venture – a miffel-fur farm, largely on capital borrowed from Councillor Onswud – the future had looked very black. It had even included a probable ten-year stretch of penal servitude for 'wilful and negligent abuse of entrusted monies.' The laws of Nikkeldepain were rough on debtors.

'But you've always been looking for someone to take out the old *Venture* and get her back into trade!' Illyla reminded her father tearfully.

'Hm-m-m, yes! But it's in the blood, my dear! His great uncle Threbus went the same way! It would be far better to let the law take its course,' Councillor Onswud said, glaring at Pausert who remained sulkily silent. He had *tried* to explain that the mysterious epidemic which suddenly wiped out most of the stock of miffels wasn't his fault. In fact, he more than suspected the tricky hand of young Councillor

Rapport who had been wagging futilely around Illyla for the last couple of years!

'The *Venture*, now—!' Councillor Onswud mused, stroking his long, craggy chin. 'Pausert can handle a ship, at least,' he admitted.

That was how it happened. Were they ever going to be surprised! For even the captain realized that Councillor Onswud was unloading all the dead fish that had gathered the dust of his warehouses for the past fifty years on him and the *Venture*, in a last, faint hope of getting *some* return on those half-forgotten investments. A value of eighty-two thousand maels was placed on the cargo; but if he'd brought even three quarters of it back in cash, all would have been well.

Instead – well, it started with that lucky bet on a legal point with an Imperial official at the Imperial capital itself. Then came a six-hour race fairly won against a small, fast private yacht – the old *Venture* 7333 had been a pirate chaser in the last century and could still produce twice as much speed as her looks suggested. From there on, the captain was socially accepted as a sporting man and was in on a long string of jovial parties and meets.

Jovial and profitable – the wealthier Imperials just couldn't resist a gamble; and the penalty he always insisted on was that they had to buy!

He got rid of the stuff right and left! Inside of twelve weeks, nothing remained of the original cargo except two score bundles of expensively built but useless tinklewood fishing poles and one dozen gross bales of useful but unattractive all-weather cloaks. Even on a bet, nobody would take them! But the captain had a strong hunch those items had been hopefully added to the cargo from his own stocks by Councillor Rapport; so his failure to sell them didn't break his heart.

He was a neat twenty per cent net ahead, at that point—

And finally came this last-minute delivery of medical supplies to Porlumma on the return route. That haul alone would have repaid the miffel-farm loss three times over!

*　　*　　*

The captain grinned broadly into the darkness. Yes, they'd be surprised – but just where was he now?

He checked again in the narrow street, searching for the port-beacon in the sky. There it was – off to his left and a little behind him. He'd got turned around somehow!

He set off carefully down an excessively dark little alley. It was one of those towns where everybody locked their front doors at night and retired to lit-up, enclosed court-yards at the backs of the houses. There were voices and the rattling of dishes nearby, and occasional whoops of laughter and singing all around him; but it was all beyond high walls which let little or no light into the alley.

It ended abruptly in a cross alley and another wall. After a moment's debate, the captain turned to his left again. Light spilled out on his new route a few hundred yards ahead, where a courtyard was opened on the alley. From it, as he approached, came the sound of doors being violently slammed, and then a sudden, loud mingling of voices.

'Yeeee-eep!' shrilled a high, childish voice. It could have been mortal agony, terror, or even hysterical laughter. The captain broke into an apprehensive trot.

'Yes, I see you up there!' a man shouted excitedly in Universum. 'I caught you now – you get down from those boxes! I'll skin you alive! Fifty-two customers sick of the stomach-ache – YOW!'

The last exclamation was accompanied by a sound as of a small, loosely built wooden house collapsing, and was fol-lowed by a succession of squeals and an angry bellowing, in which the only distinguishable words were '... threw the boxes on me!' Then more sounds of splintering wood.

'Hey!' yelled the captain indignantly from the corner of the alley.

All action ceased. The narrow courtyard, brightly illumi-nated under its single overhead bulb, was half covered with a tumbled litter of what appeared to be empty wooden boxes. Standing with his foot temporarily caught in one of them was a very large, fat man dressed all in white and waving a stick. Momentarily cornered between the wall and two of the boxes, over one of which she was trying to climb, was a smallish, fair-haired girl dressed in a smock of some kind, which was also white. She might be about fourteen, the captain thought – a helpless kid, anyway.

'What *you* want?' grunted the fat man, pointing the stick with some dignity at the captain.

'Lay off the kid!' rumbled the captain, edging into the courtyard.

'Mind your own business!' shouted the fat man, waving his stick like a club. 'I'll take care of her! She—'

'I never did!' squealed the girl. She burst into tears.

'Try it, Fat and Ugly!' the captain warned. 'I'll ram the stick down your throat!'

He was very close now. With a sound of grunting exasperation, the fat man pulled his foot free of the box, wheeled suddenly and brought the end of the stick down on the top of the captain's cap. The captain hit him furiously in the middle of the stomach.

There was a short flurry of activity, somewhat hampered by shattering boxes everywhere. Then the captain stood up, scowling and breathing hard. The fat man remained sitting on the ground, gasping about '. . . the law!'

Somewhat to his surprise, the captain discovered the girl standing just behind him. She caught his eye and smiled.

'My name's Maleen,' she offered. She pointed at the fat man. 'Is he hurt bad?'

'Huh – no!' panted the captain. 'But maybe we'd better—'

It was too late! A loud, self-assured voice became audible now at the opening to the alley: 'Here, here, here, here, here!' it said in the reproachful, situation-under-control tone that always seemed the same to the captain, on whatever world and in whichever language he heard it.

'What's this all about?' it inquired rhetorically.

'You'll all have to come along!' it replied.

Police court on Porlumma appeared to be a business conducted on a very efficient, around-the-clock basis. They were the next case up.

Nikkeldepain was an odd name, wasn't it – the judge

222

smiled. He then listened attentively to the various charges, countercharges, and denials.

Bruth the Baker was charged with having struck a citizen of a foreign government on the head with a potentially lethal instrument – produced in evidence. Said citizen had admittedly attempted to interfere as Bruth was attempting to punish his slave Maleen – also produced in evidence – whom he suspected of having added something to a batch of cakes she was working on that afternoon, resulting in illness and complaints from fifty-two of Bruth's customers.

Said foreign citizen had also used insulting language. The captain admitted under pressure to 'Fat and Ugly'.

Some provocation could be conceded for the action taken by Bruth, but not enough. Bruth paled.

Captain Pausert, of the Republic of Nikkeldepain – everybody but the prisoners smiled this time – was charged (a) with said attempted interference, (b) with said insult, (c) with having frequently and severely struck Bruth the Baker in the course of the subsequent dispute.

The blow on the head was conceded to have provided a provocation for charge (c) – but not enough.

Nobody seemed to be charging the slave Maleen with anything. The judge only looked at her curiously and shook his head.

'As the court considers this regrettable incident,' he remarked, 'it looks like two years for you, Bruth; and about three for you, Captain. Too bad!'

The captain had an awful sinking feeling. He had seen something and heard a lot of Imperial court methods in the fringe systems. He could probably get out of his three-year rap; but it would be expensive.

He realized that the judge was studying him reflectively. 'The court wishes to acknowledge,' the judge continued, 'that the captain's chargeable actions were due largely to a natural feeling of human sympathy for the predicament of the slave Maleen. The court, therefore, would suggest a settlement as follows, subsequent to which all charges could be dropped: That Bruth the Baker resell Maleen of Karres – with whose services he appears to be dissatisfied – for a reasonable sum to Captain Pausert of the Republic of Nikkeldepain.'

Bruth the Baker heaved a gusty sigh of relief. But the captain hesitated. The buying of human slaves by private citizens was a very serious offence in Nikkeldepain! Still, he didn't have to make a record of it. If they weren't going to soak him too much—

At just the right moment, Maleen of Karres introduced a barely audible, forlorn, sniffling sound.

'How much are you asking for the kid?' the captain inquired, looking without friendliness at his recent antagonist. A day was coming when he would think less severely of Bruth; but it hadn't come yet.

Bruth scowled back but replied with a certain eagerness: 'A hundred and fifty m—' A policeman standing behind him poked him sharply in the side. Bruth shut up.

'Seven hundred maels,' the judge said smoothly. 'There'll be court charges, and a fee for recording the transaction—' He appeared to make a swift calculation. 'Fifteen hundred and forty-two maels—' He turned to a clerk. 'You've looked him up?'

The clerk nodded. 'He's right!'

'And we'll take your cheque,' the judge concluded. He gave the captain a friendly smile. 'Next case.'

The captain felt a little bewildered.

There was something peculiar about this! He was getting out of it much too cheaply. Since the Empire had quit its wars of expansion, young slaves in good health were a high-priced article. Furthermore, he was practically positive that Bruth the Baker had been willing to sell for a tenth of what the captain actually had to pay!

Well, he wouldn't complain. Rapidly he signed, sealed, and thumbprinted various papers shoved at him by a helpful clerk, and made out a cheque.

'I guess,' he told Maleen of Karres, 'we'd better get along to the ship.'

And now what was he going to do with the kid, he

pondered, padding along the unlighted streets with his slave trotting quietly behind him. If he showed up with a pretty girl-slave in Nikkeldepain, even a small one, various good friends there would toss him into ten years or so of penal servitude – immediately after Illyla had personally collected his scalp. They were a moral lot.

Karres—?

'How far off is Karres, Maleen?' he asked into the dark.

'It takes about two weeks,' Maleen said tearfully.

Two weeks! The captain's heart sank again.

'What are you blubbering about?' he inquired uncomfortably.

Maleen choked, sniffed, and began sobbing openly.

'I have two little sisters!' she cried.

'Well, well,' the captain said encouragingly. 'That's nice. You'll be seeing them again soon. I'm taking you home, you know!'

Great Patham – now he'd said it! But after all—

But this piece of good news seemed to be having the wrong effect on his slave! Her sobbing grew much more violent.

'No, I won't,' she wailed. 'They're here!'

'Huh?' said the captain. He stopped short. 'Where?'

'And the people they're with are mean to them too!' wept Maleen.

The captain's heart dropped clean through his boots. Standing there in the dark, he helplessly watched it coming:

'You could buy them awfully cheap!' she said.

II

In times of stress, the young life of Karres appeared to take to the heights. It might be a mountainous place.

The Leewit sat on the top shelf of the back wall of the crockery and antiques store, strategically flanked by two expensive-looking vases. She was a doll-sized edition of Maleen; but her eyes were cold and grey instead of blue and tearful. About five or six, the captain vaguely estimated. He wasn't very good at estimating them around that age.

'Good evening,' he said, as he came in through the door. The Crockery and Antiques Shop had been easy to find. Like Bruth the Baker's, it was the one spot in the neighbourhood that was all lit up.

'Good evening, sir!' said what was presumably the store owner, without looking around. He sat with his back to the door, in a chair approximately at the centre of the store and facing the Leewit at a distance of about twenty feet.

'... and there you can stay without food or drink till the Holy Man comes in the morning!' he continued immediately, in the taut voice of a man who has gone through hysteria and is sane again. The captain realized he was addressing the Leewit.

'Your other Holy Man didn't stay very long!' the diminutive creature piped, also ignoring the captain. Apparently, she had not yet discovered Maleen behind him.

'This is a stronger denomination – much stronger!' the store owner replied, in a shaking voice but with a sort of relish. '*He'll* exorcise you all right, little demon – you'll whistle no buttons off him! Your time is up! Go on and whistle all you want! Bust every vase in the place—'

The Leewit blinked her grey eyes thoughtfully at him.

'Might!' she said.

'But if you try to climb down from there,' the store owner went on, on a rising note, 'I'll chop you into bits – into little, little bits!'

He raised his arm as he spoke and weakly brandished what the captain recognized with a start of horror as a highly ornamented but probably still useful antique battle-axe.

'Ha!' said the Leewit.

'Beg your pardon, sir!' the captain said, clearing his throat.

'Good evening, sir!' the store owner repeated, without looking around. 'What can I do for you?'

'I came to inquire,' the captain said hesitantly, 'about that child.'

The store owner shifted about in his chair and squinted at the captain with red-rimmed eyes.

'You're not a Holy Man!' he said.

'Hello, Maleen!' the Leewit said suddenly. 'That him?'

'We've come to buy you,' Maleen said. 'Shut up!'

'Good!' said the Leewit.

'Buy it? Are you mocking me, sir?' the store owner inquired.

'Shut up, Moonell!' A thin, dark, determined-looking woman had appeared in the doorway that led through the back wall of the store. She moved out a step under the shelves; and the Leewit leaned down from the top shelf and hissed. The woman moved hurriedly back into the doorway.

'Maybe he means it,' she said in a more subdued voice.

'I can't sell to a citizen of the Empire,' the store owner said defeatedly.

'I'm not a citizen,' the captain said shortly. This time, he wasn't going to name it.

'No, he's from Nikkel—' Maleen began.

'Shut up, Maleen!' the captain said helplessly in turn.

'I never heard of Nikkel,' the store owner muttered doubtfully.

'Maleen!' the woman cried shrilly. 'That's the name of one of the others – Bruth the Baker got her. He means it, all right! He's buying them—'

'A hundred and fifty maels!' the captain said craftily, remembering Bruth the Baker. 'In cash!'

The store owner looked dazed.

'Not enough, Moonell!' the woman called. 'Look at all it's broken! Five hundred maels!'

There was a sound then, so thin the captain could hardly hear it. It pierced at his eardrums like two jabs of a delicate needle. To right and left of him, two highly glazed little jugs went 'Clink-clink!' showed a sudden veining of cracks, and collapsed.

A brief silence settled on the store. And now that he looked around more closely, the captain could spot here and there other little piles of shattered crockery – and places where similar ruins apparently had been swept up, leaving only traces of coloured dust.

The store owner laid the axe down carefully beside his chair, stood up, swaying a little, and came toward the captain.

'You offered me a hundred and fifty maels!' he said rapidly as he approached. 'I accept it here, now, see – before witnesses!' He grabbed the captain's right hand in both of his and pumped it up and down vigorously. 'Sold!' he yelled.

Then he wheeled around in a leap and pointed a shaking hand at the Leewit.

'And NOW,' he howled, 'break something! Break anything! You're his! I'll sue him for every mael he ever made and ever will!'

'Oh, do come help me down, Maleen!' the Leewit pleaded prettily.

For a change, the store of Wansing, the jeweller, was dimly lit and very quiet. It was a sleek, fashionable place in a fashionable shopping block near the spaceport. The front door was unlocked, and Wansing was in.

The three of them entered quietly, and the door sighed quietly shut behind them. Beyond a great crystal display counter, Wansing was moving about among a number of opened shelves, talking softly to himself. Under the crystal of the counter, and in close-packed rows on the satin-covered shelves, reposed a many-coloured jewel gleaming and glittering and shining. Wansing was no piker.

'Good evening, sir!' the captain said across the counter.

'It's morning!' the Leewit remarked from the other side of Maleen.

'Maleen!' said the captain.

'We're keeping out of this,' Maleen said to the Leewit.

'All right,' said the Leewit.

Wansing had come around jerkily at the captain's greeting, but had made no other move. Like all the slave owners the captain had met on Porlumma so far, Wansing seemed

228

unhappy. Otherwise, he was a large, dark, sleek-looking man with jewels in his ears and a smell of expensive oils and perfumes about him.

'This place is under constant visual guard, of course!' he told the captain gently. 'Nothing could possibly happen to me here. Why am I so frightened?'

'Not of me, I'm sure!' the captain said with an uncomfortable attempt at geniality. 'I'm glad your store's still open,' he went on briskly. 'I'm here on business—'

'Oh, yes, it's still open, of course,' Wansing said. He gave the captain a slow smile and turned back to his shelves. 'I'm making inventory, that's why! I've been making inventory since early yesterday morning. I've counted them all seven times—'

'You're very thorough,' the captain said.

'Very, very thorough!' Wansing nodded to the shelves. 'The last time I found I had made a million maels. But twice before that, I had lost approximately the same amount. I shall have to count them again, I suppose!' He closed a shelf softly. 'I'm sure I counted those before. But they move about constantly. Constantly! It's horrible.'

'You've got a slave here called Goth,' the captain said, driving to the point.

'Yes, I have!' Wansing said, nodding. 'And I'm sure she understands by now I meant no harm! I do, at any rate. It was perhaps a little— But I'm sure she understands now, or will soon!'

'Where is she?' the captain inquired, a trifle uneasily.

'In her room perhaps,' Wansing suggested. 'It's not so bad when she's there in her room with the door closed. But often she sits in the dark and looks at you as you go past—' He opened another drawer, and closed it quietly again. 'Yes, they do move!' he whispered, as if confirming an earlier suspicion. 'Constantly—'

'Look, Wansing,' the captain said in a loud, firm voice. 'I'm not a citizen of the Empire. I want to buy this Goth! I'll pay you a hundred and fifty maels, cash.'

Wansing turned around completely again and looked at the captain. 'Oh, you do?' he said. 'You're not a citizen?'

229

He walked a few steps to the side of the counter, sat down at a small desk, and turned a light on over it. Then he put his face in his hands for a moment.

'I'm a wealthy man,' he muttered. 'An influential man! The name of Wansing counts for a great deal on Porlumma. When the Empire suggests you buy, you buy, of course. But it need not have been I who bought her! I thought she would be useful in the business. And then, even I could not sell her again within the Empire. She has been here for a week!'

He looked up at the captain and smiled. 'One hundred and fifty maels!' he said. 'Sold! There are records to be made out—' He reached into a drawer and took out some printed forms. He began to write rapidly. The captain produced identifications.

Maleen said suddenly, 'Goth?'

'Right here,' a voice murmured. Wansing's hand jerked sharply, but he did not look up. He kept on writing.

Something small and lean and bonelessly supple, dressed in a dark jacket and leggings, came across the thick carpets of Wansing's store and stood behind the captain. This one might be about nine or ten.

'I'll take your cheque, Captain!' Wansing said politely. 'You must be an honest man. Besides, I want to frame it.'

'And now,' the captain heard himself say in the remote voice of one who moves through a strange dream, 'I suppose we could go to the ship.'

The sky was grey and cloudy; and the streets were lightening. Goth, he noticed, didn't resemble her sisters. She had brown hair cut short a few inches below her ears, and brown eyes with long, black lashes. Her nose was short and her chin was pointed. She made him think of some thin, carnivorous creature, like a weasel.

She looked up at him briefly, grinned, and said, 'Thanks!'

'What was wrong with *him*?' chirped the Leewit, walking backwards for a last view of Wansing's store.

'Tough crook,' muttered Goth. The Leewit giggled.

'You premoted this just dandy, Maleen!' she stated next.

'Shut up,' said Maleen.

'All right,' said the Leewit. She glanced up at the captain's face. 'You been fighting!' she said virtuously. 'Did you win?'

'Of course, the captain won!' said Maleen.

'Good for you!' said the Leewit.

'What about the takeoff?' Goth asked the captain. She seemed a little worried.

'Nothing to it!' the captain said stoutly, hardly bothering to wonder how she'd guessed the takeoff was the one operation on which he and the old *Venture* consistently failed to cooperate.

'No,' said Goth, 'I meant when?'

'Right now,' said the captain. 'They've already cleared us. We'll get the sign any second.'

'Good,' said Goth. She walked off slowly down the hall toward the back of the ship.

The takeoff was pretty bad, but the *Venture* made it again. Half an hour later, with Porlumma dwindling safely behind them, the captain switched to automatic and climbed out of his chair. After considerable experimentation, he got the electric butler adjusted to four breakfasts, hot, with coffee. It was accomplished with a great deal of advice and attempted assistance from the Leewit, rather less from Maleen, and no comments from Goth.

'Everything will be coming along in a few minutes now!' he announced. Afterwards, it struck him there had been a quality of grisly prophecy about the statement.

'If you'd listened to me,' said the Leewit, 'we'd have been done eating a quarter of an hour ago!' She was perspiring but triumphant – she had been right all along.

'Say, Maleen,' she said suddenly, 'you premoting again?'

Premoting? The captain looked at Maleen. She seemed pale and troubled.

'Spacesick?' he suggested. 'I've got some pills—'

'No, she's premoting,' the Leewit said, scowling. 'What's up, Maleen?'

'Shut up,' said Goth.

231

'All right,' said the Leewit. She was silent a moment, and then began to wriggle. 'Maybe we'd better—'

'Shut up,' said Maleen.

'It's all ready,' said Goth.

'What's all ready?' asked the captain.

'All right,' said the Leewit. She looked at the captain. 'Nothing,' she said.

He looked at them then, and they looked at him – one set each of grey eyes, and brown, and blue. They were all sitting around the control room floor in a circle, the fifth side of which was occupied by the electric butler.

What peculiar little waifs, the captain thought. He hadn't perhaps really realized until now just how *very* peculiar. They were still staring at him.

'Well, well!' he said heartily. 'So Maleen "premotes" and gives people stomach aches.'

Maleen smiled dimly and smoothed back her yellow hair. 'They just thought they were getting them,' she murmured.

'Mass history,' explained the Leewit, offhandedly.

'Hysteria,' said Goth. 'The Imperials get their hair up about us every so often.'

'I noticed that.' The captain nodded. 'And little Leewit here – she whistles and busts things.'

'It's *the* Leewit,' the Leewit said, frowning.

'Oh, I see,' said the captain. 'Like *the* captain, eh?'

'That's right,' said the Leewit. She smiled.

'And what does little Goth do?' The captain addressed the third witch.

Little Goth appeared pained. Maleen answered for her.

'Goth teleports mostly,' she said.

'Oh, she does?' said the captain. 'I've heard about that trick, too,' he added lamely.

'Just small stuff really!' Goth said abruptly. She reached into the top of her jacket and pulled out a cloth-wrapped bundle the size of the captain's two fists. The four ends of the cloth were knotted together. Goth undid the knot. 'Like this,' she said, and poured out the contents on the rug between them. There was a sound like a big bagful of marbles being spilled.

'Great Patham!' the captain swore, staring down at what was a cool quarter million in jewel stones, or he was still a miffel farmer.

'Good gosh,' said the Leewit, bouncing to her feet. 'Maleen, we better get at it right away!'

The two blondes darted from the room. The captain hardly noticed their going. He was staring at Goth.

'Child,' he said, 'don't you realize they hang you without trial on places like Porlumma, if you're caught with stolen goods?'

'We're not on Porlumma,' said Goth. She looked slightly annoyed. 'They're for you. You spent money on us, didn't you?'

'Not that kind of money,' said the captain. 'If Wansing noticed— They're Wansing's, I suppose?'

'Sure!' said Goth. 'Pulled them in just before the takeoff!'

'If he reported, there'll be police ships on our tail any—'

'Goth!' Maleen shrilled.

Goth's head came around and she rolled up on her feet in one motion. 'Coming,' she shouted. 'Excuse me,' she murmured to the captain. Then she, too, was out of the room.

But again, the captain scarcely noticed her departure. He had rushed to the control desk with a sudden awful certainty and switched on all screens.

There they were! Two sleek, black ships coming up fast from behind, and already almost in gun range! They weren't regular police boats, the captain recognized, but auxiliary craft of the Empire's frontier fleets. He rammed the *Venture*'s drives full on. Immediately, red and black fire blossoms began to sprout in space behind him. Then a finger of flame stabbed briefly past, not a hundred yards to the right of the ship.

But the communicator stayed dead. Porlumma preferred risking the sacrifice of Wansing's jewels to giving them a chance to surrender! To do the captain justice, his horror was due much more to the fate awaiting his three misguided charges than to the fact that he was going to share it.

He was putting the *Venture* through a wildly erratic and, he hoped, aim-destroying series of sideways hops and forward lunges with one hand, and trying to unlimber the turrets of the nova guns with the other, when suddenly—!

No, he decided at once, there was no use trying to understand it. There were just no more Empire ships around. The screens were all blurred and darkened simultaneously; and, for a short while, a darkness went flowing and coiling lazily past the *Venture*. Light jumped out of it at him once, in a cold, ugly glare, and receded again in a twisting, unnatural fashion. The *Venture*'s drives seemed dead.

Then, just as suddenly, the old ship jerked, shivered, roared aggrievedly, and was hurling herself along on her own power again!

But Porlumma's sun was no longer in evidence. Stars gleamed and shifted distantly against the blackness of deep space all about. The patterns seemed familiar, but he wasn't a good enough navigator to be sure.

The captain stood up stiffly, feeling a heavy cloud. And at that moment, with a wild, hilarious clacking like a metallic hen, the electric butler delivered four breakfasts hot, one after the other, right onto the centre of the control room floor.

The first voice said distinctly, 'Shall we just leave it on?'

A second voice, considerably more muffled, replied, 'Yes, let's! You never know when you need it—'

The third voice, tucked somewhere in between them, said simply, '*Whew!*'

Peering about the dark room in bewilderment, the captain realized suddenly that the voices had come from the speaker of an intership communicator, leading to what had once been the *Venture*'s captain's cabin.

He listened; but only a dim murmuring came from it now, and then nothing at all. He started toward the hall, then returned and softly switched off the communicator. He went quietly down the hall until he came to the captain's cabin. Its door was closed.

He listened a moment, and opened it suddenly.

There was a trio of squeals: 'Oh, don't! You spoiled it!'

The captain stood motionless. Just one glimpse had been given him of what seemed to be a bundle of twisted black wires arranged loosely like the frame of a truncated cone on – or was it just above? – a table in the centre of the cabin. Where the tip of the cone should have been burned a round, swirling, orange fire. About it, their faces reflecting its glow, stood the three witches.

Then the fire vanished; the wires collapsed. There was only ordinary light in the room. They were looking up at him variously – Maleen with smiling regret, the Leewit in frank annoyance, Goth with no expression at all.

'What out of Great Patham's Seventh Hell was that?' inquired the captain, his hair bristling slowly.

The Leewit looked at Goth; Goth looked at Maleen. Maleen said doubtfully, 'We can just tell you its name—'

'That was the Sheewash Drive,' said Goth.

'The what drive?' asked the captain.

'Sheewash,' repeated Maleen.

'The one you have to do it with yourself,' the Leewit said helpfully.

'Shut up,' said Maleen.

There was a long pause. The captain looked down at the handful of thin, black, twelve-inch wires scattered about the table top. He touched one of them. It was dead cold.

'I see,' he said. 'I guess we're all going to have a long talk.' Another pause. 'Where are we now?'

'About three light-years down the way you were going,' said Goth. 'We only worked it thirty seconds.'

'Twenty-eight!' corrected Maleen, with the authority of her years. 'The Leewit was getting tired.'

'I see,' said Captain Pausert carefully. 'Well, let's go have some breakfast.'

III

They ate with a silent voraciousness – dainty Maleen, the exquisite Leewit, supple Goth, all alike. The captain, long finished, watched them with amazement and – now at last – with something like awe.

'It's the Sheewash Drive,' explained Maleen finally, catching his expression.

'Takes it out of you!' said Goth.

The Leewit grunted affirmatively and stuffed on.

'Can't do too much of it,' said Maleen. 'Or too often. It kills you sure!'

'What,' said the captain, '*is* the Sheewash Drive?'

They became reticent. People did it on Karres, said Maleen, when they had to go somewhere else fast. Everybody knew how there.

'But of course,' she added, 'we're pretty young to do it right!'

'We did it pretty good!' the Leewit contradicted positively. She seemed to be finished at last.

'But how?' said the captain.

Reticence thickened almost visibly. 'If you couldn't do it,' said Maleen, 'you couldn't understand it either.'

He gave it up, for the time being.

'I guess I'll have to take you home next,' he said; and they agreed.

Karres, it developed, was in the Iverdahl System. He couldn't find any planet of that designation listed in his maps of the area, but that meant nothing. The maps were old and often inaccurate, and local names changed a lot.

Barring the use of weird and deadly miracle-drives, that detour was going to cost him almost a month in time – and a good chunk of his profits in power used up. The jewels Goth had illegally teleported must, of course, be returned to their owner, he explained. He'd intended to look severely at the culprit at that point; but she'd meant well, after all! They were extremely peculiar children, but still children – they couldn't really understand.

He would stop off en route to Karres at an Empire planet with banking facilities to take care of that matter, the captain added. A planet far enough off so the police wouldn't be likely to take any particular interest in the *Venture*.

A dead silence greeted this schedule. It appeared that the representatives of Karres did not think much of his logic.

'Well,' Maleen sighed at last, 'we'll see you get your money back some other way then!'

The junior witches nodded coldly.

'How did you three happen to get into this fix?' the captain inquired, with the intention of changing the subject.

They'd left Karres together on a jaunt of their own, they explained. No, they hadn't run away; he got the impression that such trips were standard procedure for juveniles in that place. They were on another planet, a civilized one but beyond the borders and law of the Empire, when the town they were in was raided by a small fleet of slavers. They were taken along with most of the local youngsters.

'It's a wonder,' he said reflectively, 'you didn't take over the ship.'

'Oh, brother!' exclaimed the Leewit.

'Not that ship!' said Goth.

'That was an Imperial slaver!' Maleen informed him. 'You behave yourself every second on those crates.'

Just the same, the captain thought as he settled himself to rest in the control room on a couch he had set up there, it was no longer surprising that the Empire wanted no young slaves from Karres to be transported into the interior! Oddest sort of children— But he ought to be able to get his expenses paid by their relatives. Something very profitable might even be made of this deal—

Have to watch the record entries though! Nikkeldepain's laws were explicit about the penalties invoked by anything resembling the purchase and sale of slaves.

He'd thoughtfully left the intership communicator adjusted so he could listen in on their conversation in the captain's cabin. However, there had been nothing for some time beyond frequent bursts of childish giggling. Then came a succession of piercing shrieks from the Leewit. It appeared she was being forcibly washed behind the ears by Maleen and obliged to brush her teeth, in preparation for bedtime.

It had been agreed that he was not to enter the cabin, because – for reasons not given – they couldn't keep the Sheewash Drive on in his presence; and they wanted to have it ready, in case of an emergency. Piracy was rife beyond the Imperial borders, and the *Venture* would keep beyond the border for a good part of the trip, to avoid the more pressing danger of police pursuit instigated by Porlumma. The captain had explained the potentialities of the nova guns the *Venture* boasted, or tried to. Possibly, they hadn't understood. At any rate, they seemed unimpressed.

The Sheewash Drive! Boy, he thought in sudden excitement, if he could just get the principles of that. Maybe he would!

He raised his head suddenly. The Leewit's voice had lifted clearly over the communicator: '. . . not such a bad old dope!' the childish treble remarked.

The captain blinked indignantly.

'He's not so old,' Maleen's soft voice returned. 'And he's certainly no dope!'

He smiled. Good kid, Maleen.

'Yeah, yeah!' squeaked the Leewit offensively. 'Maleen's sweet onthu-ulp!'

A vague commotion continued for a while, indicating, he hoped, that someone he could mention was being smothered under a pillow.

He drifted off to sleep before it was settled.

If you didn't happen to be thinking of what they'd done, they seemed more or less like normal children. Right from the start, they displayed a flattering interest in the captain and his background; and he told them all about everything and everybody in Nikkeldepain. Finally, he even showed them his treasured pocket-sized picture of Illyla – the one with which he'd held many cosy conversations during the earlier part of his trip.

Almost at once, though, he realized that was a mistake. They studied it intently in silence, their heads crowded close together.

'Oh, brother!' the Leewit whispered then, with entirely the wrong kind of inflection.

'Just what did you mean by that?' the captain inquired coldly.

'Sweet!' murmured Goth. But it was the way she closed her eyes briefly, as though gripped by a light spasm of nausea.

'Shut up, Goth!' Maleen said sharply. 'I think she's very sweet— I mean, she looks very nice!' she told the captain.

The captain was disgruntled. Silently, he retrieved the maligned Illyla and returned her to his breast pocket. Silently, he went off and left them standing there.

But afterwards, in private, he took it out again and studied it worriedly. His Illyla! He shifted the picture back and forth under the light. It wasn't really a very good picture of her, he decided. It had been bungled! From certain angles, one might even say that Illyla did look the least bit insipid.

What was he thinking, he thought, shocked.

He unlimbered the nova gun turrets next and got in a little firing practice. They had been sealed when he took over the *Venture* and weren't supposed to be used, except in absolute emergencies. They were somewhat uncertain weapons, though very effective, and Nikkeldepain had turned to safer forms of armament many decades ago. But on the third day out from Nikkeldepain, the captain made a brief notation in his log: 'Attacked by two pirate craft. Unsealed nova guns. Destroyed one attacker; survivor fled—'

He was rather pleased by that crisp, hard-bitten description of desperate space adventure, and enjoyed rereading it occasionally. It wasn't true, though. He had put in an interesting four hours at the time pursuing and annihilating large, craggy chunks of substance of a meteorite cloud he found the *Venture* ploughing through. Those nova guns were fascinating stuff! You'd sight the turrets on something; and so long as it didn't move after that, it was all right. If it did move, it got it – unless you relented and deflected the turrets first. They were just the thing for arresting a pirate in midspace.

*   *   *

239

The *Venture* dipped back into the Empire's borders four days later and headed for the capital of the local province. Police ships challenged them twice on the way in; and the captain found considerable comfort in the awareness that his passengers foregathered silently in their cabin on these occasions. They didn't tell him they were set to use the Sheewash Drive – somehow it had never been mentioned since that first day – but he knew the queer orange fire was circling over its skimpy framework of twisted wires there and ready to act.

However, the space police waved him on, satisfied with routine identification. Apparently, the *Venture* had not become generally known as a criminal ship, to date.

Maleen accompanied him to the banking institution that was to return Wansing's property to Porlumma. Her sisters, at the captain's definite request, remained on the ship.

The transaction itself went off without a visible hitch. The jewels would reach their destination in Porlumma within a month. But he had to take out a staggering sum in insurance. 'Piracy, thieves!' smiled the clerk. 'Even summary capital punishment won't keep the rats down.' And, of course, he had to register name, ship, home planet, and so on. But since they already had all that information in Porlumma, he gave it without hesitation.

On the way back to the spaceport, he sent off a sealed message by radio relay to the bereaved jeweller, informing him of the action taken, and regretting the misunderstanding.

He felt a little better after that, though the insurance payment had been a severe blow! If he didn't manage to work out a decent profit on Karres somehow, the losses on the miffel farm would hardly be covered now.

Then he noticed that Maleen was getting uneasy.

'We'd better hurry!' was all she would say, however. Her face grew pale.

The captain understood. She was having another premonition! The hitch to this premoting business was, apparently, that when something was brewing, you were informed of the bare fact but had to guess at most of the details. They grabbed an aircab and raced back to the spaceport.

They had just been cleared there when he spotted a small group of uniformed men coming along the dock on the double. They stopped short and then scattered, as the *Venture* lurched drunkenly sideways into the air. Everyone else in sight was scattering, too.

That was a very bad takeoff – one of the captain's worst! Once afloat, however, he ran the ship promptly into the nightside of the planet and turned her nose toward the border. The old pirate chaser had plenty of speed when you gave her the reins; and throughout the entire next sleep period, he let her use it all.

The Sheewash Drive was not required that time.

Next day, he had a lengthy private talk with Goth on the golden rule and the law, with particular reference to individual property rights. If Councillor Onswud had been monitoring the sentiments expressed by the captain, he could not have failed to rumble surprised approval. The delinquent herself listened impassively; but the captain fancied she showed distinct signs of being rather impressed by his earnestness.

It was two days after that – well beyond the borders again – when they were obliged to make an unscheduled stop at a mining moon. For the captain discovered he had already miscalculated the extent to which the prolonged run on overdrive after leaving the capital was going to deplete the *Venture*'s reserves. They would have to juice up.

A large, extremely handsome Sirian freighter lay beside them at the moon station. It was half a battlecraft really, since it dealt regularly beyond the borders. They had to wait while it was being serviced; and it took a long time. The Sirians turned out to be as unpleasant as their ship was good-looking – a snooty, conceited, hairy lot who talked only their own dialect and pretended to be unfamiliar with Imperial Universum.

The captain found himself getting irked by their bad manners, particularly when he discovered they were laughing over his argument with the service superintendent about the cost of repowering the *Venture*.

'You're out in deep space, Captain!' said the superintendent. 'And you haven't juice enough left even to travel back to the border. You can't expect Imperial prices here!'

'It's not what you charged *them*!' The captain angrily jerked his thumb at the Sirian.

'Regular customers!' the superintendent shrugged. 'You start coming by here every three months like they do, and we can make an arrangement with you, too.'

It was outrageous – it actually put the *Venture* back in the red! But there was no help for it.

Nor did it improve the captain's temper when he muffed the takeoff once more, and then had to watch the Sirian floating into space, as sedately as a swan, a little behind him!

An hour later, as he sat glumly before the controls, debating the chance of recouping his losses before returning to Nikkeldepain, Maleen and the Leewit hurriedly entered the room. They did something to a port screen.

'They sure are!' the Leewit exclaimed. She seemed childishly pleased.

'Are what?' the captain inquired absently.

'Following us,' said Maleen. She did not sound pleased. 'It's that Sirian ship, Captain Pausert—'

The captain stared bewilderedly at the screen. There *was* a ship in focus there. It was quite obviously the Sirian and, just as obviously, it was following them.

'What do they want?' he wondered. 'They're stinkers but they're not pirates. Even if they were, they wouldn't spend an hour running after a crate like the *Venture*!'

Maleen said nothing. The Leewit observed, 'Oh, brother! Got their bow turrets out now – better get those nova guns ready!'

'But it's all nonsense!' the captain said, flushing angrily. He turned suddenly toward the communicators. 'What's that Empire general beam-length?'

'Point zero zero four,' said Maleen.

A roaring, abusive voice flooded the control room im-

mediately. The one word understandable to the captain was
'*Venture*'. It was repeated frequently, sometimes as if it
were a question.

'Sirian!' said the captain. 'Can you understand them?' he
asked Maleen.

She shook her head. 'The Leewit can.'

The Leewit nodded, her grey eyes glistening.

'What are they saying?'

'They says you're for stopping,' the Leewit translated
rapidly, but apparently retaining much of the original
sentence structure. 'They says you're for skinning alive . . .
ha! They says you're for stopping right now and for only
hanging. They says—'

Maleen scuttled from the control room. The Leewit
banged the communicator with one small fist.

'Beak-Wock!' she shrieked. It sounded like that, anyway.
The loud voice paused a moment.

'Beak-Wock?' it returned in an aggrieved, demanding
roar.

'Beak-Wock!' the Leewit affirmed with apparent delight.
She rattled off a string of similar-sounding syllables. She
paused.

A howl of inarticulate wrath responded.

The captain, in a whirl of outraged emotions, was yelling
at the Leewit to shut up, at the Sirian to go to Great
Patham's Second Hell – the worst – and wrestling with the
nova gun adjustors at the same time. He'd had about
enough! He'd—

SSS-whoosh!

It was the Sheewash Drive.

'And where are we now?' the captain inquired, in a voice of
unnatural calm.

'Same place, just about,' said the Leewit. 'Ship's still on
the screen. Way back though – take them an hour again to
catch up.' She seemed disappointed; then brightened. 'You
got lots of time to get the guns ready!'

The captain didn't answer. He was marching down the
hall toward the rear of the *Venture*. He passed the captain's

cabin and noted the door was shut. He went on without pausing. He was mad clean through. He knew what had happened!

After all he'd told her, Goth had teleported again.

It was all there, in the storage. Items of half a pound in weight seemed to be as much as she could handle. But amazing quantities of stuff had met that one requirement – bottles filled with what might be perfume or liquor or dope, expensive-looking garments and clothes in a shining variety of colours, small boxes, odds, ends and, of course, jewellery!

He spent half an hour getting it loaded into a steel space crate. He wheeled the crate into the rear lock, sealed the inside lock and pulled the switch that activated the automatic launching device.

The outside lock clicked shut. He stalked back to the control room. The Leewit was still in charge, fiddling with the communicators.

'I could try a whistle over them,' she suggested, glancing up. She added, 'But they'd bust somewheres, sure.'

'Get them on again!' the captain said.

'Yes, sir,' said the Leewit surprised.

The roaring voice came back faintly.

'SHUT UP!' the captain shouted in Imperial Universum. The voice shut up.

'Tell them they can pick up their stuff – it's been dumped out in a crate!' the captain told the Leewit. 'Tell them I'm proceeding on my course. Tell them if they follow me one light-minute beyond that crate, I'll come back for them, shoot their front end off, shoot their rear end off, and ram 'em in the middle.'

'Yes, SIR!' The Leewit sparkled. They proceeded on their course.

Nobody followed.

'Now I want to speak to Goth,' the captain announced. He was still at a high boil. 'Privately,' he added. 'Back in the storage—'

Goth followed him expressionlessly into the storage. He closed the door to the hall. He'd broken off a two-foot length from the tip of one of Councillor Rapport's over-priced tinklewood fishing poles. It made a fair switch.

But Goth looked terribly small just now! He cleared his throat. He wished for a moment he were back on Nikkel-depain.

'I warned you,' he said.

Goth didn't move. Between one second and the next, however, she seemed to grow remarkably. Her brown eyes focused on the captain's Adam's apple; her lip lifted at one side. A slightly hungry look came into her face.

'Wouldn't try that!' she murmured.

Mad again, the captain reached out quickly and got a handful of leathery cloth. There was a blur of motion, and what felt like a small explosion against his left kneecap. He grunted with anguished surprise and fell back on a bale of Councillor Rapport's all-weather cloaks. But he had retained his grip. Goth fell half on top of him, and that was still a favourable position. Then her head snaked around, her neck seemed to extend itself, and her teeth snapped his wrist.

Weasels don't let go—

'Didn't think he'd have the nerve!' Goth's voice came over the communicator. There was a note of grudging admiration in it. It seemed that she was inspecting her bruises.

All tangled up in the job of bandaging his freely bleeding wrist, the captain hoped she'd find a good plenty to count. His knee felt the size of a sofa pillow and throbbed like a piston engine.

'The captain is a brave man,' Maleen was saying reproachfully. 'You should have known better—'

'He's not very *smart*, though!' the Leewit remarked suggestively.

There was a short silence.

'Is he? Goth? Eh?' the Leewit urged.

'Perhaps not very,' said Goth.

'You two lay off him!' Maleen ordered. 'Unless,' she added meaningly, 'you want to *swim* back to Karres – on the Egger Route!'

'Not me,' the Leewit said briefly.

'You could still do it, I guess,' said Goth. She seemed to be reflecting. 'All right – we'll lay off him. It was a fair fight, anyway.'

IV

They raised Karres the sixteenth day after leaving Porlumma. There had been no more incidents; but then, neither had there been any more stops or other contacts with the defenseless Empire. Maleen had cooked up a poultice which did wonders for his knee. With the end of the trip in sight, all tensions had relaxed; and Maleen, at least, seemed to grow hourly more regretful at the prospect of parting.

After a brief study, Karres could be distinguished easily enough by the fact that it moved counterclockwise to all the other planets of the Iverdahl System.

Well, it would, the captain thought.

They came soaring into its atmosphere on the dayside without arousing any visible interest. No communicator signals reached them; and no other ships showed up to look them over. Karres, in fact, had all the appearance of a completely uninhabited world. There were a large number of seas, too big to be called lakes and too small to be oceans, scattered over its surface. There was one enormously towering ridge of mountains that ran from pole to pole, and any number of lesser chains. There were two good-sized ice caps; and the southern section of the planet was speckled with intermittent stretches of snow. Almost all of it seemed to be dense forest.

It was a handsome place, in a wild, sombre way.

They went gliding over it, from noon through morning and into the dawn fringe – the captain at the controls, Goth and the Leewit flanking him at the screens, and Maleen behind him to do the directing. After a few initial squeals, the Leewit became oddly silent. Suddenly the captain realized she was blubbering.

Somehow, it startled him to discover that her home-

246

coming had affected the Leewit to that extent. He felt Goth reach out behind him and put her hand on the Leewit's shoulder. The smallest witch sniffled happily.

' 'S beautiful!' she growled.

He felt a resurge of the wondering, protective friendliness they had aroused in him at first. They must have been having a rough time of it, at that. He sighed; it seemed a pity they hadn't got along a little better!

'Where's everyone hiding?' he inquired, to break up the mood. So far, there hadn't been a sign of human habitation.

'There aren't many people on Karres,' Maleen said from behind his shoulder. 'But we're going to The Town – you'll meet about half of them there!'

'What's that place down there?' the captain asked with sudden interest. Something like an enormous lime-white bowl seemed to have been set flush into the floor of the wide valley up which they were moving.

'That's the Theatre where – *ouch*!' the Leewit said. She fell silent then but turned to give Maleen a resentful look.

'Something strangers shouldn't be told about, eh?' the captain said tolerantly. Goth glanced at him from the side.

'We've got rules,' she said.

He let the ship down a little as they passed over 'the Theatre where—' It was a sort of large, circular arena, with numerous steep tiers of seats running up around it. But all was bare and deserted now.

On Maleen's direction, they took the next valley fork to the right and dropped lower still. He had his first look at Karres animal life then. A flock of large, creamy-white birds, remarkably terrestrial in appearance, flapped by just below them, apparently unconcerned about the ship. The forest underneath had opened out into a long stretch of lush meadowland, with small creeks winding down into its centre. Here a herd of several hundred head of beasts was grazing – beasts of mastodonic size and build, with hairless, shiny black hides. The mouths of their long, heavy heads were twisted up into sardonic, crocodilian grins as they blinked up at the passing *Venture.*

'Black Bollems,' said Goth, apparently enjoying the

247

captain's expression. 'Lots of them around; they're tame. But the grey mountain ones are good hunting.'

'Good eating, too!' the Leewit said. She licked her lips daintily. 'Breakfast—!' she sighed, her thoughts diverted to a familiar track. 'And we ought to be just in time!'

'There's the field!' Maleen cried, pointing. 'Set her down there, Captain!'

The 'field' was simply a flat meadow of close-trimmed grass running smack against the mountainside to their left. One small vehicle, bright blue in colour, was parked on it; and it was bordered on two sides by very tall, blue-black trees.

That was all.

The captain shook his head. Then he set her down.

The town of Karres was a surprise to him in a good many ways. For one thing, there was much more of it than you would have thought possible after flying over the area. It stretched for miles through the forest, up the flanks of the mountain and across the valley – little clusters of houses or individual ones, each group screened from all the rest and from the sky overhead by the trees.

They liked colour on Karres; but then they hid it away! The houses were bright as flowers, red and white, apple green, golden brown – all spick and span, scrubbed and polished and aired with that brisk, green forest smell. At various times of the day, there was also the smell of remarkably good things to eat. There were brooks and pools and a great number of shaded vegetable gardens to the town. There were risky-looking treetop playgrounds, and treetop platforms and galleries which seemed to have no particular purpose. On the ground was mainly an enormously confusing maze of paths – narrow trails of sandy soil snaking about among great brown tree roots and chunks of grey mountain rock, and half covered with fallen needle leaves. The first six times the captain set out unaccompanied, he'd lost his way hopelessly within minutes, and had to be guided back out of the forest.

But the most hidden of all were the people! About four

thousand of them were supposed to live in the town, with as many more scattered about the planet. But you never got to see more than three or four at any one time – except when now and then a pack of children, who seemed to the captain to be uniformly of the Leewit's size, would burst suddenly out of the undergrowth across a path before you, and vanish again.

As for the others, you did hear someone singing occasionally; or there might be a whole muted concert going on all about, on a large variety of wooden musical instruments which they seemed to enjoy tootling with, gently.

But it wasn't a real town at all, the captain thought. They didn't live like people, the Witches of Karres – it was more like a flock of strange forest birds that happened to be nesting in the same general area. Another thing: they appeared to be busy enough – but what was their business?

He discovered he was reluctant to ask Toll too many questions about it. Toll was the mother of his three witches; but only Goth really resembled her. It was difficult to picture Goth becoming smoothly matured and pleasantly rounded; but that was Toll. She had the same murmuring voice, the same air of sideways observation and secret reflection. And she answered all the captain's questions with apparent frankness; but he never seemed to get much real information out of what she said.

It was odd, too! Because he was spending several hours a day in her company, or in one of the next rooms at any rate, while she went about her housework. Toll's daughters had taken him home when they landed; and he was installed in the room that belonged to their father – busy just now, the captain gathered, with some sort of research of a geological nature elsewhere on Karres. The arrangement worried him a little at first, particularly since Toll and he were mostly alone in the house. Maleen was going to some kind of school; she left early in the morning and came back late in the afternoon; and Goth and the Leewit were just plain running wild! They usually got in long after the captain had gone to bed and were off again before he turned out for breakfast.

It hardly seemed like the right way to raise them! One afternoon, he found the Leewit curled up and asleep in the chair he usually occupied on the porch before the house. She slept there for four solid hours, while the captain sat nearby and leafed gradually through a thick book with illuminated pictures called *Histories of Ancient Yarthe*. Now and then he sipped at a cool, green, faintly intoxicating drink Toll had placed quietly beside him some while before, or sucked an aromatic smoke from the enormous pipe with a floor rest, which he understood was a favourite of Toll's husband.

Then the Leewit woke up suddenly, uncoiled, gave him a look between a scowl and a friendly grin, slipped off the porch, and vanished among the trees.

He couldn't quite figure that look! It might have meant nothing at all in particular, but—

The captain laid down his book then and worried a little more. It was true, of course, that nobody seemed in the least concerned about his presence. All of Karres appeared to know about him, and he'd met quite a number of people by now in a casual way. But nobody came around to interview him or so much as dropped in for a visit. However, Toll's husband presumably would be returning presently, and—

How long had he been here, anyway?

Great Patham, the captain thought, shocked. He'd lost count of the days!

Or was it weeks?

He went in to find Toll.

'It's been a wonderful visit,' he said, 'but I'll have to be leaving, I guess. Tomorrow morning, early—'

Toll put some fancy sewing she was working on back in a glass basket, laid her thin, strong witch's hands in her lap, and smiled up at him.

'We thought you'd be thinking that,' she said, 'and so we – You know, Captain, it was quite difficult to find a way to reward you for bringing back the children?'

'It was?' said the captain, suddenly realizing he'd also clean forgotten he was broke! And now the wrath of Onswud lay close ahead.

'Gold and jewel stones would have been just right, of course!' she said, 'but unfortunately, while there's no doubt a lot of it on Karres somewhere, we never got around to looking for it. And we haven't money – none that you could use, that is!'

'No, I don't suppose you do,' the captain agreed sadly.

'However,' said Toll, 'we've all been talking about it in the town, and so we've loaded a lot of things aboard your ship that we think you can sell at a fine profit!'

'Well now,' the captain said gratefully, 'that's fine of—'

'There are furs,' said Toll, 'the very finest furs we could fix up – two thousand of them!'

'Oh!' said the captain, bravely keeping his smile. 'Well, that's wonderful!'

'And essences of perfume!' said Toll. 'Everyone brought one bottle of their own, so that's eight thousand three hundred and twenty-three bottles of perfume essences – all different!'

'Perfume!' said the captain. 'Fine, fine – but you really shouldn't—'

'And the rest of it,' Toll concluded happily, 'is the green Lepti liquor you like so much, and the Wintenberry jellies!' She frowned. 'I forgot just how many jugs and jars,' she admitted, 'but there were a lot. It's all loaded now. And do you think you'll be able to sell all that?' she smiled.

'I certainly can!' the captain said stoutly. 'It's wonderful stuff, and there's nothing like it in the Empire.'

Which was very true. They wouldn't have considered miffel furs for lining on Karres. But if he'd been alone he would have felt like he wanted to burst into tears.

The witches couldn't have picked more completely un-saleable items if they'd tried! Furs, cosmetics, food, and liquor – he'd be shot on sight if he got caught trying to run that kind of merchandise into the Empire. For the same reason that they couldn't use it on Nikkeldepain – they were that scared of contamination by goods that came from uncleared worlds!

He breakfasted alone next morning. Toll had left a note

beside his plate, which explained in a large, not-too-legible script that she had to run off and fetch the Leewit, and that if he was gone before he got back she was wishing him goodbye and good luck.

He smeared two more buns with Wintenberry jelly, drank a large mug of cone-seed coffee, finished every scrap of the omelet of swan hawk eggs, and then, in a state of pleasant repletion, toyed around with his slice of roasted Bollem liver. Boy, what food! He must have put on fifteen pounds since he landed on Karres.

He wondered how Toll kept that sleek figure.

Regretfully, he pushed himself away from the table, pocketed her note for a souvenir, and went out on the porch. There a tear-stained Maleen hurled herself into his arms.

'Oh, Captain!' she sobbed. 'You're leaving—'

'Now, now!' the captain murmured, touched and surprised by the lovely child's grief. He patted her shoulders soothingly. 'I'll be back,' he said rashly.

'Oh, yes, do come back!' cried Maleen. She hesitated and added, 'I become marriageable two years from now. Karres time—'

'Well, well,' said the captain, dazed. 'Well, now—'

He set off down the path a few minutes later, with a strange melody tinkling in his head. Around the first curve, it changed abruptly to a shrill keening which seemed to originate from a spot some two hundred feet before him. Around the next curve, he entered a small, rocky clearing full of pale, misty, early-morning sunlight and what looked like a slow-motion fountain of gleaming rainbow globes. These turned out to be clusters of large, vari-hued soap bubbles which floated up steadily from a wooden tub full of hot water, soap and the Leewit. Toll was bent over the tub; and the Leewit was objecting to a morning bath, with only that minimum of interruptions required to keep her lungs pumped full of a fresh supply of air.

As the captain paused beside the little family group, her red, wrathful face came up over the rim of the tub and looked at him.

'Well, Ugly,' she squealed, in a renewed outburst of rage, 'who you staring at?' Then a sudden determination came into her eyes. She pursed her lips.

Toll upended her promptly and smacked the Leewit's bottom.

'She was going to make some sort of a whistle at you,' she explained hurriedly. 'Perhaps you'd better get out of range while I can keep her head under. And good luck, Captain!'

Karres seemed even more deserted than usual this morning. Of course it was quite early. Great banks of fog lay here and there among the huge dark trees and the small bright houses. A breeze sighed sadly far overhead. Faint, mournful bird cries came from still higher up – it could have been swan hawks reproaching him for the omelet.

Somewhere in the distance somebody tootled on a wood instrument, very gently.

He had gone halfway up the path to the landing field, when something buzzed past him like an enormous wasp and went *clunk*! into the bole of a tree just before him.

It was a long, thin, wicked-looking arrow. On its shaft was a white card; and on the card was printed in red letters:

STOP, MAN OF NIKKELDEPAIN!

The captain stopped and looked around slowly and cautiously. There was no one in sight. What did it mean?

He had a sudden feeling as if all of Karres were rising up silently in one stupendous, cool, foggy trap about him. His skin began to crawl. What was going to happen?

'Ha-ha!' said Goth, suddenly visible on a rock twelve feet to his left and eight feet above him. 'You did stop!'

The captain let his breath out slowly.

'What else did you think I'd do?' he inquired. He felt a little faint.

She slid down from the rock like a lizard and stood before him. 'Wanted to say goodbye!' she told him.

Thin and brown, in jacket, breeches, boots, and cap of grey-green rocklichen colour, Goth looked very much in her element. The brown eyes looked up at him steadily; the mouth smiled faintly; but there was no real expression on her face at all. There was a quiverful of those enormous arrows slung over her shoulder, and some arrow-shooting gadget – not a bow – in her left hand.

She followed his glance.

'Bollem hunting up the mountain,' she explained. 'The wild ones. They're better meat.'

The captain reflected a moment. That's right, he recalled; they kept the tame Bollem herds mostly for milk, butter, and cheese. He'd learned a lot of important things about Karres, all right!

'Well,' he said, 'goodbye, Goth!'

They shook hands gravely. Goth was the real Witch of Karres, he decided – more so than her sisters, more so even than Toll. But he hadn't actually learned a single thing about any of them.

Peculiar people!

He walked on, rather glumly.

'Captain!' Goth called after him. He turned.

'Better watch those takeoffs,' Goth called, 'or you'll kill yourself yet!'

The captain cussed softly all the way up to the *Venture*. And the takeoff was terrible! A few swan hawks were watching but, he hoped, no one else.

V

There wasn't the remotest possibility, of course, of resuming direct trade in the Empire with the cargo they'd loaded for him. But the more he thought about it now, the less likely it seemed that Councillor Onswud was going to let a genuine fortune slip through his hands on a mere technicality of embargoes. Nikkeldepain knew all the tricks of interstellar merchandising; and the councillor himself was undoubtedly the slickest unskinned miffel in the Republic.

More hopefully, the captain began to wonder whether some sort of trade might not be made to develop eventually

254

between Karres and Nikkeldepain. Now and then, he also thought of Maleen growing marriageable two years hence, Karres time. A handful of witch notes went tinkling through his head whenever that idle reflection occurred.

The calendric chronometer informed him he'd spent three weeks there. He couldn't remember how their year compared with the standard one.

He found he was getting remarkably restless on this homeward run; and it struck him for the first time that space travel could also be nothing much more than a large hollow period of boredom. He made a few attempts to resume his sessions of small talk with Illyla, via her picture; but the picture remained aloof.

The ship seemed unnaturally quiet now – that was the trouble! The captain's cabin, particularly, and the hall leading past it had become as dismal as a tomb.

But at long last, Nikkeldepain II swam up on the screen ahead. The captain put the *Venture* 7333 on orbit, and broadcast the ship's identification number. Half an hour later, Landing Control called him. He repeated the identification number, and added the ship's name, his name, owner's name, place of origin, and nature of cargo.

The cargo had to be described in detail.

'Assume Landing Orbit 21,203 on your instruments,' Landing Control instructed him. 'A customs ship will come out to inspect.'

He went on the assigned orbit and gazed moodily from the vision ports at the flat continents and oceans of Nikkeldepain II as they drifted by below. A sense of equally flat depression overcame him unexpectedly. He shook it off and remembered Illyla.

Three hours later, a ship ran up next to him, and he shut off the orbital drive. The communicator began buzzing. He switched it on.

'Vision, please!' said an official-sounding voice. The captain frowned, located the vision stud of the communicator screen, and pushed it down. Four faces appeared in vague outline on the screen, looking at him.

'Illyla!' the captain said.

'At least,' young Councillor Rapport said unpleasantly, 'he's brought back the ship, Father Onswud!'

'Illyla!' said the captain.

Councillor Onswud said nothing. Neither did Illyla. They both seemed to be staring at him, but the screen wasn't good enough to permit the study of expression in detail.

The fourth face, an unfamiliar one above a uniform collar, was the one with the official-sounding voice.

'You are instructed to open the forward lock, Captain Pausert,' it said, 'for an official investigation.'

It wasn't till he was releasing the outer lock to the control room that the captain realized it wasn't customs who had sent a boat out to him, but the police of the Republic.

However, he hesitated for only a moment. Then the outer lock gaped wide.

He tried to explain. They wouldn't listen. They had come on board in contamination-proof repulsor suits, all four of them; and they discussed the captain as if he weren't there. Illyla looked pale and angry and beautiful, and avoided looking at him.

However, he didn't want to speak to her before the others anyway.

They strolled back to the storage and gave the Karres cargo a casual glance.

'Damaged his lifeboat, too!' Councillor Rapport remarked.

They brushed past him down the narrow hallway and went back to the control room. The policeman asked to see the log and commercial records. The captain produced them.

The three men studied them briefly. Illyla gazed stonily out at Nikkeldepain II.

'Not too carefully kept!' the policeman pointed out.

'Surprising he bothered to keep them at all!' said Councillor Rapport.

'But it's all clear enough!' said Councillor Onswud.

They straightened up then and faced him in a line. Councillor Onswud folded his arms and projected his craggy chin. Councillor Rapport stood at ease, smiling faintly. The policeman became officially rigid.

Illyla remained off to one side, looking at the three.

'Captain Pausert,' the policeman said, 'the following charges – substantiated in part by this preliminary investigation – are made against you—'

'Charges?' said the captain.

'Silence, please!' rumbled Councillor Onswud.

'First: material theft of a quarter-million value of maels of jewels and jewelled items from a citizen of the Imperial Planet of Porlumma—'

'They were returned!' the captain protested.

'Restitution, particularly when inspired by fear of retribution, does not affect the validity of the original charge,' Councillor Rapport quoted, gazing at the ceiling.

'Second,' continued the policeman. 'Purchase of human slaves, permitted under Imperial law but prohibited by penalty of ten years to lifetime penal servitude by the laws of the Republic of Nikkeldepain—'

'I was just taking them back where they belonged!' said the captain.

'We shall get to that point presently,' the policeman replied. 'Third, material theft of sundry items in the value of one hundred and eighty thousand maels from a ship of the Imperial Planet of Lepper, accompanied by threats of violence to the ship's personnel—'

'I might add in explanation of the significance of this particular charge,' added Councillor Rapport, looking at the floor, 'that the Regency of Sirius, containing Lepper, is allied to the Republic of Nikkeldepain by commercial and military treaties of considerable value. The Regency has taken the trouble to point out that such hostile conduct by a citizen of the Republic against citizens of the Regency is likely to have an adverse effect on the duration of the treaties. The charge thereby becomes compounded by the additional charge of a treasonable act against the Republic.'

He glanced at the captain. 'I believe we can forestall the accused's plea that these pilfered goods also were restored. They were, in the face of superior force!'

'Fourth,' the policeman went on patiently, 'depraved and licentious conduct while acting as commercial agent, to the detriment of your employer's business and reputation—'

'WHAT?' choked the captain.

'—involving three of the notorious Witches of the Prohibited Planet of Karres—'

'Just like his great-uncle Threbus!' nodded Councillor Onswud gloomily. 'It's in the blood, I always say!'

'—and a justifiable suspicion of a prolonged stay on said Prohibited Planet of Karres—'

'I never heard of that place before this trip!' shouted the captain.

'Why don't you read your Instructions and Regulations then?' shouted Councillor Rapport. 'It's all there!'

'Silence, please!' shouted Councillor Onswud.

'Fifth,' said the policeman quietly, 'general wilful and negligent actions resulting in material damage and loss to your employer to the value of eighty-two thousand maels.'

'I've still got fifty-five thousand. And the stuff in the storage,' the captain said, also quietly, 'is worth half a million, at least!'

'Contraband and hence legally valueless!' the policeman said. Councillor Onswud cleared his throat.

'It will be impounded, of course,' he said. 'Should a method of resale present itself, the profits, if any, will be applied to the cancellation of your just debts. To some extent, that might reduce your sentence.' He paused. 'There is another matter—'

'The sixth charge,' the policeman said, 'is the development *and* public demonstration of a new type of space drive, which should have been brought promptly and secretly to the attention of the Republic of Nikkeldepain!'

They all stared at him – alertly and quite greedily.

So *that* was it – the Sheewash Drive!

'Your sentence may be greatly reduced, Pausert,' Councillor Onswud said wheedlingly, 'if you decide to be reasonable now. What have you discovered?'

'Look out, Father!' Illyla said sharply.

'Pausert,' Councillor Onswud inquired in a fading voice, 'what is that in your hand?'

'A Blythe gun,' the captain said, boiling.

There was a frozen stillness for an instant. Then the policeman's right hand made a convulsive movement.

'Uh-uh!' said the captain warningly.

Councillor Rapport started a slow step backwards.

'Stay where you are!' said the captain.

'Pausert!' Councillor Onswud and Illyla cried out together.

'Shut up!' said the captain.

There was another stillness.

'If you'd looked,' the captain said, in an almost normal voice, 'you'd have seen I've got the nova gun turrets out. They're fixed on that boat of yours. The boat's lying still and keeping its little yap shut. You do the same—'

He pointed a finger at the policeman. 'You got a repulsor suit on,' he said. 'Open the inner port lock and go squirt yourself back to your boat!'

The inner port lock groaned open. Warm air left the ship in a long, lazy wave, scattering the sheets of the *Venture*'s log and commercial records over the floor. The thin, cold upper atmosphere of Nikkeldepain II came eddying in.

'You next, Onswud!' the captain said.

And a moment later: 'Rapport, you just turn around—'

Young Councillor Rapport went through the port at a higher velocity than could be attributed reasonably to his repulsor units. The captain winced and rubbed his foot. But it had been worth it.

'Pausert,' said Illyla in justifiable apprehension, 'you are stark, staring mad!'

'Not at all, my dear,' the captain said cheerfully. 'You and I are now going to take off and embark on a life of crime together.'

'But, Pausert—'

'You'll get used to it,' the captain assured her, 'just like I did. It's got Nikkeldepain beat every which way.'

'Pausert,' Illyla said, whitefaced, 'we told them to bring up revolt ships!'

'We'll blow them out through the stratosphere,' the captain said belligerently, reaching for the port-control switch. He added, 'But they won't shoot anyway while I've got you on board!'

Illyla shook her head. 'You just don't understand,' she said desperately. 'You can't make me stay!'

'Why not?' asked the captain.

'Pausert,' said Illyla, 'I am Madame Councillor Rapport.'

'Oh!' said the captain. There was a silence. He added, crestfallen, 'Since when?'

'Five months ago, yesterday,' said Illyla.

'Great Patham!' cried the captain, with some indignation. 'I'd hardly got off Nikkeldepain then! We were engaged!'

'Secretly ... and I guess,' said Illyla, with a return of spirit, 'that I had a right to change my mind!'

There was another silence.

'Guess you had, at that,' the captain agreed. 'All right – the port's still open, and your husband's waiting in the boat. Beat it!'

He was alone. He let the ports slam shut and banged down the oxygen release switch. The air had become a little thin.

He cussed.

The communicator began rattling for attention. He turned it on.

'Pausert!' Councillor Onswud was calling in a friendly but shaking voice. 'May we not depart, Pausert? Your nova guns are still fixed on this boat!'

'Oh, that—' said the captain. He deflected the turrets a trifle. 'They won't go off now. Scram!'

The police boat vanished.

There was other company coming, though. Far below him but climbing steadily, a trio of revolt ships darted past on the screen, swung around and came back for the next turn of their spiral. They'd have to get a good deal closer before they started shooting; but they'd try to stay under him so as not to knock any stray chunks out of Nikkeldepain.

He sat a moment, reflecting. The revolt ships went by once more. The captain punched in the *Venture*'s secondary drives, turned her nose toward the planet and let her go. There were some scattered white puffs around as he cut through the revolt ships' plane of flight. Then he was below them, and the *Venture* groaned as he took her out of the dive.

The revolt ships were already scattering and nosing over for a counter-manoeuvre. He picked the nearest one and swung the nova guns towards it.

'—and ram them in the middle!' he muttered between his teeth.

SSS-whoosh!

It was the Sheewash Drive – but, like a nightmare now, it kept on and on!

VI

'Maleen!' the captain bawled, pounding at the locked door of the captain's cabin. 'Maleen – shut it off! Cut it off! You'll kill yourself. Maleen!'

The *Venture* quivered suddenly throughout her length, then shuddered more violently, jumped and coughed, and commenced sailing along on her secondary drives again. He wondered how many light-years from everything they were by now. It didn't matter!

'Maleen!' he yelled. 'Are you all right?'

There was a faint *thump-thump* inside the cabin, and silence. He lost almost a minute finding the right cutting tool in the storage. A few seconds later, a section of door panel sagged inwards; he caught it by one edge and came tumbling into the cabin with it.

He had the briefest glimpse of a ball of orange-coloured fire swirling uncertainly over a cone of oddly bent wires. Then the fire vanished, and the wires collapsed with a loose rattling to the table top.

The crumpled small shape lay behind the table, which was why he didn't discover it at once. He sagged to the floor beside it, all the strength running out of his knees.

Brown eyes opened and blinked at him blearily.

'Sure takes it out of you!' Goth grunted. 'Am I hungry!'

'I'll whale the holy, howling tar out of you again,' the captain roared, 'if you ever—'

'Quit your bawling!' snarled Goth. 'I got to eat.'

She ate for fifteen minutes straight, before she sank back in her chair and sighed.

'Have some more Wintenberry jelly,' the captain offered anxiously. She looked pretty pale.

Goth shook her head. 'Couldn't – and that's about the first thing you've said since you fell through the door, howling for Maleen. Ha-ha! Maleen's *got* a boyfriend!'

'Button your lip, child,' the captain said. 'I was thinking.' He added, after a moment, 'Has she really?'

'Picked him out last year,' Goth nodded. 'Nice boy from town – they get married as soon as she's marriageable. She just told you to come back because she was upset about you. Maleen had a premonition you were headed for awful trouble!'

'She was quite right, little chum,' the captain said nastily.

'What were you thinking about?' Goth inquired.

'I was thinking,' said the captain, 'that as soon as we're sure you're going to be all right, I'm taking you straight back to Karres!'

'I'll be all right now,' Goth said. 'Except, likely, for a stomach-ache. But you can't take me back to Karres.'

'Who will stop me, may I ask?' the captain asked.

'Karres is gone,' Goth said.

'Gone?' the captain repeated blankly, with a sensation of not quite definable horror bubbling up in him.

'Not blown up or anything,' Goth reassured him. 'They just moved it! The Imperials got their hair up about us again. But this time, they were sending a fleet with the big bombs and stuff, so everybody was called home. But they had to wait then till they found out where we were – me and Maleen and the Leewit. Then you brought us in; and they had to wait again, and decide about you. But right after you'd left – *we'd* left, I mean – they moved it.'

'Where?'

'Great Patham!' Goth shrugged. 'How'd I know? There's lots of places!'

They probably were, the captain admitted silently. A scene came suddenly before his eyes – the lime-white, arena-like bowl in the valley, with the steep tiers of seats around it, just before they'd reached the town of Karres – 'the Theatre where—'

But now there was unnatural night-darkness all over and about that world; and eight thousand-some Witches of Karres sat in circles around the Theatre, their heads bent towards one point in the centre, where orange fire washed hugely about the peak of a cone of curiously twisted girders.

And a world went racing off at the speeds of the Shee-wash Drive! There'd be lots of places, all right. What peculiar people!

'Anyway,' he sighed, 'if I've got to start raising you – don't say, "Great Patham" any more. That's a cuss word!'

'I learned it from you!' Goth pointed out.

'So you did, I guess,' the captain acknowledged. 'I won't say it either. Aren't they going to be worried about you?'

'Not very much,' said Goth. 'We don't get hurt often – especially when we're young. That's when we can do all that stuff like teleporting, and whistling, like the Leewit. We lose it mostly when we get older. They're working on that now so we won't. About all Maleen can do right now is premote!'

'She premotes just dandy, though,' the captain said. 'The Sheewash Drive – they can all do that, can't they?'

'Uh-huh!' Goth nodded. 'But that's learned stuff. That's one of the things they already studied out.' She added, a trace uncomfortably, 'I can't tell you about that till you're one yourself.'

'Till I'm what myself?' the captain asked, becoming puzzled again.

'A witch, like us,' said Goth. 'We got our rules. And that won't be for four years, Karres time.'

'It won't, eh?' said the captain. 'What happens then?'

'That's when I'm marriageable age,' said Goth, frowning at the jar of Wintenberry jelly. She pulled it towards her

263

and inspected it carefully. 'I got it all fixed,' she told the jelly firmly, 'as soon as they started saying they ought to pick out a wife for you on Karres, so you could stay. I said it was me, right away; and everyone else said finally that was all right then – even Maleen, because she had this boy-friend.'

'You mean,' said the captain, stunned, 'this was all planned out on Karres?'

'Sure,' said Goth. She pushed the jelly back where it had been standing, and glanced up at him again. 'For three weeks, that's about all everyone talked about in the town! It set a perceedent—'

She paused doubtfully.

'That would explain it,' the captain admitted.

'Uh-huh,' Goth nodded relieved, settling back in her chair. 'But it was my father who told us how to do it so you'd break up with the people on Nikkeldepain. He said it was in the blood.'

'What was in the blood?' the captain said patiently.

'That you'd break up with them. That's Threbus, my father,' Goth informed him. 'You met him a couple of times in the town. Big man with a blond beard – Maleen and the Leewit take after him.'

'You wouldn't mean my great-uncle Threbus?' the captain inquired. He was in a state of strange calm by now.

'That's right,' said Goth. 'He liked you a lot.'

'It's a small galaxy,' said the captain philosophically. 'So that's where Threbus wound up! I'd like to meet him again some day.'

'We'll start after Karres four years from now, when you learn about those things,' Goth said. 'We'll catch up with them all right. That's still thirteen hundred and seventy-two Old Sidereal days,' she added, 'but there's a lot to do in between. You want to pay the money you owe back to those people, don't you? I got some ideas—'

'None of those teleporting tricks now!' the captain warned.

'Kid stuff!' Goth said scornfully. 'I'm growing up. This'll be fair swapping. But we'll get rich.'

'I wouldn't be surprised,' the captain admitted. He thought a moment. 'Seeing we've turned out to be distant relatives, I suppose it is all right, too, if I adopt you meanwhile—'

'Sure,' said Goth. She stood up.

'Where are you going?' the captain asked.

'Bed,' said Goth. 'I'm tired.' She stopped at the hall door. 'About all I can tell you about us till then,' she said, 'you can read in those Regulations, like the one man said – the one you kicked off the ship. There's a lot about us in there. Lots of lies, too, though!'

'And when did you find out about the communicator between here and the captain's cabin?' the captain inquired.

Goth grinned. 'A while back,' she admitted. 'The others never noticed!'

'All right,' the captain said. 'Good night, Witch. If you get a stomach-ache, yell and I'll bring the medicine.'

'Goodnight.' Goth yawned. 'I will, I think.'

'And wash behind your ears!' the captain added, trying to remember the bedtime instructions he'd overheard Maleen giving the junior witches.

'All right,' said Goth sleepily. The hall door closed behind her – but half a minute later, it was briskly opened again. The captain looked up startled from the voluminous stack of *General Instructions and Space Regulations of the Republic of Nikkeldepain* he'd just discovered in one of the drawers of the control desk. Goth stood in the doorway, scowling and wide awake.

'And you wash behind yours!' she said.

'Huh?' said the captain. He reflected a moment. 'All right,' he said. 'We both will, then.'

'Right,' said Goth, satisfied.

The door closed once more.

The captain began to run his finger down the lengthy index of K's – or would it be under W?

RESURRECTION

A. E. Van Vogt

One of the most interesting recurrent ideas in science fiction is the one we have already seen brilliantly developed in 'Who Goes There?' – the monster, the last of its race, dead but revived, and now ready to destroy again. Here is a story which has its roots in 'Who Goes There?' and also in another Don A. Stuart story, 'Forgetfulness'. Again, aliens come to Earth – but this time the monster is a man.

THE great ship poised a quarter of a mile above one of the cities. Below was a cosmic desolation. As he floated down in his energy bubble, Enash saw that the buildings were crumbling with age.

'No signs of war damage!' The bodiless voice touched his ears momentarily. Enash tuned it out.

On the ground he collapsed his bubble. He found himself in a walled enclosure overgrown with weeds. Several skeletons lay in the tall grass beside the rakish building. They were of long, two-legged, two-armed beings with skulls in each case mounted at the end of a thin spine. The skeletons, all of adults, seemed in excellent preservation, but when he bent down and touched one, a whole section of it crumbled into a fine powder. As he straightened, he saw that Yoal was floating down nearby. Enash waited until the historian had stepped out of his bubble, then he said, 'Do you think we ought to use our method of reviving the long dead?'

Yoal was thoughtful. 'I have been asking questions of the various people who have landed, and there is something wrong here. This planet has no surviving life, not even insect life. We'll have to find out what happened before we risk any colonization.'

Enash said nothing. A soft wind was blowing. It rustled through a clump of trees nearby. He motioned toward the trees. Yoal nodded and said, 'Yes, the plant life has not been harmed, but plants after all are not affected in the same way as the active life forms.'

There was an interruption. A voice spoke from Yoal's receiver: 'A museum has been found at approximately the centre of the city. A red light has been fixed on the roof.'

Enash said, 'I'll go with you, Yoal. There might be skeletons of animals and of the intelligent being in various stages of his evolution. You didn't answer my question. Are you going to revive these things?'

Yoal said slowly, 'I intend to discuss the matter with the council, but I think there is no doubt. We must know the cause of this disaster.' He waved one sucker vaguely to take in half the compass. He added as an afterthought, 'We shall proceed cautiously, of course, beginning with an obviously early development. The absence of the skeletons of children indicates that the race had developed personal immortality.'

The council came to look at the exhibits. It was, Enash knew, a formal preliminary only. The decision was made. There would be revivals. It was more than that. They were curious. Space was vast, the journeys through it long and lonely, landing always a stimulating experience, with its prospect of new life forms to be seen and studied.

The museum looked ordinary. High-domed ceilings, vast rooms. Plastic models of strange beasts, many artifacts – too many to see and comprehend in so short a time. The life span of a race was imprisoned here in a progressive array of relics. Enash looked with the others, and was glad when they came to the line of skeletons and preserved bodies. He seated himself behind the energy screen, and watched the biological experts take a preserved body out of a stone sarcophagus. It was wrapped in windings of cloth, many of them. The experts did not bother to unravel the rotted material. Their forceps reached through, pinched a piece of skull – that was the accepted procedure. Any part of the skeleton could be used, but the most perfect revivals, the most complete reconstructions resulted when a certain section of the skull was used.

Hamar, the chief biologist, explained the choice of body. 'The chemicals used to preserve this mummy show a sketchy knowledge of chemistry. The carvings on the sarcophagus indicate a crude and unmechanical culture. In such a civilization there would not be much development of the potentialities of the nervous system. Our speech experts have been analysing the recorded voice mechanism which is a part of each exhibit, and though many languages are involved – evidence that the ancient language spoken at the time the body was alive has been reproduced – they found no difficulty in translating the meanings. They have now adapted our universal speech machine, so that anyone who wishes to need only speak into his communicator, and so will have his words translated into the language of the revived person. The reverse, naturally, is also true. Ah, I see we are ready for the first body.'

Enash watched intently with the others as the lid was clamped down on the plastic reconstructor, and the growth processes were started. He could feel himself becoming tense. For there was nothing haphazard about what was happening. In a few minutes a full-grown ancient inhabitant of this planet would sit up and stare at them. The science involved was simple and always fully effective.

Out of the shadows of smallness, life grows. The level of beginning and ending, of life and – not life; in that dim region matter oscillates easily between old and new habits. The habit of organic, or the habit of inorganic. Electrons do not have life and un-life values. Atoms form into molecules, there is a step in the process, one tiny step, that is of life – if life begins at all. One step, and then darkness. Or aliveness.

A stone or a living cell. A grain of gold or a blade of grass, the sands of the sea or the equally numerous animalcules inhabiting the endless fishy waters – the difference is there in the twilight zone of matter. Each living cell has in it the whole form. The crab grows a new leg when the old one is torn from its flesh. Both ends of the planarian worm elongate, and soon there are two worms, two identities, two digestive systems each as greedy as the original, each a whole, unwounded, unharmed by its experience. Each cell can be the whole. Each cell remembers in detail so intricate that no totality of words could ever describe the completeness achieved.

But – paradox – memory is not organic. An ordinary wax record remembers sounds. A wire recorder easily gives up a duplicate of the voice that spoke into it years before. Memory is a physiological impression, a mark on matter, a change in the shape of a molecule, so that when a reaction is desired the *shape* emits the same rhythm of response.

Out of the mummy's skull had come the multi-quadrillion memory shapes from which a response was now being evoked. As ever, the memory held true.

A man blinked, and opened his eyes.

'It is true, then,' he said aloud, and the words were translated into the Ganae tongue as he spoke them. 'Death is merely an opening into another life – but where are my attendants?' At the end, his voice took on a complaining tone.

He sat up, and climbed out of the case, which had automatically opened as he came to life. He saw his captors. He froze, but only for a moment. He had a pride and a very special arrogant courage, which served him now. Reluctantly, he sank to his knees and made obeisance, but doubt must have been strong in him. 'Am I in the presence of the gods of Egypt?' He climbed to his feet. 'What nonsense is this? I do not bow to nameless demons.'

Captain Gorsid said, 'Kill him!'

The two-legged monster dissolved, writhing in the beam of a ray gun.

The second revived man stood up, pale, and trembled with fear. 'My God, I swear I won't touch the stuff again. Talk about pink elephants—'

Yoal was curious. 'To what *stuff* do you refer, revived one?'

'The old hooch, the poison in the hip pocket flask, the

juice they gave me at that speak – my lordie!'

Captain Gorsid looked questioningly at Yoal. 'Need we linger?'

Yoal hesitated. 'I am curious.' He addressed the man. 'If I were to tell you that we were visitors from another star, what would be your reaction?'

The man stared at him. He was obviously puzzled, but the fear was stronger. 'Now, look,' he said, 'I was driving along, minding my own business. I admit I'd had a shot or two too many, but it's the liquor they serve these days. I swear I didn't see the other car – and if this is some new idea of punishing people who drink and drive, well, you've won. I won't touch another drop as long as I live, so help me.'

Yoal said, 'He drives a "car" and thinks nothing of it. Yet we saw no cars. They didn't even bother to preserve them in the museums.'

Enash noticed that everyone waited for everyone else to comment. He stirred as he realized the circle of silence would be complete unless he spoke. He said, 'Ask him to describe the car. How does it work?'

'Now, you're talking,' said the man. 'Bring on your line of chalk, and I'll walk it, and ask any questions you please. I may be so tight that I can't see straight, but I can always drive. How does it work? You just put her in gear, and step on the gas.'

'Gas,' said Engineering Officer Veed. 'The interal combustion engine. That places him.'

Captain Gorsid motioned to the guard with the ray gun.

The third man sat up, and looked at them thoughtfully. 'From the stars?' he said finally. 'Have you a system, or was it blind chance?'

The Ganae councillors in that domed room stirred uneasily in their curved chairs. Enash caught Yoal's eye on him. The shock in the historian's eye alarmed the meteorologist. He thought, 'The two-legged one's adjustment to a new situation, his grasp of realities, was unnormally rapid. No Ganae could have equalled the swiftness of the reaction.'

Hamar, the chief biologist, said, 'Speed of thought is not necessarily a sign of superiority. The slow, careful thinker has his place in the hierarchy of intellect.'

But Enash found himself thinking it was not the speed; it was the accuracy of the response. He tried to imagine himself being revived from the dead and understanding instantly the meaning of the presence of aliens from the stars. He couldn't have done it.

He forgot his thought, for the man was out of the case. As Enash watched with the others, he walked briskly over to the window and looked out. One glance, and then he turned back.

'Is it all like this?' he asked.

Once again, the speed of his understanding caused a sensation. It was Yoal who finally replied.

'Yes. Desolation. Death. Ruin. Have you any ideas as to what happened?'

The man came back and stood in front of the energy screen that guarded the Ganae. 'May I look over the museum? I have to estimate what age I am in. We had certain possibilities of destruction when I was last alive, but which one was realized depends on the time elapsed.'

The councillors looked at Captain Gorsid, who hesitated; then, 'Watch him,' he said to the guard with the ray gun. He faced the man. 'We understand your aspirations fully. You would like to seize control of this situation and ensure your own safety. Let me reassure you. Make no fake moves, and all will be well.'

Whether or not the man believed the lie, he gave no sign. Nor did he show by a glance or a movement that he had seen the scarred floor where the ray gun had burned his two predecessors into nothingness. He walked curiously to the nearest doorway, studied the other guard who waited there for him, and then, gingerly, stepped through. The first guard followed him, then came the mobile energy screen, and finally, trailing one another, the councillors.

Enash was the third to pass through the doorway. The room contained skeletons and plastic models of animals. The room beyond that was what, for want of a better term,

Enash called a culture room. It contained the artifacts from a single period of civilization. It looked very advanced. He had examined some of the machines when they first passed through it, and had thought, Atomic energy. He was not alone in his recognition. From behind him, Captain Gorsid said to the man, 'You are forbidden to touch anything. A false move will be the signal for the guards to fire.'

The man stood at ease in the centre of the room. In spite of a curious anxiety, Enash had to admire his calmness. He must have known what his fate would be, but he stood there thoughtfully, and said finally, deliberately, 'I do not need to go any farther. Perhaps you will be able to judge better than I of the time that has elaspsed since I was born and these machines were built. I see over there an instrument which, according to the sign above it, counts atoms when they explode. As soon as the proper number have exploded it shuts off the power automatically, and for just the right length of time to prevent a chain explosion. In my time we had a thousand crude devices for limiting the size of an atomic reaction, but it required two thousand years to develop those devices from the early beginnings of atomic energy. Can you make a comparison?'

The councillors glanced at Veed. The engineering officer hesitated. At last, reluctantly, he said, 'Nine thousand years ago we had a thousand methods of limiting atomic explosions.' He paused, then even more slowly, 'I have never heard of an instrument that counts out atoms for such a purpose.'

'And yet,' murmured Shuri, the astronomer, breathlessly, 'the race was destroyed.'

There was silence. It ended as Gorsid said to the nearest guard, 'Kill the monster!'

But it was the guard who went down, bursting into flame. Not just one guard, but the guards! Simultaneously down, burning with a blue flame. The flame licked at the screen, recoiled, and licked more furiously, recoiled, and burned brighter. Through a haze of fire, Enash saw that the man had retreated to the far door and that the machine that counted atoms was glowing with a blue intensity.

Captain Gorsid shouted into his communicator, 'Guard all exits with ray guns. Spaceships stand by to kill alien with heavy guns.'

Somebody said, 'Mental control. Some kind of mental control. What have we run into?'

They were retreating. The blue flame was at the ceiling, struggling to break through the screen. Enash had a last glimpse of the machine. It must still be counting atoms, for it was a hellish blue. Enash raced with the others to the room where the man had been resurrected. There another energy screen crashed to their rescue. Safe now, they retreated into their separate bubbles and whisked through outer doors and up to the ship. As the great ship soared, an atomic bomb hurtled down from it. The mushroom of flame blotted out the museum and the city below.

'But we still don't know why the race died,' Yoal whispered into Enash's ear, after the thunder had died from the heavens behind them.

The pale yellow sun crept over the horizon on the third morning after the bomb was dropped, the eighth day since the landing. Enash floated with the others down on a new city. He had come to argue against any further revival.

'As a meteorologist,' he said, 'I pronounce this planet safe for Ganae colonization. I cannot see the need for taking any risks. This race has discovered the secrets of its nervous system, and we cannot afford—'

He was interrupted. Hamar, the biologist, said dryly, 'If they knew so much why didn't they migrate to other star systems and save themselves?'

'I will concede,' said Enash, 'that very possibly they had not discovered our system of locating stars with planetary families.' He looked earnestly around the circle of his friends. 'We have agreed that was a unique accidental discovery. We were lucky, not clever.'

He saw by the expressions on their faces that they were mentally refuting his arguments. He felt a helpless sense of imminent catastrophe. For he could see that picture of a great race facing death. It must have come swiftly, but not so swiftly that they didn't know about it. There were too many skeletons in the open, lying in the gardens of magnificent homes, as if each man and his wife had come out to wait for the doom of his kind. He tried to picture it for the council – that last day long, long ago, when a race had calmly met its ending. But his visualization failed somehow, for the others shifted impatiently in the seats that had been set up behind the series of energy screens, and Captain Gorsid said, 'Exactly what aroused this intense emotional reaction in you, Enash?'

The question gave Enash pause. He hadn't thought of it as emotional. He hadn't realized the nature of his obsession, so subtly had it stolen upon him. Abruptly now, he realized.

'It was the third one,' he said slowly. 'I saw him through the haze of energy fire, and he was standing there in the distant doorway watching us curiously, just before we turned to run. His bravery, his calm, the skilful way he had duped us – it all added up.'

'Added up to his death!' said Hamar. And everybody laughed.

'Come now, Enash,' said Vice-captain Mayad good-humouredly, 'you're not going to pretend that this race is braver than our own; or that, with all the precautions we have now taken, we need fear one man?'

Enash was silent, feeling foolish. The discovery that he had had an emotional obsession abashed him. He did not want to appear unreasonable. He made a final protest. 'I merely wish to point out,' he said doggedly, 'that this desire to discover what happened to a dead race does not seem absolutely essential to me.'

Captain Gorsid waved at the biologist. 'Proceed,' he said, 'with the revival.'

To Enash he said, 'Do we dare return to Gana, and recommend mass migrations – and then admit that we did not actually complete our investigations here? It's impossible, my friend.'

It was the old argument, but reluctantly now Enash admitted there was something to be said for that point of view. He forgot that, for the fourth man was stirring.

The man sat up. And vanished.

There was a blank, horrified silence. Then Captain Gorsid said harshly, 'He can't get out of there. We know that. He's in there somewhere.'

All around Enash, the Ganae were out of their chairs, peering into the energy shell. The guards stood with ray guns held limply in their suckers. Out of the corner of his eye, he saw one of the protective screen technicians beckon to Veed, who went over. He came back grim. He said, 'I'm told the needles jumped ten points when he first disappeared. That's on the nucleonic level.'

'By ancient Ganae!' Shuri whispered. 'We've run into what we've always feared.'

Gorsid was shouting into the communicator. 'Destroy all the locators on the ship. Destroy them, do you hear!'

He turned with glaring eyes. 'Shuri,' he bellowed. 'They don't seem to understand. Tell those subordinates of yours to act. All locators and reconstructors must be destroyed.'

'Hurry, hurry!' said Shuri weakly.

When that was done they breathed more easily. There were grim smiles and a tensed satisfaction. 'At least,' said Vice-captain Mayad, 'he cannot now ever discover Gana. Our great system of locating suns with planets remains our secret. There can be no retaliation for—' He stopped, said slowly, 'What am I talking about? We haven't done anything. We're not responsible for the disaster that has befallen the inhabitants of this planet.'

But Enash knew what he had meant. The guilt feelings came to the surface at such moments as this – the ghosts of all the races destroyed by the Ganae, the remorseless will that had been in them, when they first landed, to annihilate whatever was here. The dark abyss of voiceless hate and terror that lay behind them; the days on end when they had mercilessly poured poisonous radiation down upon the unsuspecting inhabitants of peaceful planets – all that had been in Mayad's words.

'I still refuse to believe he has escaped.' That was Captain Gorsid. 'He's in there. He's waiting for us to take down our screens, so he can escape. Well, we won't do it.'

There was silence again as they stared expectantly into the emptiness of the energy shell. The reconstructor rested on metal supports, a glittering affair. But there was nothing else. Not a flicker of unnatural light or shade. The yellow rays of the sun bathed the open spaces with a brilliance that left no room for concealment.

'Guards,' said Gorsid, 'destroy the reconstructor. I thought he might come back to examine it, but we can't take a chance on that.'

It burned with a white fury. And Enash, who had hoped somehow that the deadly energy would force the two-legged thing into the open, felt his hopes sag within him.

'But where can he have gone?' Yoal whispered.

Enash turned to discuss the matter. In the act of swinging around, he saw that the monster was standing under a tree a score of feet to one side, watching them. He must have arrived at *that* moment, for there was a collective gasp from the councillors. Everybody drew back. One of the screen technicians, using great presence of mind, jerked up an energy screen between the Ganae and the monster. The creature came forward slowly. He was slim of build, he held his head well back. His eyes shone as from an inner fire.

He stopped as he came to the screen, reached out and touched it with his fingers. It flared, blurred with changing colours. The colours grew brighter, and extended in an intricate pattern all the way from his head to the ground. The blur cleared. The pattern faded into invisibility. The man was through the screen.

He laughed, a soft curious sound; then sobered. 'When I first awakened,' he said, 'I was curious about the situation. The question was, what should I do with you?'

The words had a fateful ring to Enash on the still morning air of that planet of the dead. A voice broke the silence, a voice so strained and unnatural that a moment passed before he recognized it as belonging to Captain Gorsid.

'*Kill him!*'

When the blasters ceased their effort, the unkillable thing remained standing. He walked slowly forward until he was only a half dozen feet from the nearest Ganae. Enash had a position well to the rear.

The man said slowly, 'Two courses suggest themselves, one based on gratitude for reviving me, the other based on reality. I know you for what you are. Yes, *know* you – and that is unfortunate. It is hard to feel merciful. To begin with,' he went on, 'let us suppose you surrender the secret of the locator. Naturally, now that a system exists, we shall never again be caught as we were.'

Enash had been intent, his mind so alive with the potentialities of the disaster that was here that it seemed impossible that he could think of anything else. And yet, a part of his attention was stirred now. 'What did happen?' he asked.

The man changed colour. The emotions of that far day thickened his voice. 'A nucleonic storm. It swept in from outer space. It brushed this edge of our galaxy. It was about ninety light-years in diameter, beyond the farthest limit of our power. There was no escape from it. We had dispensed with spaceships, and had no time to construct any. Castor, the only star with planets ever discovered by us, was also in the path of the storm.' He stopped. 'The secret?' he said.

Around Enash, the councillors were breathing easier. The fear of race destruction that had come to them was lifting. Enash saw with pride that the first shock was over, and they were not even afraid for themselves.

'Ah,' said Yoal softly, 'you don't know the secret. In spite of all your great development, we alone can conquer the galaxy.' He looked at the others, smiling confidently. 'Gentlemen,' he said, 'our pride in a great Ganae achievement is justified. I suggest we return to our ship. We have no further business on this planet.'

There was a confused moment while their bubbles formed, when Enash wondered if the two-legged one would try to stop their departure. But when he looked back, he saw that the man was walking in a leisurely fashion along a street.

That was the memory Enash carried with him, as the ship began to move. That and the fact that the three

277

atomic bombs they dropped, one after the other, failed to explode.

'We will not,' said Captain Gorsid, 'give up a planet as easily as that. I propose another interview with the creature.'

They were floating down again into the city – Enash and Yoal and Veed and the commander. Captain Gorsid's voice tuned in once more:

'... As I visualize it' – through the mist Enash could see the transparent glint of the other three bubbles around him – 'we jumped to conclusions about this creature, not justified by the evidence. For instance, when he awakened, he vanished. Why? Because he was afraid, of course. He wanted to size up the situation. *He* didn't believe he was omnipotent.'

It was sound logic. Enash found himself taking heart from it. Suddenly, he was astonished that he had become panicky so easily. He began to see the danger in a new light. Only one man alive on a new planet. If they were determined enough, colonists could be moved in as if he did not exist. It had been done before, he recalled. On several planets, small groups of the original populations had survived the destroying radiation and taken refuge in remote areas. In almost every case, the new colonists gradually hunted them down. In two instances, however, that Enash remembered, native races were still holding small sections of their planets. In each case, it had been found impractical to destroy them because it would have endangered the Ganae on the planet. So the survivors were tolerated. One man would not take up very much room.

When they found him, he was busily sweeping out the lower floor of a small bungalow. He put the broom aside and stepped onto the terrace outside. He had put on sandals, and he wore a loose-fitting robe made of very shiny material. He eyed them indolently but he said nothing.

It was Captain Gorsid who made the proposition. Enash had to admire the story he told into the language machine. The commander was very frank. That approach had been decided on. He pointed out that the Ganae could not be expected to revive the dead of this planet. Such altruism would be unnatural, considering that the ever-growing Ganae hordes had a continual need for new worlds. Each vast new population increment was a problem that could be solved by one method only. In this instance, the colonists would gladly respect the rights of the sole survivor of this world.

It was at this point that the man interrupted. 'But what is the purpose of this endless expansion?' He seemed genuinely curious. 'What will happen when you finally occupy every planet in this galaxy?'

Captain Gorsid's puzzled eyes met Yoal's, then flashed to Veed, then Enash. Enash shrugged his torso negatively, and felt pity for the creature. The man didn't understand, possibly never could understand. It was the old story of two different viewpoints, the virile and the decadent, the race that aspired to the stars and that race that declined the call of destiny.

'Why not,' urged the man, 'control the breeding chambers?'

'And have the government overthrown!' said Yoal.

He spoke tolerantly, and Enash saw that the others were smiling at the man's naïveté. He felt the intellectual gulf between them widening. The creature had no comprehension of the natural life forces that were at work. The man spoke again: 'Well, if you don't control them, we will control them for you.'

There was silence.

They began to stiffen. Enash felt it in himself, saw the signs of it in the others. His gaze flicked from face to face, then back to the creature in the doorway. Not for the first time, Enash had the thought that their enemy seemed helpless. 'Why,' he decided, 'I could put my suckers around him and crush him.'

He wondered if mental control of nucleonic, nuclear, and gravitonic energies included the ability to defend oneself from a macrocosmic attack. He had an idea it did. The exhibition of power two hours before might have had limitations, but if so, it was not apparent. Strength or weakness could make no difference. The threat of threats had been made: 'If you don't control – we will.'

The words echoed in Enash's brain, and, as the meaning penetrated deeper, his aloofness faded. He had always regarded himself as a spectator. Even when, earlier, he had argued against the revival, he had been aware of a detached part of himself watching the scene rather than being a part of it. He saw with a sharp clarity that that was why he had finally yielded to the conviction of the others. Going back beyond that to remoter days, he saw that he had never quite considered himself a participant in the seizure of the planets of other races. He was one who looked on, and thought of reality, and speculated on a life that seemed to have no meaning. It was meaningless no longer. He was caught by a tide of irresistible emotion, and swept along. He felt himself sinking, merging with the Ganae mass being. All the strength and all the will of the race surged up in his veins.

He snarled, 'Creature, if you have any hopes of reviving your dead race, abandon them now.'

The man looked at him, but said nothing. Enash rushed on, 'If you could destroy us, you would have done so already. But the truth is that you operate within limitations. Our ship is so built that no conceivable chain reaction could be started in it. For every plate of potential unstable material in it there is a counteracting plate, which prevents the development of a critical pile. You might be able to set off explosions in our engines, but they, too, would be limited, and would merely start the process for which they are intended – confined in their proper space.'

He was aware of Yoal touching his arm. 'Careful,' warned the historian. 'Do not in your just anger give away vital information.'

Enash shook off the restraining sucker. 'Let us not be unrealistic,' he said harshly. 'This thing has divined most of our racial secrets, apparently merely by looking at our bodies. We would be acting childishly if we assumed that he has not already realized the possibilities of the situation.'

280

'*Enash!*' Captain Gorsid's voice was imperative.

As swiftly as it had come, Enash's rage subsided. He stepped back. 'Yes, Commander.'

'I think I know what you intended to say,' said Captain Gorsid. 'I assure you I am in full accord, but I believe also that I, as the top Ganae official, should deliver the ultimatum.'

He turned. His horny body towered above the man. 'You have made the unforgivable threat. You have told us, in effect, that you will attempt to restrict the vaulting Ganae spirit.'

'Not the spirit,' said the man.

The commander ignored the interruption. 'Accordingly, we have no alternative. We are assuming that, given time to locate the materials and develop the tools, you might be able to build a reconstructor. In our opinion it will be at least two years before you can complete it, *even if you know how.* It is an immensely intricate machine, not easily assembled by the lone survivor of a race that gave up its machines millennia before disaster struck.

'You did not have time to build a spaceship. We won't give you time to build a reconstructor.

'Within a few minutes our ship will start dropping bombs. It is possible you will be able to prevent explosions in your vicinity. We will start, accordingly, on the other side of the planet. If you stop us there, then we will assume we need help. In six months of travelling at top acceleration, we can reach a point where the nearest Ganae planet would hear our messages. They will send a fleet so vast that all your powers of resistance will be overcome. By dropping a hundred or a thousand bombs every minute, we will succeed in devastating every city so that not a grain of dust will remain of the skeletons of your people.

'That is our plan. So it shall be. Now, do your worst to us who are at your mercy.'

The man shook his head. 'I shall do nothing – now!' he said. He paused, then thoughtfully, 'Your reasoning is fairly accurate. Fairly. Naturally, I am not all-powerful, but it seems to me you have forgotten one little point. I won't tell you what it is. And now,' he said, 'good day to you. Get back to your ship, and be on your way. I have much to do.'

Enash had been standing quietly, aware of the fury building up in him again. Now, with a hiss, he sprang forward, suckers outstretched. They were almost touching the smooth flesh – when something snatched at him.

He was back on the ship.

He had no memory of movement, no sense of being dazed or harmed. He was aware of Veed and Yoal and Captain Gorsid standing near him as astonished as he himself. Enash remained very still, thinking of what the man had said: '... *forgotten one little point*'. Forgotten? That meant they knew. What could it be? He was still pondering about it when Yoal said, 'We can be reasonably certain our bombs alone will not work.'

They didn't.

Forty light-years out from Earth, Enash was summoned to the council chambers. Yoal greeted him wanly. 'The monster is aboard.'

The thunder of that poured through Enash, and with it came a sudden comprehension. 'That was what he meant we had forgotten,' he said finally, aloud and wonderingly. 'That he can travel through space at will within a limit – what was the figure he once used – of ninety light-years.'

He sighed. He was not surprised that the Ganae, who had to use ships, would not have thought immediately of such a possibility. Slowly, he began to retreat from the reality. Now that the shock had come, he felt old and weary, a sense of his mind withdrawing again to its earlier state of aloofness. It required a few minutes to get the story. A physicist's assistant, on his way to the storeroom, had caught a glimpse of a man in a lower corridor. In such a heavily manned ship, the wonder was that the intruder had escaped earlier observation. Enash had a thought.

'But after all, we are not going all the way to one of our planets. How does he expect to make use of us to locate it if we only use the video—' he stopped. That was it, of course. Directional video beams would have to be used, and the man would travel in the right direction the instant contact was made.

Enash saw the decision in the eyes of his companions, the only possible decision under the circumstances. And yet, it seemed to him they were missing some vital point. He walked slowly to the great video plate at one end of the chamber. There was a picture on it, so sharp, so vivid, so majestic that the unaccustomed mind would have reeled as from a stunning blow. Even to him, who knew the scene, there came a constriction, a sense of unthinkable vastness. It was a video view of a section of the Milky Way. Four hundred *million* stars as seen through telescopes that could pick up the light of a red dwarf at thirty thousand light-years.

The video plate was twenty-five yards in diameter – a scene that had no parallel elsewhere in the plenum. Other galaxies simply did not have that many stars.

Only one in two hundred thousand of those glowing suns had planets.

That was the colossal fact that compelled them now to an irrevocable act. Wearily, Enash looked around him.

'The monster has been very clever,' he said quietly. 'If we go ahead, he goes with us, obtains a reconstructor, and returns by his method to his planet. If we use the directional beam, he flashes along it, obtains a reconstructor, and again reaches his planet first. In either event, by the time our fleets arrived back here, he would have revived enough of his kind to thwart any attack we could mount.'

He shook his torso. The picture was accurate, he felt sure, but it still seemed incomplete. He said slowly, 'We have one advantage now. Whatever decision we make, there is no language machine to enable him to learn what it is. We can carry out our plans without his knowing what they will be. He knows that neither he nor we can blow up the ship. That leaves us one real alternative.'

It was Captain Gorsid who broke the silence that followed. 'Well, gentlemen, I see we know our minds. We will set the engines, blow up the controls, and take him with us.'

They looked at each other, race pride in their eyes. Enash touched suckers with each in turn.

An hour later, when the heat was already considerable, Enash had the thought that sent him staggering to the communicator, to call Shuri, the astronomer. 'Shuri,' he yelled, 'when the monster first awakened – remember Captain Gorsid had difficulty getting your subordinates to destroy the locators. We never thought to ask them what the delay was. Ask them ... ask them—'

There was a pause, then Shuri's voice came weakly over the roar of the static. 'They ... couldn't ... get ... into the ... room. The door was locked.'

Enash sagged to the floor. They had missed more than one point, he realized. The man had awakened, realized the situation; and, when he vanished, he had gone to the ship, and there discovered the secret of the locator and possibly the secret of the reconstructor – if he didn't know it previously. By the time he reappeared, he already had from them what he wanted. All the rest must have been designed to lead them to this act of desperation.

In a few moments, now, *he* would be leaving the ship, secure in the knowledge that shortly no alien mind would know his planet existed. Knowing, too, that his race would live again, and this time never die.

Enash staggered to his feet, clawed at the roaring communicator, and shouted his new understanding into it. There was no answer. It clattered with the static of uncontrollable and inconceivable energy. The heat was peeling his armoured hide as he struggled to the matter transmitter. It flashed at him with purple flame. Back to the communicator he ran, shouting and screaming.

He was still whimpering into it a few minutes later when the mighty ship plunged into the heart of a blue-white sun.

Science Fiction in Pan

Ghost & Horror in Pan

Occult and
Supernatural

Ira Levin

ROSEMARY'S BABY   25p

> 'At last I have got my wish. I am ridden by a
> book that plagues my mind and continues to
> squeeze my heart with fingers of bone. I swear
> that *Rosemary's Baby* is the most unnerving
> story I've read' – KENNETH ALLSOP

> '. . . if you read this book in the dead of night,
> do not be surprised if you feel the urge to keep
> glancing behind you' – QUEEN

> 'A darkly brilliant tale of modern deviltry that,
> like James' *Turn of the Screw*, induces the
> reader to believe the unbelievable. I believed it
> and was altogether enthralled'
>   – TRUMAN CAPOTE

A KISS BEFORE DYING   25p
THIS PERFECT DAY   35p

These and other PAN Books are obtainable
from all booksellers and newsagents. If you
have any difficulty please send purchase price
plus 7p postage to PO Box 11, Falmouth,
Cornwall.
While every effort is made to keep prices low,
it is sometimes necessary to increase prices at
short notice. PAN Books reserve the right to
show new retail prices on covers which may
differ from those advertised in the text or
elsewhere.